Just Kids

Novel one in the

Our Wandering Paths

series.

Stay up to date with the latest books, special offers, and exclusive content from Rachel Jackson by following her on Goodreads, Amazon, BookBub or busybeemedia.org/RachelJackson.

JUST KIDS

Rachel Jackson

Busy Bee Media, London, England

ISBN: 978-1-913985-25-7

First published in 2025 by Busy Bee Media, London, England

'A twisting and compelling story filled with suspense… a believable and simmering thriller.'

— LoveReading (UK)

For Emily.

'I won't lie, you're not everyone's cup of tea, but at the end of the day, when all's said and done, you're tidy. And I know it's been complicated, you and me. All this, like. But I loves it. And if truth be told… I loves you.'

– Nessa to Smithy, Gavin and Stacey

Prologue

Present Day

I RECOGNISED HIM BEFORE HE SAW ME. It wasn't his face at first. It was the way he was standing—too still, like he had nowhere else to be. He was thinner than I remembered, his hair cropped close to his skull, his face covered in lines and harder somehow. As though prison had stripped away whatever softness he'd once had.

He stood outside the off-licence, one hand shoved deep in his pocket, the other lazily trying to obscure the spliff that he was so obviously smoking. He was watching people come and go. Not browsing. Just watching.

I slowed, then stopped walking altogether.

Oh, crap.

I couldn't believe this day had finally come.

Crap. Crap. Crap.

Suddenly, I felt very exposed. As though I were the only one on the busy street, even though people were still passing by, casually getting on with their days. A car door slammed nearby and scared the living daylights out of me.

He looked up.

For a moment, his face didn't register anything at all. But then, recognition settled in, unmistakably.

'Hello Trouble,' he said.

Hearing my old nickname sent a familiar shiver through my body. Nobody called me Trouble anymore and hadn't done for years.

My chest tightened, and my breath caught before I could help it.

'Did you think I wouldn't remember you?' His voice was calm. Almost casual. Like this was a coincidence. Like we were two people who'd simply run into each other.

I didn't say anything.

He smiled then, just slightly, at some unspoken joke.

'It's funny,' he said. 'I've had a lot of time to think about you.'

My stomach jolted. I felt the implication in his words. He'd been rehearsing this moment for a long time.

He pushed himself away from the wall and took a step towards me.

I instinctively took a step back.

I didn't wait to see what he would do next. Instead, I turned and fled, my heart pounding harder than my feet were hitting the pavement. I didn't turn around or slow down. All I could think was that I'd waited too long. That I should never have stopped in the first place.

Some instincts are learned the hard way.

Belonging

1
Lightning

March 1998

WALKING INTO TOM'S LOUNGE, I prayed that the boy from last week would be there. My head was so high on life right then that I could have lived for a week on nothing but that feeling. As I passed the edge of the door and the room came into view, I could see him sitting on the sofa.

Nick.

My stomach flipped around like I was on a fairground ride. Our eyes locked, and for a moment, the rest of the world disappeared.

'Sarah!' He jumped to his feet with puppy-like enthusiasm, and before I'd had time to think, he'd wrapped me in an exaggerated hello, lifting me clean off the floor.

Must. Be. Cool, I reminded myself, as I so often did back then, always so eager to be liked

'Nick!' I laughed, trying to sound as confident as my feet dangled briefly before he set me back down.

Everything about him made the moment feel suddenly bigger than it should have been, and I didn't yet know what to do with feelings like that. People say that teenage feelings don't last. But standing there in that lounge, it felt like the most important thing in the world.

I'd met Nick and the rest of the boys at the cinema a week earlier. Emma McCarthy and Jennifer Wren, my two closest girlfriends, had introduced us. Emma was the one who knew everyone; Jennifer had arrived early to save us seats at the end of the back row. Emma and I were late, as usual, and crept in halfway through the first scene, scooting past the unseen boys in the dark.

No sooner had we sat down than drinks and popcorn arrived, passed down by the shadowy outlines of the boys. We shared our nachos and pick 'n' mix sweets before settling back to watch the film.

Now, call me a square, but when I watch a film, I actually watch it. I'd been brought up to be quiet and respectful in cinemas, so when loud laughter and rustling started behind us, irritation prickled. I leaned forward to see who it was and caught the outline of a boy sitting with a girl on either side of him.

He froze and stared straight back at me.

'Shhh!' I pressed my fingers to my lips.

He raised his hands apologetically, still staring, while the girls beside him dissolved into laughter. I sank back into my seat, annoyed.

Moments later, Emma handed me a soda. 'From Nick. He says sorry,' she whispered.

I took a sip from his straw, trying not to smile. *That's the first time a boy's ever sent me a drink,* I noted, astonished. I passed it back and met his gaze again, warmth blooming where irritation had been.

He can't be so bad.

The film itself wasn't great from a sixteen-year-old's perspective—all violence and very little heart—and by the end, we were fidgeting. When the lights came up, I slipped past the boys without looking at them. The boy from before was sitting alone now, the other girls gone, and I felt his head follow me as I walked past. It's not that I was rude or that I didn't want to say hi; it's just that I suddenly felt so awkward that I preferred to slip on by.

As we filed down the steps, I thought about how lucky I was to have found Emma and Jennifer. They'd been best friends since Year

Seven, both at the same Catholic school. I was the newcomer, the shy girl who'd joined Emma's youth theatre group at The Bull Theatre a year earlier, and somehow, against all odds, ended up belonging.

When I first started at the youth theatre, I'd been painfully shy, all nerves and self-consciousness. But my nerves had given way to a slightly mad sense of humour, and now I dreamed of being a Hollywood actress and sticking it to everyone at school who'd ever been horrible to me.

'I didn't really see the point in it,' Jennifer huffed, dissecting the film. 'So, she died—big surprise—and he survived. Why is it always the woman who dies or gets brutally murdered somehow?'

'And only after she's done drugs and had sex,' Emma added. 'I mean, isn't the message getting a bit old already? "Bad" girls are worth nothing in Hollywood. It's like—you have sex—and suddenly they kill you off. Or stop inviting you to parties, at least.'

'What do you mean they stop inviting you to parties?' I asked.

'Well, like, in *Friends,*' she explained, referring to the popular television sitcom. 'When Joey sleeps with someone, suddenly that woman never gets invited to another party again. The whole group just abandons her. It's mad.'

I listened, absorbing it all, filing it away carefully as fact. Glancing behind me at Jennifer, I noticed her lips had drawn thin, and her eyebrows had drawn together in a deep frown.

Uh oh. I racked my brain for something mollifying to say, but it was too late.

'I don't think that was the point I was making,' Jennifer cut in, her mouth tightening. 'I was talking about violence, not sex, *actually*.'

It had been like this for weeks, the pair of them squabbling whenever Emma mentioned sex. Ever since Emma had decided it was time to start dating and going to parties and hanging out with the mysterious boys, who were now coming down the stairs behind us. As a strict Catholic, Jennifer was far more reserved and emphatically disapproved of Emma's choices. Both girls identified as feminists and owned their choices, but seemed to increasingly wish that the other would change tack and join them on their own path, by either loosening up massively or becoming far more restrained.

As for me, Miss Piggy in the middle, I was just relieved to be included at all. At school, I'd been the class loner not so long ago. Now, I was part of something, and I wasn't about to jeopardise it.

So, I did what I always did: smoothed things over.

Just as Emma was opening her mouth to retort, I scoffed and cut her off. 'Ha! The whole entertainment industry is run by *sexist old men*,' I shook my head vehemently and looked back up at Jennifer. 'They wouldn't know a new idea if it hit them squarely between the eyes,' I snorted.

'That's true!' laughed Emma, as she trotted down the stairs. 'They don't have a clue what it's like to be like us.'

Slowly, Jennifer smiled and put her arms around my shoulders as we filed out through the cinema doors. In the lobby, Emma herded us together. That was the first time I saw the boys properly. A tall boy with flame-red hair and a face full of acne smiled kindly and shook my hand, putting me instantly at ease.

'Hey Emma, who's your friend?' he asked kindly.

'Hey Tom, this is Sarah,' Emma made the introduction. 'Sarah, this is Tom…'

'Hiya, how's it going?' I smiled, closed-mouthed, trying not to show the enormous double gaps in my teeth.

'….and this is Johnnie,' Emma concluded, as a second boy, much shorter than Tom, with black, gelled curtains plastered to either side of his forehead, stepped forward and bustled him aside. I recognised him immediately.

'Hiya, Sarah…' he started.

'Hey! Don't you go to my school?' I asked, my four front teeth bursting through my closed smile like Bugs Bunny's. Johnnie glanced at them, briefly startled—something that happened a lot back then. I was still waiting for my braces, embarrassingly late, while most people in my year had already had theirs on and off again.

Johnnie seemed to catch himself and met my eyes. 'Hey. Yeah, I've seen you around,' he said, darting in for a quick, limp handshake before retreating again, hands shoved into his pockets as he scuffed his trainers along the floor. 'Funny—we've never actually spoken.'

I laughed, a little nervously.

'So, what shall we do now, then?' Emma cut in, flicking her poker-straight blonde hair. 'We can go back to mine if you want. My parents don't mind.'

'Yeah, that works for me,' Johnnie began, adding something about needing to be home for synagogue.

But I barely heard him.

I turned, and that was when I saw the boy who had sent me his soda properly for the first time. He was well over six feet tall with broad, solid shoulders, baggy jeans, and a loose shirt worn casually open at the neck. He had the kind of face you noticed instantly: piercing eyes, an easy confidence, and a jaw so square it looked like it belonged in a men's shaving advert.

Most striking of all was that he was looking right at me. And then he walked towards me.

Oh wow. He's gorgeous, I thought, and snapped my mouth shut at once to hide my gappy teeth.

Time seemed to stretch as he crossed the lobby, the rest of the group blurring into background noise. I stared for half a second too long, then panicked and looked away, fixing my attention on the cinema posters as though they were suddenly fascinating. Someone asked me a question—Johnnie, I think—but I couldn't have repeated it if my life depended on it.

'Hi,' he said, stopping right in front of me. 'I'm Nick.'

He smiled and held out his hand.

I blinked up at him, momentarily stunned, as though I'd been struck by lightning and was still humming from the impact.

This must be what love feels like, I thought dazedly.

When my brain finally kicked back in, I smiled—a huge, determinedly closed-mouthed smile—and slipped my hand into his.

'Hiya! I'm Sarah,' I breathed, shaking his hand wildly.

At sixteen, I had never properly talked to a boy I fancied before. The fact that he was standing here, talking to me like this, felt unreal.

'I haven't seen you around,' Nick said easily. 'How do you know Emma?'

'Drama,' I replied. 'She introduced me to Jennifer a few months ago. And Tom and Johnnie… just now. Today.'

I could hear myself babbling and hated it.

Nick smiled as though he found it charming. Jennifer glanced over from the other side of the group and leaned in to whisper something in Emma's ear.

'That movie was crap,' Nick said, shifting closer, close enough that I had to tilt my head back slightly to look at him. My heart began to race. I noticed the silver chain against his tanned skin, the way his dark-blonde hair fell just messily enough to look deliberate.

'Yeah,' I said weakly. 'Really… rubbish. Properly bad.'

Emma's voice cut through the moment. 'If we're going back to mine, we have to run—the bus is here in five minutes!'

There was a flurry of agreement, and Jennifer grabbed my arm, tugging me forward so the three of us walked ahead of the boys. I felt absurdly relieved—and instantly bereft.

I was acutely aware of Nick walking just behind me, or at least I hoped he was.

Don't trip. Don't trip. Don't trip.

We hurried along in our tight jeans, tight tops, and towering platform heels, the unofficial uniform of teenage North London, and although my feet burned with pain, I felt as though I were floating.

The spell broke when Nick reluctantly peeled away to catch his bus home. His parents, apparently, didn't allow him to stay out after dark, a fact that only made him more intriguing. He glanced back and waved as he climbed the stairs to the top deck. We waved back.

One moment, I was blissed out beyond reason. The next, already hollowed out by his absence. *Will I ever see you again?* I wondered forlornly.

The rest of the boys came with us back to Emma's house, where her parents were waiting, and we all went upstairs to look at her treasured graffiti wall. It was the absolute coolest thing I had ever seen, and I admired it profoundly.

One side of her bedroom was dedicated entirely to signatures and tags from friends and family who had stopped by and left some form of wisdom or nonsense behind.

'Live every day as though it's your last, love deeply, and laugh wildly, Gina XXX,' read one.

'F U NE M? S, V F M. F U NE X? S, V F X. I'LL F X N M,' wrote another great wit.

'Love ya, babe,' wrote Stephanie B., straightforward and to the point.

Sadly, I imagined my mum's reaction if I wanted to do the same. As a highly effective schoolteacher, she'd developed an iron grip over her children, and things like graffiti walls were definite no-nos.

A few hours later, I was home, and all I could think about was Nick. I picked up the phone and called Emma. I imagined telling her how I felt and how surprised she'd be, but shockingly, she already knew.

'Have you put your eyes back in your sockets yet, hon?' she teased, before adding that there was a chance he felt the same. 'I'm not saying he doesn't like you, because he might. But maybe he's just good for a snog, rather than boyfriend material.'

Disappointment gnawed at my stomach, but I was far too curious to let it go. 'Why's that, Em?' I asked.

'Those two girls he was with? He'd literally just met them in the car park before the film. He is a genuinely nice guy and everything, but he's always up to something.'

'Oh really?' I felt myself being pulled further into Nick's orbit. 'Like what?'

'Well, once he got expelled from a boarding school after he was caught playing drinking games in the girls' dorm,' Emma explained. 'He climbed across the roof, his sister let him in through a window, and they all got drunk on vodka and Red Bull she'd asked him to bring. Then he went to Tom's school for a while—until he was caught smoking weed out the back and tried to buy more from a sixth former who reported him.'

I was surprised. I'd never met anyone who smoked weed before. 'Is that why he had to go home early today?' I asked, suddenly worried for my new friend.

'Yeah. He's still in the doghouse about it. But he's trying really hard now. His mum's obsessed with him going to medical school and becoming a doctor. She's constantly riding him to keep him in line. It's savage.'

'Does he even want to be a doctor?' I asked.

'I don't think so,' Emma said. 'Honestly, I haven't got a clue what Nick actually wants to do. I don't think he does either.'

I came off the phone feeling sad for Nick, and intrigued, as I'd never been before.

Before I knew it, three days had passed. He left my mind for all of ten seconds when I crossed the road and almost walked straight into moving traffic. In that brief moment, my short life flashed before my eyes, and I felt strangely happy and peaceful.

Other than that, Nick was always there—always with me—like a longing that couldn't be satisfied, and an indescribable high I'd never felt before.

It must be a crush, I kept telling myself. *I'll get over it soon. That's what they say. A teenage crush will pass.*

At home, Mum was always hammering on at me for something. The daughter she seemed to hate, who hadn't turned out as she expected. I wondered exactly how she had wanted me to be. Clearly, school grades were important to her, but I always got straight As, although I never did my homework. Perhaps it was that that pissed her off. But really, the depths of her bitterness seemed to stem from my inability to tidy or clean my room properly.

She seemed to revel in telling me how stupid I was when 'doing exactly as I'm told,' joining in with the family chores. 'You take everything *off* the table *before* you dust it,' she scolded and mocked as she re-dusted the immaculate glass coffee table. It seemed to me that I wasn't the one being stupid in that situation. But I no longer cared; I had my medicine.

I thought of Nick while she talked. I thought of him walking home from school, in the shower, in bed. I replayed the way he'd crossed the cinema lobby, that loose, confident sway, the casual way his lips had formed the words, *that movie was crap.*

In my head, the scene kept going. Only this time, he said, *I want you, Sarah. You look so beautiful. I don't care about your teeth. Kiss me!*

And I replied smoothly, *You're not too bad yourself, Nick.*

Reluctantly, I dragged myself out of my daydream and sat cross-legged on my bedroom floor with my revision notes. The school year had reached the point where studying was no longer optional. GCSEs loomed, mock exams were on the horizon, and I was already behind.

I stared at the page but nothing went in.

How are you meant to concentrate when you're in love? I thought miserably. *Not love,* another part of me snapped back. *A crush. On a boy you've met once. Who probably doesn't even remember you exist.*

As if on cue, my little sister Bethany came bounding up the stairs carrying a plastic bag. At just eight, she always wanted to be a part of what I was doing, and I wasn't always kind about it. But right then, I was grateful for the interruption.

'What's up Beth-Peth?' I asked.

'Oh, nothing,' she sighed dramatically. 'Stacey Bunn said that my bag was very ugly at school today, so I thought I'd try and make it nicer.'

'She said your bag was ugly?' I asked, immediately protective. Stacey Bunn was the undisputed leader of Bethany's friendship group. 'That's not very nice. Did you tell the teacher?'

'No. But Mum said we could decorate it,' she said, peering into the bag.

'Can I help?' I asked, already eyeing the glitter glue pens and forgetting all about revision.

'Yes!'

We disappeared into her room and set about transforming the bag with glitter, stickers, and plastic flowers, giving it what Bethany proudly declared a 'crafty look'.

A while later, I checked the time and realised I had to leave for drama. Back in my room, I refreshed my overdone makeup, grabbed my bag, and headed for the bus stop.

The bus rattled through the green belt that hemmed London in, past fields and quiet stretches of road, before depositing me on High Barnet High Street—Tudor pubs rubbing shoulders with greasy spoon cafés, charity shops, and American fast-food joints.

I hurried into the theatre and straight into the thick of it: teenage chatter, nervous energy, hormones hanging in the air. Class had started, and everyone was limbering up with some improv and vocal exercises. Emma spotted me and waved enthusiastically, as if we hadn't spent an hour on the phone together after school. As I swayed on the spot, pretending to be a howling tree, Emma drifted over in dramatic twirls, playing moonlit wind.

'Hey,' she whispered. 'What are you doing this weekend? We're going to the fairground—me, Jennifer, and the boys. My parents said I could. Do you want to come?'

'Yes!' I said instantly.

My heart thudded. I couldn't believe I was going to see Nick again.

I was so excited I could barely keep my roots on the ground.

2

Really Quite Annoying

AND SO, THERE I WAS, HUGGING NICK in Tom's lounge, so high on life that I felt like a ping-pong ball in a hurricane.

'You look nice,' he put me down from our embrace to look at me.

'Thank you!' I could have burst with happiness.

'What's this in your hair?' He pulled at the brown, plastic zig-zagging Alice band, holding the hair back from my forehead in what look like unplaited corn rows. Before I could answer, a smooth, deep voice came from behind us as Tom's older brother Andy filled the doorway.

'What are you guys up to today?' He asked. Andy was two school years above us but seemed infinitely wiser. He had gone to the same posh private school as Tom but was expelled for lighting a bin on fire in the chemistry lab and, in doing so, had become a fabled legend. Now, having just turned eighteen, he worked full-time in an off-license like a fully-fledged adult—but one with access to alcohol—adding further to his mystique.

For a moment, I was lost in the aftermath of Nick's embrace, and I could still smell him and feel his warmth. Then I came to my senses, and I was back on earth and in the room again. Emma, Jennifer and Tom had gotten up from the sofas lining the walls, and it was hugs all around. I hadn't even had a chance to greet them before Nick leapt up to meet me when I entered.

'Hey, man. We're going to the funfair,' Nick piped up, his admiration for Andy as clear as day. 'You should come!'

'No, you kids have fun. I got stuff to do,' Andy sauntered cockily into the room.

'This is Sarah' piped up Tom, and I smiled nervously and shook Andy's hand when he offered it to me. The two brothers were strikingly tall and broad, with red hair. Tom's hair was flame red, whereas Andy's was a strawberry-ash blonde. Andy sported a layer of stubble, and his eyes were calm and knowing.

'Hey, nice to meet you.' He smiled casually and sat down at the table in the middle of the room, taking his time and keeping the floor's attention.

'*Page*.' I felt the need to clarify. 'I mean, my name is Sarah *Page*.' My face started burning at my outburst. 'Nice to meet you, too,' I added, trying to hide the gaps in my teeth. When he looked up at me, he seemed to see me. Or that was how it felt, at least.

'Oh. Well, hello, *Miss Page*,' Andy regarded me with a sparkle in his eyes. 'I'm *Mister East*,' he said with a small tip-of-the-cap gesture, and everyone in the room (except me) laughed—though not unkindly. With that, I flushed beetroot red, and the conversation moved on, although I felt like a bit of an idiot.

We talked about the series Ally McBeal on TV and the Dancing Baby episode that just aired.

'Anyone who hallucinates dancing babies in the toilets is insane and should not be a practising lawyer,' asserted Emma. 'Back me up here, Sarah.'

'Isn't that just a symptom of schizophrenia?' I laughed, and to my delight, everyone else laughed, too. I felt a small, fizzing thrill at being the one who'd made it happen.

'And let's not forget she's in love with a married man,' huffed Jennifer, 'somehow, we're supposed to dislike his wife just because Ally McBeal has a crush on her husband? Oh, please!'

Tom screwed up his face and put on a dramatic voice. 'Yeah, but apparently he's so sexy though…' he said, rolling his eyes and finishing with an exaggerated sigh. We laughed again, our spirits lifting even higher in anticipation of the fairground.

A little later, Johnnie joined us from his parents' house a few doors up, and we piled out together, catching the bus across town.

When we got off, Emma, Jennifer, and I walked arm in arm, chatting, while the boys followed behind. Ahead of us, the funfair glowed at the end of a tree-lined path—bright lights flickering, a rollercoaster rattling overhead, the air thick with the smell of candy floss and popcorn.

A warm fuzzy feeling flooded me, and I felt so lucky to have found some wonderful friends at last after two years of being an outcast at school. Theatre classes had saved my life from a lonely and sad direction, and I would be forever grateful for the confidence, social skills and people they brought into my life.

Always aware of where he was, Nick was walking just behind us. He was close enough that I could feel him there, close enough that it was distracting, and I had the odd sense of being observed.

'You know what I've just realised?' he said, suddenly, loud enough for the others to hear.

I glanced back. 'What?'

He looked me up and down, grinning. 'You're actually really… sweet.'

There were a few amused noises from behind us.

'Sweet?' I repeated.

'Yeah,' he said easily. 'Like, properly innocent. It's strange.'

I laughed because that seemed like the correct response, even though something about it didn't sit right.

'Not in a bad way,' he added quickly. 'You just seem…' He searched for the word. 'A bit soft.'

Hmmm.

'Soft?' I repeated.

'Yeah,' he said easily. 'Like, if we weren't here, I'd expect you to get mugged on the way home... or lost, or something.'

Johnnie snorted from behind us. My smile froze.

I stopped walking. 'Right,' I said, turning round. 'So that's what you think of me.'

Nick blinked. 'What?'

'That I'm strange. And helpless, and a bit clueless,' I said. 'That I'd fall over if someone looked at me funny.'

'That's not what I said,' he protested.

'It's what you meant,' I shot back, my face hot now. 'You didn't say Emma or Jennifer were strange or would get mugged. Just me.'

'Don't be weird,' he laughed. 'I mean, you're just very… *you*.'

Johnnie let out a low, delighted 'Oof.'

Emma winced. 'Nick…'

Nick ran a hand through his hair, still half-laughing. 'You're taking this way too seriously.'

There it was again.

'Funny how it's "too seriously" when someone doesn't laugh along,' I said. 'But sure—whatever.'

The mood shifted, and the easy buzz evaporated.

'God,' Nick scoffed. 'You're intense.'

The word landed hard.

'And you're arrogant,' I snapped. 'So, I guess we're even. There. Who's soft now?'

For a second, neither of us spoke. We were standing too close now, the air between us crackling.

Suddenly, Jennifer stepped between us with a face like thunder. 'Are you quite done?' she whispered, sounding alarmingly like my mum. But Nick and my eyes remained locked in a death glare over Jennifer's shoulder.

'Oh, get a room, you two!' groaned Johnnie from the sidelines, and Tom sniggered.

Nick and I whirled around to glare at them.

'Pah! I wouldn't go anywhere alone with her!' he sneered.

'Good! Me too! You're not invited anyway!' I tossed back.

But the group was already drifting off towards the fair. Nick watched them go and turned back to me, hotly.

'God! What is wrong with you!? I was joking!!' he implored, his voice rising to a shout.

'Well, then say something funny, and I'll laugh!' I quipped, and suddenly Nick was bridling with a restless energy like he didn't quite know what to do with himself.

Exasperated, Jennifer stepped between us again, clicking her fingers harshly in the space between our faces. Yet still our eyes remained adamantly locked. 'That is *quite* enough, both of you! People are looking. Just… shut up already and let's just go to the fair. Jesus!'

Reluctantly, we trudged the rest of the way in sullen silence, separated by a wall of well-meaning friends. Once inside the gates, we drifted between rides and snacks, eventually piling onto the roller coaster, the Waltzer, and finally a giant spinning cylinder that pinned us to the wall like flies on sticky paper as the floor dropped away.

I tried not to look at Nick, but it was impossible.

He stood opposite me, next to Emma, who was laughing at Johnnie, saying he felt sick. Every time our eyes met, I felt a direct flow of energy between us, and a heat that I'd never felt before. Which was strange, because I'd decided he was a total idiot.

The feeling appeared to be mutual, and after the ride, Nick stormed off ahead and dragged Jennifer on the bumper cars alone. Johnnie, looking suspiciously pale, erupted with pink candy floss vomit next to me, and some of it landed on my trainers.

That's just great, I thought to myself, and took him to the refreshment stand to buy a bottle of water. Thankfully, he could walk, as he was about half a foot taller than me. I'd have had no hope of carrying him if he took a turn for the worse, despite the fact that he was yet to fill out his wiry frame.

'Sorry.' Johnnie looked at my pink-stained shoe. I shrugged as I tried to get the pink off by wiping it on the grass.

'Don't worry about it,' I put my arm through his to reassure him. 'Pink is definitely my colour.'

Johnnie groaned and sat out the next ride. Still, I felt magnetically drawn to Nick and was secretly disappointed when he spent the rest of the afternoon ignoring me and going on rides with Jennifer while I watched from a distance with Emma, Johnnie, and Tom, telling myself that I didn't care.

Things could not have gotten much worse, except that the next day, I was going to get my braces put on. Double train tracks on the top and bottom, and I needed them for a whole, terrible year.

***

The following Saturday was cold but brilliantly sunny. We were all hanging out at Tom's—already my favourite place—and had just come back from a game of football in the churchyard. Johnnie had managed to kick the ball straight into my face, and my teeth were killing me. Not only had I had my braces for less than a week, but now my lips were all cut up, too.

On the plus side, the boys had decided to call me *Trouble* after my run-in with Nick and I wore it like a badge of honour.

'Sorry again, Trouble,' Johnnie said, handing me a cup of water and looking genuinely guilty, despite having teased me earlier for being 'a girl who can't play football' at the time of the injury. Never mind that I was playing a better game than him.

'We're heading to the corner shop if you want anything?' Johnnie offered sheepishly, gesturing towards Nick, who was regarding me suspiciously nearby.

For some reason, my heart still pounded a million times a minute whenever Nick was nearby. Or when I thought about him. Or when he looked at me. Or smiled. But I still hadn't forgiven him for calling me strange and soft, and we both seemed quite wary of each other.

'I'll have a chocolate Yoohoo and some cherry drops, please.' I said, fishing out some change. Maybe I'd like Nick again if he brought me sweets. Although I wasn't sure he was particularly eager to be liked.

Tom asked for a lilt and a cornetto and dropped the exact change into Johnnie's hand.

'Cornetto, in March?' I exclaimed dubiously, raising an eyebrow.

Nick laughed suddenly, leaning forward and tugging on my sleeve in mock play. 'Cornetto any time of the year, baby!' he declared, and for a moment we were laughing together again—not because nothing had happened, but because his energy was too infectious to resist.

'Alright. Later, losers,' Johnnie said, once he'd gathered the orders and Nick lobbed the football at the back of his head as they left.

A moment later, we heard thudding feet and raised voices outside. Tom, Emma, Jennifer and I looked at each other.

'Are they fighting?' I asked.

'Just mucking about,' Tom said, but we all went to look, nonetheless.

'So immature,' tutted Jennifer, her eyes wide as she trotted out quickly beside me, with Emma slightly in front.

'They're always doing this kind of thing,' Emma shook her head disapprovingly, trying to get a better view as she passed the front hedge.

On the pavement, next to a neighbour's parked car, Johnnie submitted to Nick reluctantly, as Emma knelt next to him and encouraged him to fight back. Tom, eager not to let the games pass him by, tried to help Johnnie and piled in on top of Nick. But Nick sent him flying effortlessly, and soon Tom was sprawled across the tarmac, clutching his shin, groaning but insisting he was fine and still smiling.

Just then, Andy returned from work, wrapped in a giant fleece, his cheeks red from the cold. He greeted us calmly, and I felt absurd and childish, standing there watching the boys wrestle.

But Nick sensed a golden opportunity.

'Come on, man!' he goaded. 'Let's see what you got!'

All eyes turned expectantly to Andy as Nick squared up to him, wearing a big, goofy grin, and Andy's slow smile took on a cocky quality.

'You think you have what it takes?' he goaded, stepping nose to nose with Nick like a boxer in a ring, and we couldn't believe our luck!

Be. Cool, I told myself as a ticker tape parade went wild in my brain.

The pair smiled and circled each other, urging the other to make the first move. And for a few glorious minutes, it was Nick versus Andy—moves and defences, kicks and grabs—as the two tried to topple each other, pulling each other's clothes and exposing bare midriffs and backs and all sorts of rippling flesh to my innocent, starving eyes.

Then, with a cry of 'pull his trousers down!' Johnnie ruined it all by piling back in. With that, Andy laughed, called it a day and left the younger boys to it.

Buzzing with an extraordinary energy, and with the boys showing no sign of letting up from their roughhousing, I finally decided to go to the shop without the boys. Emma and Jennifer said they'd come too, and I ran back inside to get our handbags.

Andy was in the kitchen, and as I nervously neared the open door, our eyes met, and that slow, knowing smile touched his lips for a moment and was gone.

'Nice to see you again, *Miss Page*.'

'Hi Andy, you too!' I gushed, running awkwardly past with my mouth clamped shut to hide my braces and cross with myself for sounding so soft.

Damn! What is it with this guy? I thought, grabbing the bags and rushing out to join my friends.

A short while later, Emma and I got back from the shop without Jennifer, who had been picked up early by her dull-as-dishwater dad. Nick was the only one still outside, sitting on the churchyard wall opposite Tom's house. He pulled out a cigarette and put it in his mouth, watching me as I walked over to him on jellied legs.

'You know, you really shouldn't smoke,' I told him, seriously, handing him a banana Yoohoo and a packet of gummies.

'You know, you really should think about trying one,' he quipped, his voice so smooth I felt lightheaded all of a sudden. 'Might loosen you up a bit,' he added, sparking it up and offering it to me.

'Smoking is terrible for your health,' I lectured, giving myself away as a giant nerd.

'Yeah, well,' he shrugged, and as he did so, I pulled the lit cigarette from his fingers and broke it in front of his face. 'Sarah—' he sighed. 'Don't do that.' He looked at me and then down at his broken cigarette and managed to control himself by clenching his chiselled jaw and looking away.

Then he pulled out another one. 'You know… you really are quite annoying,' he said, as I tried to grab it from him but failed.

He lit it and held it on the other side of his body just out of reach.

I can still get that.

I reached for it again, my arm grazing his, and the air between us changed.

I could smell him. Feel the heat from his body. As I looked up into his eyes, my heart thudded so hard it hurt.

We froze, our faces inches apart.

He spoke first.

'Go. Away,' he said quietly, blowing a cloud of smoke into my face and looking deep into my eyes in defiance.

For a moment, I couldn't tell if he was joking or not. But then the intensity in his eyes told me he wasn't.

My heart sank and threatened to break into a thousand shards. I turned around and walked back across the road as tears welled up, ready to spill from my eyes, ready to humiliate me, there at Tom's, in front of everyone. But just as I was about to enter Tom's house (and be swallowed by the abyss), he called out after me.

'Thank you for the Yoohoo, Trouble.'

I spun around, and he winked at me, smiling, and exhaled a vast cloud of smoke.

I nodded, trying not to show my gappy, train-tracked teeth as an enormous smile erupted on my face. Then my wounded heart fluttered and soared back to life as I headed back inside to join the rest of the gang.

3

The Off Licence

April 1998

WE WERE GOING TO SEE TOP OF THE POPS being recorded, and I couldn't believe it. Johnnie had three tickets from the new BBC website, and invited me and Emma to go one Thursday after school. I sat in maths class watching the clock, willing it to move faster. One of my brace brackets had come loose on my front tooth, again, and I wiggled it around with my tongue nervously. Mr Jennington-Smythe was going on about Pythagoras' Theorem, sharing his 'very easy' method to remember the three Pythagorean equations, which involved his arch-nemesis, Deputy Head, Mr Hope.

Finally, the bell rang, and *en masse*, a sea of teenagers erupted from the building and raced home, with me at the front. No sooner was I through the front door than the phone rang.

It was Emma.

'Eee!' I screeched, barely containing my excitement, my bare brace wire grazing my sore lips. 'Do you think we'll get on TV!?'

'Of course! Let's stand next to the presenter, and we can lean in front of the camera…'

By the time I ran into the living room to say goodbye to my family—sporting a face full of makeup, huge clip-on earrings and skin-tight pinstriped flares—I was already close to missing my bus.

Living in the sticks was the worst, especially because the buses only ran every half an hour if you were lucky.

Mum looked up at my outfit and frowned, insisting that I get back by 10:00 pm, while Dad and my big brother Lucas watched on worriedly from the sofa. The only one who looked pleased to see me was my little sister Bethany, who leapt up from her place next to Dad enthusiastically and ran over to me enthusiastically.

'Wow, you look amazing!' she said, looking me up and down carefully like a fashion inspector.

'Thanks, Beth Peth!' I blew my sister a kiss and ran towards the front door, dreading missing the bus.

'Don't be late!' called out Mum after me.

'I won't!' I called back, letting the door slam loudly by mistake and hoping she didn't think I'd done it on purpose.

When I staggered off the bus in my platform school shoes in Whetstone, Emma was already waiting for me. She looked fantastic. Her petite frame rocked combat trousers and a halter-neck top, showing just a hint of midriff, her blonde locks flowing down her back. We hugged each other excitedly, as everyone in our theatre group did religiously.

'Let's go to the offie before Johnnie gets here,' she suggested, pointing towards Victoria Wines off-license next to the Underground station. We both knew there was far less chance of getting served if we were with a boy our own age.

'Do you think they'll serve us?' I asked, unsure but excited. I'd never had a drink on a school night before. In fact, not counting the family sherry I partook in when my grandparents came to visit, I'd only had a drink with friends twice before. Both times, a single bottle of alcopop had been enough to make me quite wobbly.

'Yeah, hon, Tom's brother works there, he'll serve us!'

'Andy?'

Suddenly, I felt nervous. We tottered towards the off-license on heels that were far too high, checking our watches as we went. Johnnie's bus wasn't due for another 10 minutes, so we should have been able to buy our drinks and make it back to the bus stop before he started wondering where we were.

As Emma confidently strode into the shop, I meekly sauntered in behind her. Andy looked up at us from behind the counter, eyebrows raised, but said nothing. Emma's confidence was short-lived, and with a toss of her hair, she made a beeline for the alcopops section, with me in tow, trying not to look at Andy as he watched us with obvious amusement.

We quickly grabbed a watermelon Bacardi Breezer, a bottle of lemon Hooch, and a blue WKD for Johnnie. Then, as neither of us had the nerve to face Andy, we casually browsed the snacks. We looked at gum. I showed Emma the new menthol breeze flavour. She nodded enthusiastically, even though I knew she hated menthol. Emma took her house keys out of her pocket as though they were car keys, tossed them in the air, missed catching them, and, after picking them up off the floor, shoved them back in her pocket. I acted like it was the most natural thing in the world.

Finally, we were at the counter and face-to-face with Andy.

'Good evening, ladies,' he leaned forward, looking at us blankly.

'Just these, please, Andy.' Emma stuck her chest out and gestured towards our hoard.

'Do you have ID?' he asked, turning slowly from Emma's face to mine and smiling as I turned a deep beetroot colour.

Crap, crap, crap! 'Yes, yes. Absolutely. Yes. Right here.' I rummaged around in my bag for my wallet while Emma fished hers out and put on an elaborate pantomime of searching each card slot for her driver's license.

'Oh! I must have taken it out,' said Emma. 'Yes—I remember now. I took it out because I needed it earlier because I was speeding, and a policeman stopped me and asked me to show my ID.'

It was lame. It was awful. I was mortified. Andy nodded and smiled, looking at Emma and then at me.

'No ID, no alcohol, ladies. I'm sorry.'

This is so embarrassing.

Just then, a group of people in the back room laughed at some unseen drama playing out, and a second shop attendant emerged. He stopped mid-sentence, surprised to see us, and stared straight at Emma.

'You're in my brother's year, Emma,' explained Andy. 'And so are you, Miss Page. That makes you sixteen.' He looked over at me and shrugged as if to say, 'I don't make the rules; I just follow them,' but we could tell it was more than that. He didn't want to serve us alcohol because he was looking at us like children. I looked down at my shoes and urged the ground to swallow me up.

'I'll serve you,' the second shop attendant announced, moving to a different till. His name tag said Matthew Dyer, his hair was a mess, and he was smiling at some unspoken joke. We quickly moved to the other side of the counter without looking at Andy. As Emma handed him the money, Dyer gently touched her hand, counting out her change and laying it carefully on her palm. We thanked him wholeheartedly and bolted. Just as I was about to follow Emma out the door, I turned and looked at Andy. I smiled a little, 'sorry'. He nodded, his face unreadable, and then I was back outside.

Laughing wildly, we ran back to the bus stop and watched as Johnnie's bus came over the hill towards us.

'You got served!' exclaimed Johnnie happily as we presented him with his WKD straight off the bus. 'Girls can always get served.' Johnnie started on a typical misogynistic rant about how girls could dress up and get into nightclubs and get served in pubs when boys our age couldn't.

'Shut up, Johnnie, and help us open these; we don't have a bottle opener,' said Emma.

'What? Oh, nice one, genius!' Johnnie was clearly in the mood to moan.

For the next five minutes, the three of us wandered around, looking for something we could use to open our bottles. Johnnie tried the plastic bus stop seats, and Emma tried the back of a wooden bench, but I was finally able to pry the lid off mine on the top of a brick wall.

Try as we might, none of the other tops would come off, no matter how hard we tried.

'Use your teeth,' said Emma to Johnnie.

'No, *don't* use your teeth, Johnnie. You might break them,' I interjected, ever the annoying goodie-two-shoes. 'And then you might need braces,' I added, feeling sorry for myself and remembering the ever-present dull ache in my mouth.

'Why don't *you* use *your* teeth!' retorted Johnnie at Emma as he banged his palm on the top of his bottle. 'Double standards. Honestly. Women!'

Hands bruised, we eventually gave up and sat on the bench to share the single bottle of lemon Hooch. Around us, dusk fell, and I felt the excitement of limitless possibilities lying before me. We were young and fun, and now we were almost free.

I thought about Andy's face as I left the shop. Had he been disappointed? I remembered Nick smoking a cigarette and offering it to me, annoyed with me when I turned it down and snapped it. It seemed as though I was judged for being good and judged for being bad. *How am I meant to please everyone if everyone wants different things?* I pondered.

Later that evening, we queued up outside and brainstormed outrageous ways to appear on Top of the Pops. Needless to say, when the time came, all of us bottled out, and we stood silently, as close to the television presenters as possible.

'That Matthew Dyer was cute,' said Emma as we waited for the first act to come on stage. 'You know, I think he liked me.'

'The guy from the offie? He *so* did,' I assured her. 'He was looking at you like he was in love with you or something!'

'Well, I don't know about that,' she tutted, shooting me a glance of strained patience, 'but this weekend, I am definitely going back to Victoria Wines!'

Suddenly, the lights went up, and all of us screamed. Cameras were flying everywhere on extendable mechanical arms, and the next act came running out in front of us. We couldn't believe our eyes. Johnnie turned to us with boyish glee, and we all started dancing our hearts out. I had nothing much to compare it to, but so far it had been the best night of my life. I couldn't wait until Friday to see if we made it on TV!

***

The following Friday night, Johnnie and I got to Emma's house at about 7 pm, and Top of the Pops was going to air in half an hour. We weren't allowed to go upstairs to watch it in Emma's room because her parents were home, and boys weren't allowed upstairs.

Instead, we were in the living room, loafing on the sofas, while her parents chopped vegetables for a charity stew being served by their church group the next day. They weren't particularly happy about their front room being taken over by teenagers just after dinner. But I knew from Emma that they were trying to host her friends so that she would stay in rather than go out to other people's houses. At least while she was there, Emma said, they could keep an eye on her.

Emma called Jennifer, who was slightly put out by the fact that we went to Top of the Pops without her and was watching from home in St. Albans. Her parents didn't let her out after dark at all, and with so many events in her church youth group in her hometown to attend, she had been skipping daytime activities, too. Emma put the phone down and looked at her lap, her face tinged with annoyance.

'Is everything alright, Em?' I asked, concerned.

'Oh yeah, no worries,' she shrugged, plastering a huge smile on her face. 'I'm just going to make some popcorn. Back in a bit.'

With that, she vanished into the kitchen, leaving me to puzzle over whatever Jennifer might have said. Before long, Emma reemerged with a huge bowl of sugary popcorn and her mum in tow.

'You read my mind,' grinned Johnnie, grabbing a handful and scootching over so that Emma could sit down next to him.

Mrs McCarthy lingered in the doorway as the presenter introduced the first act, smiling at our growing excitement.

'Oh, they've finally changed the format back to how it was in the sixties!' she exclaimed, her double chins wobbling as she spoke.

'You used to watch Top of the Pops in the sixties?!' Emma blurted, turning to gape at her mum in awe.

'You'd better believe it,' she chuckled, sauntering into the room and helping herself to a fistful of popcorn. 'Your generation didn't invent all the cool stuff, you know. Your father and I used to love this. We watched it every week.'

'Wow, Mrs McCarthy, you must be so old!' Johnnie exclaimed, mouth hanging open as he stared at Emma's mum.

Mrs McCarthy visibly recoiled. 'You cheeky little…' she blustered—half smiling, half affronted. 'No more popcorn for you, young man!' She turned to me and winked. 'Sarah, you keep an eye on him.' I nodded obligingly as she disappeared back into the kitchen, muttering under her breath, '…needs a good clip round the ear, that one…' and I didn't catch the rest.

Narrowing my eyes, I turned to Johnnie and smiled. 'No more popcorn for you, Johnnie,' I teased, offering him the bowl, then slapping his hand away as he reached for it and whipping it over to Emma.

Emma's eyes suddenly flew wide as she glanced at the TV. 'This is it! We're definitely in shot on this next one!' she shouted, as the camera zoomed in on a smarmy presenter surrounded by teenage audience members.

The three of us scanned the screen, but we were nowhere to be seen. That is, until Johnnie scurried right up to the television and yelled suddenly.

'That's my elbow!'

'No, it's not,' Emma retorted, annoyed that she hadn't made the shot.

'It is!' he insisted, and as the camera began to pan back towards the stage, the corner of a shirt sleeve appeared just above the elbow. 'Look! It's my shirt!'

Johnnie pointed to his shirt on the screen and down at the very shirt he was wearing, which he'd worn again especially. Victoriously, he danced around the room, and Emma threw a cushion at him as he teased her, while my eyes were still glued to the screen.

Surely, that can't be it! I thought. *An elbow and a patch of shirt don't count as being on TV. Surely we'll make it onto the screen later, dancing around the stage.* But somehow, we never materialised.

I couldn't believe it! I had thought getting on TV would be easy. A part of me wondered whether becoming a famous Hollywood actress would also be more difficult than I expected.

Meanwhile, Johnnie was ecstatic and, as soon as the show was over, used Emma's landline to call Nick and brag. My ears pricked up, and I listened intently to the call, even though I pretended to be engrossed by the television. Johnnie passed the phone around the room to Emma—as was the habit at the time—and my stomach lurched. I knew the phone would be passed to me next, and I had no idea what I would say.

It seemed to take forever.

My heart thudded painfully in my chest.

And then it was time.

I took the receiver from Emma's outstretched hand and leaned back nonchalantly on the sofa.

'Hey,' I breathed nonchalantly.

'Hey,' came the nonchalant reply.

Then silence.

Nick broke it.

'Johnnie seems pretty excited.'

'Yeah. He practically kissed the screen when his elbow came on,' I joked, glancing at Johnnie, who froze mid-attack—cushion raised, about to whack Emma—then threw it at me instead.

Nick laughed, a magical sound, and suddenly I felt fifty pounds lighter. Smiling, I pulled the receiver closer and tucked my knees underneath me.

'So, what are you guys up to tonight?' Nick asked, he himself stuck at home under parental house arrest for skipping school the week before.

'I'm not sure yet. My dad's coming to get me at nine, so we've only got an hour.' I paused and turned to Emma. 'Hey! do you know what we're doing now, Emma?'

'I dunno. You should call your parents and tell them you're sleeping over,' she said, much to Johnnie's seeming delight.

From the kitchen, Mrs McCarthy coughed loudly, obviously listening in.

'We're very happy for Sarah to stay if her parents say so, but I'm sorry, Johnnie, you'll have to go home,' interjected Mrs McCarthy firmly, apparently reading Johnnie's mind.

Johnnie's hopes of also staying over with us were deflated like a squeaky balloon. He moped about for a moment before remembering his Cameo appearance on television earlier and perking up.

'Hopefully, I can stay over at Emma's,' I said coolly down the line to the most handsome ear in the universe.

'So… you'll still be around tomorrow, then?' he asked, with what sounded like hope in his voice.

'Yeah, I guess so,' I said, my heart pounding at the implication. Nick spent every Saturday afternoon at Tom's, just a ten-minute walk from Emma's house. My mind raced, instantly cursing the fact that I hadn't brought my full makeup bag.

'Cool. See you tomorrow then, nutcase,' Nick said breezily.

'Bye. See you tomorrow.'

I put the phone down and leaped off the sofa, high as a kite and as excited as I'd ever been.

'Nick wants to see me tomorrow!' I screamed at Emma, who jumped up with me, and we danced around the living room holding cushions.

'What?!' Johnnie stopped us short. 'No way. Sorry, Sarah—there's no way he said that.'

I stopped jumping and stared at him. 'What do you mean?' I asked, a sudden cold knot forming in my stomach.

'It's nothing,' Johnnie stammered, already backpedalling, as Emma and I turned on him. He retreated onto the sofa, squirming as we closed in.

'Go on, Johnnie,' Emma said, suddenly serious. 'Why wouldn't Nick want to see Sarah tomorrow?'

'What? What?! Don't ask me! I don't know!' He grew flustered, cracking under the lightest pressure, spilling secrets like an upended can.

I grabbed a cushion and raised it above my head as if to strike. 'Why wouldn't Nick want to see me tomorrow, Johnnie?'

Johnnie lifted his hands to shield himself just as Emma swung another cushion hard into his shoulder.

'Ow! Zip! Okay, okay! Calm down, you crazy women!' he pleaded, and finally, he caved. 'Nick said he can't stand you, Sarah.'

Ouch.

I froze, cushion in hand, as my world broke apart and my heart smashed into a thousand empty shards.

Johnnie grabbed my cushion from where it hung in mid-air above him and frowned at me. 'And I have to say, maybe he's right; you are pretty annoying.'

OUCH.

The words landed like a blade; the worst confirmation I could have received. In an instant, I was the old me again—the weirdo, the loner, the girl with no friends. Just as my mum always said. No hope of finding a boyfriend, no hope of even being liked or of being normal.

Maybe that's just who I am. No man will ever love me except my dad, I told myself—and certainly not the one who had stolen my heart.

Tears pricked in my eyes, and Emma stared at me for a moment, Johnnie too, his eyes bulging in horror as my face dropped. And then, Emma was holding me, hugging me, and I was holding back the tears like a pro. Swallowing them down, hiding the pain, and pretending everything was completely alright. I didn't know if this was a "stiff upper lip", but I'd certainly had lots of practice.

'Don't worry, I'm sure he didn't mean it,' soothed Emma in my ear.

'Oh, well, that's okay, I don't mind,' I smiled unconvincingly and pulled away as though it meant nothing, imagining Johnnie running back to Nick and describing what was happening. 'Honestly, I think he's pretty annoying too,' I added, deciding it was probably better to be on an equal footing than to look upset.

He is really quite annoying, actually.

'Yeah, right,' Johnnie interjected from the sofa before mimicking my celebration moments earlier in a high-pitched voice: *'Aaaghhhh! Nick wants to see me tomorrow!'*

'Shut up, Johnnie!' Emma growled, and Johnnie shut up, as I smiled and laughed in a forced carefree manner, sitting down delicately on the sofa again.

'Well, I suppose I'd better call my dad and tell him I'm staying over,' I said, deflecting carefully and picking up the phone.

A couple of minutes later, Dad was not pleased with the prospect of my staying out unexpectedly and asked to speak to Emma's parents. But he quickly changed his tune when they assured him they would be there the whole evening and wouldn't let us out of their sight. I overheard them loudly telling Dad that Johnnie would be going home momentarily, and I smiled at Johnnie flatly.

Taking it as his cue to make a move, Johnnie jumped up from the sofa and came over to say his goodbyes. He hugged Emma, then turned to me and pulled me into a quick hug.

'I'm sorry, Sarah; I didn't mean to upset you. Nick is an idiot. And you're not annoying. You're a good laugh,' he said, smiling.

I smiled and hugged him back. 'It's okay. I really don't like him anyway. And thank you, I think you're funny too.' I paused, waited, and added my dad's silly ending for when things get slightly too sweet. 'Huh. Funny *looking*.'

Johnnie groaned, smiled, and headed out the door into the dusky evening, leaving Emma and me to make plans for the weekend. Making sure that her mum wasn't listening, Emma leaned towards me.

'I've been thinking about tomorrow,' she smiled. 'Let's go to Tom's house and then let's get some booze from Victoria Wines.' She pulled an excited grimace as she said 'Victoria Wines' as though she couldn't quite contain herself.

'And who are you expecting to see? Anyone in particular?' I teased, knowing exactly who she was going there for. "Anyone in particular?"

***

The next morning, Emma and I were woken up at ten o'clock by her mum banging on her bedroom door.

'Emma! Your hair is clogging the shower drain—AGAIN!' Mrs McCarthy yelled through Emma's closed bedroom door.

I opened my eyes as Emma slowly stirred on the other side of her double bed, a smudge of black mascara under her eyes, squinting against the light and the invasive sound of her mum.

'Oh God,' she groaned. 'I forgot to clean out the shower drain.' She closed her eyes like her life was a nightmare and ran her hand through her hair wearily.

'Can you come out here, please?' insisted Mrs McCarthy outside the door. 'You're supposed to clean it out every week. You know that. Or it floods.'

'Coming, just a minute!' answered Emma loudly, her voice croaky.

'NOW, please Emma!'

'OKAY! JEEZ!' Emma threw back the duvet, and a rush of chilly air hit me, shocking me awake. I desperately wanted to go back to sleep. 'She's like a flippin' dog with a bone!' grumbled Emma to me quietly as she climbed out of bed and headed to the door.

Later that morning—shower drain cleaned—we had toast, watched MTV, and then Emma was interrogated by her mum about where we would be spending our Saturday. Emma said we'd be heading over to Tom's, but Mrs McCarthy looked unconvinced, as though she could smell something else on the cards and refused to let the matter drop. Her instinct was spot on. Emma was indeed planning to go back to Victoria Wines to try to chat up Matthew Dyer. But how could Mrs McCarthy have known that?

Feeling guilty, I contemplated coming clean, but then thought better of it. It was Emma's mum and Emma's life, after all. Eventually, we headed back upstairs to get ready to go to Tom's. Since I only had the clothes I'd arrived in the night before, Emma immediately took charge.

Digging through her wardrobe, she handed me a floaty skirt and a strappy top, adding a cardigan and a clatter of silver bangles.

'I know you say you don't like Nick anymore,' she said, 'which I don't believe for a second, by the way, but what's the harm in his thinking you look fit?'

I raised an eyebrow, suddenly struck by how much she thought like her mum: same instincts, totally different application. She had a point, though. Looking good didn't mean admitting anything.

After I'd gotten changed, she took a step back to assess me.

'No,' she decided firmly. 'Too boring.'

We laughed in unison, pleased by how in sync we'd become.

Emma buzzed around me like a professional stylist, and in the end, we settled on a blue-and-white tartan maxi dress layered over a white long-sleeved top, with my hair pulled into two low pigtails.

She dusted gold shimmer across my cheekbones, then pulled on her own outfit—dungarees, a cropped top, bright red lipstick—before declaring us ready.

Marching down the stairs, we shrugged our enormous coats on, and all our efforts disappeared beneath a blanket of fabric and stuffing.

'Bye, Mum! We're off to Tom's!' Emma shouted as we headed out the front door.

'Come back! Let me have a look,' came the reply. Emma's mum insisted that we show her what we were wearing under our coats.

'You look very nice, girls,' she said, eyes taking in Emma's red lips and my iridescent cheeks. 'Just to Tom's house, is it?'

'Of course, Mum,' Emma replied brightly. 'We're just going to watch a film.' Mrs McCarthy turned to me, and I felt my face grow hot. If she questioned me about our plans, I had no doubt I would spill the beans.

Look natural. Smile! Make eye contact.

I could feel her beady eyes on my face.

Eventually, she nodded.

'Alright. Have fun, girls, don't be late back!' she said, smiling thinly.

Once outside, I let out a breath I hadn't realised I was holding. 'Your mum is terrifying,' I whispered. 'I honestly thought she was reading my mind.'

'Tell me about it. It's like living with Sherlock Holmes,' laughed Emma.

Skipping down the steps, a bright, crisp April day awaited us. The sun was already high in the sky, but its power was limited, so we could barely feel much heat on our faces. Emma's road was lined with enormous silver birch trees, still bare from the winter but sporting the tiniest sprinkling of green buds. We barrelled down a hill, a bundle of energy, chatting and laughing as we went.

As we got to the end of Tom's Road, my heart started to beat faster at the knowledge that Nick might be there, and I felt a sharp pang of pain as I thought about what Johnnie had said the night before. If Nick couldn't stand me, why did he ask if I would be around today? Was it just so that he could avoid me? A bitter feeling of rejection joined the cacophony of emotions swirling around in my stomach.

I hopped down the steps to Tom's front door and rang the bell, with Emma following closely behind. Andy answered the door majestically.

'Miss Page.' He nodded down at me with his knowing Buddha smile.

'Hi, Andy.' I felt myself beaming suddenly, all braces and gappy teeth.

'Not driving today, Miss McCarthy?' He looked over my shoulder at Emma and at the road where no car was parked.

'Oh. No. My parents needed the car today,' Emma lied badly.

Andy nodded along knowingly and looked back at me. 'Of course. Well, Tom is in the back room. If you'll excuse me, ladies, I have to get to work.'

'Bye, Andy!' Emma and I both chimed at the same time. A look passed between us as he went, and we silently acknowledged the same thing. Andy was tooth-achingly cool.

In the back living room, we found Tom and Johnnie, but no Nick. My heart sank, and I felt desperately disappointed. Still, I was so glad to see the rest of my friends. We settled in for a chat, and later, we headed out with a football to a local green space known creatively as 'The Green'. Some people who lived around the edge were already out on the grass, and Emma knew some of them, so she introduced us all. Before long, we were having a fantastic game of football, followed by pizza on the field from a little pizzeria on the corner. Finally, Emma said she wanted to go to the off-license to bring back some booze.

'You'll never get served,' one of our new friends, Jamie-from-The-Green, chimed in. 'Good luck with that!'

To us, it felt like a challenge, which we eagerly accepted. Emma and I headed off together in the direction of Victoria Wines, and as we approached, I noticed a sign in the window that said anyone under eighteen would not be served. I was immediately transported back to the last time we were there.

'Maybe this is a bad idea, Em,' I said, feeling nervous and pointing to the sign. 'Andy is obviously working now, and there's no way he'll serve us.'

Emma paused, deep in thought. 'Okay, how's this?' she said, as though struck by a wave of inspiration. 'We pass by on the opposite side of the road and look to see if Matthew Dyer is working. We can wait until Andy's out the back restocking or whatever. Then, we go in. Otherwise, we can just leave and try the other offie up the road,' she suggested. 'What do you reckon?'

'Okay, that sounds good,' I conceded. I had to give it to Emma, after years of outsmarting her parents, she came up with cunning plans impressively quickly.

We sidled up outside Victoria Wines and casually stopped in front of a house on the opposite side of the road. Emma pretended to see someone in the upstairs window and waved theatrically up at them. Meanwhile, I bent down to tie my shoelace and peered carefully in the shop window from afar. It was darker inside than out, but I could just about make out the counter.

'Matthew Dyer's there, Em,' I whispered. 'No sign of Andy… Let's go!'

Emma let out a giggle under her breath. She waved again at the pretend person in the house and then stepped into the road. But just as I was getting up, my eyes caught sight of Andy at the other end of the counter, already watching me. With a surge of adrenaline, I froze.

'Crap. Andy's there!' I muttered under my breath.

But Emma either hadn't heard me, or she didn't care, because before I could stop her, she was already pushing open the door.

'Andy's there! Andy's there!' I called after her without moving my lips, attempting to abort the mission. But Emma was inside the shop already. I had no choice other than to go in after her.

By the time I caught up, Dyer was smiling at Emma as though all his Christmases had come at once. He was wearing the same messy hairstyle as last time, and he was still laughing at some unspoken joke. He smirked at Andy, who didn't smile back, and I felt suddenly ill at ease. For some reason, it felt as though the joke might be on Emma, or on both of us. I glanced over at Andy myself, and he watched me, his expression unreadable, and something hung heavily in the air between us.

Dyer turned back to Emma, and his smile widened. 'Hello, beautiful,' he said, and she positively simpered in front of him. 'What can I help you with today?'

'We're not sure. Maybe you can help us pick out a wine?' Emma twiddled with her hair and stuck her chest out, and Dyer stopped to notice, not taking his eyes off her for a second.

'Wine for sophisticated girls, hey?' he laughed and came out from behind the counter, guiding Emma off to a case of shelves on one side of the shop.

I watched them leave, not sure if I should follow, then looked at Andy, who was still watching me coolly. I felt awful. I managed a small smile, and he sent a small smile back, but it wasn't the same one as before.

Andy watched Dyer and Emma at the wine cabinet as Dyer put his hand on the small of her back to guide her. Dyer looked back at me and grinned. I fidgeted in my shoes and turned back to Andy, thinking about what to say.

'We're playing football at The Green,' I blurted, needing to fill the silence.

Andy's expression softened a little. 'That's nice,' he said, gently.

'What time do you finish?' I asked clumsily, feeling silly and wishing I'd never come in. 'Maybe we'll still be there, and you can play with us.'

Play with us!? What am I, like, five!?

'I'll be done in a couple of hours,' he nodded noncommittally, his eyes moving back to Dyer and Emma at the wine cabinet.

From the darkened doorway of the back room, someone stepped into view. He looked about the same age as Dyer—nineteen, maybe twenty—with dark hair clipped close to his scalp and a long, pale scar running cleanly down one cheek, as though it had once been split open by a knife. The overhead light caught on a tattoo that stretched across the back of his neck in a black gothic banner. He leaned one shoulder against the doorframe, loose and unhurried.

His eyes found me immediately, and they didn't flick away, although mine did. Straight to the floor. And back up again, just to be polite. But his eyes… his eyes stayed steady. I could feel them travelling slowly down my body, exploring every inch of me, while a smile tugged at one corner of his mouth. Not a friendly smile. And not amused, either. Something else. Something that made my arms prickle and a heavy weight settle low in my stomach, as though the air around him had curdled.

Andy followed my line of sight. 'You've got nothing to do back there?' he said evenly.

The man let out a short, humourless laugh through his nose—a sneer more than a sound—and pushed himself off the frame, disappearing back into the shadows without a word.

Silence fell between us until Dyer and Emma returned to the counter with a bottle of wine, a six-pack of beer and some Bacardi Breezers. Then, Dyer rang them up delightedly. Andy watched hawkishly for a moment as though considering what to do.

Then he sighed and headed over to the till.

'Have you asked these ladies for ID, Dyer?' he asked, his voice low and calm. Matthew Dyer stopped, turned to Andy and laughed.

'Are you joking?' he demanded incredulously.

'No, I'm not joking. We can't serve these girls without ID. They're clearly under eighteen.'

'Mate, you didn't care the other day. What the hell, man!?' Dyer bristled, agitated.

'Well,' Andy shrugged, as he moved in to occupy the space between Dyer and the till. 'I do now. You're not going to serve them until they are old enough to have ID.'

Dyer paused, considering his next move and Emma and I watched on, open-mouthed and alarmed. Something funny was going on. Something I didn't fully understand. I flashed back to the boyish roughhousing in the street the week before, and this felt a million miles from that. I was frightened that the pair might start fighting, and I didn't want Andy to get hurt. I mean, how would I explain to Tom that his brother had been injured because of something that Emma and I did?

After what felt like an age, Dyer put his hands up and backed away from the till, walking silently into the back room. Cool as a cucumber, Andy put the unpurchased bottles behind the counter and deleted the order from the cash register.

'Can I get you something non-alcoholic, ladies?' he asked flatly, only the slightest upturned corner of his mouth betraying his underlying amusement.

Emma and I looked at each other, defeatedly. 'Just some lemonade and some Doritos, please,' huffed Emma.

'Certainly.'

Andy rang up our new order, handed us our bag, and leaned on the counter with one elbow and a widening smile as we meekly exited the shop.

Outside, Emma was livid.

'Oh my God. What an ARSEHOLE!' she exclaimed, 'Can you believe that?'

I felt torn. On the one hand, I wanted to agree with my friend, but on the other hand, I wasn't so sure.

'That was weird,' I said, managing to describe how I felt without agreeing or disagreeing about Andy's arsehole status. Emma continued to rant and rave as we walked to another off-licence to try again.

'Well, Andy will be done in a couple of hours, and then Dyer will be there alone if you want to go back?' I told her and instantly regretted it. Emma was thrilled and decided to go back to Victoria Wines later, after my dad had picked me up.

'You really shouldn't go back there alone,' I said, wishing I'd never said anything.

'It'll be fine! Honestly, don't worry about it!' Emma told me, exasperatedly. 'I'll call you when I get home anyway and tell you how it went.'

'Make sure that you do,' I insisted as we entered a second shop.

Fifteen minutes later, we triumphantly rejoined our friends sitting on the grass, carrying a stash of Bacardi Breezers.

***

When Emma called me at home at 10 pm that night, she announced that she'd gone back to Victoria Wines to see Dyer, and she was already unmistakably smitten.

'Oh my God, he's *so* amazing, Sarah,' she gushed. 'He took me out the back, and we smoked a joint. Then, all of a sudden, we were all over each other, right there in the alley behind the shop. He's such a good kisser!'

My mind reeled. Emma had smoked weed with Dyer.

The elderly part of my brain—the one that sounded suspiciously like a headmistress—wondered what kind of adult gave drugs to a sixteen-year-old girl and then kissed her in an alleyway.

'You smoked weed?' I asked, stunned.

'Oh, come *on*, Sarah.' Emma said, her voice tightening before relaxing again. 'Yes. I smoked weed. It's not a big deal. It was *fun*! I'm meeting him again tomorrow after school—he's taking me to the cinema!'

'That's a bit quick, isn't it?' I ventured, feeling confused and oddly hurt that she seemed to think I was being childish.

'I know,' she squealed. 'He said he couldn't wait to see me again!'

Maybe he wasn't so bad.

'Well, if you think he really likes you,' I conceded.

Emma assured me that he did, and from that day on, she couldn't stop talking about Matthew Dyer. They became inseparable. Wherever one went, the other followed. Matthew Dyer could do no wrong. Matthew Dyer was her everything.

Matthew Dyer was Emma's new God.

4
The Fork in the Road

May 1998

THE DINING ROOM TABLE AT EMMA'S HOUSE had become a war zone of textbooks, notes, and empty cups. The usual laughter and banter had been replaced by the rustle of pages and the occasional frustrated sigh—a soundtrack to the collective stress of GCSE exams looming over us like a dark cloud.

I sat there, trying to appear focused on a physics textbook, but in reality, my mind was in a frenzy of distraction. Around me, the atmosphere was tense. Tom was tapping his pen against the table in a nervous rhythm while Emma and Jennifer were arguing over the proper way to approach a tricky maths problem. Meanwhile, Johnnie, reclining back in his chair, was inputting data into a calculator with a resigned concentration.

We were all in the same boat: adrift on a sea of mock exams and practice papers, each trying desperately to find some solid ground upon which to rest our hopes for the future. Yet my attention felt as divided as my interests. My braces, freshly tightened, added a dull throb to my jaw that I tried to ignore. But that was only part of the problem. The real issue was Nick. He sat across from me, completely absorbed in writing out a pile of Biology flashcards. To him, I was just another study compatriot, but to me, he was at the centre of my universe.

As I read and reread the same paragraph, I could see him in the corner of my vision all the time. Giddy just from being near him, I struggled to sit still but kept glancing at the top of his head.

Exasperated, I closed the book on star formation and poured myself a glass of water from a jug in the middle of the table. Then, as if reading my mind, Nick looked across at me and nodded to get my attention.

'Can you test me again?' he whispered, offering up a pile of freshly written flashcards and sitting back in his chair expectantly.

'Sure, what subject this time?' I asked, trying not to show my excitement.

'Biology,' he said, doom featuring heavily in his voice. 'The exam is on Monday. I have to do well if I'm going to be a doctor someday.'

I nodded sympathetically. *I wonder what he actually wants to study*, I thought, remembering what Emma had told me about his mum pressuring him.

Just then, there was a knock at the dining room door. It was Matthew Dyer for Emma. Jennifer looked up, scowling as Emma leapt up from the table to greet him in the hallway. Emma's mum stood behind him, looking unhappy about the visit, and I noticed her dart a heated glance at Jennifer.

As though on cue, Jennifer spoke. 'Matthew, we're studying; Emma has exams next week; can you come back later?' she asked pointedly.

'Yes, Matthew, it's really not a good time,' Mrs McCarthy chimed in.

Emma smiled. 'It won't take long, Mum,' she cooed, pulling Dyer into the dining room, wrapping her arms around his neck and kissing him.

The whole room recoiled slightly in disgust, unprepared for such public displays of affection, and Mrs McCarthy looked positively queasy.

'That's enough of that, you two,' Mrs McCarthy said, going red in the face and raising her voice. 'Your friends are studying. They don't need the pair of you making a spectacle of yourselves.'

Tension poured into the dining room, and no one was paying attention to their notes anymore. But Jennifer was not to be deterred. Her gaze sharpened, boring holes into the back of Emma's head.

'We were halfway through a maths practice paper, Emma,' she said.

Dyer smirked. 'Calm down, Jennifer! I can help,' he oozed, looking at Jennifer with satisfaction, his joke on the world still something only he knew. 'What's the question?'

Jennifer bristled with indignation and ignored him, staring directly at Emma, who blinked back at her blankly before reluctantly walking back to the table.

'I won't be long, *my love*,' said Emma, 'we just have a couple of questions left, and then I can take a break.'

Satisfied, Dyer came further into the dining room and stood in front of our study table for a moment, looking at Nick. 'Wanna go for a ciggie?' he asked, and Nick nodded and got up from the table to join him.

'What about Biology?' I called after him, anxious not to lose Nick to Dyer and his cigarettes.

Nick turned around, thought for a moment and gestured for me to come out, too. 'Bring the cards,' he said, so I grabbed them and jumped up, my heart soaring at the idea of spending some extra time with him.

We walked past a scowling Mrs McCarthy and through the hallway with Dyer leading the way.

'There'll be no smoking in the garden, boys,' warned Mrs McCarthy.

As we reached the front door, Nick stood back and held it open for me. It was such a small gesture, and yet it felt so unexpectedly sweet that my braces pressed hard against my lips as I fought the urge to smile. As I passed, he looked down at me openly, and my heart soared. Finally, Nick was looking at me the way I wanted him to.

At the end of the driveway, we turned left along the broad, leafy avenue. A little further down, there was a wooded patch with a bench tucked discreetly behind a line of trees. We sat, and I pulled out my deck of flashcards to quiz Nick.

'What is the name of the organelle that releases energy in human cells?' I asked.

Nick lit a cigarette and scrunched up his nose, thinking hard, a habit I found irresistibly cute. Having gotten used to the fact that he smoked, I couldn't have felt happier until, with a sudden thrill, I realised he'd draped his arm along the back of the bench, behind me. I was about to lean into it when I noticed movement beside him.

Dyer was breaking a cigarette into a small rectangle of white paper in his lap. Then, he pulled out a little bag of green herbs and crumbled them on top. Marijuana. I'd never seen anyone roll a joint before, but having not been born on the moon, it was immediately obvious what it was.

'What the hell are you doing?' I blurted out, unable to hide my alarm. 'We're revising for our exams on Monday! Why are you making... *that*?'

Dyer ignored me and smiled. 'Just relax, Page,' he said. 'Emma's tried it, she likes it. It's no big deal. You should really just chill out and try some.' Then he rolled the paper into a cigarette shape between his fingers.

Nick shifted in his seat uncomfortably and sighed heavily before speaking. 'Sarah is right. We should probably just stick to the cigarettes today, mate.' Nick sounded anything but determined as we watched Dyer roll the joint.

'Mate, it'll help you concentrate,' Dyer giggled, a strange sound I could imagine coming from a villain in a children's cartoon.

'You're insane!' I protested. 'We're going back inside; we've got loads of work to do.' I jumped up from the bench and gestured for Nick to come, too.

But he didn't.

Nick stayed where he was.

'I'll be in in a minute, Trouble,' he looked at me, his hands in his pockets and his eyes tinged with sadness, like a puppy hopping onto a vet's table that knows it's about to be put to sleep.

'What? No! Nick, come on, I'll test you in Biology; you've got the exam on Monday…' But even as I protested, I knew it was too late. I looked from Nick's resigned eyes to Dyer's dancing ones and cursed him from the depths of my soul.

Then, a figure emerged from the shadows of the trees, his hands tucked into the pockets of his hoodie.

'Thought I might find you here,' he said lazily.

'Yo!' Dyer tossed back.

It was the same man from the shop—the one with the long scar slicing down his cheek. He moved with an easy, unhurried confidence, like someone who was used to getting what he wanted.

'Still not allowed to smoke in the Holy Vatican household, eh?' the man added with a crooked grin.

Dyer gave a half-laugh, and then the man's eyes shifted and landed on me. They stayed there, openly assessing me, as though I were something unexpected he hadn't accounted for.

'You alright?' he said, the question directed at me now.

I didn't answer.

Instead, I turned back to Nick.

'Come on. Come in. *Please,*' I pleaded, all my attention fixed on the person who had stolen my heart.

For a fraction of a second, I sensed it—the faintest change in the air. The man's smile faltered slightly. Not like he was wounded or embarrassed. Perhaps just a little… intrigued.

Nick shoved his hands deeper into his pockets.

'Just go in without me, Sarah. It'll be alright. I'll be back in a minute. I promise.'

With that, I turned and left without another word.

Nick never came back.

5

Cutting Loose

June 1998

DAYS BLURRED INTO NIGHTS, and before long, the exams were in mid-flow—a whirlwind of forgotten meals and late-night cramming and, finally, the last turning of papers and the collective exhale of relief as we left the exam room for the last time.

I remember it so clearly, such a beautiful day, with the sun beaming down as if to congratulate us. Finally, our GCSEs were behind us, and for those planning to take A-levels, school was over for six whole weeks. The summer lay ahead of us like a land of limitless possibilities, and in celebration, we picked up our pens and ran around signing each other's white shirts and blouses, writing sweet messages of good luck and best wishes.

Later that day, as soon as I got home, I ran to the telephone to call Emma and found my older brother Lucas using it with my little sister Bethany watching nearby. With his hair worn in blonde curtains, my brother was a dead ringer for David Beckham, the Manchester United player. The only thing missing was a Spice Girl on his arm to pose with.

Urging him to hurry up and get off the phone, he reluctantly obliged, and Bethany and Lucas started reading the notes on my shirt with amusement as I made my call. Inspired, Bethany ran to her room and got a green felt-tip pen and added three hearts to my sleeve. Feeling happy, I planted a kiss on her cheek for each one.

Lucas, who was two years older than me, took up the pen and wrote me a note of congratulations for finishing my exams, signing it off by saying he would miss me when he went away to university in September.

'I'll miss you, too!' I smiled as I put down the phone and ran to my bedroom to get ready to go out.

'Where are you going?' called Lucas, curious about my burgeoning social life, which seemed to have emerged from nowhere and surprised everyone in my family over the past year.

'We're going to have a barbecue to celebrate finishing our exams!' I cried, already buzzing with excitement.

Less than an hour later, I hopped on the bus in the bright sunshine wearing pinstriped bootcut leggings, wedges, and a black puff-sleeved gypsy top. I gingerly applied my makeup as the driver hurtled through leafy green-belt avenues, trying not to poke myself in the eye as fields rolled past and the distant outline of the Big Smoke hovered on the horizon. Even from my hometown, way out in the sticks, as Johnnie liked to say, London's financial district was visible.

When I arrived at New Barnet station, Emma was already waiting (for once). Thrilled that the torture of studying was finally over, we squealed, hugged, and jumped up and down like lunatics.

'Is Jennifer coming?' I asked once we'd calmed down.

'She can't,' Emma groaned. 'She's got some church social in St Albans.'

'Oh no! That's such a shame—she's going to miss all the fun,' I said. Jennifer seemed to be absent more and more these days.

'Yeah, I feel like her parents are getting worse or something,' Emma tutted. 'Come on. Let's get some booze. They serve Johnnie in here, so we'll be fine.'

A few minutes later, we emerged triumphant, clutching a bag of alcopops and beer.

This is going to be the most epic night of our lives, I thought as we tottered down the road towards The Green. At least it would be until the Youth Summer Ball at Alexandra Palace, which was two weeks away and felt like an entire lifetime.

When we arrived at The Green, Johnnie and Tom had set up camp on the grass, and when they saw us approaching, they jumped up and hugged us joyously. Some of the kids who lived around the edge had wired up a stereo to play music from their driveway. It couldn't have felt more like summer.

'Where's Nick?' I asked, Tom subtly looking around for him, as we sat in a circle on the grass next to the younger kids playing football.

'He's bringing the barbecue,' Tom explained, unwrapping a packet of hamburgers and a bottle of ketchup from a carrier bag. That reminded me. Opening my bag, I pulled out a pack of sausages and mustard, and Tom and I made a little pile in the middle of the circle. Beside me, Emma pulled out a pack of marinated chicken legs and a bottle of barbecue sauce and added them to the heap, while Johnnie looked on worriedly.

'I couldn't get anything, guys,' he said, shaking his head morosely. 'I'm sorry, my mum forgot to go shopping.' Tom and I exchanged a knowing look. Johnnie's mum had *not* forgotten to go shopping: he'd forgotten to *ask* her to buy something. 'It's okay, I'll get some pizza from the shop in a bit,' Johnnie gestured towards Reno's, the pizzeria on the corner, and we let out a little cheer because Reno's pizza was the best.

'Does anyone have a bottle opener?' asked Tom, pulling out a bottle of beer from his carrier bag.

'I've got one!' came a voice approaching from behind us.

It was Nick! He and Jamie-from-The-Green were coming across the grass with a disposable barbecue and a clinking carrier bag full of bottles. The gang greeted them excitedly, everyone except me jumping up to hug them. The kids stopped their game for a moment to swarm Nick, ever the big, friendly giant, and then he plopped himself opposite me in the circle and gave me a friendly nod.

'Alright, Trouble?' he asked casually, looking me in the eye with a playful glint that made my stomach do flips.

'Yeah, not bad,' I replied nonchalantly, tossing my straightened hair over my shoulder and waiting for my turn with the bottle opener to open my pineapple Bacardi Breezer. 'How did your exams go?'

'Crap,' Nick replied matter-of-factly. 'How about yours?'

'Not too bad, I don't think,' I said truthfully. 'But I'm really glad they're over.'

'Cheers to that, we're free for the summer!' he exclaimed. We clinked our bottles and took a long sip; neither of us sure what to say next, so we sat there in silence for a moment. Then Nick regarded me for a moment. 'You look nice today,' he said warmly, and I felt myself getting giddy. He looked at my hand. 'Is that new?' he said, gesturing to a ring my mum had just given me. 'Can I have a look?'

'Sure. It's coral.'

Too nervous to give him my hand, I passed him the pink carved ring, and he inspected it carefully. 'It's beautiful,' he said, 'I like the colour.' Then, like a magician doing a slight of hand trick, he clicked his fingers, and the ring had disappeared. 'Do you mind if I keep it?' He asked deadpan, and I blinked at his empty palm, amazed.

'Oh, wow!' I gushed, impressed. *Nick knows magic tricks!?* 'That was amazing! Where's it gone?'

Nick smiled, and then, with another slight of hand, the ring reappeared in his palm. But rather than give it back to me, he slipped it into his pocket with a smile and looked away as though he knew nothing about any ring.

'So mature,' I rolled my eyes, suppressing a grin and crossing my arms. 'Can I have it back, please?'

'What, you mean, this?' he teased playfully, predictably pulling it out and holding it up in front of me.

Uh. Oldest routine in the world! I tried to tell myself. But the rest of my brain was already doing backflips with the circus.

I rolled my eyes and tried not to smile. 'Real mature!' I faux-moaned.

As Nick eased the ring towards me, I made a grab for it, the front of my body pressing against his arm as I leaned across him to grab it, and suddenly, there were sparks flying between us. Nick pulled it away with an easy smile, so that it was always just out of reach.

'You can have that back *later*…' he winked, pocketing it again. '…But right now, it's time to spark up this bad boy,' he said, gesturing to the barbecue and pulling a lighter out of his pocket, instead of my ring.

Incredulous but far too proud to beg, I looked around for Emma to tell her that Nick had stolen my ring and saw her disappearing with Johnnie into Reno's Pizza. Alone with Nick and Tom, I cradled my Bacardi Breezer. I took a minuscule sip, aware of my lightweight status and not wanting to do anything embarrassing.

Soon, Nick was expertly flipping burgers on the barbecue, the sizzle and aroma making my stomach rumble with anticipation while Tom fiddled with the stereo and played us nostalgic tunes. Much to our delight, as the sunset painted the sky in hues of orange, Johnnie and Emma returned triumphantly with a pizza and garlic bread from Reno's. We all dug in, enjoying the food and each other's company as the afternoon bled seamlessly into the evening. I eagerly grabbed a slice of garlic bread, the crunchy crust and lush garlicky butter melting in my mouth with each bite.

In the dusk, Nick, Tom and Emma got up to kick a ball around before it got dark, and Johnnie and I lounged contentedly, too full to want to move much. Johnnie tossed a pizza crust into his box and turned to me with a playful grin.

'Do us all a favour and find some gum, will you, Trouble? You've got garlic breath that could knock out a cow,' he teased, waving his hand dramatically in front of his nose.

Horrified, I searched my bag for some gum but found none. 'Is it really that bad?' I asked, embarrassed.

'Awful,' laughed Johnnie. 'Not that different from normal, actually.'

I rolled my eyes and smiled. 'Shut up, or I'll breathe on you!' I quipped and jumped up to go to the corner shop. As I stood, I could feel that I'd gotten a little tipsy, and I could see everyone else had, too. 'I'm going to go and buy some gum, then. Do you want anything?' I asked.

'I'll have a pack as well if you're going,' winked Johnnie, and I realised I'd done exactly what he wanted me to do.

'You're so lazy!' I bent over and threw a pizza crust at him, but he dodged it and lay back on the grass smugly in the sun's fading glow as I walked off.

Spotting me alone, Nick ran over to join me. 'Mind if I tag along?' he asked, his eyes glinting with his familiar playful charm. I nodded, trying to act naturally despite the intense fluttering in my chest. Together, we wandered away from the group, and my eyes fixated on the corner shop: the Promised Land of Gum. My minty salvation from garlic breath. Who knew what might happen between Nick and me if I could get hold of some? I suppressed a smile as my head swam with luscious possibilities.

But much to my alarm, Nick gently guided me to sit on a garden wall just out of everyone's view.

What's he doing? Is he… are we… having a moment? NOW!? When I stink like garlic? My heart started pounding as I realised what was happening.

'Thanks for all the help with my revision,' Nick began as he sat down next to me—placing himself between me and the shop. I glanced achingly at it over his shoulder. So close and yet so far away.

'Maybe we should…' I pointed at the door intently.

'I know I wasn't always the best student,' Nick continued, gently taking my hand in his and stroking it with his thumb.

Oh my. We're really doing this! My skin came alive at his touch, and I found myself lost in Nick's eyes, inches from mine. I was so swept away, I almost forgot about my breath.

Turn away! You stink like garlic! I berated myself. I quickly bowed my head demurely and smiled, hoping I wasn't giving off "rejection" vibes.

Nick seemed to find my coyness irresistible. Fixing me with a smouldering gaze, he lifted my hand to his lips and kissed it tenderly. Unable to help myself, my eyes were drawn up to him like a magnet. But I couldn't let our first kiss be disgusting and smelly!

I considered getting up and yanking him towards the shop. But I couldn't bring myself to break the moment. Who knew if I'd get another chance again? So, I gave up on my mission of gum and angled my body so that we were sitting side by side on the wall.

'I'm just glad the exams are over,' I confided to the empty street, my hand still in Nick's and my heart pounding a million beats a minute. Unable to kiss him or to break free from his spell, I seized the moment to abate my curiosity about his life instead. 'How's it going with Matthew Dyer these days?' I asked, glancing up at him sideways. With horrified yet delicious glee, I realised he was gazing intently at my lips, apparently intent on seducing me. 'He seemed to be leading you astray before the exams,' I added, shakily.

Nick squeezed my hand and laughed softly, a sound that caused my heart to skip. 'It's alright. My mum doesn't like him, but then, she doesn't like me much right now,' he admitted, his face growing more serious. 'I haven't told anyone except Tom this, but actually…' Nick paused as though he wasn't sure about whether he should continue. 'The police arrested us a few weeks ago.' I swung my head to face him in alarm and swung it right back before he could smell me.

'Crap, no way!' I exclaimed to the road.

Nick nodded gravely. 'They searched us, and we both had some weed on us. My dad had to come and get me from the police station. This time, they let me off with a warning; next time, they said I wouldn't be so lucky.' Nick's thumb kept gently rubbing my hand as he spoke. 'My mum absolutely hit the roof when she found out. She kept screaming that I can't get into medical school if I have a criminal record.'

'Do you actually want to be a doctor?' I asked, my eyes darting up to meet his before darting back to my feet again.

Nick's eyes glazed over for a moment as though he were lost in a painful memory. Then he sighed, let go of my hand and faced the street head-on, the same as me. His seduction apparently abandoned, we were just two people sitting on a wall, finally getting to know each other.

'Not really,' he admitted, shrugging. 'But then, I don't really know what else I would do. So, I reckon, why not? If it keeps my mum off my back. But it's so much pressure. I really don't know I'm clever enough, but it's like she doesn't even want to know,' he scoffed, and I nodded sympathetically. Then he turned to me. 'What about you? Do you know what you want to do?' he asked, glancing sideways at me.

'No not really,' I chuckled, beginning to feel more at home with Nick than I ever had before. 'Although I was thinking the other day it might be cool to be a journalist.'

'Oh, I can totally see that. You'd be good at that,' agreed Nick, giving me a playful nudge with his shoulder. 'You're very tenacious! I can imagine you chasing down a story.'

'Ha! I thought you said I was soft?' I laughed, thinking back to our run-in at the funfair. 'And that I'd get mugged if you weren't around?'

Nick cracked up at the reference. 'Ha! What the hell did I know!? You're anything but soft! But you're sweet,' he reassured me with a grin. 'And you're also smart. And persistent.' He paused. 'You certainly didn't give up on me too easily when we were revising,' he said, taking my hand again, a touch of a smile touching his lips.

A warm glow throbbed in my chest as I realised I had actually helped him. We talked then, for over an hour, my hand in his, as the sun set around us and the street grew dark. At last, it felt so much easier to talk to him. I wondered if he felt the same.

'You know, you can always talk to me about anything if you need to,' I said softly.

Leaning into me, Nick brushed a stray lock of hair off my cheek, a mounting silence building between us. 'You're sweet, you know?' he said, shifting closer so that his leg was pressed against mine and his arm encircled me, his hand resting on the wall.

No longer thinking clearly—intoxicated by his embrace and his body heat—my head started swimming. My thumb started caressing Nick's hand encouragingly. He leaned in further, his fingers tracing lightly along my cheek and down to my neck, where he placed a soft kiss. The sensation sent a thrill through me, and all I wanted was to turn and kiss him back.

Maybe a kiss right now wouldn't be so bad. Maybe he won't notice that I taste horrible. I contemplated looking up into his face, and I knew what would happen if I did. He was waiting for me to do it. Willing me to. I could feel it. My heart pounded as I considered whether to kiss him.

Just then, Johnnie's voice pierced the charged silence. 'Oi! Where's my gum, you two lovebirds?' he teased, strolling past our position on the wall with a knowing grin. 'Oh, I see what's going on here,' he chuckled to himself before heading towards the shop.

The interruption left Nick and me suspended in a moment we couldn't quite bring ourselves to act on. I felt breathless with the urge to finally taste his lips and succumb to the kiss I craved. But reluctantly, I pulled away, flashing an apologetic smile, and made up a lame excuse to run after Johnnie.

'I'll be back!' I shouted back at him as he watched me running away.

When I reached the shop, thrilled to have finally reached gum, a clock on the wall brought home how late it was, and I realised with horror that I'd lost all track of time. The last bus would be leaving

New Barnet Station within a few minutes, and I'd be stranded if I didn't run to catch it.

Running out of the shop, I noticed for the first time that it had gotten completely dark while I'd been sitting on the wall with Nick. Running back to the wall, Nick was no longer there.

Where is he?

I ran to The Green, but Nick was nowhere to be seen. Rushing up to our circle of friends still sitting around the glowing embers of our barbecue, I grabbed my bag from the middle and told Emma I would miss the last bus if I didn't run. My mum had already insisted I go home that night rather than stay at Emma's.

Leaping up, Emma grabbed her bag too, and we ran at full pelt through the streets until we reached the top of the hill overlooking New Barnet station. The 84 bus was resting there, and the driver had just turned the lights on. I hugged Emma and ran down the hill, jumping on board just as the driver started the engine.

Momentarily exhilarated to have made it in time, I grinned back at Emma breathlessly, just as the boys emerged over the crest of the hill, Nick out in front. He stared at me, ashen-faced as I mounted the bus, and I waved at him cheerily, but he just stood there, motionless, as the bus pulled away. Watching the outlines of my friends disappear in the distance, something inside me sank. I couldn't shake the feeling that Nick was somehow lost forever. But then, when I looked down at my hands, I noticed my bare-naked finger and felt a stirring of hope.

Nick still had my coral ring.

6

The Water Fight

A WEEK OR SO LATER, I hadn't seen or heard from Nick, and I found myself hanging out at Tom's. With the sun high in the sky and a blanket of balmy heat covering the neighbourhood, Tom and I were crouching behind the massive oak tree in his back garden, his 'Super-Soaker' water gun poised and ready. I stifled a laugh as Andy appeared from behind the garden shed with his own Super-Soaker, completely unaware of our presence. Tom pushed a finger to his lips, and together, we peered out at his brother as he scouted the exterior of the house, trying to work out where we were hiding.

The game had begun a few minutes earlier, when Tom had soaked his unsuspecting brother as he got home from work. Realising that I was there, and ever the gentleman when girls were present, Andy had gone easy on his brother, and instead of a physical altercation breaking out, he'd chased him out into the garden and soaked him with the hose.

With Tom attempting to outmanoeuvre Andy, a plan had hatched in my mind, and I had run quickly upstairs. Clutching a large tub of water gleefully, I crept up to the bathroom window and pushed the pane gently outward. With a quick flick of my wrist, I had upended the tub, drenching Andy completely. In the commotion, Tom had made his escape and hidden in the coal store under the house.

Momentarily stunned, Andy had turned and stared at me in disbelief, hose still in hand, before calmly following his brother to the coal store and locking him inside. Then he had cockily strutted back to the garden and stared straight back up at me.

'You're going to regret that, Miss Page,' he had warned, narrowing his eyes and smiling. 'My brother's not the only one with a Super Soaker around here.'

'I'm really scared!' I had mocked blatantly as I refilled the tub with water, planning to soak him again if I could. Secretly, I had felt more than a little scared of Andy but had really enjoyed the thrill of it, not that I would have admitted it to anyone.

Andy had just returned from a week in the Scottish Highlands, where he had pitched his tent on the top of a lonely hill and built fires, cooked and written—although what he had been writing about, he wouldn't tell a living soul. Impressed and inspired by his free spirit, I decided that as soon as I had my own car, I would drive it wherever the wind took me. I imagined boarding a ferry to France and sleeping in my car or a tent wherever I felt like it across Europe.

When I looked back down, heart pounding in my chest, Andy had disappeared somewhere beneath the window ledge, leaving only the sound of his retreating footfalls. Wary of his impending revenge, I had snuck down and let Tom out of the coal store.

Now, here we were, watching as Andy reemerged, carrying his own Super-Soaker and on the prowl. He paused and looked around when he discovered the coal store door wide open, his brother long-since escaped. Tom shot me a conspiratorial grin, and together, we darted from our hiding spot, unleashing a torrent of water towards him, and Andy ducked for cover behind the old greenhouse.

'Nice try, but it won't be that easy this time!' he called, his voice carrying above our footsteps. But our ambush had momentarily thrown him off balance.

Tom, seizing the opportunity, signalled for me to run up the back steps and into the living room, where I locked the door behind me, and he slipped silently towards the kitchen side door. His plan was to lock Andy out, because if we weren't able to, he knew we would be in for the soaking of our lives.

Realising Tom's plan, Andy rushed out of hiding just as I locked the back door. I watched as he ran around to the kitchen, where Tom was struggling to fit a key into the lock, but he turned it just as Andy grabbed the handle and rattled the door. Then there was silence. Eerie, terrifying silence. Tom and I reconvened breathlessly in the hallway.

'We did it!' I laughed, ecstatic with the joy of winning.

But Tom, all too familiar with the depth of his brother's resourcefulness, was already running towards the stairs, far from celebrating.

'He knows every way into this house!' he exclaimed, pulling shut the side window next to the stairs with a bang and locking it tight. 'We have to lock all the doors and windows! Quickly!'

Tom ran to the front door and bolted it before checking that the front room windows were secure. Then he ran back to the living room and bolted all the windows before checking the kitchen windows.

The house was eerily quiet, and Andy was nowhere to be seen.

We reconvened in the hallway, feeling nervously elated.

'What about the upstairs bathroom window?' I suggested, remembering that I had left it open.

Tom nodded. 'You close that. I'll go and check his bedroom windows.'

We headed up the stairs, out of breath but thrilled to be winning the game. After closing the bathroom window with a bang, I met Tom on the upstairs landing, and together we took a deep breath.

'Ha! Victory is ours!' exclaimed Tom, and we high-fived like Americans.

Then we relaxedly started walking down the stairs. Until, an unsettling dread crept over me.

'Tom, what about *your* room!?' I blurted, eyes wide with the realisation of an accessible weak spot we had overlooked.

Heart racing, I sprinted back upstairs just as a stealthy arm emerged around the windowpane, like a scene out of a horror film. Andy was edging across a narrow ledge from the kitchen's flat roof towards the open window, his fingers feeling blindly for purchase. Caught up in the moment and half-terrified by the sight of him there, I ran to the window and slammed it shut with a yelp.

For a split second, nothing happened.

Then his hand vanished.

There was a sharp, hollow crash—and Andy dropped out of sight.

'Andy!' I shouted, fearing I might have killed him. 'Andy!'

I flung open the window and leaned out, my heart hammering. I could see Andy's protruding head and shoulders below, the only parts of him still visible above the broken conservatory roof, his body dangling somewhere underneath.

'Oh my God,' I whispered. 'Are you okay?' I shouted, but Andy didn't reply. He didn't look up either; he simply dropped through the roof to the floor, and then all that was left of him was an Andy-shaped hole.

I stood frozen, not knowing what to do next.

Where was Tom?

Fearing that Andy might be hurt, I turned and bolted for the stairs, my chest tight with panic…

…only to skid to a halt as Andy burst out of the living room, drenched and looking like a crazed maniac, his water gun clutched in one hand.

'*Now I've got you, Miss Page*!' he grinned, as he came straight for me, soaking me with a jet from his water gun.

Screaming, I turned and fled back up the stairs and into Andy's bedroom, slamming the door behind me.

'*Let me in, Miss Page, the game's up*!' he yelled as I screamed and pushed hard against the door. It was no use. No matter how hard I leaned into it, Andy was pushing harder, forcing his way into the room despite my squeals of hysterical laughter and frantic attempts to keep him out.

Out of options, I glanced wildly around his room and spotted his stereo on a shelf beside the bed. Seizing on the only leverage I had, I jumped and threw myself onto the mattress in front of it just as Andy burst through the door, water gun raised, grinning like a madman.

'Get off the bed, Miss Page, it's time to pay the price,' he goaded me.

'Don't shoot! Don't shoot!' I pleaded, already soaked from the stairs. I pressed myself up against his stereo. 'Take your pick; you can soak your mattress or your stereo,' I said breathlessly. 'What will it be, *Mister East*?' I demanded, my eyes sparkling with a mixture of mischief and apprehension.

Somewhat taken aback, Andy looked at me as though he had underestimated me, and we both knew he didn't want to soak either. Not wanting to be beaten, he came towards me tentatively, and I could see that he was thinking carefully about trying to manoeuvre me away from the bed.

One step ahead, I sank back against the mattress and held my ground, my heart thudding as the air between us thickened. He leaned over me, uncertain now, hovering. Then he reached for my hand. I pulled it away, so he tried for my shoulder instead, inching closer. I could feel the heat of him, the brush of his arms, the solid weight of him looming above me. His skin was warm, his scent sharp and unfamiliar, and everything inside me went strangely quiet and loud at the same time.

For a moment, I didn't move. I didn't even laugh. I just lay there, caught between wanting to escape and not wanting to go anywhere. I wondered what it would be like to push my lips against his passionately. But instead, I grabbed his gun and ran for it.

Bounding down the stairs, I saw Andy standing motionless in his bedroom, red-faced and staring after me in disbelief. Then, I was running through the living room, out of the conservatory with the hole in the roof, and outside in the garden again with Tom. He had run to check on Andy after he'd fallen through the conservatory roof and, seeing that he was fine, ducked outside to hide, unseen.

Now in possession of both guns, Tom and I waited for Andy to reemerge so we could soak him one last time. But when he finally did, he came at such speed that we barely knew what was happening. He made it to the side of the house when, suddenly, Tom charged out after him. Pulling himself up onto the garage roof, Andy ran around to the front of the house and disappeared from our sight, with Tom in hot pursuit.

Never one to be left behind, I followed the brothers to the garage, but being much shorter, I struggled to scale the wall and hovered uselessly for a moment, watching them get away. Then I noticed a small window halfway up, with a narrow ledge beneath it—the glass already cracked and broken.

Trying not to think too hard about it, I pulled myself up, careful not to cut my hands, planted one foot on the ledge and hauled myself onto the roof after Tom. Adrenaline buzzing through me, I ran across the garage roof and then felt a sudden, sharp sting in my foot.

I stopped dead and realised I was bleeding.

Looking down, I saw blood pooling against the white strap of my flimsy summer sandal.

Urgh, I thought, my stomach lurching. I must have caught my foot on the jagged edge of the broken window. Shocked, I sat on the edge of the roof, inspecting my poor, injured foot and wondered how I was going to get down.

'Are you bleeding?' Andy's voice floated up from just below me, and I looked over the edge to see him peering up from a well-concealed hiding place next to the garage.

'I must have cut my foot on the window,' I admitted, suddenly feeling a bit woozy.

For a second, he just looked at me—assessing, deciding.

Then, before I knew it, Andy had jumped up and scooped me off the roof and carried me into the kitchen. Without saying a word, he placed me on a chair, filled a bowl with water, tore off some kitchen towel, and quietly washed my wound. When Tom burst in moments later, still holding his gun and grinning, he stopped dead at the sight of the pink-tinged water in the bowl.

'What happened?' he asked, his smile dropping away.

'I cut my foot on the garage window,' I confessed, embarrassed, but feeling a bit like a princess as Andy bent down in front of me, washing and drying my toes.

Andy was known more for his aloofness than acts of compassion, and yet here he was, focused entirely on me. The warmth of it spread through my chest in a way I hadn't expected.

A few minutes later, my foot was bandaged and throbbing painfully—but I found myself hungry for more of his attention.

Seizing the moment, I fished my Filofax out of my bag and asked him for a note. He hesitated, rolled his eyes slightly, then relented. After a moment's thought, he wrote two.

AN ILLUSTRATION OF ZEN

THE ZEN MASTER WAS ASKED THE SOLEMN QUESTION, 'WHAT IS BUDDHA?' SO, HE TOOK HIS SANDAL OFF, PUT IT ON HIS HEAD AND WALKED AWAY.

A NOTE ABOUT WOMEN

I LIKE WOMEN BECAUSE I LIKE THEIR EYES. I LIKE THEIR LEGS. WOMEN CAN TAKE A MAN TO THE EDGE BUT SELDOM DO. WOMEN CAN GIVE PLEASURE LIKE ONE GIVES CANDY TO A BABY, BUT HE WON'T BE THERE THE NEXT MORNING BECAUSE HE'S AFRAID SHE KNOWS HIM BETTER THAN HE KNOWS HIMSELF.

I stared at the page, deflated. That wasn't what I'd expected him to write. Far from it. There was nothing sweet, nothing personal.

I looked up at Andy, and he seemed oblivious to my puzzlement and very happy with his notes. I thought about taking my bloodstained sandal off, putting it on my head, and walking away. But I didn't. Instead, I called my mum from Tom and Andy's landline and told her I'd cut my foot.

Unmoved, Mum told me that unless I'd lost a leg, I was to get on the bus and come home. As I limped out of the driveway towards the bus stop with Tom, his mother arrived home, and I nervously said hello before hurriedly exiting. Hobbling down the street, we could hear her start to shout about the hole in her conservatory roof and the blood on her carpet. I wondered what poor Andy was saying.

Tom looked at me glumly. 'I'm going to tell her you broke the garage window,' he warned. 'Or she really might kill us when she sees that.'

'Sure,' I said, curious whether Tom or Andy had actually broken it. 'But just out of interest, was it you?'

Tom denied having broken the window, and Andy later denied it, too. That day, the boys fibbed and told their mother I'd started the water fight, broken the garage window and soaked everything. Whether she believed them or not—and most likely, she knew her sons better than to do so—the next time I saw her, she was surprisingly welcoming towards me.

7
The Dealer's Sister

Late June 1998

A FEW DAYS LATER, THE GANG WAS INVITED to Jamie-from-The-Green's seventeenth birthday bash. To mark the occasion, Emma and I hatched one of our most ambitious schemes yet. At the supermarket, while gathering supplies, Emma suggested we charm the manager into letting us borrow a shopping trolley. Slightly bewildered but seemingly unwilling to dampen our enthusiasm, he agreed, provided we returned it the next day (which, amazingly, we did).

Delighted with our success, we cheerfully manoeuvred our new 'vehicle' down the High Street, deftly dodging puzzled pedestrians despite its rebellious, squeaky wheel. Inside, we had an assortment of sweets, one too many bottles of alcopops, and a heap of crisps and snacks. The trolley felt like a symbol of our daring spirit—or at least, it did at sixteen. We proudly decorated it with flowers and leaves picked from trees and gardens along the way and charged onward down the street.

'Do you really think Jamie-from-The-Green's going to appreciate the flowers?' I asked, laughing, as Emma dodged a pothole.

She waved her hand in the air majestically, declaring with a grin, 'Of course, hon! Who doesn't love flowers on their birthday?'

By the time we rolled into Jamie-from-The-Green's street, the party was already in full swing. Stepping inside, my eyes immediately found Nick, Tom, and Johnnie huddled together. Nick cut a striking figure, looking tall and effortlessly stylish in his baggy jeans and loose t-shirt. Tom caught sight of us, turning with a friendly wave, which we returned eagerly. I silently hoped Nick might also glance our way, but his attention was fixed on a rather tipsy Johnnie. Nick had lined up three shots of a potent amber liquid and was convincing Johnnie that they should knock them back together. True to his nature, Johnnie accepted the challenge despite his already inebriated state.

Once settled inside the party, Emma and I stuck with our 'whacky' theme and assumed the role of whimsical mixologists, convincing everyone to participate in our 'sweeties in the drink' experiment. Much to our friends' great reluctance (and annoyance in some cases), we circulated the party, sprinkling sugary jelly tots and Liquorice All Sorts into their cups as we went, under the misguided impression that we were being funny and cute.

A few minutes later, with a bag of sweets in hand, I arrived where Nick and Tom were standing, trying to revive a not-so-well Johnnie with some coffee. The room buzzed with grins and lively banter, but Nick remained quiet, his gaze fixed on me with a cool, enigmatic expression.

Once Tom had reluctantly agreed to drop some jelly tots into his beer, I shifted my attention to Nick.

'What do you say? A few of these will make your drink irresistible,' I suggested, nodding towards his glass of whisky and cola.

He pulled his glass back defensively, a smirk playing on his lips. 'As if,' he scoffed, eyes narrowing slightly.

'Please?' I coaxed, leaning in with a coy smile, my eyes wide and lips gently pouting. Nick paused, his face softening as if caught off guard. His gaze, once cool, grew warmer, charged with an undeniable spark.

'Everyone else is trying it,' I murmured, glancing down demurely before locking eyes with him again, letting a hint of seduction lace my voice.

Holding my gaze, Nick slowly extended his cup towards me. I dropped a few jelly tots and a Liquorice All Sort into the drink, my fingers lightly brushing against his. I flashed a sweet, teasing smile, fluttering my lashes in gratitude. 'Thank you,' I whispered, our eyes locked for a lingering moment before I sauntered away to my next target. As I moved, I could feel his gaze trailing me, a silent acknowledgement that, at last, I had captured his attention completely.

Having completed our round of the party, Emma and I regrouped with the boys, regaling them with tales of our brazen escapades and how we'd shamelessly wielded our feminine charm for mischief. As we recounted our exploits, I noticed a shift in Nick's demeanour; his mouth set in a hard line, annoyance flickering in his eyes. Without a word, he stepped away from the group, heading outside for a cigarette.

My gaze followed him with a mix of disappointment and intrigue, watching keenly through the patio doors. The last time I had spoken to him, on that glorious night on The Green, he had been inches from my face, stroking my cheek and gently kissing my neck. My mind searched for an explanation for his departure and found several. Perhaps he had misconstrued my sudden exit to catch the bus and thought I had given him the brush off. Or maybe he'd been jealous that I'd run around the party with Emma, convincing everyone there to let us put sweets in their drinks, too. We had been more than a little flirtatious in doing so.

Just as I was about to join him, a petite, pretty blonde appeared next to him, casually pulling out a cigarette and leaning in to ask for a light. My breath caught as I watched them, their conversation quickly sparking into laughter. This unexpected twist was definitely not in my plan!

After a moment, Emma noticed me staring and turned to see what I was looking at. Surprised, she leaned in conspiratorially.

'Who's that?' she whispered, gesturing at the new girl.

'I don't know, I've never seen her before,' I whispered back tensely. 'But she's very pretty, whoever she is.'

Just then, our host, Jamie-from-The-Green, came over and, seeing us whispering and gesturing at the pair, joined our conversation. 'Alright, girls?' he shouted in my ear above the music, his thick Cockney accent stronger than usual as he enjoyed his birthday celebration. 'Have you met Tiffany yet?'

We shook our heads that we hadn't, and Jamie-from-The-Green continued. 'You'll never guess 'ow old she is,' he giggled and put a finger to his lips. 'She really shouldn't be here, but her brother brought her, and he's my weed dealer, so I couldn't exactly turn her away.'

Emma and I looked at each other, then at Tiffany, who was animatedly chatting to Nick. From the side, she looked sixteen, the same age as us. She was wearing a lot of makeup and a short skirt. But from Jamie's question, we knew she had to be younger, so I threw a number into the air.

'Fourteen,' I declared, feeling sure she could not be that young.

'Nope.' Jamie-from-The-Green paused for dramatic effect. 'Twelve.'

At the sudden news, Emma spluttered on her drink, and my jaw almost hit the floor. 'What! You're kidding?' I exclaimed as Emma burst into uncontrollable laughter at Nick's situation. 'Oh my God, she's just a kid! She looks our age!' We laughed loudly, without restraint, catching Nick and Tiffany's attention through the glass, and he shot me a dirty look. Quickly, I stifled my laugh with my hand.

'Worst of all,' Jamie-from-The-Green confided quietly, 'her brother's nowhere to be found. Muggins 'ere is stuck babysitting!'

Our laughter vanished as quickly as it had come, replaced by a wave of shame and regret for our callousness. 'Ah, that's a shame,' I mumbled. It must have been intimidating to be left alone at a party with older teens at just twelve years old. I wondered where her mum was and why Tiffany had been allowed at a seventeen-year-old's birthday party. I couldn't imagine letting my sister Bethany attend a party like this in a few years. Resolving to make amends, I decided to caution Nick about her age and introduce myself kindly to her.

But before I could go out to join them, the front door burst open, and Dyer came in. He was accompanied by the young man from the off licence, with the scar on his cheek. Jamie identified him as Derrick, his weed dealer and Tiffany's older brother.

Emma rushed to greet them and, after kissing Dyer passionately, received a playful slap on the bottom as he winked at Derrick over her shoulder. Feeling fiercely protective of my friend, I watched as Derrick leered at Emma with a degrading smirk, a look of pure objectification. A slow chill slid down my spine, pooling cold and uncomfortable in my chest.

Slowly, Dyer and Derrick scanned the room. It was then that Derrick spotted me, and I quickly looked away. From the corner of my eye, I saw him whisper something to Dyer, who laughed, and the pair started moving towards me. Looking for an escape, I glanced around at Nick and Tiffany, still talking on the other side of the glass and decided now was the perfect time to interrupt.

Poking my head around the door with a small smile, I stopped the conversation mid-flow. 'Hey, Nick, what ya doin'?' I asked playfully.

Nick pursed his lips and looked at me apathetically. I turned to Tiffany and smiled. 'Hi, we haven't met,' I walked out and raised my hand in a little wave. 'I'm Sarah, you must be Tiffany.'

She smiled, and beneath the makeup, adult clothes and high-heeled shoes, I detected a childlike nervousness I hadn't noticed from inside. 'Hiya, nice to meet you,' she said, blushing sweetly.

'Your brother is here, by the way,' I mentioned, nodding towards Derrick through the glass. Gratefully, she made her excuses and slipped back inside, leaving Nick and me alone on the porch.

Silence settled between us. Nick watched me suspiciously, his eyes tracing over my face with an intensity that made my heart skip.

Then he casually pulled out a cigarette and lit it with deliberate slowness, a mischievous glint in his eyes.

'You look pretty tonight,' he offered, testing the water.

I felt my face light up, betraying how much the compliment meant to me. 'Thank you,' I blushed, looking down momentarily to hide my smile and braces.

'Jennifer couldn't make it, then?' he asked casually, a flicker of disappointment crossing his face.

'No, her parents wouldn't let her come out again,' I said sadly, feeling sorry that Jennifer was missing most events that summer.

'Shame. They seem crazy strict,' Nick shrugged and paused, a silence stretching between us that made me feel suddenly nervous. 'So, what happened to you the other night?' he asked abruptly. 'One minute, you were going to the shop, telling me to wait for you; the next, you'd run away and disappeared into the night.'

'I'm sorry,' I stammered, caught off guard, thinking about how I'd left him sitting on a wall, waiting for me. 'I had to run and get my bus.'

Nick leaned towards me, examining my face for a moment and thinned his eyes slightly. 'Not sure I believe you, Trouble,' he smiled flatly.

'It's the truth!' I exclaimed, panicking that he seemed so annoyed with me, electricity surging between us.

'I was there with you on that wall all night. We had a really nice talk—I thought we had a connection.' Nick looked hurt and confused, and the full scale of the misunderstanding struck me.

Feeling nervous and embarrassed, I wondered whether to tell him about my garlic breath. Still, I couldn't bring myself to because it seemed so ludicrous. So, I just stood there, lost for words, looking like a deer in the headlights. Nick seemed to glean some kind of meaning from the silence as though it confirmed his suspicions and took a deep drag on his cigarette.

Seeing the gap widening between us, I took a deep breath and prepared myself to admit the embarrassing truth, hoping that it would fix things. But before I could, Nick released a swirling cloud of smoke into the air between us. I recoiled, coughing slightly, the acrid scent clawing at my throat. Annoyed, I wondered whether he'd done it on purpose. There was no way I was going to admit something embarrassing if he was intentionally being an arse. So, I warned him about Tiffany instead.

'I thought you should know; your little friend is only twelve,' I stated, innocently. Nick's eyes widened as he choked on his cigarette. Stifling a triumphant smile, I opened the patio door and poised to make a poignant exit. 'You're welcome,' I teased.

Nick stepped forward and put his hand on the door. 'Wait a moment, please. You seem like quite the flight risk, Sarah,' he frowned down at me assertively, and angry sparks flew between us. Then Nick softened. 'Look. I'm sorry about the smoke. I forgot you don't like it. You were about to say something. What is it?'

I could feel my heart pounding in my chest, my breathing becoming shallow as he moved in. 'I'm sorry,' I stammered, swallowing hard but unable to look down. 'I really did have to run and get my bus… because I…'

Nick stepped closer and spoke softly as I trailed off: 'You know, if you weren't interested, you could have just told me,' he said more softly, offering what appeared to be an olive branch. 'I wouldn't have been offended. What offends me is that you don't want to tell me the truth, and instead, you make up some excuse.'

The thought was the furthest thing from the truth. I had desperately wanted to kiss him. Panicking, I decided to kiss him right there and then to show him just how much I liked him. But it was easier to think about than to bring myself to act.

Nick continued on his monologue, oblivious to my intention, as I stared at his lips. '…and every time I tried to kiss you, you changed the subject or turned away… asking about Dyer or my mum or whatever… then all of a sudden you had to go to the shop… and then you ran away!'

Just as I was about to go in for the kill, the patio door clicked open behind us, and Nick looked up as a group of people poured into the garden to join us. Thankfully, Dyer and Derrick weren't with them.

'Oh, not this again,' piped up Johnnie, bringing up the rear and slurring as he staggered into the garden clutching a pint glass of water. 'Get a room, you two,' he laughed, prodding me on the shoulder and spilling a slug of water down my front. With that, everyone who had just come outside snapped their heads around to look at us, and suddenly, we were the centre of attention.

'Don't think she's interested, mate,' muttered Nick, looking away and then back at me, sadly. 'Not in *me*, anyway.'

'I had to get my bus!' I insisted, trying to mop up the water from my top and yet flabbergasted at how nothing I said seemed to make him believe me.

'Yeah! So you keep saying!' he exclaimed exasperatedly as Tom sidled up beside us.

'Alright, alright—break it up, you two.' Tom moved in and pulled Nick away to the other side of the patio, and Emma took me to one side to talk.

'What's going on with you two tonight?' asked Emma curiously.

'Nick thinks I ran away and left him on The Green because I wasn't interested. I was *literally* just about to kiss him, and then you lot came out and interrupted us.'

Emma nodded, a look of understanding spreading across her face. 'Did you tell him about your pizza breath?' she asked matter-of-factly.

'No, I bottled it,' I groaned, feeling ridiculous. 'I tried, but then he blew smoke in my face, and I thought—it's Nick—so maybe he'd done it on purpose.'

'Jesus, you two. You're like a couple of old hens pecking at each other,' Emma observed, and I cringed at the image. 'You know what that is, don't you?' she teased.

I shook my head and glanced over at Nick, who happened to glance back broodily right at that moment.

'That's sexual frustration right there. What you actually want to do is rip each other's clothes off.'

I laughed. 'Do we, though?' I asked sarcastically, raising an eyebrow, imagining how wonderful it would be to rip Nick's shirt off and pull his jeans down with my teeth and then…

'Well, you have to talk to him, hon,' Emma insisted, bringing me rudely back to the room. 'He obviously likes you, and you like him. You can't just leave it like this.'

Reluctantly, I agreed. As much as my stomach was in knots at the idea, I knew that Emma was right. I took some deep breaths and steeled myself to be brave. But as I turned around to go over, I saw Nick slipping out of the front door with Derrick and Tiffany just as Dyer was running over to us.

'Babe!' came Dyer's shout as he reached us and grabbed Emma, kissing her roughly on the lips. 'I'm heading to Derrick's to get weed. I'll catch up with you tomorrow, okay?'

'What? Can't you get weed tomorrow?' exclaimed Emma, upset at being abandoned.

'He's only got a bit of the good stuff left, babe,' explained Dyer, turning and following Derrick, Nick and Tiffany out of the door, leaving Emma staring after him. She turned to me, exasperated.

'I can't believe it!' Emma sulked. 'I haven't seen him all week, and he said we were gonna spend time together tonight.'

I took her hand in mine and stroked it.

'Now I'm not going to see him at all until the ball next week!' she exclaimed.

'Sorry, Em,' I commiserated, wondering whether Dyer was too old for the upcoming Alexandra Palace Youth Summer Ball.

Just then, Johnnie (who was standing nearby with Tom and Jamie-From-The Green) bent over and was promptly sick in the corner, vomit covering the spotless beige carpet and spraying up the magnolia walls.

Jamie recoiled in horror. 'Mate! That's my mum's new carpet!' he cried as he and Tom rushed to get a cloth.

'Sorry, Jamie,' moaned a pitiful Johnnie and closed his eyes as though he were about to take a nap.

'Up you get!' I coaxed, as Emma and I pulled him up and propped him against the fireplace. Turning to Emma, I took the opportunity to share my newly acquired insights about Dyer.

'Emma, do you really think Dyer is right for you? Did you see him tonight with that Derrick bloke?' I asked, lowering my voice and speaking intensely, hoping to make her understand. 'I really didn't like the way they were looking at you. Do you think that maybe he's a bit… You know… dodgy?'

Overhearing us, Johnnie stirred from his stupor and piled on. 'Yeah, Dyer's a scumbag,' he swayed and pointed a finger at her. 'You're way too good for him, Emma. You're…' he paused and closed his eyes in a long blink. 'You're… you deserve to be… you're so beautiful.'

Emma and I stared at him momentarily, a look passing between us. This was unexpected. 'Okay there, Johnnie, have some water,' I grabbed Johnnie's glass of water from the table, and he took a sip and fell silent, closing his eyes again.

Emma looked back at me, slightly stunned, and then rallied her thoughts. 'How were they looking at me?' she asked, eyes wide.

I gulped nervously and told her the truth, even though I thought it might hurt her feelings. 'Like you were, you know, a piece of meat or something,' I explained, unsure whether I'd said enough. I hesitated, then said it anyway. 'Dyer was kind of showing off to Derrick when he slapped your bum. It just didn't look very respectful.'

'Not very respectful. *At ALL,*' Johnnie slurred, tipping sideways.

Emma frowned, staring at the carpet. 'He was just messing about,' she said, but without much conviction, then paused. 'I'll ask him. I mean, he'll probably laugh when I tell him.' She gave a small shrug and smiled at me as if to reassure me. 'Honestly, he didn't mean anything by it.' Then we half-carried Johnnie to the sofa, and as Emma wiped his black, greasy curtains back from his forehead, I rang his mum to come pick him up.

8

Summer Ball

Early July 1998

THE EVENT OF THE SUMMER WAS FINALLY happening. Alexandra Palace, the global birthplace of television, was hosting the fifth annual Youth Summer Ball for fifteen to nineteen-year-olds. Affectionately known as Aly Pally, or the 'People's Palace', half the teenage population of North London was going to be there. The boys were hiring tuxes, and the girls were begging, borrowing and stealing from their mum's and sister's wardrobes or heading to the shops to find the perfect dress.

Generously, Emma had convinced her mum to take Jennifer and me shopping with them, and now we were getting ready in Emma's bedroom. This was going to be my first-ever Ball, and I was more excited than I'd ever been in my life. I imagined that tonight would be the night Nick and I finally shared our first kiss. I had pictured it a thousand times: how he would reach down and touch my cheek, tell me how beautiful I looked, and finally, *finally,* lean down to kiss me. It was going to be perfect.

Downstairs, Nick, Dyer and Tom were in the front room waiting for Johnnie to arrive and had been barred by Emma's parents from coming upstairs. We hadn't seen them yet, as we'd been getting ready for over an hour. As I applied a light shade of eyeshadow to my brow bone, I thought back to when Nick had tried to kiss me less than two weeks before. We'd been sitting on a wall next to The Green. I could remember everything about him that night: his eyes, his lips, how his fingers had felt as they caressed my cheeks. I saw the curve of his neck and how his silver chain sat against his tanned skin.

'Hello?' Jennifer's sharp voice pierced my daydreams. She looked irritated, as though she'd been trying to get my attention. 'Pass me the hair straighteners, will you?'

Embarrassed, I stopped applying eyeshadow and passed her the straighteners. 'Sorry! I was miles away!'

'You're very distracted tonight,' she muttered, and I smiled to appease her, unsure of whether she was annoyed and, if so, what I'd done wrong.

Emma cut in, breaking the tension. 'What do you think, girls?' she asked, having pulled the neckline down on her dress and hitched her bra up as high as it would go.

Jennifer frowned and shook her head. 'Put them away, Emma, that's too much.'

Emma turned to me, smiling. 'What do you think, Sarah?'

I looked down at her heaving cleavage. 'Your mum would *never* let you out like that,' I concluded, rendering the question moot.

Emma turned to look at herself in the mirror. 'Hmmm. You're probably right.' With that, she loosened her bra straps and tucked herself away a little.

'Mmmmmm. Beautiful!' Dyer commented from the doorway, having snuck upstairs while Emma's parents were distracted. Still, only in her underwear, Jennifer leapt out of sight behind Emma's bed.

'Get out! Get out, Matthew!' she yelled loudly as Dyer tried to shush her so his cover wouldn't be blown. Jennifer was having none of it, though. 'Mrs McCarthy! Mrs McCarthy! Matthew is upstairs! We're not dressed!'

A look of pure terror struck Dyer's face as he plunged away from the doorway and down the stairs as fast as he could. But it was too late. Mrs McCarthy's voice boomed up from the kitchen.

'Matthew! GET DOWN HERE. NOW.'

Emma doubled over with laughter while Jennifer peeled herself up from the bedroom floor. When we finally finished getting ready and went downstairs, I felt like a butterfly emerging from its cocoon for the first time. My knee-length, burgundy satin dress had a scoop neck and was pleated in the gypsy style of the time. Jennifer's classic A-line black dress hugged her waist and billowed out towards her knees, highlighting her slim figure and pretty face. Looking gorgeous, Emma floated down the stairs in a long shimmering silver dress with a slit up her right thigh. Clutching our small bags, we breezed into the living room in front of the boys on a cushion of air, and they immediately stopped talking, stood up and stared at us, open-mouthed.

'Wow.' Nick and Tom said simultaneously.

'You all look amazing,' gushed Tom excitedly.

We stared right back at them, impressed by how dashing they looked in their formal wear. The transformation was striking, a sharp departure from the casual sportswear, jeans, and jumpers they typically wore. Nick, in particular, was captivating in his black jacket, crisp white shirt, and bow tie, leaving me momentarily breathless. Our eyes locked from across the room, a charged connection sparking between us as if the rest of the world had faded away.

But then, Jennifer stepped further into the room, and Nick's gaze shifted. I felt a sudden chill, watching as his eyes traced the length of Jennifer's dress. He looked up at her face, and they both smiled gently as if having a little moment of their own. A pang of uncertainty gnawed at me. Why wasn't he looking at me? Shouldn't his attention be solely on me if he truly felt something for me?

Suddenly, Dyer jumped forward, grabbed hold of Emma—who squealed—and pulled her down onto his lap on the sofa. But he quickly let her go again as he heard Mrs McCarthy's voice approaching. Before she could enter the room, the doorbell went, and within moments, Johnnie was bounding around, looking sharp in his tux and kippah, and boy, didn't he know it.

After a few minutes filled with lively chatter about how wonderful we all looked, Mrs McCarthy and Johnnie ushered us out the door.

'Whoever's riding with me, hop in!' Mrs McCarthy called out as she stepped outside and unlocked her practical people carrier. She waved cheerfully to Johnnie's Mum, who was playing chauffeur number two, waiting in her luxury car on the driveway.

'Who's coming with me, then?' Johnnie asked, checking his kippah and bow tie briefly in the hallway mirror, and as if on cue, Tom, Dyer, and Emma headed over to the other car. Mrs McCarthy seemed a bit wounded seeing her daughter opt for the alternative ride, but I couldn't help thinking that it would probably be better for her nerves if she didn't have to watch Dyer and her daughter in the back seat.

This left Nick, Jennifer, and me to join Mrs McCarthy, and suddenly, a palpable tension filled the air as we slid into the car in silence. I felt incredibly nervous, unsure of how to compose myself. Seeming to sense the atmosphere, Mrs McCarthy glanced back at Jennifer and me in the back while Nick gazed coolly out the front passenger window.

'How were your exams, Nick?' asked Mrs McCarthy politely, 'Do you think you'll be able to take the sciences at A-level?'

Nick sat up straight, fiddled with his seat belt and smiled respectfully as he spoke. 'Fine, thank you, Mrs McCarthy, although I wouldn't say I did all that well. I'll just have to wait and see.'

I couldn't help but smile as I watched him longingly from the backseat, everything about him igniting a yearning within me. From here, the angle of his chiselled jawline looked so masculine that it made my head feel fuzzy just to look at it. Feeling flustered, I turned to Jennifer, hoping for some conversation, but she'd barely said anything to me all day, and it didn't seem like she was going to start now.

When we arrived, Mrs McCarthy was directed to pull up outside the Palm Court Entrance on the West side of the Palace. I could barely contain my glee as I watched the magnificent arches of the entrance rear up ahead of us, with Alexandra Palace's grand glass domes towering over it. Dressed-up teenagers were swarming around the entrance and filing inside slowly. As we stepped out of the car and waved Mrs McCarthy goodbye, there was an electric sense of excitement in the air. We looked around us, found Tom, Johnnie and Dyer, walked up the steps to the entrance and entered the enormous Great Hall to a cacophony of music and chatter.

We gasped at the sight that lay before us. The Great Hall's domed glass ceiling bore a canopy of twinkling lights, and the hall's elegant arched windows were dressed in decorative drapes. Thousands of partygoers filled the hall, dressed up 'to the nines' and countless eyes scanned the room on the lookout for someone special. Perhaps they would be lucky enough to find love, or perhaps just a pair of willing lips to kiss. Everyone was hoping for something incredible to happen, and the atmosphere was buzzing with possibilities.

By the entrance, the bar was packed ten people deep, selling non-alcoholic soft drinks in clear plastic cups. The liquor was still there, teasing us, but it was safely protected behind a rolling security grill at the back of the bar. We queued up together and slowly jostled our way to the front, all of us on the lookout for a gap in front of us to slip into. Dyer reached the bar first, put in our order and passed back our cups before leaving the scuffle.

'Who wants a little extra in their cola?' asked Dyer, winking, pulling out a bottle of white rum from his jacket. Thrilled, all of us but Jennifer cheered his good thinking, and then Nick surprised us with a bottle of whisky from his jacket, and Emma held up a secret bottle of amaretto. Excited, we snuck to the toilets to spike our drinks, and it seemed as though everyone else in the venue had had exactly the same idea.

Jennifer watched Emma like a hawk as she poured a drop of amaretto into her cup. 'That's enough!' She stopped her by grabbing the neck of the bottle. 'Okay, I'll pour yours,' she announced and dribbled a tiny slug of amaretto into Emma's cup, too.

'And the rest!' Emma protested, pushing the end of the bottle upwards and splashing the sugary liquid all over Jennifer's hands and feet below, with some of it landing in her cup.

'Oi!' Jennifer protested, her hands wet. 'That's going to be really sticky.' She handed Emma her cup and took hold of mine, filling it to the brim with a huge pour from the bottle. 'There you go,' she said, smiling, handing me back my cup.

'Wow. That's a lot!' I laughed nervously, aware of my lightweight status.

Jennifer's smile widened, and she stroked my arm. 'Don't worry, it's not very strong. Tonight is supposed to be fun! And anyway, Mrs McCarthy is going to pick us up at midnight. Loosen up!'

I sipped the sweet, mellow liquid and could barely taste the alcohol over the sugar. 'Mmm, it's nice,' I giggled, pleased to be in Jennifer's good books again and her eyes lit up.

'Drink up, then,' she gestured. 'There's plenty more where that came from!'

Then, she linked her arm around mine as we followed Emma back into the Great Hall to join the boys. For a while, we moved around the sides of the room until we found a perfect little space for ourselves on the dancefloor. Then, we girls twirled and danced around each other, our handbags in a pile on the floor while the boys thrashed around as though they were at a mosh pit or rave dancing to The Prodigy. The crowd went wild as Intergalactic by Beastie Boys came over the speakers, and we shouted along while doing our best 'robot' moves. I was having a fantastic time. The lights were bright, the music buzzing, my friends all around, and the love of my life right here with me. My head felt light and happy, and I didn't ever want to stop dancing. But all good things must come to an end, and at the end of the song, a boyband ballad sounded, and the energy mellowed. Emma and I swayed to the music, singing to each other with huge smiles on our faces.

Then, from the corner of my eye, I saw Nick lean in towards Jennifer and whisper something in her ear. Then he gestured to Dyer, who whispered in Emma's ear, too, and the four started moving off towards a side door. Tom, Johnnie and I followed along passively behind. As we exited onto a long balcony, we were greeted by breathtaking views of lights, the city of London sprawling across the horizon far below us.

Despite it being July, the air had gotten surprisingly chilly. I took another sip of my drink and hugged myself, turning to Johnnie to chat for a while. Behind Johnnie, Dyer removed his jacket and placed it over Emma's shoulders. Then Nick took his jacket off, too. But instead of offering it to me, like he had done a thousand times in my dreams, he placed it over Jennifer's shoulders.

And then, everyone stopped dancing.

The music stopped playing.

People stopped talking.

Even the world stopped turning.

Life took a funny turn as history played out *completely wrongly*.

Slowly, Nick took Jennifer's hand.

They were slow dancing.

A few moments passed, and right before my eyes, Nick leaned down and gently gave *my* long-awaited kiss to *Jennifer*.

First, he kissed *her* cheek.

Then he kissed *her* mouth.

I watched as *Jennifer* put her arms around Nick's neck and pulled him gently into her.

My world shattered, and a pain unlike anything I'd ever felt before ripped through my chest. Burning tears welled in my eyes and threatened to spill down my cheeks in front of everyone.

Johnnie turned around to see what I was gawping at and let out a little gasp of surprise. But before he could look back at me, I was gone. I ran back to the toilets, threw open the door of an empty bathroom stall and slammed it behind me, hiding, ashamed of my tears. Ashamed of myself. Utterly heartbroken. Completely lost in my pain. I let out a little sob, unable to contain it.

And then, without warning, Dyer's grotesque, mocking head appeared over the side of the stall wall. He looked down at me, crying, and tried not to laugh, the expression on his face a mask of smirking sympathy.

'She's in here!' He called out to Emma and then looked back down at me. '*What's the matter, Trouble*?'

'Nothing, Dyer, I'm fine; go away!' I sobbed uncontrollably, completely exposed in the toilet stall, with nowhere left to hide.

'Tell me,' cooed Dyer as Emma knocked on the door.

'Sarah, are you okay?' Emma's soothing tones did nothing to make me feel better but only added to my embarrassment and shame. All I wanted to do was be alone in my misery, but it didn't seem like that was going to happen. 'Come down, Matthew,' she told Dyer off, and he disappeared, leaving me alone again. 'Can I come in, hon?' she asked sympathetically.

'No, just leave me alone,' I demanded. I sat on the toilet seat, holding my head in my hands and cried. 'Everybody, just leave me alone!'

There was silence as my friends left the bathroom, and I had a moment to think. How could this be happening? How could he have given my kiss to her?

The image of them dancing and kissing, of her wearing his jacket, flashed in my mind's eye, and fresh tears escaped like waterfalls down my cheeks. I couldn't bear the thought of seeing Nick or Jennifer again tonight, and I didn't think I'd be able to answer anyone else's questions about what the matter was without crying. So, instead, I hatched a plan that meant I wouldn't have to do either, and that seemed like the best all around.

Feeling dizzy and drunk, I carefully stood on the toilet and looked over the stall door into a sea of strangers' faces queuing up to use the facilities. A ray of hope gripped me as I saw that all of my friends had left. I climbed back down, wiped under my eyes with a tissue, and slipped out of the stall. Leaving the toilet block, I could see Emma and Dyer standing with Johnnie nearby, but I silently slipped past unseen, heading back towards the entrance towards freedom and my escape into the night.

Just as I was about to pass through the arches and out into the night, I turned back one last time to drink in the scene of my heartbreak. By chance, Dyer, who was still standing outside the toilets, glanced up and spotted me from a distance, pointing me out to the gang. Startled, I turned and fled down the steps and took off down the hill at top speed.

After a few moments, I could hear Dyer behind me, calling after me, and although he seemed to be gaining on me, I didn't dare stop. I was mortified enough as it was. I would run all the way home if I had to, despite it being miles away and not knowing exactly where Aly Pally was.

'Page! Page! Wait! Where are you going?' Dyer's footsteps got closer, but his breathing became laboured, and it seemed like he was about to give up. 'Page!' he shouted, 'Slow down!'

It wasn't until Nick's voice called out from behind Dyer that I stopped, sat on the curb and sobbed. Dyer ran up and stood near me, bent double and trying to catch his breath. Nick ran up a few moments later, stood panting for a moment, and then sat down next to me on the curb.

'Jesus Christ, Trouble, you never said you could leg it like Linford Christy,' exclaimed Nick between gasps. He held me as I turned towards him and buried my head in his chest, not sobbing anymore, but feeling safe with him there and more than a little drunk. 'What's the matter? Why did you run away?'

'It doesn't matter,' I sniffed, shaking my head and leaning against him. 'I can't tell you. I'm fine.'

Nick held my head gently. 'Yeah. You really seem fine. Where did you think you were going?'

'Home.'

'From here?'

'Yes.'

'Do you even know where you are?'

'No—but I'd find my way back. It's in that direction. I'd be fine,' I sniffed and looked around at the dark street, pointing down the hill.

'Oh, I see. Well, why don't you come back inside with us?' Nick was being really kind, but there was no way I wanted to go back inside. All I wanted was to go home. I felt humiliated, and if Nick was going to be with Jennifer, I knew I couldn't stand by and watch without crying again.

In the distance, Emma and Jennifer approached. Jennifer was still wearing Nick's jacket and looked positively livid, and Emma looked deeply concerned. Dyer went back up to meet them halfway, and after speaking for some moments, he convinced them to turn around, and the three of them went back to the Ball, leaving Nick and me alone. Grateful to Dyer, for once, I looked up at Nick with a profound aching in my chest.

'I just want to go home,' I said meekly, watching the others leave.

Nick kissed the top of my forehead sweetly. 'Are you sure?' he asked quietly, and I nodded, feeling ever so sad.

Then, he pulled out his new mobile phone, the first of our group to get one, and called Emma's landline, arranging for Mrs McCarthy to come and pick me up and take me back to my parents' house. Shivering in the cold night air without his jacket, he stayed with me until she arrived. Then, he apologised to Mrs McCarthy profusely, waved us off, turned and walked back up the hill to the Ball.

On the drive back, Mrs McCarthy was uncharacteristically quiet, her face a picture of concern, rather than anger or annoyance, as I had expected. She asked me if I was okay, and in my tipsy state, I began to open up to her.

'I think I might be in love,' I confessed, believing she couldn't know who I was talking about. 'But the person I love doesn't love me back.'

'I'm so sorry,' she said, looking across at me as I stared teary-eyed out of the window. 'Loving someone who doesn't feel the same is so painful. How do you know that you love them?' she asked curiously.

'I don't. I'm not sure. But the moment I saw them, I felt like I'd been struck by lightning, and I haven't been able to stop thinking about them ever since.' I dropped my head pathetically, tears welling in my eyes as I thought about how Nick had given his jacket to Jennifer, slow dancing with her, and then kissing her.

She nodded slowly, gripping the steering wheel at the ten o'clock and two o'clock positions and studying the dark road ahead quietly. 'Well, how do you know he doesn't love you back? It is a 'he', isn't it?' She feigned ignorance as to who I was referring to, and I believed her.

'He kissed another girl tonight,' I sniffed and felt suddenly worried that she might work out that I was talking about Nick. 'He goes to my school,' I added slyly, 'I didn't realise he was going to be there tonight.'

She nodded again and gave me a consolatory rub on the shoulder. 'Of course, of course. Well, if it helps, I had my heart broken, too, when I was sixteen. I loved the older brother of my best friend, but he didn't feel the same way either. Now, I barely even think of him. He's old news. Time passes, and you'll learn to love again.'

As she spoke about brothers, an image of Tom's older brother, Andy, flickered through my mind and momentarily warmed my bleeding heart. And then I thought about how Andy barely even knew I existed, that he thought of me as a child still, and the small flame flickered and went out again, leaving me wallowing in my misery with no end in sight.

As she dropped me outside my house, I thanked her for the millionth time, and she wished me luck, smiled and drove away into the darkness. That night, I slept like a log. The next day, I sobbed all over the house, but I hid it from everyone in my family. Sadness was kept behind closed doors in our house, so I cried in the shower, I cried in my bedroom, I even cried in the garden, but nothing seemed to make me feel better.

Was Mrs McCarthy right? Would I eventually learn to love again? I hoped so. I wished it would all just hurry up because I was ready to love now, but I had no one to give my love to. Certainly not anyone who wanted to love me back.

9
The Golden Couple

Late-July 1998

EMMA BROKE THE DEVASTATING NEWS over the phone. Since snogging at the Ball, Jennifer and Nick had become an item. Miserable, I asked if Jennifer had liked him before that night, while my little sister, Bethany, watched me cradle the receiver morosely from the corner of the living room.

'She denied it, but I could tell there was something there,' admitted Emma. 'I didn't tell you because Jennifer has been my best friend for so long, and she didn't want me to. I told her you liked Nick, and she said that she knew because it was so obvious. I'm so sorry, hon. I can imagine how upset you must be. Are you okay?'

'Yeah, I'm fine,' I lied, tears streaming down my cheeks. Bethany ran over and gave me the kind of hug that only little sisters can give. Sweet, innocent and full of the purest kind of love. I smiled down at her and felt a bit better.

Later that day, Jennifer called, and I was determined not to let our friendship be affected. Putting on a brave face, I asked how she was, how Nick was and how things were going between them. Gleefully, she recounted the story of their first date; how he'd fearfully met her dad before taking her to the cinema to watch 'Armageddon', where they'd shared a carton of sweet popcorn. She gushed about how the movie title track, 'I Don't Want to Miss a Thing' by Aerosmith, was now her favourite song.

'That's wicked, Jennifer. I'm so happy for you,' I smiled, fighting the nausea and trying my best to mean it for the sake of my friend.

'Thanks!' Jennifer paused. 'How are you, by the way?' She asked tentatively, with what sounded like a hint of guilt in her voice. 'What happened to you the other night at Aly Pally? One moment, you were fine; the next, you were running away crying.' She paused before adding quietly, 'Did you get drunk or something?'

I laughed nervously. Secretly, we both knew why I had run away: because Nick had chosen her over me. Embarrassed, and for the sake of peace, I buried the truth deep inside and attempted to sweep it under the carpet.

'I was just having some trouble at home,' I insisted, not realising that my lie would soon become a reality. 'Honestly, as soon as I got back and went to bed, I was fine. I just got a bit tipsy after that whopping drink you poured me!' I giggled nervously, wondering if it had been her intention that I get drunk.

Whether Jennifer bought it or not, the conversation moved on. But seeing her together with Nick a week later at Tom's house was the hardest thing I'd ever had to do in my life. At least that time, though, I had advanced warning.

I walked from the bus stop to Tom's, feeling as though somebody had died and I was in a funeral procession. As I approached the front door, my stomach threatened to empty its contents onto my shoes as I thought about what might be waiting for me inside. I knocked, and Tom opened the door cheerfully.

'Sarah! Come in, come in, we're just trying to decide what film to watch.' He ushered me into the front room, where the nauseating view of Nick and Jennifer cuddling on the sofa greeted me. They didn't get up. Too wrapped up in each other's *amazingness*, no doubt.

Thankfully, my nerves worked in my favour that time, and I found myself experiencing an incredible burst of energy that had me on top form and pulled me through the encounter on a wave of comedy gold. I'd never been so funny before. Despite my pain, a part of me seriously started wondering whether I should pursue a career as a stand-up comedian. Perhaps I could laugh myself to sleep rather than cry.

An hour later, I found myself sitting quietly with Tom on one sofa while Nick and Jennifer had the other. As the four of us sat together in the darkened room, Tom and I stared fixedly at the television screen, trying not to hear the playful little noises coming from their side of the room.

Nick wanted Jennifer to sit on his lap, but she wouldn't, so they had a little wrestle, ending in a big, sloppy kiss and Jennifer giggling. Jennifer wanted some of Nick's drink, so he held the cup for her while she took a long, appreciative sip. Nick wanted some of Jennifer's popcorn, so she fed it to him like a baby. Unfortunately, neither of them choked.

Inside, I was dying, but my eyes never left the screen. When the film was finally over, the lovebirds jumped up and left together, with plans to go to Covent Garden for a romantic walk around the market. Tom cheerily waved them goodbye and then turned to me.

'How sickening was that?' he scrunched up his face and laughed, holding his stomach as though it was all he could do not to be sick. 'I've never seen such a nauseating public display of affection.'

I laughed, grateful to my friend for saying so, and so glad I wasn't the only one feeling that way. We got up and went to the kitchen to make coffee, and leaning against the countertop, Tom regarded me carefully.

'Are you alright, Sarah? That must have been really hard,' he asked, filling the kettle and pulling a jar of instant coffee from the cupboard.

'What do you mean?' I asked, wide-eyed and innocent.

'Oh, come on. Because of Jennifer and Nick.'

I shrugged, feigning innocence and insisted that Nick was old news, but Tom was buying none of it. Just then, the front door banged, and Andy sauntered into the kitchen.

My pulse jumped.

He was back from work and ravenously hungry. During those early months, Andy didn't like socialising with us young 'ns much. He never wanted to play football or go out. Instead, he left us to our own devices, much like older brothers do, relishing his year-and-a-bit-wiser status. I longed for the day Andy would want to spend more time with us. Still, the only time I saw him was at his house—coming or going from work, watching a film or TV, and occasionally, he'd play board games with us.

'What's all this, then?' Andy asked casually, taking a loaf of bread from the cupboard and buttering a slice. 'Are you back to break another window, Miss Page?'

I blushed, thinking back to the day of the water fight. An image of Andy carrying me into the kitchen and nursing my injured foot made me giddy with excitement. Tom turned to his brother conspiratorially.

'Sarah's got a thing for Nick, but Nick is going out with Jennifer,' he blurted out, raising his eyebrows at me in defiance as I whirled around to give him a death glare.

Andy looked up at me, highly amused, before busily buttering a second slice of bread and slathering peanut butter on both. 'Oh, really? Does Nick float your boat, Miss Page? Is he *really, really* dreamy?'

He let out a laugh as he entertained himself and watched me squirm uncomfortably, smiling broadly at my embarrassment. Unable to resist the bait, I insisted that I didn't care for Nick and was not bothered *at all* by his relationship with Jennifer. But the more I protested, the more the brothers piled on, taking it in turns, until eventually, I could do nothing but stand in their kitchen trying not to react as they mimicked a pair of teenage girls in love, talking about boys and how dreamy they are and even doing slapstick kissy kissy noises. Finally, as I went beetroot red and couldn't roll my eyes any more exaggeratedly, Andy threw me a lifeline and drew the teasing to a close.

'How does the rebel in love take her coffee, then?' he asked, taking over coffee duties, one eyebrow raised as he landed one last jab.

'Milk, one sugar, please,' I sighed. Andy shot me a consolatory wink and reached into the cupboard, pulling out his Disney mug with the broken handle. I watched it longingly, wondering, not for the first time, whether he might hand it to me instead.

He didn't.

Tom picked up his coffee and headed into the living room. I followed with my plain white mug, and Andy brushed past me in the hallway.

'Don't worry about Nick, Miss Page,' he murmured, taking an enormous bite of buttered bread and washing it down with a slug of coffee from the Disney mug. 'He's just being a typical boy.'

Then he sauntered upstairs without looking back, leaving me staring after him, wondering what it meant to be a *typical boy*, exactly.

Later that day, when I got home, Emma rang to let me know she was proud of me for how I handled things with Nick and Jennifer. Despite having been upset in the heat of the moment at Aly Pally a week before, this time I had chosen a peaceful, respectful path that kept the group together. Now, we could all stay friends and keep hanging out. Perhaps it wasn't my responsibility to keep the group together, but losing 'The Crew', who had saved me from a life of loneliness and isolation, was too crushing a thought to bear. I desperately wanted everything to stay just the same, and I wasn't ready to let anyone go.

But deep in my heart, I was bruised. Whenever I heard about Nick and Jennifer, I felt like crying. He was still on my mind all the time, and the pain was yet to fade. Something had changed, though. Now, when I thought of him, Andy's words came to mind, that Nick was 'being a typical boy'. And, in those moments, things didn't feel quite as awful.

Summer progressed, and the days ticked by as I nursed my broken heart. In my anguish, I stayed home more, not wanting to run into the Golden Couple. It was then that, for the first time, my friends came to visit me in my hometown, which felt wonderful.

One day, Emma, Johnnie and Tom caught the bus together and arrived unannounced to surprise me. With Mum and Dad at work, together we set up a waterslide in the back garden and made a bonfire to cook jacket potatoes. We had so much fun together that I almost forgot about Nick for an evening.

But as summer wore on, I had no idea what was going to happen next with Nick out of reach, and my focus shifted. The day of our GCSE exam results kept creeping ever closer, until finally, one morning in August, we all headed off to our respective schools to discover our academic fates.

10
Results Day

August 1998

AT OUR SCHOOL, JOHNNIE AND I left my dad and his mum in the lobby with the other parents and went inside the Assembly Hall to queue up for our results together. We stood in silence, for once, nerves getting the better of us, and nothing seemed important enough to say. A boy at the head of the line whooped with joy, having surpassed his expectations, while his friend clapped him on the back despite nursing a look of personal disappointment.

The wait was excruciating, and the reactions from our fellow students ranged from gut-wrenching to thrilling. As we approached the front, a long-lost friend of mine from Maths class squealed. Ecstatic with her results and having no one with her, she turned around and threw her arms around Johnnie, who feigned a long-suffering look of patience. But I could tell he was thrilled.

'I got two A-stars and seven As!' she said, jumping up and down in his arms. Johnnie winked at me over her shoulder, and I couldn't help but roll my eyes.

'Well done!' I congratulated her, and she abandoned Johnnie for me. Johnnie took the opportunity to head for the results desk, where Ms Sermina from the Art Department was handing out envelopes with Mr Patel watching on. I couldn't tell if he was admiring her, but

I decided he couldn't be. Happily married men didn't look at other women. Not like that.

Johnnie opened his envelope beside me and nodded, satisfied but not thrilled.

'Yeah, not too shabby,' he said. 'As I expected, really.'

I hugged him quickly, pleased that he was happy, before stepping forward myself, my palms sweating. Ms Sermina sorted through the 'P' surnames and handed me an envelope.

Here we go, I thought, closing my eyes for a moment to settle my jittery tummy before ripping open the paper.

The world fell away as my eyes focused on the lines of results.

Six A stars and four As.

A shockwave of disbelief shot through me. I had never expected such high marks! It felt unreal!

'Whoa, look at that!' Johnnie shouted, pointing them out to anyone within earshot. A small group gathered, voices tumbling over one another in astonishment and congratulations.

I had never felt so proud in all my life! In the lobby, our parents ran over to greet us, my dad pulling me to one side excitedly.

'So, how did you do?' he asked, a sparkle in his eyes.

My dad had kept every school report card, notebook and picture I'd ever made, my brother and sister, too. His filing cabinet was full of our achievements. Every morning, he'd waved us off to school as our mum drove down the road. I could see that this day was extra special to him.

'I got six A-stars and four As!' I said, showing him the results paper.

My dad grabbed the paper, his face lit up like the sky on Guy Fawkes night. 'You're joking! Oh my God, Sarah, that's incredible! I'm so proud of you!' He grabbed me and kissed me crushingly hard on my forehead, and for a moment, I forgot to be 'cool'. I beamed, thrilled at having pleased him so much.

We waved goodbye to Johnnie and his mum, who was looking at me in a new light, with what appeared to be admiration in her eyes. It felt so strange and yet so… wonderful.

As we jumped in Dad's car and pulled out of the school gates, I felt like a million pounds. Then, Dad hit play on his new in-car CD player, and Fat Boy Slim's debut album 'You've Come a Long Way Baby' blasted out of the speakers and windows as we raced past the school. Dad started head-banging to the electronic dance music, and my jubilation turned instantly to mortification as parents and pupils turned to watch us drive past.

'Dad!' I shouted, grabbing for the volume control, 'Turn it down! Everyone's looking!'

'Who cares!' he yelled, beeping his car horn rhythmically as we drove past the sports fields. 'My daughter's a genius!' he turned his face up and looked at me as he spoke, and I laughed and gave in and started head-banging, too. As we drove home that day, singing and dancing to 'Gangster Trippin', one of my favourite memories of my dad was formed. A memory I would treasure forever. And despite the hard family times that were soon to follow, that day would remind me of how lucky I was to have him as my dad.

At home, Mum was thrilled and started cooking my favourite, homemade lasagne, for dinner. Coming off the upstairs phone with Emma, I bellowed an update down to Mum and Dad.

'EMMA IS A BIT DISAPPOINTED, BUT SHE PASSED ALL HER EXA-AMS!'

'TELL HER CONGRATULATIONS!' Dad shouted back from the living room.

'STOP SHOUTING AND COME DOWNSTAIRS!' called Mum from the kitchen. 'DINNER'S NEARLY READY!'

'OK-AY—I'VE GOT ONE MORE PHONE CALL!' I yelled, holding my breath.

Apparently, good exam results buy you a bit of leeway.

With the household in good spirits, I joyously picked up the phone to dial Tom's house. It rang for a long time, and just as I was about to hang up, Andy answered.

'I'm sorry, Miss Page, Tom's not here; he's playing football with the lads.'

The sound of his voice made me feel oddly flustered.

'Thanks, Andy!' I said quickly, unsure what to add.

'How did you do in your exams?' he asked, before I could escape.

'Pretty well, actually. I got six A-stars and four As,' I said, trying to sound casual as I waited for his reaction.

'Wow,' Andy sounded genuinely impressed. 'Well, look at you, you little brainiac!'

I grinned down the line.

'Hold on, I'll tell my mum; maybe she'll let you off for wrecking our house,' he added dryly. I tittered nervously, never quite sure whether Andy was teasing me or not. 'Mum! It's Sarah,' I heard him shout in the background. 'She got six A-stars and four As!'

I heard murmurs of approval from afar, and when Andy came back, he told me his mother sent her congratulations. Relief washed over me. I wasn't sure whether it was the grades or just time that had softened things—but I wasn't about to question it.

'Does that mean she's forgiven me for pushing you through the conservatory roof, as well?' I joked.

'Don't push your luck, Miss Page,' he jibed. Then more quietly, 'And anyway, she's not the one you need to be worried about.'

I laughed again—a little too quickly—and imagined another water fight with Andy, only this time, when we reached his bedroom, and he cornered me on the bed, I didn't run away.

'Well done again,' Andy said, and before I could think of anything else to say, he wished me good night and hung up.

I sat there for a moment, phone still in my hand, then quietly wished him one too. I dialled Johnnie's new mobile, the second in our group to get one, and he picked up after a few rings, sounding out of breath from football.

He passed me over to Tom, who was thrilled to have achieved the results he needed to one day become an architect. Then, without warning, Nick grabbed the phone, and my heart was beating in my throat.

'Hello, Trouble! I heard about your results,' Nick gushed down the phone. 'Well done!'

My heart warmed instantly. 'Thanks, Nick,' I said.

'Maybe one day, when we're married, you can earn all the money,' he said lightly.

The thought thrilled me—and then landed awkwardly. Jennifer flashed through my mind. Was that a joke, or was he doing that thing where he blurred lines and pretended not to notice?

'I didn't do so well,' he went on. 'Mum had an absolute fit. But whatever. Hopefully, this new college will sort me out next year. Assuming I don't get expelled.'

'I'm sure you'll be fine,' I said, my heart softening. 'Even Einstein had problems at school, you know,' I offered, cringing at myself for being so cheesy.

'Ha! Thanks, Trouble, you're sweet.' He paused. 'You coming down to Tom's this weekend?'

'I can't, my grandparents are visiting. We're going out to celebrate .'

'Nice. Well, catch you soon,' he said. 'Don't do anything I wouldn't do!'

The line went dead.

I went downstairs to dinner feeling oddly hollow, unsure who I wanted more—though it hardly mattered. Nick was with Jennifer, and Andy had shown no interest at all.

11

Pancakes and a Broken Home

Late-August 1998

IT WAS A STRANGE AFTERNOON. The kind that sticks with you, although it started innocently enough. Partway through generously buttering a plate full of toast, my brother Lucas flicked his blonde David Beckham curtains out of his eyes as he looked up from the kitchen counter and out of the window.

'Who's this, then?' he asked me, as a young woman with a hooked nose walked up the driveway to the front door of our house.

'No idea,' I said, beating him to the fridge to grab the marmalade. I waggled my eyebrows triumphantly and looked at the woman as she passed. 'She's smoking, though,' I noticed, with keen interest.

The doorbell rang, and as I closed the fridge door, my brother commandeered the marmalade before I'd had a chance to use it.

I heard the front door open.

My mum's voice.

I don't remember what she said. I just remember she was shouting.

And then suddenly, everyone in the house was in the hallway: Mum, Dad, me, Lucas, and the woman. Thankfully, my sister Bethany was at a friend's house.

Mum gripped the woman tightly by the hair and dragged her inside, screaming, 'This is the tramp your father has been sleeping with!'

As the strange woman tried to fight Mum off, Dad emerged, stricken-faced from his office, and I stood, stunned, unable to process what was happening. But Lucas barely missed a beat. He leapt into action immediately, pulling the woman to safety in the living room and locking the door behind him, with my mum on the other side.

My mind reeled as it came back online.

What the hell is going on!?

Mum went wild. She beat on the door with her fists, grabbed at the brass door handle, and, only God knows how, bent the thick, solid piece of metal so that the handle was forever deformed.

'GET HER AWAY FROM MY *SON*!' Mum bellowed as she battered her body against the living room door, trying to reach the young woman.

Dad took hold of Mum by the shoulders, battling with her unseemly strength and pulled her away from the door. Mum turned and started screaming at him hysterically. Words that never registered as I stood gaping in the hallway watching, the chaos scorching itself into my mind.

Then, Dad grabbed Mum by the wrists, and as she tried but failed to hit him with her fists, he pulled her downward onto the floor. Mum screamed and squirmed, and something broke in my mind.

What's he doing!? I thought helplessly as I clasped my head in my hands, eyes wide with terror.

Then he straddled her. The next thing I knew, Dad had Mum pinned to the floor by the wrists while she struggled and screamed at him to get off of her.

Mum's tortured face was too much for me. I spun around, looking for a way to help her. Then, I ran to the hallway cupboard and grabbed a large broom. From there, it was like I was watching the scene on television.

'Get off my mother!' I yelled, threatening my dad with the broom handle. Dad's head jerked up to look at me, and my parents froze. They lay there for a moment on the floor, wide-eyed and staring at me like they didn't know what I was going to do next. Then, Dad let Mum go, and the pair of them slowly got up. I watched the scene from far-far-away as this strange girl threw the broom on the ground and ran out into the front garden, crying.

I didn't go far. I sat on the rockery opposite the front door and wept. Then I threw little stones at my dad's BMW—his stupid pride and joy. I wanted to throw a rock at it and smash it, but I didn't have the guts. I was too scared of getting in trouble.

About an hour later, long after the strange woman had run out—leaving the door hanging open like the guts of our family—there was ominous silence from the house. Eventually, Lucas emerged into the hallway, and as I watched from the garden through the open front door, I saw him go into the kitchen with Dad, closing the door behind them.

Out on the rockery, it had grown peaceful. There was a gentle breeze, and the bushes around me were swaying slightly. The grass near my feet was full of clover, buttercups, and daisies. I'd started scraping some mildew off one of the rocks with a stick, and then I'd found a small group of woodlouse living there. I was gently picking up a woodlouse with a stick, transferring them onto my hand, and putting them back down again.

After a while, Lucas emerged from the kitchen and walked solemnly across the hall, disappearing out of view as he went back into the lounge. Then, Dad appeared in the doorway, looked out at me meekly, his face pale and his eyes red.

'Can you come into the kitchen, please, Sarah?' he asked quietly, his mouth turned down at the sides in an upside-down U, instead of his usual jubilant smile.

I put the woodlouse down and followed Dad silently into the kitchen.

'I'm so sorry that you had to see that, Sarah,' he said as he placed himself opposite me at the table. I silently hugged my knees to my chest and ignored him, staring unblinkingly at the floor. 'Being married is hard,' he continued, 'you might understand that one day. It's not as simple as it looks.'

I felt confused. *Surely marriage is easy if you love each other.*

'Look at me, Sarah,' Dad moved around the side of the table and knelt before me on the floor, trying to position himself in front of where my eyes were glazing over. But I couldn't bear to look at him. All I could feel was disdain. So, I moved my gaze down and to the side, so that Dad was just a blurry shape at the side of my vision.

'Please look at me,' Dad asked again and began to cry. The sound of it cracked my heart, and the enormous sadness of our poor family leaked into the sides of my awareness. A tear rolled down my cheek for my poor Dad. I looked up at him, through tears, and he took my hands in his.

'Are you going to keep seeing her?' I asked.

'If your mother won't take me back as a man, then I'll have to,' he said, and I instantly felt revolted. Dad slowly got up again, positioning himself opposite me at the table.

'Why did you do it?'

'It's just what men do, Sarah,' he said, and I recoiled, shocked. 'Men cheat, it's instinctual. We're driven to sow our seed,' he said, as though there was nothing that could be done to change it.

Even as he said it, I knew that he was wrong. Because if he wasn't, the future I wanted for myself and for my future daughters lay before me in tatters.

Men like YOU cheat. I thought angrily to myself as I stared at him.

And you think all men cheat because all of YOUR disgusting friends cheat, too.

But NOT all men are the same.

I crossed my arms, sickened. Although he might be right that a lot of men cheat on their wives and have affairs, he couldn't possibly be right about all of them. In that moment, as I sat and listened to my dad painting a grotesque picture of what the future held for me, I promised myself I would look for men at the better end of the spectrum who strive for a higher, purer kind of love.

***

A painful and confusing week later, I still hadn't confided in anyone about what had happened at home that day. Not even Emma. It was the final Saturday before schools and sixth-form colleges reopened for the new school year, and the crew had decided to see the summer off in style with a party down at The Green.

We sat in Tom's bedroom getting ready, music buzzing softly from his stereo. I sat by the window, staring out at the garden as Emma sat cross-legged on Tom's bed, holding up t-shirt options for him to wear.

My silence went unnoticed by Tom and Emma until, out of nowhere, I sniffed quietly, tears streaming uncontrollably from my eyes. Emma glanced my way. The sight of my tears stopped her mid-sentence.

'Hon, what's wrong?' Emma asked, concern lacing her voice as she set the t-shirt aside.

I attempted to smile, but the effort was too much. 'My parents are separating,' I confided, my words laden with the weight of reality. Emma put her arm around me soothingly, and Tom turned away from his closet, a look of shared pain in his eyes. He crossed the room and sat beside us, offering a silent but steady presence of support.

'Sarah, I'm so sorry,' he said, unsure of what else could ease a hurt so profound.

'What happened?' asked Emma, before adding, 'You don't have to talk about it if you don't want to.'

'Dad was having an affair,' I sobbed. 'He's going to move out to live by himself.'

As Emma slowly rubbed my back, whispering gentle assurances that I wouldn't face this alone, Tom passed me some tissues so that I could mop up the gross mess that was oozing out of my nose. Their kindness overwhelmed me, and my tears fell thick, silent and fast.

Emma and Tom looked shocked as I went on to recount the story of how Dad's mistress had come to our house.

'He told me: "It's what men do", but I don't think *all* men do that,' I shook my head, determined that my dad wasn't going to be right as Emma gently rocked me from side to side.

'Of course, he's not right,' she said, brushing some hair away from my cheek. 'My dad isn't like that. Jennifer's dad isn't either, nor is Matthew. There are loads of men who make wonderful, loving partners, without cheating,' she assured me.

I nodded. I knew she was right, and my dad was wrong, but it terrified me to think just how many men were probably in his club.

'I think it's just about being able to tell which ones are which,' I sniffed and wiped my eyes. 'Surely, there must be a way to tell.'

It was at that moment that Andy walked by, wearing a backward baseball cap and heading for the stairs. Catching the tension in the room, he lingered at the door.

'What's going on?' he asked, his voice softer than usual. Tom and Emma exchanged looks, and after glancing at me to check I was okay, Tom filled Andy in, delivering the news that my parents were breaking up with a gravity not often found in his voice. Andy hesitated, uncharacteristically unsure of how to react.

'Sorry, Sarah,' he said quietly and paused before continuing to the staircase. Moments later, he was back. 'Want some Scottish pancakes? I make some mean ones,' he offered awkwardly, more comfortable in doing than saying.

I looked up, surprise cutting through my sorrow. I managed a weak smile. 'Scottish pancakes?' I'd never heard of them, and Andy, as ever, intrigued me.

He smirked, already heading down to the kitchen. 'They're like American pancakes, except their real name is drop scones, the Americans just stole the idea and rebranded them. But... you'll have to be the judge.'

I got to my feet, flanked by Emma and Tom, and, drying my eyes, I followed him down the stairs. The clinking of pans and the smell of batter soon filled the kitchen, mixing with the quiet reassurance of friendship that gently enveloped me. I found myself feeling happy quite suddenly, drawn out of my sadness, as Andy ladled a thick batter into a frying pan and made what looked suspiciously like an American pancake.

Tom and Emma joined me at the kitchen table, and we watched Andy cooking with surprising ease, the usual cockiness absent from his demeanour. He even let me use his Disney mug with the broken handle. As the first stack of golden-brown pancakes hit the table, I felt a flutter of something new, a warmth that spread from the pit of my stomach to the tips of my fingers.

'These are actually amazing,' I commented, trying to keep my voice light as I took a bite, savouring the taste and the unexpected attention Andy granted me. Andy grinned, pleased to have helped.

'Told you. Scottish style always wins,' he said with a cheeky wink, taking a seat opposite me.

The conversation ebbed and flowed around us, but my focus was on Andy. I studied him with a new perspective, a faint blush creeping up my cheeks as I realised how much I liked being around him.

With everything at home unravelling—Dad preparing to move out, Mum always crying—an unforeseen softness in Andy had brought a small but significant comfort. I felt cared for in a way I hadn't realised I'd been missing, and once I noticed it, I didn't want to let it go.

As it was Andy's night off, we invited him to join us at the party on The Green, but as usual, he didn't want to come. Instead, he went to see a friend of his own, and as we left for the party later that night, I felt like I was leaving a little part of me behind with him.

'Lucky you,' exclaimed Tom to me quietly as we walked. 'Andy's not usually that nice to anyone; you got the special treatment,' he teased.

'What do you mean?' I asked curiously.

'Well, our parents split up when we were little, before I can really remember—but Andy remembers it. He was always getting in trouble at school. I think it really affected him.'

'So… you think that's why he made me the pancakes?'

Tom nodded thoughtfully. 'He doesn't talk much about his feelings, but occasionally, he'll do something that definitely shows them. I think we just witnessed that tonight.'

That night, I went back to Emma's house and didn't go home. I didn't call either, not wanting to start an argument or get in trouble. When I got back home the next day, the house was empty, but my sister had left me a note under my pillow.

Dear Sarah,

I just wanted to say that I love you. You are the best sister in the dodeciverse. Please don't ever run off again. I missed you more than the whole world.

Sorry about that smudge, it is one of my tears.

Mum keeps telling me off for crying and keeps saying that I am thick if I miss you. She keeps saying that we act like we are God and that you have turned me into a cow. It is getting dangerous to write now. I think mum is suspecting something.

With all the love in the world,

Bethany

xxxxxxxxxxxxxx

Bethany still didn't know about Mum and Dad's plans to split up yet. They would tell her when the moment was right. But the note was so sweet and heartfelt; I stared at it for a long time before tears started streaming down my face.

I was crying for all of us, for Lucas and Bethany, for my parents, for myself. Then I squirrelled the note away in my secret shoebox of memorabilia and decided that I should think more carefully about Bethany, who was caught in the middle of everybody else's chaos.

Transitions

12

The Revelation

September 1998

SEPTEMBER WAS EXCRUCIATING. My parents kept arguing while my dad was looking for a place of his own; Nick and Andy were on my mind constantly, and at school, A-levels were far more intense than GCSEs had been. But as is the way with life, it took with one hand and gave with the other.

Despite my abundance of friends outside school, nothing much changed for me inside until sixth form. But when our cohort moved into the newly refurbished sixth form building that first day back at school, an array of new faces joined our year from other schools. One of them was Kate, who joined my Form Room and quickly became a good friend. She was fun, smart, and stunningly gorgeous to boot.

After the first bell rang, all of the classrooms emptied into the bright, open-plan common room. Kate and I exited together, chatting. Seeing Johnnie sitting with some mates at one of the tables, we headed over. The previous year, I'd barely seen Johnnie at school. He was usually playing football while I hid out in the art block, pretending to be busy.

'Hey Johnnie, fancy seeing you here!' I joked, and we hugged each other briefly. 'This is Kate; she's new,' I introduced my new friend and watched on incredulously as Johnnie became uncharacteristically bashful and quiet.

'Alright? How's it going?' murmured Johnnie, looking at his shoes, up at me awkwardly, and then side-glancing at Kate.

Kate tried to engage Johnnie in easy conversation but failed miserably. When the second bell rang, she awkwardly made her excuses and left to go to her next class. I turned to Johnnie with a look of theatrical horror on my face.

'What the hell was that!?' I laughed as soon as Kate was out of earshot. Johnnie shuffled in his shoes and scratched his head. 'It's like you forgot how to talk or something,' I teased, and as Johnnie relaxed, his senses came back.

'I don't know,' he admitted, smiling embarrassedly. 'Man, she is really fit,' he added, gazing in the direction that she'd walked.

'Yeah, alright, put your tongue back in your mouth,' I mocked, pulling my Filofax out of my bag to check what class I had next.

'Ooh. Watch out. The Filofax is back,' Johnnie quipped, and I gave him a retaliatory prod.

'Hey, Sarah!' called out Lisa, a trendy girl in my class. Despite having shared a Form Room for five years, Lisa and I hadn't spoken much since we were about twelve. 'Was that you I saw in Whetstone over the summer, running along with a shopping trolley covered in flowers?' she asked curiously.

'Oh yeah, I was on my way to a party,' I explained matter-of-factly, and Lisa looked at me as though she were seeing me for the first time.

'Cool,' she laughed and smiled. 'Whose party was it?'

'Oh, just some friends from outside of school,' I breezed, and Lisa's eyes sparkled with what seemed like curiosity. I looked over at Johnnie, who smiled and winked at me sweetly. Things were off to a good start already!

***

About a week into that first year of sixth form, I arrived home from school to a Post-It note from Dad on the mirror. Peeling it off, I read that Emma had called with something she needed to tell me. But when I called her back, no one answered.

'Everything alright?' asked Dad, concerned.

'She's not answering,' I explained moodily, as I'd barely spoken to Dad since news of his affair surfaced and wasn't looking forward to him moving out. 'I'll see her tonight at drama class, so I suppose I'll talk to her then.'

With that, we headed upstairs to see Lucas, who was packing some boxes in his room, closely observed by Bethany. The next morning, he was leaving for university in Bristol to study Finance, and Dad wasn't taking it so well.

'I can't believe my son is going to university,' said Dad, choking up, and Lucas shot him a sympathetic look.

'Calm down, Dad, don't cry about it!' Lucas laughed, and Dad laughed too and sat on his son's bed.

'Are you going to take Mister Bear?' Dad teased, pointing up at a battered blue teddy bear that had been stuffed on top of the wardrobe. 'That'll impress the girls,' he winked, and I frowned to myself.

Seems like girls are all he thinks about.

'I don't want you to go!' cried Bethany suddenly, flinging herself at Lucas' legs.

'I'll be back before you know it,' promised Lucas. 'And everything will be totally back to normal,' he added, breezily ruffling her hair.

With that, Bethany calmed down, but I looked at Dad reproachfully.

Will it, though?

***

Later that evening, acting classes reopened at mine and Emma's theatre group after the summer break. Liam, our enthusiastic young drama teacher, had written a play, and the theatre buzzed with the familiar energy of a new production. Scripts rustled as the group prepared to audition while laughter and dialogue filled the air. I scanned the room, my heart light at trying out for one of the leading roles.

My gaze landed on Emma, absently fidgeting with the staple holding her script together. Her usual bright demeanour seemed muted, and she looked worried. During a break in warm-up exercises, I wove through a throng of animated group members and approached her. Emma looked up from her spot in the corner, giving me a forced smile and a wave that did little to disguise the angst in her eyes.

'Hey, Em,' I said, trying to sound casual but unable to hide my concern. 'I got your message. Everything okay?'

Emma hesitated, glancing around to ensure privacy. The theatre's lively backdrop provided little chance for eavesdropping, so she spoke freely. 'It's kind of complicated,' she started, her voice barely above a whisper amidst the bustling activity. 'But I think you should know.'

My curiosity sharpened, my mind already racing with possibilities. 'Did you split up with Dyer?' I trailed off, hoping I hadn't sounded too keen on the idea.

She shook her head, her expression a mix of sympathy and uncertainty. 'It's about Jennifer and Nick. They broke up. It wasn't pretty,' she admitted softly, meeting my eyes directly. 'And it involves you more than you might think.'

The impact of Emma's words hit me like a tidal wave, my mind reeling with the news of Jennifer and Nick's breakup. To my shock, Nick was suddenly entangled with me in a way I couldn't begin to imagine. My chest tightened with a volatile mix of curiosity and anticipation. What could this mean? I was desperate to understand why Nick and Jennifer's breakup somehow had me at its centre. But before Emma could explain, Liam burst onto the scene with his usual flair.

Clapping his hands, he boomed, 'Alright, everyone! Gather round. Auditions start now—I need absolute silence!'

The room hushed instantly. Emma shot me an apologetic look, and I nodded; this would have to wait. As Liam launched into his animated monologue, I tried to focus, but my attention kept drifting back to Emma, frustration buzzing under my skin.

Ninety minutes later, the torture ended. Emma and I grabbed our coats and headed out into the cool evening air, making a beeline for a McDonalds just down the street. The bright, busy hum of the restaurant enveloped us as we settled into a corner booth, the smell of fries and grilled patties comforting in its familiarity.

Emma took a deep breath, finally ready to spill. 'Jennifer found Nick wearing your ring on a chain around his neck,' she began, her voice low but steady. 'That's what triggered the breakup.'

I blinked, her words sinking in slowly. 'My ring? The coral one?' Mixed feelings washed over me—surprise, disbelief, and a flicker of hope.

Emma nodded. 'He told her it means something important to him. That's when things got really bad between them.'

I slouched back against the booth, trying to process it all. This revelation shifted everything. The thought that Nick might have feelings for me sparked a warmth that spread through my entire being. But despite the involuntary thrill, a wave of guilt doused my happiness, reminding me that this revelation wasn't just about me—it involved Jennifer's feelings, too.

Emma resumed her story, her tone sobering. Jennifer had confronted Emma, her emotions raw, accusing her of holding back the truth and insisting she must have known more about Nick's feelings for me. She said Emma had changed since meeting Dyer and me—that she barely even knew her anymore.

The accusations had clearly stung. Emma broke down in the booth, and I pulled her into me, murmuring that it would be okay, that Jennifer was probably just upset but would calm down eventually. But Emma shook her head and continued.

Jennifer had gone on to Emma's parents, claiming I was a bad influence—that I did drugs, slept around, smuggled a bottle of whisky into the Alexandra Palace Ball, got completely drunk and attempted to run away with Matthew Dyer, Emma's own boyfriend.

'But I didn't do any of those things!' I burst out. 'I've never even *had* a boyfriend! I've only kissed two boys. I've never even *smoked* a cigarette, and I drank the drink that *she* poured for me!'

Emma sighed, shaking her head. 'I know. And mum knows too, because she said it was so obvious you were in love with Nick that night.'

I winced. *So obvious? Ouch.*

Emma went on. 'Jennifer's trying to convince my parents to keep me away from you and Matthew. Matthew is effectively banned from our house now. Mum hasn't said the same about you—but she's considering it.'

I felt sick with indignation and fear for our friendship. And yet, a part of me felt pleased that Jennifer had managed to warn Emma's parents about Dyer. I couldn't stop myself from saying it out loud.

'Well, Em…' I said softly, my heart pounding, aware that Emma was going to react badly. 'You know you can't trust him…'

She raised a hand, eyes shining with tears. 'Please! Sarah. Not you, as well. I've been getting enough of this at home.'

I felt awful, but as I leaned in to hug her again, Emma slid out of the booth and left the restaurant, saying she needed some space.

I sat there alone, the table suddenly too big, the noise around me too loud. Whatever flicker of excitement I'd felt about Nick drained away, leaving something duller underneath—worry for Emma, and the sour weight of Jennifer's accusations. Too much had shifted at once, and I had no idea what I was supposed to feel first.

Later that night, when I got home, I considered whether to call Emma and apologise. I picked up the receiver, the dial tone humming softly in my ear as I hesitated. My fingers hovered over the numbers, my mind spiralling through countless scenarios. But fear of making things worse, of misunderstanding or deepening the hurt, paralysed me. She'd asked for some space, and I decided I should give it to her. The weight of our fractured friendship loomed too large. Silence was safer for now, at least until I could sort through my own confused feelings.

I thought about Jennifer and wondered if I could salvage our friendship despite the hurtful things that she had been saying about me. What would I even say? That I was sorry for something I couldn't have known about?

After a few moments of restless pacing, I couldn't put it off any longer, and my thoughts inevitably landed on Nick. I picked up the receiver again, a flutter of nerves mixing with excitement. I imagined asking him about why he wore my ring on a chain, and in my mind, he told me everything I wanted to hear. My heart raced as I dialled his number, half-hoping and half-dreading he'd pick up.

Instead, his dad answered, his voice deep and unfamiliar.

Disappointment pricked at my excitement as I learned Nick wasn't home—he was at Derrick's house, the dealer from the party.

I paused. Derrick wasn't exactly the kind of person you went to for a quiet night.

I thanked his dad and hung up, left to sit with my racing thoughts and a faint, unfamiliar knot in my stomach.

And still, the same question lingered. Now that Nick had split up with Jennifer, was he thinking about me?

13
EUPHORIA

October 1998

MY SEVENTEENTH BIRTHDAY OFFERED my family a brief respite from the recent turmoil. Mum and Dad were united and happy again for a day, and as I opened my cards and blew out the candles on my birthday cake, they shared a tender moment together as though nothing had happened between them. I was particularly delighted when I opened a card from my parents saying that I would start taking driving lessons soon.

Yet beneath the celebration and appreciated generosity, there was a quiet ache: Emma still hadn't called. Not even to wish me a happy birthday.

Eventually, I caved and rang her. The next day, she was waiting for me at an outdoor table in a pretty café in Covent Garden, down some steps in the middle of the square. We hadn't seen each other for almost a month since she'd rushed out of the burger restaurant crying, and I was feeling terribly nervous.

Nearby, a violinist played a wistful melody to a crowd of onlookers looking down from above into the sunken alcove. We were wearing our winter coats already, which felt symbolic somehow, a testament to not only the changing seasons but also to our friendship, having moved on from the easy breeziness of summer into something different. I worried that I had lost her and that things would never again be the same between us.

As I rushed to greet her, I nearly knocked over one of the tables on the outskirts of the café, spilling the drinks of the people sitting there. I apologised profusely and helped to mop up the mess with serviettes while Emma came over to help us, which was just like her. Smiling at each other awkwardly, we returned to her table, and I sat down.

'You always knew how to make an entrance,' she joked, and I laughed, the ice broken between us.

'It's good to see you; I'm so glad you're here,' I confessed, and she reached out and took my hand before leaning in for a big hug. 'I thought you might not want to see me again,' I sniffled, which seemed to trigger Emma into sniffling too.

'I could never stay angry at you,' she smiled. 'It's just that things are really hard right now,' she continued. 'Jennifer still isn't speaking to me. Mum's like a dog with a bone, interfering in my life. She gets these theories and thinks she's right about everything,' Emma tutted. 'She's convinced Matthew is a loser. I barely even see him anymore now he's banned from our house. He's spending more and more time at Derrick's house smoking weed with Nick. They've even started doing mushrooms. The other day, I called him, and they were out in a field, hunting for them!'

'As in.... magic mushrooms?' I repeated, startled.

'Yes! Exactly,' Emma shook her head in disbelief. 'And it wasn't the first time. I'm really worried about him. I feel like I'm losing him, and I don't know what to do.' Emma started sniffing at the table, and her eyes filled with tears. I took her hands and comforted her as best I could.

'It's okay, Em. I'm sure you're not losing him,' I rubbed her arm tenderly. 'Maybe it's just something he's trying for a while.'

At that, Emma seemed to feel better. 'Maybe you're right,' she smiled and sniffed just as the waitress came over to take our drinks orders, and we ordered replacement coffees for the table I'd knocked into, as well as cappuccinos for us. When she had gone, Emma continued. 'I really love him, you know. Everyone seems to be against us right now. Please, can you promise me that you'll be nice to him? I couldn't cope if you were against us too.'

Emma looked deep into my eyes as she pleaded, and despite my better judgment, I nodded anyway.

'Of course, Em. I can give him another chance if you need me to,' I smiled and rubbed the top of her hand. 'Although I'm going to have to ask Nick about the mushrooms,' I pondered.

Our cappuccinos arrived, and Emma started to look much brighter and happier.

'How are things with you? Have you spoken to Nick yet about the ring?' she asked, her face animated and lively again, more like her usual self.

'We've spoken on the phone a few times,' I admitted excitedly. 'Last night, we were talking for nearly two hours. But I haven't asked him about Jennifer or the ring yet, and he hasn't said anything.' I paused, furrowing my brow, confused. 'The thing is, I'm the one who always calls him. And he's never actually asked me out. What do you think that means?'

Emma was stumped. Neither of us had gotten to grips with the confounding world of men yet—their strange ways, how they seemed interested in you one moment, and the next, they were cold and distant.

'Seems like the perfect thing to ask him at Euphoria next weekend. You are coming, aren't you?' Emma giggled excitedly.

'Hell yeah! Wouldn't miss it!' I exclaimed, 'I can't believe Johnnie's actually gotten around to organising it; he's been talking about it for so long,'

'Woohoo! Teenie-boppers clubbing in a church!' Emma feigned mockery, but I knew she was as excited about the upcoming event as I was.

I paused, 'I wonder what Nick will say when I ask him,' I pondered.

'I do think he has feelings for you, Sarah,' divulged Emma. 'Otherwise, why would he wear your ring around his neck?' She paused for a moment and thought. 'Maybe he thinks you're a bit intense, though,' she offered, shifting uncomfortably in her seat.

Looking at her, I knew that she was repeating what Dyer had told her straight from Nick himself, and I felt wretched as soon as she said it.

'What do you mean, intense?' I asked defensively, feeling wounded.

Emma continued to fidget, and I could see that she was struggling to express herself. 'Well, I mean, it's not like you've always gotten along, is it?'

Emma was looking at me apologetically, but all I could feel was miserable. 'I'm not intense,' I said intensely, fiddling with my teaspoon before sitting perfectly still. I stared morosely at the sugar bowl before taking a sip of my coffee.

'Anyway,' she smiled slyly. 'It looked to me like Nick isn't the only one on your radar. What's going on with you and Andy these days?'

Caught off guard, I coughed, and coffee spilt from my cup, blazing a brown trail down my new cream coat with faux-fur collar.

'What?! Nothing!' I protested loudly, dabbing at the stain as Emma laughed. 'Why would you think something is going on with Andy and me?' I asked innocently. Emma's eyes narrowed, and she examined me from a distance.

'Oh, come on, hon, *puh-lease*,' she sniffed. 'Pancakes?' she raised an eyebrow as she said it, and I paused to think for a moment.

'Yeah, that was really sweet of him, wasn't it?' I chuckled, feeling a warmth spread through me just thinking about it. 'He really made me feel taken care of. Like, he knew just what to do to make everything right.' I smiled, and Emma made an excited 'ooh' noise, which was half mockery and half genuine. 'The thing about Andy is that he's just so intriguing. Normally, he's so distant, but every now and then, he'll just do something incredibly sweet—like the pancakes—or incredibly sexy.'

'Sexy?' perked up Emma raunchily. 'Do go on!'

As Emma took a gulp of her coffee, I recounted the day of the water fight and how, in Andy's bedroom, I'd thrown myself on his mattress, and he'd put his arms around me to try to gently remove me. Even though nothing had happened between us, I'd thought about that moment often.

'But Andy sees me as a kid, though,' I sighed wistfully. 'He is quite a bit older than us, after all.'

'He's really not, actually,' Emma pointed out, not to be put off. 'He's a year and a bit older than you. He's eighteen—you're seventeen. *Trust* me, hon. It's *nothing*,' she shrugged nonchalantly, having been in a relationship herself for six months with Dyer, who was a year older than Andy.

I looked at Emma and hoped that my face wasn't betraying how disgusted Dyer made me feel and how frustrating it was not to say so. The last thing I wanted was to fall out again. I wanted to believe her about Andy, but deep in my heart, despite our age difference meaning less now, I knew he still saw me as a kid. Even if I let myself dream about him, I feared that I'd end up disappointed.

I decided my best option was to distract Emma with a spot of teasing, before she drove me mad with it. Mimicking her voice and body language exaggeratedly, I replied and contradicted her directly:

'*Trust* me, hon. It's *something*.'

Emma laughed and swatted at me theatrically. 'Stop, stop,' she laughed, clearly enjoying my skit.

Encouraged, I threw in a few more of Emma's mannerisms—a theatrical hand flap, a dramatic eyebrow waggle—until she started giggling and doing her own impressions of me. In a spoof of my clumsiness, she knocked the napkin holder over, apologised profusely like a bumbling female Hugh Grant character, before bringing her fist down forcefully on the handle of her teaspoon, which was perched on the edge of her saucer. I gasped and froze mid-laugh.

Immediately regretting the decision, we watched in horror as the teaspoon hurtled into the air and landed with a clang at the feet of the violinist, who kept playing but shot us the filthiest of looks. Nearby, a group of German tourists looked on—one laughing, one scowling, one stunned.

Clamping a hand over our mouths to stop ourselves laughing, I retrieved the teaspoon apologetically and fled into the café to pay at the till rather than wait for the waitress.

***

The following weekend, Emma and I pranced around her room, singing at the top of our voices as we got ready to go to Euphoria. Tonight was the night. Finally, I would ask Nick about his feelings for me and tell him I knew he wore my ring around his neck. I imagined us falling into each other's arms on the dance floor and never being apart again, but a part of me knew it wouldn't be that easy.

'How do I look?' asked Emma, wearing a pair of leopard-print spandex flares and enormous black platform shoes, topped off with a black gypsy top that showed both of her shoulders.

'Amazing!' I gasped, admiring her outfit. 'I love your flares. They're so cool!'

'Five pounds… half price from C&A,' boasted Emma, issuing the standard British response to a compliment: anytime someone said something nice about an item you were wearing, you had to say that it was a bargain, and if it had been expensive, you had to confess that you could hardly afford it. If you couldn't denigrate the item, the rule was that you had to denigrate yourself. It was a conversational paradigm we had both become masters of. 'I love your earrings!' chimed in Emma.

'Thanks! It was 'buy a pair, get one free!' I said masterfully as I tied my hair into a pair of low pigtails and lined my eyes with gold eyeshadow. Pulling on a pair of tight, white pedal pushers and a vest top lined with tiny beads, I followed Emma down to where Mrs

McCarthy was waiting to inspect our outfits. Then, the three of us hopped into the family car with Emma in the driver's seat—having finally gotten her provisional license—and we inched our way to the party.

We aimed to get down to the church hall at seven to see if Johnnie needed help setting things up. But by the time we arrived, it was almost eight o'clock, and a hoard of scantily clad teenagers were already braving the elements without coats, waiting for the doors to open. Pulling into the car park, a long line of cars started to accelerate past, the drivers frowning harshly at Emma as they went.

Holding a clipboard and assuming an air of authority as the organiser, Johnnie was calmer than I'd ever seen him, and it was only when we got a little closer that we realised how excited he was; he was simply playing it cool.

'Wow, this is incredible, Johnnie,' I gushed, hugging him. 'Look how many people there are!'

Johnnie stifled a celebration and turned his back to the queue so that no one could see his face. 'I was so worried no one would come!' he whispered. 'But I've sold half of the tickets already, and the doors aren't even open yet!'

Laughing, Emma looked up at the church hall where she'd attended so many events as a child. 'The church secretary was quite surprised when my parents asked if our Jewish friend could hire the hall for a teenagers club night,' she said matter-of-factly. 'I think that's a first on both fronts!'

We jumped a little in the cold to keep ourselves warm, and Johnnie ushered us up the driveway. 'Time to open the doors!' He exclaimed. 'Do you want to be first in?'

We jumped at the chance, and inside the hall, we found a loud sound system blaring out Jay-Z. The hall was almost completely dark, except for coloured spotlights that were flashing while a giant disco ball sent shards of light bouncing atmospherically around the room. Near the entrance, stretching up to the stage along the side of the hall, was a gently lit bar selling soft drinks. At the foot of the hall, breaking up the space, two large wooden platforms had been placed for people to dance on.

Impressed, we turned to Johnnie. 'How did you manage all this? This is wicked!' I asked, in awe of his setup.

'I've never seen it look like this before!' Emma gasped. 'Who's playing DJ tonight?'

Looking slightly embarrassed, Johnnie pointed to the left of the stage, at a small storage cupboard crammed with sports equipment, where his mum sat wedged inside with an alarming number of CDs and a CD player.

'Mum's under very strict orders to only play music from the list tonight,' he said, scowling as though she had had opinions of her own about what music to play. 'If you hear anything from the '70s, come and get me immediately,' he ordered, and we nodded, hiding the smiles that involuntarily crept onto our faces.

As Johnnie left and teenagers started trickling in, we noticed Father O'Brien, the church priest, behind the bar and went over.

'Hello, Father,' we both chimed simultaneously, Emma doing an almost imperceptible curtsey.

'Hello, my dears, nice to see you; how lovely you both look,' Father O'Brien replied politely. 'What can I get you to drink this evening?'

'A Sprite and a Coke, please,' I asked and awkwardly grinned as we took our drinks. Behind us, we noticed with glee that the dancefloor was beginning to fill up as a steady stream of people entered the hall.

In the cupboard, Johnnie's mum stumbled across a crowd-pleaser, and as 'Ghetto Supastar' came over the sound system, the first girls started to dance, glancing around them to see if any of the boys were watching. At the end of the song, the dancefloor suddenly became packed as people standing around the edge flocked to the middle when Abba's 'Dancing Queen' started playing. Hearing it, Johnnie rushed up to the cupboard with a face like thunder, and much to everyone's disappointment, it was quickly replaced by a new Garage track.

A few songs later, Emma and I had met up with Kate and Lisa from my school, and with no sign of Nick and Tom, we were dancing together on top of the wooden boxes, with the party in full swing all around us.

'I just pulled *the* fittest guy outside,' gushed Kate loudly into my ear as Emma chatted animatedly with Lisa.

'Oh really?' I asked, my eyes sparkling with excitement. 'Which one?'

I scanned the room with her, but we couldn't see him. 'Maybe he's still outside,' she shouted matter-of-factly into my ear, preferring instead to recount all the juicy details of how he'd seduced her and kissed her. As she was talking, Nick and Tom walked into the hall. I met Nick's gaze and waved, a warm smile slowly spreading across my face, looking forward to finally getting to the bottom of why he wore my ring around his neck.

But rather than smiling back, Nick froze, like a rabbit in headlights, just as Kate turned and pointed at him.

'There he is,' she squealed. 'Isn't he gorgeous? Don't look! He'll know we're talking about him,' she panicked, looked away and tried to act naturally.

My heart sank—again—as it had done when he'd kissed Jennifer at the Ball. But this time, the disappointment wasn't as overpowering. I pushed it down and kept dancing with Kate as Nick watched on. He seemed to be waiting for something. But I no longer cared. I turned away and spent the rest of the night laughing and dancing with my girlfriends. It wasn't until the end of the evening that he cornered me alone on my way to the bathroom.

'Sarah!' he pounced on me from the corner of the hallway, full of people. 'How's it going?' His eyes lingered on mine in the same way that my dad's did when he was trying to work out whether he'd been caught in a lie.

'Fine, thanks,' I smiled broadly and started to pull away. 'I'm busting for the loo, though!'

Nick stepped in line with me, partially blocking me, seemingly desperate to keep me engaged in our conversation. 'Did you have a good night?' he asked urgently. 'I saw you dancing with Kate earlier,' he mentioned, finally arriving at his point. 'Do you two know each other?'

'Oh yeah. Nice girl.' I side-stepped him and pushed open the toilet door. 'Big fan of yours, I believe.'

Out of the corner of my eye, I saw Nick's head drop down as I let the bathroom door swing shut behind me. I'd be damned if I was going to ask him about my ring tonight. And when I did ask, perhaps I should simply ask to have it back.

14
CONNECTION

The week before Christmas, December 1998

IT WAS FINALLY THE CHRISTMAS HOLIDAYS, and for the first time in my life, I had the whole house to myself. Mum had taken Bethany away on holiday, Dad had moved out, and Lucas was celebrating Christmas with university friends.

Come Friday night, everyone had gathered at my place, and inside, the party was in full swing. Music pumped from the stereo, my parents' CD collection was being pawed through by Tom, who was acting as DJ, and Johnnie and Jamie-from-The-Green were testing out childish wrestling moves on the furniture.

'Guys, if you break the sofa, I'm dead,' I asserted, tucking my new Rachel-from-Friends hairstyle behind my ear and pulling my flimsy little black dress (LBD) as low as it would go in a vain attempt to cover my legs up a bit. I wasn't cold—I'd whacked the heating on full blast (thanks Mum)—but I'd never really been one for short skirts or dresses. I felt wildly exposed as the hemline of my first LBD seemed to have a mind of its own.

Tutting, I noticed that Dyer had used one of my parents' CDs as a coaster. Not the case. The actual CD.

Pig.

I got up, picked up his full glass, and carried it towards the kitchen to pour it down the sink. As I went, I wondered where Nick had gone. Things had been pretty good between us in the weeks since Euphoria. No drama, no heavy conversations about rings, breakups, kisses or feelings. Nothing except friendship and good times, actually. It was like our vibe had finally mellowed.

In the hallway, I snuck to the mirror, pulled out a sparkly pink lip gloss and slathered my lips in a thick, iridescent layer. Just then, Nick appeared from the kitchen wearing a snazzy Rudolph jumper and carrying a Jack Daniel's and Coke in one hand.

'It's hopeless, Sarah,' he quipped, having seen me preening myself and deciding to get a dig in. 'Give it up, man. You're hideous.' Whirling around from the mirror to face him, my face lit up as he approached.

'Er, rude!' I slapped him on the shoulder, and he poked me in the arm, laughing.

'Come and stand with me while I smoke?' he asked warmly, gesturing for me to join him as he headed to the front door. He had that familiar teasing glint in his eye, the kind that made my heart race despite my best efforts at maintaining indifference. I nodded, but as soon as he was outside, I closed the door behind him, giggling, and looked out at him through the letterbox.

'Can I help you?' I asked, sniggering. Nick looked down at me and rolled his eyes, trying not to smile. Then, he got down on his knees, and suddenly, his eyes were an inch from mine, looking straight back at me through the gap.

My breath went in and never came out again.

Wow, his eyes are amazing.

'Let me in, Trouble,' he whispered gently in a voice so persuasive I almost just opened the door without thinking.

Shaking my head, I warmed to my game. 'I'm sorry, we didn't order any of what you're selling.'

Nick stared into my eyes intensely through the letterbox—so close that an electric connection between us seemed to transcend everything around us. 'If you let me in, I promise you'll want what

I'm selling.' He waited for a moment, and before I had time to think, like a sucker, I opened the door.

Nick slipped inside, firmly but gently pushed me out, and clicked the door shut softly behind me.

I stood blinking under the porch light in the cold night air for a moment before what had just happened sank in.

'Nick!' I yelled, flipping around and pressing my face to the letterbox, where his own had been moments earlier.

Nick's smug face dropped casually into view, his smiling eyes filling the small rectangle between us. 'Yes?' he asked, his face a mask of innocence and impossible to resist. 'You gonna beg?' he challenged, not mean-spirited but with a boyishness that got under my skin.

'Very funny, open the door,' I insisted, half-rolling my eyes but unable to break his gaze.

Actually, I wasn't sure if I wanted him to open the door or not. Despite being freezing, with no shoes and just my LBD to keep me warm, I didn't want the moment to end.

Just then, I heard the familiar purr of a car in the street and then pulling into the driveway. Spinning around, I saw my dad's BMW, with the shadowy figure of a woman in the passenger seat, unmistakable even through the windshield's gleam. Why were they pulling into the driveway of our house, knowing that Mum and Bethany were away on holiday?

Nick let the door swing open, but I ignored it and stayed outside, staring at the car.

My eyes locked with my dad's across the darkened front lawn, and his expression shifted—a look of horror spreading across his face as the tyres crunched suddenly into reverse. On Fridays, I was usually out in North London with my friends; I was never usually home.

Dad backed out onto the street and was about to drive off, but he hesitated as I approached. I bent down slowly and looked deep into the car.

As the window rolled down, my dad's face became plastered with a desperate smile. His passenger—the same woman as before—stared straight ahead.

'Dad? What are you doing here?' I asked and looked across at his passenger.

'I was just giving Amanda a lift home,' he said, 'and I saw you in the driveway and thought I'd check that you were okay.'

Liar.

How dare he bring that woman here while Mum is away?

I nodded silently.

Then I remembered an unopened box of chocolates he'd given me when he moved out. Disgusted, I ran back inside to fetch them so I could throw them back in his car. But as I came back outside holding them, the driveway and street were empty.

Nick appeared in the doorway; his grin faded to a look of concern. 'Hey,' he said softly, stepping outside to meet me. 'Are you okay?'

I let out a deep breath and leaned against the doorframe to steady myself, suddenly feeling chilled to the bone, my arms covered in goosebumps and my feet like blocks of ice.

Seeing that I was upset, Nick reached out to me and led me inside, his presence comforting in the midst of my swirling thoughts. We settled on a plush, well-worn sofa in the back room, far away from the ruckus of the party. The room was dimly lit, casting soft shadows across Nick's face. I couldn't help but feel a sense of relief enveloping me, his warmth juxtaposing with the cold shock of seeing my father's car earlier and that woman sitting next to him.

'Are you okay, Sarah? Was that your dad?' Nick asked, nudging me gently with his shoulder, a subtle gesture which prompted me to speak.

'Yeah… with the woman who split my parents up in the passenger seat,' I revealed, feeling numb with the shock. Nick raised his eyebrows and let out a little gasp at the news, before putting his arm around me gently as if to reassure me that I wasn't alone. 'He said that it was over between them,' I continued. 'What am I supposed to tell my mum when she gets back from holiday?' Nick listened attentively as my shock wore off, replaced with confusion and frustration. 'It's just... everything's upside down right now,' I admitted, holding my head in my hands, trying to find the words buried beneath my turmoil. 'Between my parents breaking up, my dad's cheating, and... well, *you*.'

'Me?' He frowned, surprise filling his voice.

'Yes, you,' I looked up, frowning, my heart pounding, but a part of me feeling so good for finally being brave. 'I heard that you and Jennifer broke up because of, well,' I hesitated, feeling a bit ridiculous bringing it up, 'because you wear my coral ring around your neck.'

The stunned look on Nick's face told me he had no idea I'd heard about him wearing my ring. His hand instinctively touched the small, vibrant piece of coral hidden beneath his shirt. There was something intimate in his gesture, a tenderness that matched his tone when he finally spoke.

'Well, that's embarrassing,' he laughed gently, looking at me in the eyes and then looking away, flushed. It was the first time I'd ever seen him blush before. The first time I'd ever seen him look vulnerable.

'Sorry,' I stammered immediately. 'Maybe I shouldn't have said anything.'

'No, no. I'm glad that you did. I've worn it since that night on The Green,' he confessed quietly. 'When I stole it from you,' he added a gentle laugh and an apologetic smile.

I smiled back. 'Yes, you did steal it from me, didn't you?' I teased, tucking my head to one side and then falling silent, letting my eyes linger on his for a while.

'Here, you can have it back if you like,' he said, putting his hands to the back of his neck. But before he could undo the chain, I stopped him.

'No, it's okay. I think it's sweet. I like the fact that you wear it.'

Nick looked at me, and his eyes softened. He gently picked up my hands in his and stroked them gently with his thumb before continuing. 'I guess… I guess I've had feelings for you. Feelings I couldn't ignore, even then,' he admitted. 'You've always wanted the best for me. It's really sweet. Wearing it this way, I kept you close without you even realising it.'

My heart skipped a beat, the heat between us suddenly palpable. 'Nick, I've had feelings for you, too. I've been trying to look out for you. I worry about you, especially with Dyer hanging around. And the weed… the other drugs? School's important, and—'

'Hey,' he interrupted softly, taking my hand. 'Stop worrying so much about me. You've got enough on your plate already. Dyer's a bit chaotic, but I'm okay. I know you worry because you care, and I really appreciate that.'

Before I could reply, Nick leaned in closer, his breath warm against my skin. When his lips met mine, every thought I'd been holding back seemed to fall away. The kiss was gentle but full, tender and electric all at once.

I melted into him as his hands cupped my face, pulling me closer, as if we were both finally admitting what we'd been circling for months. When we pulled apart, something quiet and certain passed between us.

Our fingers laced together as we stood and walked back into the living room. Tom was still DJing, and Emma, Dyer and Johnnie were sprawled on the sofa with a couple of guys from The Green. When everyone saw us, a chorus of whoops went up. Emma jumped up and squealed in delight, much to Dyer's disdain.

Wrapped in our friends' cheers, Nick and I turned to each other and started to dance.

Together, Nick and I grinned, knowing this was just the beginning.

15
Highs and Lows

BY THE TIME MUM AND BETHANY RETURNED from holiday, I'd worked myself into a panic about how to tell her what had happened with Dad. I put it off, telling myself I'd wait until after the New Year rather than ruin everyone's Christmas. By Christmas Eve, I was a bundle of nerves—but a date with Nick eclipsed everything.

I curled my 'Rachel' hair into soft waves and kept my makeup mostly restrained. In my messy bedroom, I tried on half my wardrobe before—like always—circling back to the first thing I'd put on anyway.

As I waited for Nick, my heart pounded with nervous excitement. My mind raced ahead, inventing versions of the evening that all ended the same way: with me grinning like an idiot and Nick deciding to friend-zone me. The minutes dragged, and I kept glancing at the clock, willing time to hurry up.

When Nick finally arrived in his clapped-out old banger, my heart felt like it might beat right out of my chest. He stepped out of the car and made his way towards me, a smile spreading across his face.

'Wow, you look stunning,' he said, his eyes filled with genuine admiration as he gave me a kiss on the cheek and opened my car door for me. My cheeks burned with pure delight. I couldn't believe I was finally on a date with Nick!

'So, where are we going?' I asked as he pulled away from the curb.

He smiled, his eyes twinkling. 'I thought you might like to see the Christmas lights in London?'

I beamed. 'That sounds perfect.'

Nick drove us to High Barnet Underground station and held my hand as we went down to the platform. I kept looking at our hands intertwined like they belonged to someone else. Then we rode to Leicester Square, and emerging from the underground, we were greeted by a sea of dazzling lights.

'Wow… it's so beautiful,' I murmured, my breath visible in the chilly night air. Nick looked at the lights, then at me, the reflections dancing in his eyes.

'I'm glad you like it,' he said softly, squeezing my hand. 'I wanted tonight to be special.'

As the cold air pinched my nose and flushed my cheeks, I could feel something warm and heady unfurling inside me. We strolled shoulder to shoulder, taking in the vibrant decorations and the bustle of the city. Eventually, we found ourselves in Trafalgar Square, where Nelson's Column towered above us, atop huge stone steps, guarded by four enormous lions.

'We have *got* to sit on a lion,' Nick grinned.

I looked up at the massive statues and hesitated. 'I don't think I can get up there!'

Nick chuckled. 'Come on,' he said, hauling himself on top of a lion, before holding out his hand.

'Oh my god!' I squealed, clambering up next to him as he pulled. 'I can't believe we're actually doing this!'

He wrapped his arms around me, warm and solid, and I felt safe and leaned back into him. His lips tenderly brushed my neck, then my cheek, until they found mine. The kiss was soft but certain, and it sent a shiver straight through me.

We stayed there, tangled together on top of the lion watching all of London pass by around us—black cabs, double-decker buses, drunken revellers—under a banner of twinkling lights.

It felt wrong to be so elated while Mum was still crying over Dad at home… and yet, somehow, here I was. For the first time in a long time, life didn't feel broken. It felt like it was just beginning, and it was all thanks to Nick.

***

Two days later, Christmas over and done with, I found myself in High Barnet High Street to meet Nick, Tom, Emma and Dyer in one of the old Tudor pubs. Tucking my coat tighter against the brisk Boxing Day air, I pushed the pub door open and was greeted by the smell of cigarette smoke and stale lager. The pub was covered with gaudy Christmas decorations, yet despite the festive atmosphere, a part of me remained uneasy. I'd promised Emma I would make an effort to get along with Dyer that evening, even though we clearly couldn't stand each other.

Emma spotted me almost instantly, flashing her infectious grin and waving me over with the exuberance only she could muster.

'Hey! Glad you made it, hon,' Emma beamed, nudging me playfully. 'Tom and Nick will be here soon. Figured we'd start without them.'

At the mention of Nick's name, a thrill went down my spine, but I hid it and instead offered a reluctant smile to Dyer, inwardly reminding myself to keep things civil.

'I wouldn't miss this for the world, Em!' I replied, forcing lightness into my voice.

Emma rolled her eyes good-naturedly. 'What're we drinking tonight?' she asked, signalling to the bartender. As I slid into the booth beside her, I noticed Dyer was somewhat more subdued than usual, but unavoidable, nonetheless. As the drinks arrived and conversation flowed, Emma shifted the focus to Dyer, eyebrows raised in mock irritation.

'You've practically moved into Derrick's house lately, always smoking with Nick. Do you ever plan on being around the rest of us?' She asked him pointedly.

Dyer smirked, shrugging off her teasing. 'Derrick's mum doesn't mind us there, babe. Less hassle than finding somewhere else to hang out.'

'Why don't you get your own place, then? You're never around anymore,' Emma pressed, a delicate balance of affection and exasperation weaving through her words.

Listening in to their conversation, I felt like an involuntary fly on the wall and wondered if I should buzz off to the toilet. In response, Dyer leaned back, crossing his arms with a hint of defensiveness.

'Okay, look, you know there's another reason we're round there all the time,' he said, a glint in his eye as he lowered his voice conspiratorially.

'Why is that?' I asked, my curiosity piqued and unable to resist despite my better judgment. Dyer turned to me, an amused look flickering across his face.

'Because Nick has been seeing Tiffany, Derrick's sister,' he giggled. 'For a couple of months now.'

My mouth fell open in shock. *Tiffany. The twelve-year-old girl from Jamie's party!?*

The revelation was like a sickening punch to the gut, disorienting and unwelcome. Tiffany—now thirteen—was a child. The thought of Nick being involved with her was not only heartbreaking but utterly revolting.

Dyer smiled into my frozen face.

I lingered to assess his expression, his posture, his credibility, but I found nothing trustworthy about Dyer whatsoever.

'No way. I don't believe you.' I blurted out, unable to mask my contempt.

Emma shot him a reproachful glance. 'Nick and Tiffany?' she asked, concern and doubt etching her features.

'It's true!' exclaimed Dyer, seemingly revelling in the moment. 'It's shocking, isn't it? A girl that young,' Dyer shook his head reproachfully, watching my face as he did so. His eyes danced as he paused and took a large gulp from his pint glass. 'But Tiffany's mum said that as she was thirteen now, she can make her own decisions.'

'That's disgusting,' Emma recoiled as she spoke, unable to comprehend how Nick could do such a thing. 'Her mum said that?'

Dyer nodded slowly and mimicked our sense of disgust.

My mind flashed back to the feel of Nick's arms around me as we'd sat on top of the lion in Trafalgar Square. I felt nauseous. I shook my head, trying to process what I was hearing.

'That's not true,' I protested angrily. 'Nick wouldn't do that.'

'Honestly, ask Derrick, Tiffany's brother,' insisted Dyer. 'He knows all about it,' he smirked and looked me in the eye as he enjoyed my suffering. 'Yeah. It's weird. Her mum thinks if Tiffany is doing it at home, then at least she's somewhere safe,' he sighed deeply and continued, 'better that than her going off somewhere else. Ya know?'

Emma turned to me and squeezed my hand, her voice breaking the tension as she attempted to pivot the conversation.

'I'm really sorry, hon, I never heard anything about this before,' she muttered, looking at Dyer with a look of scepticism. 'I have no idea if this is true or not.'

'It's not,' I insisted angrily, and Dyer visibly stifled a laugh.

'Look, maybe we should just leave before Tom and Nick get here,' Emma suggested. 'Do you want to head back to mine and invite him over? But better not do it at the pub,' she said softly, almost apologetically. My thoughts were a whirlwind as I nodded vaguely but didn't move.

Emma frowned suddenly and turned to Dyer. 'So, presuming this is true, *Matthew,* if Nick has been seeing a *child,* then what the hell are you still doing hanging out with him?' she asked accusingly.

'And why make all this up now?' I piled on defensively. Dyer shrugged.

'How is it any of my business what Nick does?' he scowled. 'If I can smoke weed at Derrick's and *his* mum's okay with that, then that's where I'm going.'

Emma stood up suddenly from the table.

'Lovely. That's *really* lovely, Matthew. What a standup bloke you *truly* are!' She growled. 'You know, sometimes…' she continued as tears swelled in her eyes, 'sometimes… I don't know why I'm with you anymore.'

Upon hearing Emma's feelings, a jolt of hope roused in me that she might be ready to leave him. Without warning, I stood up too, my chair scraping harshly against the wooden floor. I imagined, in one swift motion, lifting my glass and dousing Dyer with its contents. Then, Dyer would sit there, beer dripping from his hair, a look of bewilderment etched across his features as Emma and I stormed out.

But I controlled myself. As unconvincing as Dyer sounded, I needed to find out the truth from Nick. My heart pounded, and my head whirled as Emma and I grabbed our coats and walked out, leaving Dyer alone in the booth and staring after us.

Together, we walked swiftly back to her house and set up camp in the kitchen. I was about to call Nick when Mrs McCarthy bumbled into the kitchen, ready for bed in her pyjamas. Immediately, I felt nervous, as I knew Mrs McCarthy was still considering the terrible lies that Jennifer had said about me.

Sensing that something was wrong, rather than telling us to go to bed ourselves, Mrs McCarthy insisted on being told what the matter was. After we'd filled her in, she pursed her lips and furrowed her brow in thought for a moment.

'And Nick, this is the boy who Jennifer was seeing, until he had feelings for another girl?' she asked.

Emma and I glanced at each other pointedly.

'Um, yes. That other girl would be me,' I admitted.

Mrs McCarthy frowned and looked at me carefully. 'I see.'

'But I didn't know he had feelings for me,' I quickly blurted out.

'No, it was all completely innocent, mum,' insisted Emma, putting her hands on top of mine reassuringly.

Mrs McCarthy thought for a moment more, then nodded, her expression unreadable.

'First thing Tuesday, I'm calling Social Services,' she said resolutely, referring to the fact that Monday was a bank holiday. 'I'm sorry, girls. But if there's a kiddie at risk, and her own *mother* knows about it and is doing nothing to protect her, it needs to be reported.'

I shifted in my chair. The thought of calling Social Services without asking Nick about his involvement with Tiffany made me feel deeply uncomfortable. I had to speak up.

'Mrs McCarthy, um, I really don't trust Matthew Dyer at all,' I said, shrugging apologetically at Emma, who looked wounded, as though I'd betrayed her. 'We don't even know if it's true. We might get Nick and an innocent family in trouble.'

Mrs McCarthy wore a look of deep concern. 'I don't know if Matthew can be trusted, either, Sarah. That's why he's banned from this house.' She shot her daughter a pointed look, and Emma sat back in her chair exasperatedly. Mrs McCarthy ignored her and continued: 'But this is no laughing matter, girls.'

'But I really think we ought to ask Nick about what's going on first,' I insisted.

Mrs McCarthy patted me on the hand across the table, and I felt wonderfully hopeful that perhaps she might decide she liked me.

'Yes, of course, dear, I wasn't suggesting that you don't ask him,' she reassured me. 'I was just suggesting that we ask Social Services to investigate it, properly, as well.' She shrugged and continued. 'Look, let's be honest. People *lie*,' she said, directing another look at Emma, who so often got caught trying to pull the wool over her mother's eyes. 'And in my experience, if you ask someone about a crime—and let's not forget—that's what this is… more often than not, people don't want to incriminate themselves,' she concluded. '*Especially* teenagers,' she added, looking pointedly at her daughter and resting her case.

'Mum, you're not a detective,' Emma hissed, rolling her eyes.

'Er, yes, thank you, young lady. I never said that I *was*,' Mrs McCarthy silenced her daughter with a sharp look.

'What if it's not true?' I asked, panicking, stuck on how much I distrusted Dyer.

'If you want to try and find out the truth before Tuesday—be my guest. But if you want my advice? Don't ask a teenager to incriminate themselves! You have to find out another way.'

'But we're not detectives either!' interjected Emma.

'Then that's fine!' I looked on, dumbstruck, as Mrs McCarthy turned red. 'Either way, unless you can convince me it's not true by Tuesday—and I'm sorry, girls, Nick denying it simply wouldn't cut it—I'm calling Social Services. Because I'll be damned if a little girl has her life ruined because of actions that I failed to take!' she warned.

Emma and I looked at each other, and my mind raced, trying to think of a way that we could get to the truth before the end of the weekend.

'What about Derrick?' I suggested, directly to Emma.

'Who's Derrick?' interjected Mrs McCarthy.

'He's Tiffany's brother,' Emma explained. 'Dyer said he knew about Nick and Tiffany.'

Mrs McCarthy sat silently for a moment. 'Can you think of a reason he might lie about it?'

Emma and I shrugged.

'None that I can think of,' I said, failing to mention that Derrick was a drug dealer and not a particularly wholesome character. There was no point poking the bear.

Mrs McCarthy frowned. 'Well, if the mum knows, there's no way the brother wouldn't know. If Derrick confirms to you that his sister is seeing Nick, then we can report it. If he doesn't have a clue, then we know that Matthew was probably lying, and you can go ahead and ask Nick yourself.' Mrs McCarthy lay a comforting hand on my arm. 'But Sarah, if Derrick says Nick and Tiffany are involved, you'll have to wait until Social Services have investigated it properly before you confront him.' She placed her mug on the table and sighed. 'Otherwise, you'll be warning him to cover his tracks, which would be highly irresponsible.'

A wave of guilt hit me, and I wondered whether my dad would have covered his tracks if he'd been warned his affair was going to be uncovered.

Probably.

Sadly, I nodded obligingly at Mrs McCarthy. Who was I to put the well-being of Tiffany at risk by running straight to ask Nick what was going on?

Later, as I lay unable to sleep, staring up at Emma's bedroom ceiling in the darkness, an image of Derrick sneering at Emma like a piece of meat came to me, making my heart pound with fear. How were we going to get close to him? We'd never even spoken to the bloke before.

Then my mind strayed back to Nick and the feel of his hand in mine as we'd strolled among the Christmas lights. Unable to hold in my sadness any longer, tears rolled down my cheeks into the blackness.

Please. Don't let it be true.

16

Spies, Flies and Garibaldis

THE NEXT DAY, Tom called me on my mobile, which had been a joint present from my parents for Christmas. Emma and I quickly filled him in on what Matthew Dyer had told us about Nick going out with Tiffany. He was as sceptical as I was, considering the source was Dyer.

'We've got two days to find out whether it's true before Emma's mum calls Social Services,' I warned him, as Emma listened to our conversation from across her bedroom. 'And she says teenagers are unreliable, so if we ask Nick and he denies it, she's going to report it, anyway.' Emma looked down at her feet as I mentioned teenagers being unreliable. 'So, we were thinking of finding out what Derrick knows about Nick and Tiffany,' I continued.

'Wow.' Tom sounded amazed. 'Okay. I suppose that all makes sense. But two days? That's… not much time.'

'Yeah. Tell me about it. Do you know Derrick?' I asked. 'Emma and I have never actually spoken to him. He just seems like a weirdo to me.'

'I don't personally,' deliberated Tom. 'I just saw him that time at Jamie-from-The-Green's party. Why doesn't Emma ask Dyer if you guys can go hang out at their house with him? Isn't that where he usually hangs out these days?'

'We can't go with Dyer, he'll know we're up to something,' I pointed out. 'He only told us about Nick and Tiffany yesterday. It would look more than a little suspicious if suddenly, the next day, we wanted to go with him to Tiffany and Derrick's house.'

Emma piped up loudly from across the room so that Tom could hear her in the background. 'Yeah, and I'm not speaking to him today at all!' she said. 'I don't care how many times he calls!'

'Did you hear that?' I checked.

'Yeah, I heard. That's fair enough,' Tom agreed and fell silent for a few moments. 'Okay, give me five minutes. I've got an idea. I'll call you back!' he blurted out and hung up the phone, leaving me feeling intrigued.

A few minutes later my phone rang again. 'How's this?' said Tom with excitement in his voice. 'What if we organize an impromptu party at Johnnie's tomorrow night? His parents are away, he says he's well up for it. Jamie-from-The-Green can invite Derrick, and you and Emma can find out what he knows.'

It was perfect. As I hung up the phone, Emma came over to join me, and we hugged nervously. A lot was riding on this for both of us. If it turned out Dyer had been lying, Emma decided that it would be the end of their relationship. If it turned out he'd been telling the truth, it would be the end of me and Nick, and Emma would insist that Dyer stay away from him. If he didn't agree, she would end things between them anyway because she didn't want to be with someone who could turn a blind eye to such matters.

I picked up my phone and together we formulated a text to Jamie-from-The Green.

'Hey Jamie,' we wrote. 'Party at Johnnie's tomorrow. Can you come?'

Then we waited nervously for a reply. We didn't have long to wait. Less than five minutes later my phone beeped.

'Count me in! What's the occasion? What should I bring?'

We exchanged a look.

'Bring booze. And Derrick! Emma's friend wants to meet him. She's a real babe ;-D X' I typed. We sniggered as I hit send.

'Why doesn't she want to meet ME??' came the reply from Jamie. 'Did you tell her I'm better looking than him? LOL ;-)' Emma giggled and took hold of the phone.

'Sorry Jamie. She likes bad boys with tattoos! I still love you though!' Emma wrote, but before she could hit send, I snatched the phone back and changed it to 'Emma and I still love you though'. The last thing I needed was Jamie-from-The-Green thinking I had a thing for him. Life was complicated enough!

Within moments my phone beeped again.

'Sod you guys (just kidding)! I want the babe!' said Jamie. 'Tell her I can get a tattoo if she wants…'

Emma cracked up, and the sound was music to my ears. It meant she wasn't irreconcilably upset about Dyer.

'ROFL. See you tomorrow, Jamie. Let us know if Derrick can make it. Party starts at 8. XX'

Emma and I turned to each other. Looked like we had a party to organise! Thankfully, Johnnie was fast becoming the party king…

***

That afternoon, Emma and I went round to Tom's to organise everything. Johnnie joined us after dinner, his phone beeping constantly with messages from people saying they were coming to the party.

After a few hours, Andy got back from work and sat with us in the living room. He had light stubble and was wearing a dark blue fleece jacket over a white t-shirt and blue jeans. Seeing him made me think back to how he'd made me pancakes when my parents were splitting up.

Andy must have felt me looking at him because he glanced over at me, and I realised I must have been staring. Quickly, I darted my gaze away and felt my face getting hot. Too embarrassed to look back, I suggested we put on a film, as the party was pretty much organised by that point. Just as the film was beginning, my phone beeped.

It was a message from Jamie-from-The-Green.

'Derrick says cheers for the invite! And he wants to know who this mystery bird is.' I showed my phone screen to Emma, and we regarded each other solemnly. Then we turned to the room to share our news.

'Hey guys, Derrick's asking who the "bird" is that wants him to come to the party,' I explained, looking at Tom and Johnnie to see if they had any ideas about what to reply.

'Right, but there is no "bird", so you're screwed,' giggled Johnnie while Tom thinned his eyes, deep in thought.

'What's all this?' asked Andy, glancing around the room curiously. We filled Andy in on the events of the previous evening, how Dyer had said Nick was going out with Tiffany and our plan to find out the truth from Tiffany's brother, Derrick, before Mrs McCarthy reported the child's family to Social Services. He sat back in his chair as he listened.

'Are you sure it's a good idea to get Derrick involved in all this?' he asked, finally, scratching his stubbly jaw. 'He's not the greatest bloke in the world.'

'As we see it, we don't have much of a choice,' Tom explained.

Andy turned towards Emma solemnly. 'Emma,' he said calmly and paused. 'Forgive me if this is none of my business. But, if you feel as though you can't trust Dyer, why are you with him?'

My breath stuck in my throat as Andy verbalised the elephant in the room. I turned and waited on bated breath to see how Emma would react.

Emma looked down at her trainers. 'Because I love him,' she said simply, and spoke directly to Andy while the rest of us listened. Tom and I exchanged empathetic glances. 'If Dyer's been lying about Nick going out with Tiffany, that's really out of order,' she said. 'He would, if you think about it, have tried to sabotage Nick's life.'

A tear rolled down Emma's cheek, and I moved next to her on the sofa, pulling her into my arms for a cuddle before she continued. She turned to me and took my hands in hers.

'But if he was telling the truth… how could Sarah go out with him, now?' I nodded in agreement as Andy looked at me with a look of surprise. 'How could Tom and Johnnie be mates with someone like that?' she asked, sounding more and more like her mum as Tom and Johnnie nodded silently. 'They couldn't.' She sat back on the sofa with her arms crossed in front of her, twiddling a strand of blond hair between her fingers. 'So, yeah. If he's lying… I couldn't forgive him for that. It would be over between us,' she said, tears welling up in her eyes again.

As Emma sniffed, I took over the floor from her, speaking directly to Andy, who seemed to have developed a position of authority within the group—at least when he was around.

'It's not just about Nick, or Dyer or me and Emma. Tiffany might be taken into care if it's true,' I said, before trying to bite my thumbnail again, finding nothing there and moving on to the nail of my index finger.

'Especially if Social Services find out that Derrick deals drugs from their house,' pointed out Tom.

'We didn't mention that to Mum,' mumbled Emma, chewing her bottom lip. 'She'd never have let us approach Derrick if she knew he was a dealer. And she'd have asked a million questions about who's been smoking weed. I'd never be let out of the house again.'

I sighed. 'We should probably tell Social Services about it, though,' I said, feeling a stab of guilt. 'Even if we don't tell your mum.'

'Well, we can always do that, even if Nick isn't seeing Tiffany,' pointed out Tom. 'It's not exactly a great place for a kid to be growing up, with people smoking weed everywhere and dodgy people coming and going all the time.' The rest of us nodded, and the room fell silent as we contemplated Tiffany's pitiful childhood.

'For what it's worth,' said Andy, directly to me, 'I don't think Nick has it in him to go out with a kid.' He smiled gently. 'Not when he has a girl like you who wants to go out with him.'

A warmth spread through me, and I blushed gently at the compliment. And then I felt hopelessly confused. On the one hand, Andy's words brought back to life the promise that Nick and I might have a future together, but at the same time, they seemed to underline that there was a connection developing between Andy and me. Or was I imagining it? Because he seemed to be rooting for me and Nick to get together. Or perhaps he was just defending his friend.

'I don't think he could go out with a kid, either,' I smiled, and Andy and I shared a moment that was both warm and sad all at once.

'So, what should we reply to Jamie?' interjected Tom. Silence fell in the room as we all thought. Then, Johnnie slapped his knee mischievously.

'How about: "there is no bird, Tom's got a thing for him"?' he guffawed, and everyone except Tom laughed gratefully as the tension evaporated.

Tom scowled and then smirked. 'How about: "It's Johnnie's mum, his dad's away."'

While it was Johnnie's turn to scowl, the answer came to me in a flash.

'I've got it! Why don't we just say something like "it's a secret, she'd kill us if she knew we'd blabbed" and that he'll just have to come along to find out?' I floated to the group.

Andy nodded. 'Yeah, that works. Keep it short and sweet,' he advised with a knowing smile. 'Say: "He'll just have to come along to find out." Trust me. That'll get him there.'

Nodding, I wrote out our message and pressed send.

Nervously, we waited.

Later, when I was pouring myself a glass of water in the kitchen, Andy followed me in.

'You know, I know it's none of my business, Miss Page,' he said abruptly, his voice full of concern, 'but I really don't think you and Emma should be toying with Derrick the way you are. He's a dangerous guy,' he insisted. 'Believe me. He hangs around at Victoria Wines sometimes with Dyer. I'd steer well clear if I were you.'

Feeling intrigued by the fact that Andy seemed to care about my welfare, I turned to him reassuringly.

'We're going to be really subtle,' I said. 'He won't have a clue why he's been invited. We're just going to find out what Nick gets up to at his house with Tiffany, and that's it. Like conversation ninjas,' I laughed, and Andy smiled reluctantly.

'Okay, Miss Page. Have it your way,' he smiled his knowing smile. 'But don't say I didn't warn you.'

Just then, my phone beeped.

'It's Jamie-from-The-Green!' I exclaimed, running into the living room to open the message in front of everyone. Andy followed casually behind and leaned against the doorframe.

'Be warned,' I read aloud. 'She's gonna take one look at Derrick and choose me over him. We'll see you at 8. Smiley face.' I laughed, and suddenly my stomach was doing flips and in knots.

'Woo! Derrick is coming to the party tomorrow!' Emma declared triumphantly to the room.

'Detective Page and McCarthy are on the case!' joked Tom, and Emma and I looked at each other nervously.

The fact that there was no mystery 'bird' was a problem we'd have to face tomorrow night.

My chest tightened as I glanced up at Andy.

The trap was set.

17
The Honey Trap

THE FOLLOWING EVENING, EMMA AND I met at Tom and Andy's place before the party started. We were waiting for Johnnie to complete his elaborate beauty regimen a few doors down before we could go over, a process that somehow never changed how he looked.

As we sat in silence on opposite sofas in their living room, wearing tight jeans and spaghetti-strap vest tops, my stomach was churning wildly. Emma was as fretful as I was.

Tom and Andy brought us mugs of tea and Garibaldi biscuits—squashed-fly biscuits as Dad used to call them—to calm our nerves while we waited.

'Thanks, Andy,' I smiled, blowing on the hot tea.

'Miss Page,' he nodded, sitting beside me.

'You know, you don't have to go through with this if you don't want to,' Andy said. 'You're both looking incredibly nervous. He might figure that something is off if you start asking questions, looking like this.'

'There's a lot riding on this,' I replied, thinking about Nick and Tiffany and her family.

'For everyone,' Emma added.

Right on cue, the phone rang. It was Johnnie telling us we could go over. Andy pulled on his fleece jacket and his baseball cap (backwards) and came with us. I was glad he was coming.

'People! People!' announced Johnnie as he threw open his front door to greet us. 'Let's get this show on the road!' Johnnie rubbed his hands together joyously. Any excuse was a good excuse for a party when it came to Johnnie. He quickly ushered us into the living room, where Craig David's dulcet tones were pumping from the stereo. 'Now, everyone, please be careful of the cabinet tonight,' he warned, gesturing to his parents' display cabinet full of glass. 'The crystal in there is worth many thousands of pounds.'

Emma and I exchanged a look. Every time Johnnie had a party, the value of his parents' crystal increased.

Before long, all the sofas and seats around the lounge and dining area were full, with people crowded into the hallway and kitchen, while others were standing out in the freezing garden smoking cigarettes.

At about half past ten, Jamie-from-The-Green and Derrick arrived. I watched from a corner with Emma as Derrick pushed into the living room like a pitbull, surveying the crowd with a cold, calculating gaze. His hair had been shorn close to his scalp, and the deep scar on his cheek looked darker than ever. My heart hammered. We had to talk to him. And I was terrified.

Johnnie ran over to greet Jamie, who smiled hazily, his eyes red from smoking weed with Derrick.

'Mate! So glad you could make it!' said Johnnie, clapping him on the back. 'Sorry for such short notice... you know me, any excuse for a knees-up!'

'Cheers for the invite mate,' Jamie grinned. 'You remember Derrick don't cha?'

Johnnie shook Derrick's hand and assumed a more Cockney accent. 'Yeah, Course I do. Alright, mate?'

'Alright,' nodded Derrick, holding up a twelve-pack of Stella—or *Wife Beater* as it was affectionately known. 'Where can I shove this lot?'

'Just through there, mate,' Johnnie pointed towards the kitchen as Jamie held his own twelve-pack of Stella aloft. 'Ayyyy! That's the spirit!' Johnnie roared, then merged back into the party.

As Derrick and Jamie headed for the kitchen, I nudged Emma. 'Now. Let's get a drink.'

We hastily followed them, my heart pounding as we entered the kitchen. Jamie looked up and grinned, while Derrick stood just behind him, silent and watchful.

'Awright, girls?' asked Jamie affably, kissing us on the cheek.

'Hiya, Jamie,' Emma and I said in unison.

Derrick stood back and slowly looked me up and down before turning to Emma. 'Awright Ems?' he said, finally. 'So, is this the bird who wants to meet me, then?' he looked back at me and leered down at my chest.

Emma and I exchanged a quick glance before I stepped forward. 'She couldn't make it,' I said, keeping my voice light. 'I'm Sarah, Emma's friend.'

Jamie and Derrick both burst out laughing, Derrick's wheezy laugh breaking into a dry smoker's cough.

'I know who you are, Sarah,' Derrick said, shaking his head. 'So… this *other* bird who couldn't make it, then,' he smirked dubiously, 'what's her name?'

'That would be telling,' Emma giggled nervously. 'But really, she got food poisoning.'

Jamie and Derrick exchanged a look and made a theatrical display of laughter, making it obvious they didn't believe us. Then Derrick stepped towards me, his eyes narrowing slightly.

'I reckon it's you, Sarah,' he said, his smile as impure as a blowjob in church.

Agh! He thinks I fancy him, I panicked.

Sensing that we were dumbfounded, Derrick seemed to take it as confirmation of his suspicions and looked uncharacteristically bashful for a moment.

'No need for all the cloak and dagger stuff, Sarah. You just had to ask, you know,' he winked, and looked at me nervously. Flattered. Hopeful, even. For a moment, I found myself wondering where his life had gone so horribly wrong.

But then I paused and collected myself.

Maybe Derrick thinking I fancy him could be quite useful, I considered. After all, I needed him to trust me if I was going to get the truth out of him.

I flicked my hair from my shoulder in a faux show of comfort and forced out a small, uncertain laugh. 'I wouldn't like to say,' I deflected and reached for an open wine bottle. 'Drink?' I asked politely.

'Nah, wine's for birds,' said Derrick, relaxing a little and moving closer to me. 'I'll stick wiv me Stella,' he said, lifting his can and finishing it. 'You drink up, though, Sarah. Very classy,' he winked. 'I like a classy bird.'

Yuck.

Every instinct in my body was begging me to recoil, but I held my ground, leaning against the kitchen counter and holding my glass of wine up like a shield.

'So… how do you know Jamie?' I asked, directing us back to safer ground.

'School,' he said. Then abruptly: 'You had a thing with him or somethin'?'

'No,' I answered quickly, surprised at how much like a caveman he seemed. 'Jamie and I are just friends.'

Derrick scoffed. 'Men and women can't be friends,' he declared with conviction.

'That's not true,' I retorted. 'I've got plenty of mates who are boys. Nothing's ever happened between us.'

He smiled. 'That's because you're still innocent.'

The way he said it made my skin crawl.

I took a breath.

'Well, the only friend I ever fancied was *Nick,*' I shrugged. 'But I hear he's got a girlfriend.'

Derrick studied me. 'Yeah,' he said, smirking. 'My sister. Tiffany.'

The room tilted.

'Oh,' I said lightly, though my chest had gone tight and I felt like I was going to be sick. 'Really?'

'They've been seeing each other about a month,' he said matter-of-factly and then he stepped closer. Too close. 'And I'm very protective of my sister… So, probably best you've moved on to a real man, hey?' he winked and reached out to stroke my arm.

At his touch, my flesh crawled, and I struggled to mask my disgust. For some reason, my face instinctively plastered on an enormous, uncomfortable smile. My mind scanned for a reply that would get me away from him without arousing his suspicion, or worse, his wrath.

But before I could come up with something, a calm voice cut in.

'Hey, everything alright?'

It was Andy. He was standing in the doorway watching us, and the air shifted instantly.

'Yeah,' Derrick said, withdrawing his hand, his smile fading as though he resented the intrusion. 'Just chatting with little Sarah here.'

Andy glanced at me and nodded. 'Johnnie wants everyone in the living room,' he said, motioning for us to follow him. 'Something about a drinking game.'

Without hesitating, I leapt forward and clapped delightedly as though drinking games were my favourite thing in the world, and without saying another word, I darted out of the kitchen and followed Andy back to the lounge, staying as close to him as possible.

When I dared to glance back, Derrick was watching me, his smile evaporated, his eyes cold and calculating.

In the lounge, Johnnie clapped his hands. 'Alright, everyone in a circle,' he commanded, seeing that we were back, and we joined a grand loop of people sitting around the living room rug. With Andy on one side of me, Emma strategically positioned herself on the other side of me, so that Derrick was forced to sit several places away from us. Still, I could feel his eyes on me, scowling like he was annoyed that I'd gotten away from him.

Johnnie jumped into the centre of the circle. 'Now, has anyone *not* played *Fuzzy Duck* before?' he asked, and a girl from The Green put her hand up. There was a collective, teasing groan from the party, and the girl shrieked with laughter and covered her face in mock shame. 'Typical! There's always one!' needled Johnnie, before theatrically explaining the rules.

Andy leaned in. 'I hope I didn't come in too soon,' he whispered. 'I just overheard him say he was "very protective of his sister". Thought you might want an exit.'

I nodded. 'Thank you,' I whispered, feeling shaky but trying not to show any emotion in case Derrick was still watching. 'That was *perfect* timing!'

Emma leaned in from the other side. 'What did you find out?' She whispered.

I swallowed, my head swimming, a part of me not believing what I was about to say.

'Dyer was telling the truth.'

18
The Want

TEARS THREATENED TO WELL UP IN MY EYES, but I managed to fight them down.

'Nick is going out with Tiffany,' I confirmed, scarcely able to believe it myself.

Andy and Emma placed their hands on my back, their touch warm and reassuring.

'I'm so sorry, Sarah,' said Emma softly.

'Me too,' consoled Andy.

'Thanks, guys,' I sniffed, feeling betrayed and disgusted by how Nick could go out with someone so young, all the while stringing me along as though I were the only one.

'Heads up, Emma,' Andy nodded, as *Fuzzy Duck* approached her around the circle. I glanced across the room and noticed Derrick was now watching the three of us with a keen interest.

'Fuzzy Duck!' said a lad from The Green, sitting next to Emma.

'Does he?' asked Emma, looking at me. Confused, I was just about to answer, but the lad on the other side of her was too quick.

'Ducky Fuzz!' he exclaimed, and the game returned in the direction it had come from.

Andy leaned in. 'You know, I think you're going to have to come up with an excuse to leave early,' he said. 'Because it doesn't look like *lover boy* is giving up on you too easily,' he subtly gestured over at Derrick.

'You don't think it'll look weird?' I asked, feeling relieved at the prospect of getting out of there.

'Not at all. Time to put your acting classes to good use!' he laughed. 'And anyway, why stay? So, Derrick can hit on you again?' he shrugged. 'Best get out while the going's good if you ask me.'

I nodded straight away. 'I was going to stay at Emma's, but I could always make an excuse and catch the last bus back,' I said, looking at my watch. 'I can just about make it if I go now.'

Without hesitation, Andy jumped up from the circle, grabbed his fleece jacket, pulled on his baseball cap backwards and ran to the front door, holding it open and beckoning me to go with him. 'Let's go, Miss Page, you're going to miss the last bus!'

I made an exhibition of checking my watch, jumped up from the circle and announced to the party that I had to leave. 'My mum will kill me if I'm late!' I claimed, my face going red. 'Thanks for an amazing party, Johnnie!' I hopped forward and hugged Johnnie goodbye. 'Thanks so much for coming, Jamie. Derrick,' I waved at them across the busy living room. Derrick lifted a hand in a lazy wave, his eyes never leaving me. 'Bye, everyone! See you soon, Em!' I gushed, bending down and hugging Emma tightly.

'Bye, hon!' Emma played along. 'Get home safe!'

Then I rushed out after Andy into the cold night air. Andy was already halfway down the street as I emerged from the driveway.

'You've got to move those feet, Miss Page. Hop to it. Come on!' Then he took off at pace down the road, and I was left trailing after him. There was no way I could run the whole distance, and I was quickly out of breath trying.

We made it to the top of the hill and looked down at New Barnet Train Station, with the bus standing outside, its lights on, engine revving, getting ready to leave.

'Wait!' I ran past Andy and down the hill, waving madly at the driver not to go. The bus driver ignored me, pulled out slowly and the bus roared off ahead, leaving me standing in a cloud of exhaust. I turned around and trudged slowly back up the hill to Andy, silhouetted against the night sky.

'Crap,' I exclaimed, unsure of what to do next. 'I suppose I'd better call my dad,' I mumbled, pulling out my phone.

Dad told me to wait for him at Tom and Andy's house, and he'd be around to get me in half an hour.

'Sorry,' I apologised to Andy for his troubles. 'I bet you wish you hadn't walked me to the bus stop now!' I looked at him and grimaced, expecting him to agree, but he didn't.

'Not at all, don't worry. You know, you can always call me if you get stuck,' he said as we walked back up the hill.

'What do you mean?' I asked. 'I don't have your number.'

'You know the landline number, and here, give me your mobile…' He took my phone and entered his new mobile number into it. 'You shouldn't be walking in the dark alone,' he said. 'If you ever need anyone to walk with you or you get stuck, just call. You can stay at ours. You can have my bed; I'll sleep on the couch.'

I was so touched I felt myself beaming in the glow of the street lamps. 'Wow. Are you sure? I don't want to put you out.'

'You're a pain in my arse, Miss Page,' he thinned his eyes as he looked at me, and I felt so happy, suddenly, I could skip. In fact, I did skip for a few steps and then swung myself around a lamppost.

Andy laughed. 'Crazy girl!'

Then, without saying anything, he took off his backwards baseball cap and placed it forwards on my head, giving it a hard tug so that it almost covered my eyes. For a few minutes, the ache in my chest went quiet and we walked the rest of the way back to his house in silence. When I looked over at him, he was looking at me with his mysterious knowing smile.

Walking into the living room at Andy's house, we found Emma and Tom there unexpectedly. Emma explained that she'd left the party so she could call Dyer, and Tom had been so disappointed when he'd heard that his best friend was indeed going out with a kid, that he'd come home early to go to bed.

Nick came crashing back into my mind. The thought of him with Tiffany made my stomach twist. Whatever I felt for Andy, none of it made the hurt go away. Gutted that my future with him was over before it had begun, I wondered what was going to happen to the group now.

Tom assured Emma and me that the boys wouldn't be hanging around with Nick anymore, although when we pressed him about how he was going to handle things, he didn't know. Never one for confrontation, Tom planned to 'freeze him out'—not answer his calls, not be in when he came knocking, and generally avoid him until he stopped trying and got the message. I felt terrible. But perhaps it was for the best. I hadn't decided what I was going to do yet. I didn't even want to think about it.

As Tom and Andy chatted about how to handle freezing Nick out of the group, Emma gave me a charged look—glancing up at Andy's hat poignantly. With just my eyes, I confirmed that he had given me the hat and that I needed to talk with her urgently, but before we could break away to speak in private, her phone rang. It was Dyer calling her back.

While I sat and waited for my dad, Emma was on the phone to Dyer, insisting that he stop hanging around with Nick. He agreed—reluctantly—although he refused to stop going to smoke weed around at Derrick's house, saying that he 'drew the line' at a woman telling him whom he could and couldn't buy weed from. Instead, he assured her that whenever Nick was there, he would simply avoid talking to him.

Emma didn't tell Dyer about our plan to report Tiffany's family to Social Services. When she hung up the phone, I asked her why she hadn't mentioned it, but she just shrugged and wouldn't answer. Thinking about how much of a loose cannon Dyer was, it was probably the right decision not to tell him. I paused, wanting to say something about how much better she deserved, but afraid to. We'd fallen out the last time I'd tried to speak to her about him. But that evening I'd been struck by a wave of admiration for Andy. If he had managed to speak up and ask Emma why she was with Dyer, why hadn't I? I resolved that I would be braver—more like Andy.

'Em, are you sure you still want to be with Matthew?' I asked decisively, and Emma shot me a pained look.

'We love each other, Sarah. I know he's not perfect, but nobody is,' she lamented. 'Relationships are hard. You wouldn't really know.'

I nodded slowly, considering her words, but I wasn't giving up without a fight. 'I just think you deserve so much better,' I took Emma's hand and stroked it with my thumb.

'I know you do,' she smiled appreciatively and gave me a hug that felt like home. 'I know.'

A short while later, Dad rang the doorbell, eager to get back in my good books after his affair, and Andy came with me to open the front door. As he was about to open it, I took off his baseball cap and offered it back to him.

'Keep it,' he said, touching my hand and fixing me with an enigmatic look that sent my mind and heart racing. Then he opened the door.

'Hi. I'm Sarah's dad,' my dad introduced himself to Andy chirpily.

'Andy. Nice to meet you,' nodded Andy respectfully, shaking my dad's hand. Despite not getting along with my dad at that moment, there was something sweet about the meeting that pleased me deeply.

'Thanks for looking out for her,' added Dad, visibly warming to Andy.

'It's always a pleasure. And no trouble at all.' Andy smiled.

'Well, I'd best get this one home,' chuckled Dad, putting his arm around me patronisingly, and Andy nodded at my dad, but didn't look at me.

'Nice to meet you, Mr Page. Take care, Sarah,' Andy waved us off and closed the door.

What the hell was that!? Did I just get 'handled'?

On the drive home, my mind and body returned morosely to Nick. So, it was over between us. Before it had even begun. Tears welled up in my eyes, but rather than let my dad see them, I stared out of the window and tugged Andy's cap down lower to hide my face.

Ugh. Andy. I felt more confounded about his feelings for me than ever. Did Andy just see me as a little sister he needed to protect rather than a woman he actually wanted?

19
Revenge

January 1999

IN 1999, A WHOLE NEW WORLD of mobile phones was opening up—novelty ringtones, creative voicemails, random pocket dials. People my age used pay-as-you-go top-up vouchers, so running out of credit was constant, and running out at night, when the shops were shut, was like a form of teenage torture.

In our group, prank calls were an art form. Johnnie did voices, Dyer used his network of friends to prank each other, and Andy was a genius for elaborate set-ups, like dialling two unwitting participants into a conference call and listening on mute to the ensuing chaos. I hoped that Andy's sudden enthusiasm for pranking was a juvenile play for my attention and a sign that he wanted more. But Andy remained as inscrutable as ever, and although I still felt myself getting flushed and hopeful whenever he was around, I was getting increasingly frustrated. I wondered continuously when 'true love' would come my way.

Unbeknownst to me, Dyer was already on the case on my behalf. He sold the idea to Emma as setting me up with a boyfriend, and to his friends—whether they were single or not—I later found out he sold the concept as seducing a 'good girl' and turning her 'bad'.

One weekend about halfway through January, after a particularly unconvincing prank call, Dyer came on the line for a chat.

'Yo, Page! Gotcha… Did we get you?' he drawled, and I could hear that strange smile of his oozing down the phone line.

'Hi, Dyer. No, I didn't believe that I had won twenty thousand pounds and was on the radio,' I said flatly.

'Yeah, yeah. You believed it,' he giggled with his bizarre little laugh. 'Anyway, how's it going? Guess who I've just been hanging out with.'

My stomach tightened with anxiety, which I always seemed to feel when talking to Dyer. I already knew.

'Who?' I asked.

'Guess.'

'Just tell me.'

'Nick.'

Dyer paused for dramatic effect.

'I thought you weren't hanging out with him anymore.' I said carefully. I had become much better at not taking 'the bait' from Dyer.

'I just thought you might like to know what he was saying,' Dyer teased, ignoring my hook.

'No, not really.'

'Don't pretend, Page,' he insisted, 'don't worry, it wasn't about you.' I felt the grin on the end of the line as he knew he had me. We could both feel it: a palpable silence hanging in the air.

I clenched my jaw.

'Okay. What's he been saying?' I conceded.

'He just left, actually. He's heading to Tiffany's for some luuuurve,' he said, dragging it out.

'Great. Super. What did he say?' I felt myself getting annoyed.

'I thought you didn't care,' said Dyer provocatively.

'I don't! Look, Matthew, if you're done, I have things to be getting on with.' I finally lost my cool, and Dyer got his payoff.

'Ha! Calm down, Trouble, calm down,' Dyer drank in his win at having successfully gotten under my skin, pausing again for dramatic effect. 'He said something about having one girl for sex, another to buy his weed, and another to sit on his face. That's what women are good for.' Dyer giggled and waited for my reaction.

'What!? Did he actually say that?' I exclaimed, shocked. I had been expecting some form of regret about going out with an underaged girl, not something revolting and degrading like that.

'Yep. The guy is a sicko.' Dyer stuck the knife in deep and twisted. In the background, I heard Derrick laugh—a low, wheezy sound—before it tipped into a smoker's cough.

I shook my head in disbelief. 'He really, really is,' I agreed, fuming.

'Well, I just thought you should know, Page. By the way… a mate of mine wants to meet up with you, if you're interested. You know Derrick, right?'

The mention of Derrick threw me. Why was Dyer trying to set me up with him?

'Not interested, Dyer. But thanks for telling me about Nick,' I said politely, hanging up and deciding there and then that Nick was a sick, misogynistic paedophile. I really wanted to lay into him. But we were still waiting for Social Services to investigate Nick and Tiffany, and I'd made a promise to Emma's mum that I'd wait.

Impatiently, I grabbed the Yellow Pages, and twenty minutes later, I was told by a tired-sounding social worker that the outcome of Tiffany's case was still pending. Which meant, as he explained, they hadn't had the time or resources to investigate it yet.

Frustrated, I thanked the man, and my thoughts turned back to Nick. If social services weren't going to do anything, perhaps he deserved a little DIY karma coming his way.

***

Two hours later, I chuckled to myself as I sat at the family computer, putting the finishing touches to my malevolent marketing campaign. The printer whirred into action, and soon, a stack of fake pizza flyers with irresistible late-night deals and Nick's number at the bottom. This was going to be the prank call scheme of the century. And for such a deserving recipient!

Thrilled by how righteous it all felt, I waited for the chance to put my scheme into action. Then, after drama rehearsals the following Tuesday night, I put up the posters and handed out fliers outside a busy college. Afterwards, I stalked off to McDonald's to enjoy a celebratory Big Mac. But sitting in the booth, rather than feeling happy, I imagined Nick and wondered what he was doing. I had a strange feeling in the pit of my stomach that fate would throw us together somehow. Stirrings of guilt gripped me, but my anger overrode them. Nick was disgusting, and he deserved no sympathy from me.

Grabbing my bag, I headed for the automated doors, and as they parted, across the street and framed dead-centre in the doorway were Nick and Derrick. My eyes locked with Nick's, and before I could react, he was waving at me.

'Sarah!' he shouted and smiled, a picture of enthusiasm. But deep in the pit of my stomach, I felt nauseated. It was Nick that I was punishing. I turned and stormed away, and when I glanced back, he was staring after me sadly with Derrick smirking behind him.

Later that night, heart pounding, I picked up the phone, dialled 141 to withhold my number and sat, itching to call for a pizza. But I feared it was too early. If I were the first and he recognised my voice, he would know the whole prank was my idea. A little after midnight, I called, and a reproachful Nick answered.

'Hello?' he asked, uncertainty filling his voice.

''Ello mate,' I said, doing my best London accent to throw him off my scent. 'Can I get a twelve-inch pepperoni to Potters Bar, please?'

‘Sorry, wrong number, this is not the number for pizza,’ he replied, clearly frustrated, a sign that I was not the first caller for pizza that evening.

I stifled a laugh. ‘Oh right, but I gotta leaflet 'ere says it's two-fa-one,’ I bemoaned.

‘Yeah, must be a typo,’ he said, anxious to get off the line.

‘Awright, cheers, mate,’ I hung up and laughed myself to bed, happy that I’d pulled off my prank. This was going to be *fun*.

When the weekend rolled around, I could barely keep the secret any longer. Emma drove us to Brent Cross for a shopping trip, and as we were mulling through the racks of clothes in TK Maxx, I buckled.

‘I have something to tell you,’ I whispered playfully from across a rack of jeans, ‘but you have to promise you won’t tell Dyer,’ I raised my eyebrows, and she was immediately hooked, as I knew she would be.

‘What is it?’ she laughed.

‘No—you *really* have to promise not to tell Dyer. It's about Nick. He can never know!’ I insisted, adding to her intrigue.

‘I promise! What is it?’ she demanded, eyes wide.

I smiled, savouring the moment, before blurting out: ‘I made pizza leaflets with Nick's phone number on them.’ I let the news hang in the air between us and felt relieved to have finally told her.

‘That was you!?’ Emma screeched, momentarily speechless before continuing. ‘Matthew said Nick kept getting calls for pizza—all after eleven at night!’

I practically fell on the floor laughing, thrilled that my plot was working so well. Emma joined me.

‘Everyone keeps asking for a two-for-one deal with a free two-litre bottle of Coke!’ she guffawed, and together we laughed our way to the till.

Curiosity pricked at my glee. ‘By the way… why is Dyer still hanging out with him?’ I asked, wondering why he hadn’t turned his back on him like the rest of the guys.

'Ugh. Believe me, that drives me crazy,' Emma said, worry creeping into her voice. 'But, he doesn't really have much choice. Derrick is his weed dealer. He only goes there to smoke because Derrick's mum doesn't mind, and Nick just happens to be there smoking weed and seeing Tiffany.'

I frowned, unconvinced. 'Why are Social Services taking so long to investigate?' I asked angrily. 'We filed our report weeks ago!'

Emma shrugged. 'Mum called them to check again last week.'

Frustrated, I tutted. 'Yeah. So did I.'

Emma put her hand on my arm comfortingly. 'Well then. I suppose it falls on us to get a small amount of justice until they can be bothered to do something!'

'What do you have in mind?' I asked, grinning.

'Let's go and tell the boys about your pizza leaflet,' winked Emma, swinging her shopping bags with a skip in her step. 'We can all call Nick and order some pizza from Tom's place and listen in,' she put her arm around me as we walked.

'Em, you always know exactly what to say,' I laughed, and we headed off to Tom's for an evening of prank calls.

20

Imperfect Love

November 1999

ELEVEN MONTHS FLEW BY IN WHAT SEEMED LIKE the blink of an eye, and before I knew it, I'd turned eighteen. It was my final year of sixth form, and *everything* had changed. Nick—having been frozen out of the group—had a new mobile number, effectively ending the pizza prank; Andy was being more sociable; and I'd finally had my braces out (months later than expected). But best of all, at long last, Cupid had flown my way, and I was two weeks into my first relationship with the lovely *James*.

He was tall, with dark, thickly brill-creamed curtains and eyes that always seemed to be brooding. He was so handsome I could barely stand it, and we were completely smitten with each other. Only Emma had met him as she'd introduced us through a friend of hers, and he went to school in a neighbouring town.

James held my hand as though it mattered, as though it was something precious he might drop if he wasn't careful. He walked me to bus stops, waited with me even when it was freezing, and listened with complete seriousness to everything I said, no matter how small. When he smiled at me, slowly, as if he'd been thinking about it for a while, I felt chosen in a way I never had before. Being with him made the world feel softer and more deliberate, as though everything had finally settled into the right order.

But just as one area of my life was pulling itself together, another inevitably fell apart. One day, when I got home from school, Mum was waiting for me in the kitchen—an ominous sign indeed.

'Sarah, can you come in here a minute, please?' she asked, her tone serious.

'Sure, everything alright?' I asked, feeling on edge. It seemed that any little talk with my parents brought enormous, life-changing news.

'Yes, everything's fine,' Mum said coolly, gesturing for me to sit down at the kitchen table. 'Did you have a good day at school?'

'Yes, it was alright. Kate gave me a lift back; she passed her driving test already,' I remarked, feeling annoyed at myself for having failed my own test recently.

'I have something to talk to you about,' said Mum, taking no interest in my friends, as usual. 'Your dad is going to move back in,' she said with finality.

A moment passed while the information sank in. Telling Mum about my party and how Dad had pulled into the driveway with 'that' woman in his car was one of the most difficult things I'd ever done, but I had never regretted it. She had the right to know the truth and to draw her own conclusions.

My mum continued: 'I spoke to him about what he was doing that night you saw him in the driveway, and he said he was taking Amanda home when he saw you outside in the dark and decided to check that you were okay,' she looked me square in the eye as she spoke. 'And I believe him.'

My heart broke for my mum because I knew it wasn't true.

'I know your father. I know when he's lying. And he wasn't lying,' she assured me.

I know when he's lying more than you do, I thought to myself, furious at my dad, but saying nothing. He had been bringing the woman back so that they could have sex in Mum's bed while she was away on holiday with Bethany.

Reluctantly, I nodded, although I found it impossible to speak except to mumble the word 'okay,' until finally the conversation was over, and I escaped to the sanctuary of my room.

The following week, Dad moved back in.

'Hi, Sarah,' he said, standing teary-eyed in the hallway, holding a suitcase, peering at me through the living room door. I turned away from the blaring television to look at him, and my heart raced. My words stuck in my throat, and a silence stretched between us.

All I could think about was the day he'd left when my bedroom window had been ajar. Mum had clung to him and begged him to stay, and I'd watched him push her away, call her fat and old, and drive off without even looking back, leaving her sobbing in the driveway. After years of her loyal devotion, it was a cruelty I could never forgive him for.

'I'm back,' my dad said softly, with huge, soulful eyes, as though waiting for a hug or a warm welcome.

What do you want, a medal? I thought harshly.

I mustered a nod and a half smile, but no words could be compelled from my lips. Mum glared at me from behind him as though I were the most heartless animal on Earth—a real nasty piece of work—and then Dad withdrew, and they went upstairs together. Not long after, I could hear the familiar rhythmic creaking of the ceiling as Mum welcomed him back home.

Listening for a moment, my stomach curdled, and I jumped up, threw my coat on and headed out the door to the sanctuary of Tom's or Emma's.

As I was leaving, I promised myself that I would never let a man treat me like that and get away with it.

***

Inevitably, my vow of silence against my dad didn't last long. Mum found it too much of a strain on their marital reboot, and a couple of weeks after he'd moved back in, she was waiting for me in the kitchen again after school.

'Sarah, can you come here, please?' she asked ominously.

I went in, sat opposite her at the kitchen table, and said nothing, a curtain of iron dropping over my face to stop any emotion leaking out.

'If you don't start speaking to your father again, you're going to have to move out,' Mum said flatly. 'Perhaps you could get a job and move in with one of your *many* little *friends*.'

I was shocked. At seventeen, moving out would have meant leaving school and watching my future collapse before it had even begun. It wasn't even an option. I blinked a few times, trying to steady myself, but Mum ploughed on.

'I've told you he was telling the truth, and he's not seeing that girl anymore,' she insisted, her voice hardening into the tone she used when she was on a roll. 'Right? So that's the end of it. If you don't like it, you can lump it.'

She went on and on, about my attitude, my ingratitude, my arrogance, until it was clear this wasn't a conversation but a verdict. Eventually, she asked what my decision would be.

I mumbled that I'd start talking to Dad again.

I looked at her, expecting triumph—a smirk, a flicker of satisfaction. Instead, her eyes twitched, and her lips flattened. What I saw there wasn't victory, but disappointment.

She doesn't want me to stay.

I learned then that peace and justice weren't always the same thing.

Wary of my mum's intentions, I stayed living at home and going to school, but I took a part-time job in a Chinese buffet restaurant which meant I was out of the house more—and, for the first time, had money of my own.

By my eighteenth birthday in October, my relationship with Dad was steadier again, and he had regained my civility—if not my forgiveness—simply by being himself. We laughed. We argued about music. He drove me to work when it rained. It was confusing. None of it erased what I knew about him, and somehow none of it cancelled out the rest either.

That confusion came to a head one day after a throwaway comment as I was leaving for work. Grabbing my coat and running downstairs, I saw him standing in the hallway.

'See you later, Dad. I'm off to work.'

'Okay, be good!' he called after me.

His innocent remark sent me back to the same question I couldn't seem to put down: whether my dad was one of the good guys or the bad. To his kids, his parents, his friends, he was wonderful. Adoring and generous. He was the first to come running when we fell. But his old words to me—that cheating is what men do—rang louder now that my parents were back together, and I wondered whether James was one of the cheaters, too. I decided, perhaps too quickly, that he wasn't.

Mum, meanwhile, was struggling to let go of what had happened, and she may as well have taken up residency at the local gym. Any excess weight dropped from her like water, and she had the glow of a woman on a mission. But over time it was as though she came steaming through a healthy weight range, missed the station, and kept going until there was almost nothing left of her.

21
The Hoodie

December 1999

A COUPLE OF MONTHS LATER, in December 1999, came a night when I had double-booked myself. I was spending half the night at Tom and Andy's, where a group of us were playing *Spin the Bottle Truth or Dare* (which was essentially *Spin the Bottle*, but with *Truth or Dare* instead of kissing). Then, when the gang planned to go clubbing in central London, I was heading down the road to Whetstone, for a cast reunion of Liam's most recent theatre production.

My boyfriend, James had been invited to both parties, because all my friends were still dying to meet him, but he had decided to stay at home and watch MTV instead.

I wondered how much *less* of an effort he could possibly make. Gone were the days of him hanging on my every word and waiting with me at bus stops. I was lucky if I saw him once a week, and usually at *his* house or meeting *his* friends.

A few minutes into the game, Dyer revved up outside on a new motorbike, and Emma dragged us into the street to admire his new wheels. Eventually, windswept and exhilarated from trying it out, we tumbled back inside to resume our game.

The game felt pretty wild at the time, even though the usual kinds of questions came up: 'How many people have you kissed?' was one of the questions I asked.

'Well over a hundred,' Johnnie claimed, making Emma groan and roll her eyes.

'Would you rather be stuck on a desert island with Johnnie, or lose your phone for a year?' Tom asked.

'Lose my phone,' Emma said instantly.

'Rude,' Johnnie protested, as the rest of us laughed.

'Have you had sex, and how many people have you done it with?' Dyer asked the room, giggling creepily and adding to my conviction that he was a weirdo.

'Loads,' Johnnie boasted to a chorus of sceptical groans. 'Well into double digits by now.'

'Four,' threw out Andy.

'None,' Tom added quietly.

'None,' I said too, meeting Andy's unreadable gaze.

Dyer laughed. 'Ha! Still!? What's wrong with you, *Trouble*? No wonder you're so uptight!'

'Matthew!' Emma snapped, as my face went red with embarrassment.

Andy stirred and shot Dyer a meaningful look. 'Yeah, not cool, mate.'

Dyer apologised but kept grinning. 'Sorry, Page,' he giggled. 'I was just kidding. You're sooo *sweet*.'

The game moved on, although my annoyance at Dyer went nowhere, and I decided it was time to make a move to the cast reunion a little earlier than planned. Emma—who had borrowed the family car to play club-night chauffeur for the evening—kindly drove me to the pub.

'Say hi to everyone for me,' she said, looking a little sad, and I wondered if she regretted having left the theatre group to spend more time with Dyer.

'I will. Love you,' I replied. I blew her a kiss and ran towards the pub, eager to get out of the cold.

That night, caught up in the buzz of the reunion, I stayed longer than I intended, and by the time I stepped outside, it was gone midnight. That was when reality set in. Here I was with no money for a cab, and there were no buses running from that part of town at that hour.

How could I be so stupid?

I stood, feeling tipsy, weighing my options to get home.

James was at his, far away in a neighbouring town. The gang had gone clubbing in London, Dad was away 'on business', and Mum had been increasingly hostile lately—not someone I felt able to call. For the first time, I realised how few people there really were to rely on.

At a loss, I turned to walk down the High Street while I thought. But as I passed the closed pub on my right, the shadowy figure of a man moved in the abandoned car park. I kept walking without slowing down, and one past glanced back and saw him approaching the exit behind me. Which way was he going to turn?

I picked up my pace, walking with determination, and when I turned around again, he was following along behind me. He had his hood up, and although I couldn't see his eyes, I could feel them on me. My pulse quickened as goose bumps ran up my arms.

The voices of the Crimewatch presenters echoed in my mind, an amalgamation of past episodes and my imagination: *'She missed her bus… and was never seen alive again', 'a man in a hoodie was seen following her… and she was found dead in the bushes the next morning'*, and then the catchphrase of the show—*'don't have nightmares!'*—as if to mock any woman watching.

Petrified, I considered calling Mum again, but she was at least twenty minutes' drive away. I thought quickly. I knew this area of town well, and if I kept walking straight, in about five minutes, I'd pass through a quiet, wooded area, which I really *didn't* want to do.

Just then, I passed the closed shopfront of Victoria Wines and remembered Andy and what he'd said about being there for me if I was ever stuck. He hadn't gone into London with the others; he was probably still at home. Pulling the aerial out from my phone, I quickly dialled him, and he picked up with his usual air of mystique.

'Miss Page. To what do I owe the pleasure at this late hour?'

Curiosity filled his low, smooth voice.

'Hi, Andy. I'm sorry to call. I just passed Victoria Wines, and I'm not sure how to get home.'

'Are you okay? Is there anyone there with you?'

'Um, I don't know. I think a guy might be following me, though.'

'Walk towards mine, and I'll come get you,' Andy's voice was calm and reassuring, and I felt glad that I'd called. His house was in the direction that I was walking. 'Cross the road and see if he follows you,' he instructed.

'Okay.'

I crossed the wide yet empty highway and glanced back to see if Hoodie was crossing, too. My stomach dropped as I saw that he was.

'Crap. Crap. Crap. He's crossing over as well.' A well of panic exploded within me, and I could feel myself wanting to cry. But thankfully, Hoodie maintained his distance. A car went past, and a little girl looked out of her rear window at me.

'Okay. I'm coming now,' I heard a door bang shut as Andy left his house, so close and yet so terribly far away. And I could hear that Andy had started running. 'Sarah, you're coming up to Brook Farm Wood,' Andy's voice was urgent and louder. 'Whatever you do, don't go through the wood. You're going to have to turn off the road.'

Andy knew as well as I did that to reach each other, one of us would have to cross Brook Farm Wood. Beautiful by day, but not a place you wanted to be at night, especially not with an ominous hoodie following you.

'But the side roads are so quiet,' I stammered, scared that if I left the main road, the hoodie would come and get me.

'I know. But you can't go into the woods, Sarah.' Andy's feet were pounding the pavement, and his breath was becoming laboured. 'Turn left up Walfield Avenue and keep going. Run if you have to. It loops back round to the main road, that'll give you some time, and I'll be there literally in two minutes.' I could hear twigs and leaves crunching under his feet as he ran.

Andy was coming through the woods.

I approached Walfield Avenue on the left and took it. The quieter, narrower road had no passing traffic, no cars or passengers as witnesses. A few moments later, the hoodie turned onto the same street. I could hear my hurried footsteps echoing now in the narrow street, and I could hear the gentle scuffing of his trainers on the tarmac behind me. He was getting closer. I pulled the phone away from my ear and started running. I approached the bend as the road swept around to join the High Street again and glanced back. As I did, the hoodie suddenly started sprinting towards me, and I let out a loud shriek as I pushed forward as fast as I could go. Rounding the corner, the end of the road appeared, connecting back to the highway.

Andy appeared like a vision.

'Andy!' I shrieked as we ran towards each other.

I reached him and turned around as the hoodie emerged at the corner. He froze when he saw us together. Then, he turned and fled down an alleyway at the bend in the road. As he ran, his hood fell down behind him, the light from a streetlamp bouncing off a shaved head as he sprinted beneath it. We stared after the tiny figure in the darkness, and within moments, he had vanished out of sight.

'Jesus Christ!' Andy exclaimed, trying to catch his breath. 'Are you okay, Sarah?'

I paused and doubled over, breathing heavily, my heart pounding. 'I'm fine,' I lied, as my emotions caught up with me and I started to cry from the fear and relief of it all.

'It's okay.' Andy held me in his arms and didn't let me go. As my body collapsed into his, finally, I felt safe.

'Come on. Let's get you back to mine,' he said and led in the direction of his home.

Andy walked through the dark streets with such confidence, making me feel protected and cared for. We walked in silence for a while before I finally managed to speak.

'Andy, thank you so much for being there tonight,' I said, my voice trembling with emotion. 'I don't know what would have happened if you hadn't shown up.'

He looked at me with a gentle smile. 'You don't have to thank me, Sarah. I'm just glad you're safe.'

A knot of frustration tightened in my stomach as though I hadn't been fully understood or expressed myself well enough. I wanted to show him what this all meant to me. But when we got back to his, he took me straight up to his room, barely looking at me. I, on the other hand, couldn't peel my eyes away from him. I thought about kissing him then, but my thoughts drifted to James, filling me with guilt and shame. I didn't want to be a cheater like my father.

Andy handed me a t-shirt of his to sleep in, his fingers brushing against mine in a moment that felt both innocent and intimate. Finally, he looked up at me, and sparks flew between us.

I yearned for his touch, his embrace, but I knew we were treading dangerous waters. His gaze lingered on my lips a moment too long, then he quickly looked away. I sensed a hunger in him, a yearning that seemed to mirror my own. My heart raced at the thought that he might want me too. But as he removed a pillow for himself from his bed and walked towards the door without looking up, I felt a sharp pang of disappointment.

'Good night, Sarah,' he said softly. And then he was gone, leaving me alone in the dimly lit room.

As I lay in the dark, lost in the enormity of his t-shirt, my head on his remaining pillow, I could smell his musky scent all around me. I tried to sleep, but every time I closed my eyes, an unbearable ache stirred within me. He'd saved me when I needed him most, and he didn't ask for anything in return. The thought of his selflessness, his strength, only intensified my desire for him.

After some time, I gave up trying to sleep and switched on the light. A clock on the wall said it was half past one in the morning.

Unable to contain myself any longer, I crawled out of Andy's bed and gingerly stepped into the hall. Tom's bedroom was empty, the door wide open, with Tom yet to return from clubbing. His mum's door was firmly shut, the occupant oblivious to my presence as I carefully snuck past and down the stairs. Slowly, I edged towards the open living room door.

Peering in, I could see the top of Andy's head on the sofa, sticking out from under a blanket. I froze, not knowing whether to go in or not, but at the last moment, I chickened out and went into the kitchen. Closing the door quietly behind me, I took a deep breath and pulled Andy's Disney mug with the broken handle from the cupboard, and immediately felt relieved. Filling the mug from the tap, I gulped down the cool liquid gratefully. Then, the door handle slowly creaked downward. By the time Andy opened the door, my heart was already racing.

'Hey,' he whispered sleepily from the doorway.

'Hey,' I replied.

'That's my mug,' he said.

'Oh. Sorry. Sorry, I always use it.' I blustered and felt silly.

'That's okay, Miss Page. I give you permission to use my mug,' he smiled and came into the room, closing the door softly behind him, as my body surged to attention.

I thanked him, not sure whether he was toying with me, a little sparkle in his eye hinting that he was. His eyes darted down to the tops of my thighs, covered by his t-shirt, and then back up to my face.

'May I have some?' he asked, referring to the water in the mug, gulping it down when I handed it to him.

When he finished, there was silence between us as he handed me back the mug, and I stood not daring to breath, his eyes fixed on my face.

'I can't sleep,' I said, breaking the silence at last. I didn't want our conversation to end, a little apprehensive about what might come next.

'No?' He watched me for a while. 'No. I can't sleep either.'

We stood in the kitchen, regarding each other in a new way with a strange heat developing between us.

Andy's gaze dropped down to the tops of my thighs again and lingered there. Just knowing he was looking at my body, a hazy fog of desire descended over me. Thick. Compelling. Impossible to resist.

But before anything could happen between us, the front door banged loudly, and Tom came striding into the kitchen wearing a beanie hat and a face like thunder.

'Well, that was a bloody nightmare!' he exclaimed, swaying slightly and slurring his words.

Andy and I stood as still as statues, an unspent charge lingering between us, my body lit from head to toe.

Tom didn't notice. He went straight to the cupboard, poured himself a glass of water and downed it in one. 'Honestly, your friend…' he turned to me with his finger out, irritated.

'What do you mean?' I paused, turning to take him in at last, surprised to see him so annoyed.

'Emma.'

'What about her? What happened?' I asked, suddenly alarmed.

'God! Talk about *drama*!' Tom exclaimed and pulled out a packet of super noodles and a small saucepan, which he filled with water. 'We waited in her car for an *hour* for those two to stop screaming at each other,' he moaned, his brow furrowed. 'It was absolutely bloody freezing. That is the *last* time I go *anywhere* with those two.'

As Tom cooked his Super Noodles, I puzzled over what might have caused such an epic blow-up.

'What were they fighting about?' I asked.

'Oh *God*. He cheated on her, apparently,' he said, looking drunk and tired. 'Honestly, I'm surprised you don't know about it already. She was just calling you, like, a *million* times.'

At that, I ran quickly out of the kitchen towards the stairs to get my phone, which was on silent in my bag in Andy's bedroom. Halfway up the stairs, Andy called after me.

'Good night, Miss Page,' he said, his eyes lingering on mine as I paused. Part of me wanted to stop and turn around. To explore the desire behind those eyes.

'Good night, Andy.'

Thoughts racing, I snuck back up the stairs to his waiting, empty bed. Fishing my phone out of my bag, I had ten missed calls and six new text messages from Emma. Alarmed, I opened the first message.

'Dyer's been cheating on me!!' It said.

My mouth fell open. I hurriedly opened the second.

'Are you there??'

Without opening the rest, I quickly returned Emma's calls.

'Hey, I got your messages,' I said softly in hushed tones so as not to wake Tom and Andy's mum.

'He's been cheating on me!' Emma sobbed down the line. 'I found a G-string in his pocket!'

Stunned silence passed between us before my mind caught up.

'Oh my god, I'm so sorry, Em!' I gushed, feeling helplessly far away and wishing I could be wherever she was. 'Do you know who she is?'

'No, he won't tell me. He keeps saying it was just once with some random girl, but I know it's not true. I had a feeling before, you know, I could just tell… and I just know he's been seeing someone else…'

I stayed on the line for over an hour while Emma cried. Later that night, I hardly slept, and when I did, I was haunted by turbulent dreams. Images of Emma crying. Of the hoodie chasing me. Of Andy saving me and making love to me. Of Nick staring sadly after me when I'd seen him outside McDonald's with Derrick. I woke from my final dream with a gasp as daylight filtered in from outside.

Derrick. Derrick had been wearing the same hoodie that day I'd seen him with Nick outside McDonald's. The same hoodie as the man who had followed me last night. I was sure of it. I quickly got dressed and rushed down the stairs to the living room, pushing the door open gently as Andy stirred on the sofa.

'Hey, Andy!' I whispered. 'Are you awake?'

'Hmm?' Andy looked up at me. 'Well, I am now,' he laughed groggily, rubbing his eyes.

'Oh, I'm sorry.' I whispered and started closing the door again, but Andy stopped me.

'Come in,' he assured me, 'I'm awake now, Miss Page. What's up?'

'This is going to sound silly. But do you think that could have been Derrick last night?' I kept whispering so as not to wake Tom or their mother.

'Derrick?' repeated Andy incredulously. 'Um. I don't know. I didn't get a good enough look at him. How come?'

I hurriedly explained about my dream, and having seen Derrick wearing the same hoodie. Andy blinked for a while before speaking.

'How would Derrick know where to find you last night?' he asked. 'And why would he be waiting for you?' We both pondered Andy's questions for a while. 'Are you sure you didn't just dream that Derrick was wearing the same hoodie as the bad guy from last night?' suggested Andy softly.

I considered it. Maybe. Maybe my dream was some kind of transference. I was terrified of Derrick, after all. And there was no reason to think he would have been waiting for me one night in some random car park. After all, how would he have known I was there?

***

Later that day, back at home, a text message arrived, and I blinked twice as I realised it was from Andy, not James. I could barely believe it!

Prank calls aside, Andy had never texted me before, and I'd never texted him. The first time I'd called his mobile directly had been last night when the hoodie was following me. My stomach churned as I opened the message. Even more surprising than who it was from was what it *said*.

'My bed smells of you, Miss Page. I can smell you on my pillow.'

I stared at my screen, trying to figure out what it meant. So, I asked.

'Hi, Andy. Errrr… Is that good or bad?'

'I wouldn't like to say, Miss Page.'

I laughed out loud and then felt horribly guilty. Andy was flirting with me. And I liked it.

No.

I *loved* it.

I walked out of my room and picked up the landline, dialling Emma with lightning speed. Emma came to the phone, breathless, having run up the stairs to take the call in private.

'Emma, Andy's texting me,' I revealed, feeling puzzled, as soon as she came on the line.

'Really? What's he saying?' she asked, sniffing as though she'd been crying.

I paused, unsure of whether I should be bothering her with this. 'Are you okay, Em?'

'Yeah, of course, hon. Come on… don't keep me in suspense! What's he saying?'

'He's saying that his pillow smells of me.' Emma already knew the rest of the story.

'Interesting. What did you say?'

'I haven't said anything yet.'

We spent a few minutes debating what I should say and whether it was wrong of me to flirt back, considering that I had a boyfriend. In the end, we decided that I shouldn't flirt, but there was nothing wrong with simply telling the truth, so I picked up my phone and typed out: 'I could smell you on your pillow, too'.

The reply came back a few minutes later: 'I see. Is that good or bad?'

The truth, which I knew in my heart but was adamantly denying, was that it was very, very good. But there was no way of saying so without flirting. James certainly wouldn't have liked it if I flirted with another guy. So, I typed out: 'I wouldn't like to say, Mister East.'

As I hit send, I was struck by a profound revelation. Regardless of my feelings for Andy, was there any real future for James and me? And if not, shouldn't I just bite the bullet and end things?

22

MONOPOLY

January 2000

A COUPLE OF WEEKS LATER, in the New Year, the greatly hyped Millenium come and gone (and no sign of a computer bug that wiped out civilisation), the gang gathered at Tom and Andy's to play Monopoly. The previous week, I'd met up with James and put an end to our floundering relationship. But not wanting to be the subject of everybody's sympathy, Emma was the only one who knew.

Halfway through the evening, James' friends called me on my mobile to sing: 'Swing Low, Sweet Chaaaariot' because they were drunk and merry and wanted us to get back together. Wincing at the noise, I turned the phone to the living room, where Emma, Tom and Johnnie were getting drinks and snacks ready, and Andy was setting up the Monopoly board.

'Hi, James' friends!' everyone but Andy chorused loudly.

On the phone, we heard James in the background, frustratedly pleading with his friends to hang up. 'Come on, guys, just leave it! She's busy. You're so embarrassing!'

James' friends laughed like a bunch of drunk rugby players, which most of them were, and then Rory, one of James' best friends, came on.

'Sarah! Sarah. James is sorry. He says he loves you. Come out!'

'HE LOVES YOU, SARAH!' shouted a random slurring voice in the background. 'COME TO THE PUB!'

James grabbed the phone. 'Gimme that!' he shouted. 'Hi Sarah, sorry. They're a bit drunk; just ignore them.'

Rory and a bunch of others made kissy-kissy noises in the background as James and I said our embarrassed goodbyes and left each other to get on with our respective nights. Turning around to face the room, all eyes were on me except Emma, who was pretending as if nothing had happened.

'Trouble in paradise?' asked Johnnie with a deadpan smile, throwing a peanut in his mouth and chewing it like some kind of detective.

'No, everything's fine,' I lied, wanting to forget about my troubles. I glanced up at Andy, who was regarding me with a steady, unreadable gaze, and a wave of prickly heat surged over my body.

By ten o'clock, the game wasn't even halfway through, so I called home to say I'd be staying at Emma's. Then came the familiar sound of Dyer's motorbike outside, and anxiety gripped my stomach.

All eyes turned to Emma.

'He can go to hell,' she said convincingly.

'Yes, Emma! Girl Power!' Johnnie high-fived her, and Andy looked at me with the hint of a smile.

Our mood fell when the doorbell chimed, and I took Emma's hand to show her that she wasn't alone.

'He's not welcome,' I asserted, as Andy rose to answer the door.

'Don't worry, I'm not letting him in,' assured Andy.

Silence fell as we all tuned our ears to what was happening in the hallway, and we heard Andy open the front door with a click.

'Alright, Dyer?' we heard him say coolly.

'Yeah, not bad, mate. Yourself?'

'Can't complain.'

'Is Emma here by any chance?' Dyer reached his point quickly, and we waited on tenterhooks to hear what Andy would say.

'No, sorry, I haven't seen her.'

Just then, Emma's mobile started to ring loudly on the table, and the name 'Matthew' flashed repeatedly on the screen. We all looked at each other, wide-eyed, knowing that we'd been caught. Quickly, Emma rejected the call, and we tensely waited for what would come next. There was silence in the hall that felt like it lasted a lifetime.

'That's her ringtone,' Dyer's voice sounded quiet but urgent, charged with a strange energy I hadn't heard before.

'She doesn't want to see you, Dyer,' Andy's voice sounded firm and unwavering.

'Come on, mate, I just want to speak with her for a moment,' Dyer insisted, sounding as though he was trying to get in through the door.

'You're not coming in, Dyer,' said Andy, raising his voice, and we knew that something was happening.

Jumping up, we piled into the hallway to see Dyer and Andy outside, Andy shoving Dyer backwards up the driveway and Dyer shoving him back, bristling as though he might throw a punch. In a flash, Tom was side by side with his brother, fists at the ready.

Without thinking, Emma ran past me and out into the street. 'It's okay!' she yelled, before anything more violent than a shove could happen. 'It's okay, I'll talk to him,' she reached Tom and Andy, passed them by and stood in front of Dyer, protectively. 'Thanks, Andy. Tom,' she smiled, holding up her hands to pacify them. 'Really, thank you. So much,' she said, gratefully, and Andy nodded but didn't back down.

I ran out onto the driveway after her, and Emma smiled at me, too, peacefully, while Dyer scowled at us from over her shoulder. 'It's okay, Sarah,' she said soothingly, 'I'm just going to talk to him. I'll be back in a little while.'

As Emma and Dyer walked off down the street to talk, Tom and Johnnie ran back inside out of the cold. But Andy stood rigid at the end of the drive, his fists clenched, his whole body brimming with a strange, coiled energy. Gently, I reached out and touched him on the arm, unsure about why I was doing it. Unsure of how he would react.

At my touch, Andy loosened a little. He looked down at me tentatively, and then together, we went back inside to wait for Emma's return.

A few minutes later, I got a text message from her, saying they were going somewhere to talk. Then, we heard Dyer's motorbike start up and drive away. I texted that if she needed me, I would be there for her, but I knew Emma. I probably wouldn't hear back from her again that night.

Back in the living room, Johnnie cleared his throat and looked down at the board.

'Right,' he said mildly. 'If we're finished almost getting beaten up by Emma's boyfriend, can someone please land on my hotels?'

We laughed morosely, and Tom caught my eye with a small, reassuring smile, the kind that asked *are you okay*? without putting me on the spot. I nodded, grateful, even though I wasn't entirely sure that I was. Slowly, we let the game distract us again, slipping into it almost without noticing, as if concentrating on the board was easier than sitting with reality.

I liked the style of Monopoly we played in the East household. Andy had a special rule that you could make secret deals by passing private notes under the table whenever it was your turn to roll.

But when Andy gently kicked me under the table and handed me a note offering to buy some of my properties, I refused. Despite the fact that my pile of money had all but disappeared, I took great pleasure in writing an impudent and defiant note back, handing it over with a ten-pound note folded inside.

I'm sticking with Park Lane and Mayfair, no doubt about it (I kind of felt like winning this game!), <u>and</u> I most probably won't give up any of my properties for anything but extortionate figures (what a bitch!).

Property is not only my livelihood but my safe areas. Sorry, sweetie.

x

P.S. Buy yourself something pretty [referring to the 10-pound note]

Reading it, Andy smiled his knowing smile and took his time writing a reply while Johnnie and Tom got up to refresh their drinks.

JUST NAME WHAT I CAN OFFER YOU FOR THE ANGEL [Islington]. GOD HELP ME, I'M A COLLECTOR OF EAST END PROPERTY.

I'M SURE YOU DO WANT TO WIN THE GAME, BUT YOU MAY BE IN TROUBLE, AND OUR AMICABLE RELATIONSHIP COULD PROVE WORTHWHILE.

KEEP THE 10, YOU WOULD LOOK BETTER IN SOMETHING PRETTY.

I struggled to hide my feelings as I read his note back to me. It may have been simple, but the way he handled my sass so effortlessly reminded me of how much I adored him. Colour flowed involuntarily to my cheeks, and the more I tried to stop it, the redder I became. With only the two of us in the room, I could feel Andy's eyes on my face, reading me, and I was sure he could sense what I was feeling.

'What are you going to do, Miss Page? Your move.'

Fresh drink in hand, Tom came back from the kitchen as I reluctantly agreed to a deal. Unseen, I slipped Andy's note into my bag to keep as a memento.

'Guys, I'm not going to be able to stay until the end,' revealed Johnnie, coming back from the kitchen with his mobile in hand, 'My mum's going crazy about me staying out so late.'

Upset, we tried to get Johnnie to stay and finish the game, but he insisted he had to leave.

'And then there were three.' Andy smiled as Johnnie's properties went back to the bank and the game opened up again.

An hour later, as the clock above the fireplace chimed two in the morning, Andy beamed as he took the last of his brother's money.

'That'll be five hundred and eighty-nine pounds, please, little bro.' Andy cockily shifted in his chair as Tom scowled down at his dwindling pile of fives and ones.

'I'm going to bed,' huffed Tom, standing up from the table and stretching. I was immediately exhilarated by the thought of being alone with Andy, but I did my best to act natural. 'Don't do anything I wouldn't do.' Tom looked at me directly as he said the last part and raised his eyebrows for emphasis.

What did he mean by that? I thought, staring after him open-mouthed as he trudged up the stairs. *Am I that obvious?* I looked at my phone to see if Emma had replied to my text, but she hadn't, and she hadn't returned my missed call either.

'And then there were two,' Andy looked at me calmly over his stacks of cash and rows of hotels. Heart pounding, I tried desperately to shake off the delicious feeling that came over me from being alone with him, and I scowled intently at my meagre collection of properties. I wondered how long it would take before he put me out of my misery.

Sensing the game was as good as over, Andy switched tracks.

'What do you say to a game of truth or dare, Miss Page?' He suggested, 'I think we both know who's going to win this game.'

I looked at him for a brief moment, considering what to do, and heard myself agreeing as Andy pushed the Monopoly board to one side.

'I'll be right back,' he said, getting up and going to the kitchen.

I quickly tried Emma again, but when she didn't pick up, I sent her another message asking where she was. When Andy returned from the kitchen, he had a glass of iced water for me, and for himself, he carried his Disney mug with the broken handle. I stared at the mug longingly, wishing he had given it to me.

'Thank you.' I accepted the water gratefully. I'd only had a couple of drinks hours earlier, but sipping something would help to calm my nerves.

'Truth or dare, Miss Page?' He sat opposite me, looked me straight in the eye and steepled his fingers above the table.

'Truth,' I smiled. Andy smiled, too.

'Last time we played truth or dare, you had only kissed four people, Miss Page. Including your boyfriend, Jim.'

'James.'

'Whatever.' Andy smirked slightly, and I rolled my eyes as he pulled out the obvious "got your boyfriend's name wrong" trick. 'How many have you kissed now?'

'Still four, Andy, I didn't cheat on him,' I passionately asserted, feeling hurt that he thought I could cheat. Andy smiled and held his hands up apologetically. Then his brow furrowed, and he paused.

'Wait. *Didn't*?' he repeated. 'You *didn't* cheat on him?' he maintained eye contact and thinned his eyes at my unusual use of the past tense to describe our relationship.

'Yes, *didn't.'* Taking a sip of my water, I confessed. 'We broke up.'

Andy nodded slowly, his face unreadable. 'I'm sorry to hear that. Are you okay?'

'Yes, I'm alright. It's just been difficult, that's all. He wasn't doing any of the things that he said he would. It didn't make any sense to go on like that,' I shared quietly.

Andy looked at me gently. 'That sounds tough.'

'I'm okay, really,' I insisted, brushing it off.

A smile touched the corners of Andy's mouth. 'Well. That's good. It's your turn, Miss Page.'

'Okay. Truth or dare?'

'Truth.'

I stopped to think for a moment before inspiration struck.

'What do you look for in a girlfriend?' I asked, curious.

'Pfffff. I don't. I'm not interested in having a girlfriend, Miss Page. They are far too much trouble.'

'Okay. Interesting.' My heart sank. It wasn't like I wanted to rush into anything, but the fact that he didn't want a girlfriend really troubled me. In fact, I felt it like a physical pain in my chest. Still, I nodded along, pretending not to feel anything, as though it was an amusing factoid to find out.

'Truth or dare?'

'Truth.' I looked him straight in the eye as I said it.

'Okay. Can I ask you a sexual question?' he asked, looking down at the table for a moment to give me the space to answer.

I gave him a little nod and smiled coyly.

'Last time we played truth or dare,' he paused, not sure if he should ask, 'you were a virgin. Are you still a virgin, Miss Page?' He waited to see if I was offended. But I wasn't. I was slightly embarrassed, but I liked the feeling of talking like this with him. It felt exciting. I felt alive. I felt something awakening in me that I'd never felt before.

'Yes.' My lips prickled, and my cheeks warmed as I said it, and I shifted slightly in my seat.

'Interesting.' He looked at me with an unreadable look, and I couldn't tell if he was pleased or disappointed. Men were very strange when it came to sex, so I guessed it could have been either. 'So, what have you done?' he asked.

I tutted playfully. 'You only get one question, Andy,' I retorted. He laughed and sat back in his chair, crossing his arms cockily and spreading his legs wide under the table. 'Truth or dare?' I asked.

'Truth.'

'Why don't you want a girlfriend?' I asked and grinned victoriously, sparks flying through the air.

'What? You can't ask me that.' He shifted uncomfortably in his chair.

'I think I just did. You chose truth. Why don't you want a girlfriend, Mister East?' I used his surname playfully, and he sat back lower in his chair, shaking his head at me in mock annoyance and tapping his foot on the floor.

'Because I don't want anyone to know me better than I know myself,' he admitted, scratching his stubbly chin and smiling at me slowly. Ironically, I felt like I knew him better than ever before, but I swallowed down the urge to say so in case he clammed up. 'Truth or dare?' he smiled with a gleam in his eye.

I knew what his question would be if I chose truth.

'Dare,' I smirked, skilfully avoiding his question about the degree of my sexual experience. He smiled and dropped his head in faux defeat at my manoeuvring. Thinking for a moment, an idea struck him, and he tapped his finger against the table.

'I dare you to stay here again tonight. You can take my bed, I'll stay down here,' he said, gesturing to the sofa, a grin spreading across his face. I felt slightly taken aback, and then I realised that Emma had disappeared hours ago, and I'd probably be stranded there anyway.

'Okay.' I agreed, feeling strangely guilty about James even though we weren't together.

I studied Andy's face and wondered why he didn't want a woman to know him too well. 'Truth or dare?' I asked.

'Truth.'

'What's wrong with a woman getting to know you?'

Andy shifted his weight around under the table. 'Um. I don't know, Miss Page.' He thought for a moment, scratched his stubble, and forced himself to land on an answer. 'I don't want to get hurt, I guess.' He looked at me, and for the first time I'd known him, I saw his vulnerable side. His armour was gone, and he was right there in front of me, the real Andy. And then, he was gone again.

'Truth or dare, Miss Page?'

I paused, letting the tension build between us, a coy smile spreading across my lips.

'Truth,' I said coquettishly, taking a sip of water and bracing myself.

He sat upright respectfully in his chair and brought his hands up to his chin, fingers steepled in front of his lips.

'If you don't mind me asking, what's the furthest you've ever gone in the bedroom?' He looked at me expectantly, his expression flat, his mouth curving up slightly at the sides. I thought about it for a while, blinked a couple of times and admitted that I hadn't done much.

'We touched each other intimately,' I said, biting my bottom lip. Andy nodded gently.

'And have you ever been tempted to take things further?' he asked candidly.

'Um, yeah. Of course.' I blushed, and he apologised, sitting up straighter in his chair to make me feel comfortable again.

We were no longer playing truth or dare. It was the first real conversation I'd had about sex with anyone. And there was no one I'd rather be talking about it with.

I cleared my throat. 'Yeah. I've thought about it,' I said, smiling.

'What have you thought about?' he asked, his voice getting softer.

'What it would feel like,' I replied honestly.

'It feels good,' he said, nodding.

'Yeah?'

'Yeah, but I can't say I know what it feels like for a woman,' he said. 'I was hoping you might be able to tell me about that, but of course, you can't.' He paused and looked at me. I said nothing but held his gaze, feeling my body thrum and certain that he was feeling the same.

'Do you mind if I ask why you've decided not to do it yet?'

It seemed like he was genuinely trying to understand me. Most people our age were jumping into bed at the drop of a hat, so he was curious about why I hadn't.

I told him I didn't mind the question and explained that sex was scary to me, and it made me nervous. I didn't want to do it until I felt completely ready. He nodded respectfully, and I could sense that the respect was genuine. He saw that I owned my decisions, and I could feel that he liked that about me. He asked if a part of it was a lack of sexual drive. I laughed and shook my head.

'No,' I said. 'But there are loads of things that you can do without taking it very far.'

'Like what?' he smiled.

I'd piqued his interest, and I could feel him warming to the subject, wanting to get inside my head, to understand how I experienced desire.

I told him about the different games James and I had tried, and the way Andy looked at me made my breath catch—curious, intent, as if he were half-daring me to demonstrate.

I looked at his lips and wondered what it would be like to kiss him. But instead, I wet my lips with a sip of water. Then I surprised myself.

'Actually… I think I'm ready for bed,' I said, standing, feeling suddenly and unexpectedly adventurous.

His expression flickered.

'Are you sure?'

'I'm positive,' I said, my gaze steadily meeting his.

Andy's eyes searched mine for a moment. 'Of course, Miss Page,' he said lightly. 'Right this way.'

He led me out of the living room with exaggerated courtesy, like a host in a grand hotel. As I passed him on the stairs, his clean, masculine scent washed over me, sending a shiver through my skin. My pulse was loud in my ears, every step upward charged with a delicious sense of what I was about to do.

In his bedroom, the air felt suddenly close and intimate. I turned to him, heart racing, and without quite meeting his eyes, slipped off my jumper so that I was standing in only my bra.

'I'm going to borrow one of your T-shirts,' I said, already reaching for the drawer. I let myself stand there for a moment, Andy's eyes drinking me in, before pulling one of his soft shirts over my head. I'd never felt so reckless or alive.

And then my phone rang.

The sound cut straight through the moment like a knife. My stomach dropped. I snatched it up before it could ring again—Emma's name glowing on the screen.

For a moment, I thought about not answering it. About kissing Andy and pulling him down on top of me under the covers. But I knew I was going to answer.

'I'm so sorry,' I whispered, already stepping away, the spell breaking as fast as it had formed.

'Emma?'

'Hey, are you awake?'

'Yeah, I'm still at Tom and Andy's. Are you okay?' I looked at Andy and wanted him so badly, but Emma needed me.

'Yeah, I'm fine…' she sniffed, and it was clear she'd been crying. 'Can we talk?'

'Of course, Em… what happened?'

'I'm coming over now to get you, see you in a bit.'

I turned to Andy and explained that I was staying at Emma's after all, and for a moment, he looked disappointed. His eyes moved down and lingered on my lips like he was going to kiss me, and then he waited with me in the living room until Emma arrived.

As I went to leave, Andy gave me a warm and glorious hug goodbye, and I felt his strong, hard body pressed against mine. Then, he closed the front door with me on the other side of it, out in the freezing cold.

23
Tweedle Dum and Tweedle Dee

EMMA TOOK DYER BACK WITHIN DAYS, as if the blow-up at Tom and Andy's had never really happened, and the following week, Andy left Victoria Wines and started work at Majestic Wines, a new off license near a pub the gang sometimes went to.

The shop was enormous, like a warehouse, with the register standing like an island in the middle. You could clearly see when Andy was working through the huge glass walls—the inside lit up like a giant goldfish bowl. Emma and I would walk past on our way to or from the pub, and I'd get a thrill from seeing Andy at the counter.

'Oh Jesus, drool much?' Emma would laugh, and I'd lust after Andy as we went past, feeling far too confident that he wouldn't turn around and spot me.

One night, as a group of us walked past, I spotted Andy at the counter, and later at the pub, I couldn't stop myself from thinking about him. That was when I had an idea.

Tonight's the night I'm going to ask Andy out.

I was adamant.

I'd never asked anyone out before, and the idea made me terribly nervous. I considered telling Emma my plan, but she was busy shooting pool with Johnnie, who stood close behind her, murmuring something in her ear that made her blush before she missed the shot entirely. So, I snuck off a bit early and left Emma and Johnnie to it (which they barely seemed to notice), stopping in at Majestic Wines on my way to the bus stop.

I can't believe I'm doing this.

With my heart pounding and my body electrified, I fixed my hair, steeled myself and opened the door. A small chime sounded, but I stared straight ahead until I was sure Andy had seen me come in. Then, I turned demurely towards him and shot him a seductive half-smile. But instead of heading to the counter as I'd planned, I strode on past with a small, regal wave and a nod until I unexpectedly found myself at the back of the shop.

Well, that must have looked completely weird.

Kicking myself but tingling all over, I glanced around from the shelves at the back. Andy was watching me openly, intrigued by what I was up to. Thrilled to have caught his attention but not quite sure what to do with it, I took my time choosing a bottle of red wine, running my fingers over the cool bottles and walking slowly between the racks. I glanced up to check he was still watching, then picked out a bottle of Chianti—my parents' favourite wine.

Making my way up to the till, I tossed my hair and wound my hips like a vixen as I approached. Without saying a word, I presented him with my purchase, and he took it just as silently, a jolt of electricity passing between us.

Or maybe it was amusement.

'Hello, Miss Page.' He spoke gently, not taking his eyes off me as he tried to work out what was happening between us.

Okay. Just ask him how he is, then ask if he wants to go for a drink sometime.

But he told you—he doesn't want a girlfriend.

'Hi, Andy,' I breathed. 'How's your night going?' I tried to look tempting by playing with my hair, and that familiar enigmatic smile touched his lips as he wrapped my bottle in paper.

Oh God. Look. He knows. You're just going to embarrass yourself.

'Pretty quiet.' He glanced up at me, suggestively, then slipped the bottle into a bag. 'Except *you* turning up. Will there be anything else?' he coaxed, a charge filling the air between us.

Do it! Do it! Ask him! Do it now!

I paused. My eyes lingering on his as I handed him the money. As he gave me my change, our hands brushed, and I felt the moment open up in front of me—the kind of moment you either step into or lose forever.

'No, that's everything, thanks,' I smiled.

Then I turned on my heels and hightailed it out of the shop.

***

By the time I got home, I was replaying the moment in my mind over and over again and wishing I'd bitten the bullet. But all I had to show for myself was a bottle of red wine that would make a handy gift for my parents. The night air felt too cold on my cheeks as I let myself in, clutching the bottle of Chianti like it was some kind of talisman.

The kitchen light was on.

James was sitting at the table.

He looked up when he heard the door and stood quickly, like he'd been waiting for me for a long time.

'Oh,' I said stupidly.

What on earth is he doing here?

For a moment, I just stood there in the doorway, staring at him, my heart lurching into my throat. Then, Dad poked his head round the living room door.

'Sarah! You're back,' he said far too brightly, taking in the scene in front of him in a split second. James. Me. The tension in the air. His eyebrows shot up. Then he grinned, gave me a not-at-all-subtle wink, and clapped his hands together. 'Right. I'll leave you two to it, shall I?' And before either of us could say anything, he disappeared back into the living room and turned the television up.

I swallowed and entered the kitchen.

James shifted awkwardly. 'Hi.'

'Hi.'

We stood there for a second, neither of us knowing where to look. Then he ran a hand through his brill-creamed hair, the way he always did when he was nervous.

'I'm really glad you're here,' he said quietly. 'I really need to speak with you.'

I didn't answer. I was suddenly painfully aware of how small the kitchen felt.

'I messed everything up,' he blurted out. 'I know I did. I was a… terrible boyfriend… Sarah. I took you for granted. I just… assumed you'd always be there, and that was stupid.' He took a step closer. 'I'm kicking myself for it.'

My resolve wobbled in that stupid, familiar way it always did around him.

'I can't stop thinking about you,' he went on, his voice cracking a little. 'I just keep replaying everything in my head—all the times you were there for me, and I didn't even notice. You deserve so much better than that.'

I looked down at the floor tiles, my throat tight, and poked at a squashed pea with the toe of my shoe.

'I'm sorry,' he said. 'I really am, this time. I want to make an effort. I want to be the kind of boyfriend you actually deserve.' He looked at me intensely. 'I love you. And I swear, if you give me another chance, things will be different this time.'

As he spoke, happy memories flooded in, completely against my will. James laughing with me on the bus. James holding my hand in the cinema. James lying next to me on my bed, talking about our future like it was something we were definitely going to have. All the silly jokes. The late-night phone calls. The ways he'd once made me feel chosen.

My chest ached.

And Andy… *ugh.* Andy was just a blur of half-glances and moments that never quite became anything real. A crush. A maybe. A beautiful frustration.

James was here. Now. In front of me. Saying all the things I'd wanted to hear.

'Do you think… do you think you could forgive me?' he asked softly.

I hesitated. Could James really change? Or would I just be stepping back into the same old hurt because it was familiar and safe? I studied his face fondly, and he looked so hopeful. So sincere. I had to admit, a part of me still loved him.

'I don't know if you can change,' I said honestly. 'But… I think you at least deserve the chance to try.'

Relief spread across his face like a sunrise. He smiled, pulled me into his arms, and then he was kissing me, passionately. And for a moment, wrapped in the renewed spark of something exciting yet comforting, I let myself believe that maybe—just maybe—this was the right thing to do.

24
The Truth

February 2000

SINCE THE EPIC SUCCESS OF EUPHORIA, Johnnie had been dying to hold another club night for teeny boppers. It was the coldest night of the year so far, and Emma and I found ourselves on 'line duty', maintaining order outside the church hall, while Dyer was playing 'bouncer', asking for ID from anyone who looked like they might be over eighteen or under fifteen and barring them from entry if they couldn't prove their age (not including ourselves as 'staff members', of course).

James was supposed to go with me, but he cancelled at the last minute, saying he'd already promised to go to a party with his friends—the same excuse he always used. It had been two weeks since that night in the kitchen, and it wasn't the first time he'd let me down since then. I thought back to when James had kissed me in the kitchen and sighed.

Relationships were much harder than I'd expected. Things like not being stood up and wanting your boyfriend to meet your friends seemed like basic courtesies. It certainly didn't feel as though I had unreasonably high expectations.

As if sensing I needed a distraction from my woes, Johnnie emerged from the church and strode over to us, wearing a long black trench coat and a huge pair of black wrap-around sunglasses. Having just watched the film 'The Matrix', Johnnie had decided to dress like the main characters. He truly believed that, like in the film, we might be living through a computer program, and he regularly tried to convince us, too.

'Put your sunglasses back on,' he urged in hushed tones as he approached.

'But it's dark, we can't see!' I protested, holding them up against the light. 'Anyway, it looks ridiculous; it's nighttime, for god's sake!' I gestured to the fact that I was wearing a faux-fur-rimmed parka jacket rather than a Matrix-style trench coat, and Emma was wearing a short, white puffa jacket.

'It looks *cool*,' insisted Johnnie as he stumbled over an unseen dip in the church driveway. Emma pointed and laughed.

'Fine,' I said, rolling my eyes. 'But if we walk into something in the dark and hurt ourselves, we're suing,' I retorted, putting my sunglasses on.

'Yeah, and after tonight, we know you're loaded,' Emma teased, putting hers on, too, 'so don't even try and deny it.'

Inside the church hall, Johnnie had upped his game for the second rendition of Euphoria, organising a well-known DJ from a London club to play as part of a youth outreach program. The program aimed to encourage the future clubbers of tomorrow to discover a love of music and dance and, in doing so, keep the scene alive for years to come.

He had arrived with an enormous, incredibly loud sound system and specialised in house and Garage music, and Johnnie couldn't believe his luck. Little did he realise that this would spell the end for Euphoria, the usually peaceful church nestled in a quaint neighbourhood of Tudor and Victorian houses, their suburban occupants soon to be outraged by thumping beats and riffs surging through their walls.

Later, on the dancefloor, Emma and Dyer started grinding their bodies together in front of me, and I was struggling to avoid looking directly at them. Feeling very much like a third wheel, I started wishing that Johnnie would come over and wondering what was keeping Tom.

Then, reality took a surreal twist as Tom strolled into the hall with Nick and Jamie-from-The-Green.

What the hell? What's Nick doing here? A wave of confusion hit me. I couldn't believe Tom's betrayal. As they stood at the side searching us out in the crowd, Emma, Dyer and I stopped dancing simultaneously in surprise, and then Emma leaned over towards me.

'Don't take the bait, hon,' she shouted above the music. 'We're here for you; just ignore him,' she rubbed my back soothingly as she spoke and then started dancing again, rubbing herself suggestively all over Dyer's knee.

I didn't know which sight was worse, or where to put my eyes. Then Dyer leaned towards me with a grin and sang a little jingle he'd come up with.

'With a bag of sweets and a cheeky smile, Nick is a dirty paedophile,' he giggled, watching my face closely with glee. I eyed Dyer coldly and could see that he expected to get a rise out of me, but I gritted my teeth and refused to give it to him.

'I'm going to the bar,' I shouted in Emma's ear. 'Do you want anything?'

Emma shook her head that she didn't, and soon, I was standing in a large huddle, trying to get lost and blend in. Before long, there came an ominous tap on my shoulder. When I turned around, I dreaded seeing Nick, but it was Tom standing behind me, with no sign of Nick or Jamie at all. Relieved, yet feeling slightly betrayed, I smiled and hugged him.

'Hey, Tom. You're late!' I said and paused. 'What are you doing here with Nick?' I asked, not able to skirt around the issue for more than a moment.

'Hey, yeah. I wanted to talk to you about that,' Tom gestured over to Nick and Jamie, who were standing in a corner, watching Emma and Dyer dance. 'Can you come outside for a moment to talk?'

'With you, right? I really don't want to talk to Nick right now.' I felt a needling in the pit of my stomach. The last thing I needed was another Nick fiasco to deal with.

'Yeah, just me. Come outside,' he said, and I followed him, away from the crowd, past Nick and Jamie-from-The-Green and out into the freezing darkness. I completely blanked Nick as I passed. Just seeing him made me feel hot with indignation. But Jamie and I smiled and nodded at each other. I noticed, even in the darkness, that Jamie was sporting a huge black eye, and there was a nasty-looking cut above his lip.

Outside, a few scantily clad teenagers were shivering in the cold, smoking cigarettes and talking. At last, Tom and I could hear ourselves talk without straining. I looked up at him and realised it was one of the few times I'd seen him when he hadn't been smiling or laughing, and it was quite unnerving.

'What is it?' I asked quietly, suddenly worried.

'I'm not sure how to say this,' Tom said, looking at me and then looking away.

'Just say it,' I said gently. 'Go on, I can take it.'

'Okay. Here goes. Nick hasn't been seeing Tiffany. He never was. Dyer made it up. Tiffany already has a boyfriend, and it's not Nick.' He looked at me, his eyes wide, his mouth flat as the weight of his words sank in.

'What? Are you serious?' My jaw could have hit the floor, but instead I clamped it shut. My mind raced ahead through a thousand possibilities about what this could mean. 'How do you know?'

'Jamie smokes at Derrick's house sometimes. He hadn't seen Nick there for a while, so he asked Derrick's mum about it. She said nothing has ever happened between Nick and Tiffany. Nick used to go around to smoke because he didn't like it at home, but then stopped, and that's it. Tiffany had a boyfriend the whole time, and her mum said Nick never even looked at her that way.'

My eyes widened in alarm, thinking about how Nick had been ostracised from our group all year.

'Why would Dyer say that if it wasn't true? Why would Derrick confirm it?' I exclaimed, the horror of the situation dawning on me.

'Dyer is a weird guy,' shrugged Tom. 'You know, Andy worked with him. He said Dyer likes messing with people's lives. Gives him a strange sense of power, I guess.' Tom's eyes thinned, and he looked angry, an emotion I rarely saw on him, and I didn't like to see it now. 'As for Derrick, I have no idea why he'd lie about something like this. Maybe he believed Dyer, too? Who knows. I don't know the bloke at all.'

'This is insane!' I exclaimed, feeling light-headed, sitting down on the church steps to gather my thoughts. I thought about the pizza leaflet I'd made and how Nick had had to change his phone number because of it. Actions I'd taken because I'd believed what Dyer had said about him. How could I have been so stupid?

'Wait, it gets worse,' warned Tom, taking a breath and sitting down next to me. 'Jamie got beaten up the other day. By Derrick. Because he thought Jamie reported his mum to Social Services,' exhaled Tom, creating a huge cloud of mist with his breath that caught the light.

My hands shot up to my forehead in disbelief. 'Are you serious? When… how?'

'Social Services finally paid Tiffany's mum a visit a few days ago. Derrick thought Jamie had reported her because he was the one asking questions recently.'

'I can't believe it,' I shook my head and covered my mouth. 'This is awful!' Feeling shocked, Tom and I sat in silence for a few moments until my thoughts crystallised painfully around Nick.

'And Nick?' I gulped quietly.

'Here he is now,' said Tom, looking up as Nick came out of the hall and down the steps to join us. 'Looks like you two have got some talking to do,' conceded Tom kindly, with a poignant look on his face.

Tom got up, whispered something in Nick's ear and glanced down at me sympathetically. I nodded that it was okay if he left us alone. Then he smiled at us both and went back inside.

'Hi,' Nick said softly, gingerly, not sure whether he was okay to sit down.

I looked up at him with tears in my eyes. 'Nick, I'm so sorry!' I lamented, jumping up and wrapping my arms around him. I buried my face in his heavy winter coat. 'I didn't know!'

Nick gently stroked my hair and whispered that it was okay, his touch tender and reassuring. 'I thought I'd lost everyone,' he said quietly, his voice heavy with the weight of the past few months. The world around us seemed to slow down, the noise of the party inside fading into a distant hum. Nick sat down on the steps, and I sat next to him.

'I can't imagine what you've gone through,' I whispered, my voice trembling with emotion. 'It must have been awful for you, losing all your friends!'

Nick nodded. And in that moment, the wind picked up, swirling around us and chilling us both to the bone. I tightened my grip on him, as if trying to hold onto the moment. Nick pulled back and sighed deeply, his breath visible in the chilly air.

'I should have trusted you,' I said, my voice barely above a whisper. 'Instead, I let Dyer's lies get to me.'

Nick remained silent for a moment, his gaze fixed on the ground. 'It's not your fault,' he said quietly.

I nodded, the tears finally spilling over and running down my cheeks. Nick smiled faintly, a glimmer of hope in his eyes as he wiped away my tears with his thumb.

'Hey. Don't cry. I'm okay,' he smiled broadly. 'The truth is out, now,' he reassured me gently, and pulled me back into a deep embrace.

We sat there for what felt like an eternity, wrapped in each other's arms, as the world around us continued to turn. The cold steps beneath us, the distant sounds of the city, and the quiet, shared understanding that perhaps we might start again. But as I pulled away to look into his eyes, and felt the familiar flutter in my chest, my thoughts strayed to Andy.

Not James.

Andy.

I remembered how Andy had pulled his baseball cap onto my head and tugged it so it almost covered my eyes.

Confused and dazed, I didn't know what I felt for anyone anymore. But I knew one thing for sure: I needed some space.

Just then, the double doors to the church hall flew open, and Emma came pounding down the steps, furious and intent on leaving. Hot on her heels was Dyer, trying to reason with her, while she pushed him away and marched resolutely onward.

'You're such a liar, Matthew!' she screamed, and everyone outside the church turned to stare at them.

Seeing my friend in need, I jumped up and pulled away from Nick's potent, confusing embrace. 'I'm sorry, I have to go; Emma needs me,' I apologised, feeling completely overwhelmed.

'Can I see you tomorrow? We need to talk,' he asked, a look of deep longing in his eyes that I found impossible to resist. Unsure of whether tomorrow would be long enough to unravel how I was feeling about the mess I was in, I nodded. 'I'll pick you up at three,' he called after me, and I turned and nodded again while in hot pursuit of Emma, who was running towards her parked car.

I paused and turned around, deciding squarely that I didn't want to be like my dad when it came to relationships. Maybe James and I weren't meant to be. Maybe we were. But until the moment came when I decided what I wanted, I wasn't going to cheat on him.

'You should know. I have a boyfriend now. So tomorrow—it's just to talk,' I said.

Nick looked surprised, but nodded, and then I turned around to follow Emma, who had just slapped Dyer hard around the face, much to the astonishment and delight of the onlookers.

'Emma, wait!' Dyer called after her as she ran up to her parked car. 'I didn't know Derrick would beat up Jamie-from-The-Green! How could I know that!? Emma!' As I chased the couple, he stopped, realising it was useless to keep trying.

It took every ounce of my strength not to give him a piece of my mind as I overtook him. 'Get lost, *Matthew,*' I said, instead, using his first name like a knife, and we glared at each other viciously as I climbed into Emma's passenger seat.

As Emma pulled wobbily away from the curb, her hands resolutely at ten and two, I looked back in the wing mirror at the scene. Nick was still sitting on the steps of the church hall, staring after us. Now flanked by Tom and Jamie-from-The-Green, both scowling at Dyer, who slunk away and mounted his motorbike, driving off in the opposite direction like an ominous apparition.

***

When James called at two o'clock the following afternoon, my dad answered, but I pretended I wasn't at home, adding to the tight knot of guilt already forming in my stomach. I knew I had to come to a decision about our relationship, and sooner rather than later, but now was not the time to get into that. I quickly turned off my mobile in case James tried to get through to me on it. Putting down the landline receiver, Dad winked at me as though we were one of a kind.

Oh God.

I swore to myself that we weren't and we were never going to be.

'You look nice,' said Dad approvingly, a little confused. 'Are you going on a date?'

'No, it's not a date. I'm just meeting a friend to talk,' I corrected him, running back upstairs to choose what to wear.

'Okay. Well, if James calls again, who shall I tell him you're with?'

I sensed a level of amusement in my dad's voice, as though the tables had turned, and it prickled me. The last thing I wanted was to deceive James, but I had unfinished business with Nick, and nothing was going to happen between us—because I wasn't a cheater like Dad—so why worry James by telling him?

'No one,' I answered. 'Could you say that I've gone out, and I'll call him back when I get in?'

In my bedroom, I turned on the radio and obsessively retouched my makeup. I felt a familiar mix of nerves and excitement building within me that made Nick so thrilling to be around, but an additional sense of dread filled me, knowing I would have to come clean about the pizza leaflets. I had no idea how he was going to react.

When he finally pulled into my driveway at just after eight, I ran out and jumped into his car, still unsure about how I was going to handle the situation.

'There she is,' said Nick softly, a gentle smile touching his lips as I got in his car.

'Hey,' I smiled back, the sight of him looking at me so intently taking my breath away.

Right there and then, I resolved to end it with James. As soon as I had a chance to speak with him. He'd never had the same effect on me that Nick had. Or Andy. And I saw that he was never going to.

'You look beautiful,' said Nick.

'Thank you,' I felt myself flushing involuntarily. 'You look nice, too,' I said awkwardly, and Nick smiled.

'Does your boyfriend know you're here with me tonight?' he asked curiously.

I shifted uncomfortably in my seat. 'No, he doesn't. But I told you, this isn't a date. I just want to hear you out, and I want you to hear me out, too. There are things I need to tell you.'

There was a brief pause while Nick took in the information. 'Understood,' he nodded, 'let's go and talk.'

Nick drove in silence through the streets of my small town and pulled into a winding country lane near the entrance to my school. He stopped at the gates of an enormous house with a long, lamp-posted driveway.

'This is where we used to live before we lost it all,' he explained to my astonishment. 'I like to come here and park and remember happier times,' he said, looking up wistfully into the grounds of his childhood home. I already knew the story of Nick's family, having gone from rags to riches to rags again. Nick's father had made a fortune through financial investments before losing everything in a huge public scandal. I never imagined the estate would be so big. I could see there were tennis courts and a swimming pool; it even looked as though there was an orchard and a paddock.

'It's beautiful,' I said softly, 'It must have been wonderful to live here.' I looked across at him, and he looked sad.

'It was,' he confessed. 'It's strange knowing that the best years of your life happened when you were just a kid. It's like… nothing you do really matters or can ever make a difference because you're never going to make it back to where you were. So, why try? Ya know?'

He turned to me, and I could see that the loss had changed him. 'We lost the house when I was ten, and we had to go and live with my grandparents.'

'I'm so sorry, Nick,' I said, trying to comfort him.

'That's why losing my friends hit me so hard,' he said. 'I'd already lost so much as a kid.' Slowly, he recounted the story of what had happened between us from his perspective. 'I did wonder why you weren't in the pub that day, and everyone stopped speaking to me after that,' he started. 'It didn't really make any sense. I tried calling you, but you were always out, and you never called me back. Nobody did.' A poignant sadness fell over his features.

It all happened because of me, I thought, and fell into a deep pit of shame

'At first, Dyer told me you were a proper psycho who'd somehow turned my friends against me.' He shook his head and kept going. 'I really hated you for that,' he looked at me intensely as though a part of the memory still burned within him, and I felt my heart surge into my throat, anxiety gripping me tightly. If he could hate me for that, how would he react when I told him about the pizza leaflet?

'Then he kept giving me more and more different stuff to try. I think he liked having someone to get high with. Then, one day, he said that Emma and the rest of the group all thought I was a druggie loser and didn't want to hang out with me anymore.' Nick's set jaw was clenching and unclenching as he battled with turbulent emotions within. 'Now I find out it's because you believed a lie he told about me. How could you believe that I would go out with a thirteen-year-old?' he asked with hurt emblazoned in his eyes. 'That's sick.'

I was lost for words for a moment. 'We didn't. But then Derrick told me that it was true. It felt like he was warning me away from you to protect his sister from being cheated on. Why would he lie about that?'

Nick frowned and shook his head. 'I don't know.' He chewed his lip in silence for a moment. Then he turned the keys in the ignition, and the car burst to life. 'But screw this. I'm going to find out right now,' he said, already reversing the car.

25
DERRICK'S DEN

'WHAT ARE YOU GOING TO DO?' I asked, my voice tinged with surprise and more than a little fear.

'I'm going to ask Derrick. No time like the present,' Nick winked at me and eased the car into first gear, heading back down the country lane to the main road.

'Are you sure it's a good idea to confront him like this?' I asked, panic welling up in my chest. 'Didn't he just beat up Jamie?'

'Don't worry about it,' Nick assured me. 'We're mates. I'm just gonna ask him what the deal was—why he said that stuff to you—and we'll be sweet.'

'I don't know, Nick,' I bit my lip and hugged my arms tight to my body. 'He seems like a nutcase to me.'

'I can drop you home if you like,' Nick smiled across at me and gently squeezed my shoulder reassuringly.

'Pfff, I'm not letting you go by yourself,' I scoffed. 'What if he kills you or something? Who would clean up the mess?' I laughed to release the tension inside me, but it sounded thin even to me.

'Ha! You have quite the imagination, Sarah,' he teased. 'Honestly, Derrick and me are mates. And no offence to him, but I'm twice his size.' He looked at me sideways to gauge my reaction and winked, and I couldn't help but smile and roll my eyes exasperatedly. But underneath my amusement, an image of the scar on Derrick's cheek flashed before my eyes. I didn't think it was size you had to worry about with Derrick. More like sharp metal objects.

I nodded, my heart pounding as I chewed on my thumbnail. 'Well, if you're sure,' I conceded, putting on my big girl pants and slapping on a cheerful face. 'Drive on, then, maestro… I suppose our destiny awaits.'

'Roger that!'

Nick headed towards Barnet, and as we drove, silence fell over us. He glared at the road as he drove, and I couldn't help feeling confused. He looked so sexy driving on a mission like this. But I felt torn because of Andy, guilty because of James, and dreadful because of Derrick. *What if it was Derrick that followed me the other night?* I pondered.

Country lanes and fields quickly turned to leafy suburbs, then busy roads and concrete. Before long, we were surrounded by rows of red-brick terraced housing and high-rise flats. As we wound our way into the heart of Dollis Valley estate, where Derrick and Tiffany lived with their mum, I looked over at Nick, envious of how calm he seemed.

Finally, we entered a deserted, dead-end street, and I knew which house we were heading to before we pulled up. At the end of a row of terraced houses stood one with a garden of uncut grass with an abandoned shopping trolley in the middle of it. The window frames were flaky, the wood underneath the paint showing through as dull grey.

'Looks like Dyer's here,' pointed out Nick, gesturing towards Dyer's motorbike parked around the side. Anxiety twisted in my stomach at the thought of seeing Dyer, too.

Nick parked the car next to Dyer's motorbike, and, as we climbed out, a large pitbull dog started barking at us through the window. I gulped, my mouth dry, and I felt myself starting to sweat.

What are you doing, Sarah!? I screamed at myself, as my body came on full alert, my mind crystal clear.

A middle-aged lady with brassy blonde hair got up from below the window and stared out at us. Recognising Nick, she gave an easy wave, then sat back down again and ignored us.

'Come on,' whispered Nick, touching me on the shoulder from behind, and I startled as though he'd pulled a knife on me. 'Easy tiger!' he teased, and led me round the side of the house towards the back garden.

At the greying fence, Nick let out a whistle.

'Whassuuup!' came an instant response from within.

'Whazzzuuuuuuuuh!' Nick hollered back, sticking his tongue out and really letting rip.

'Nick! Where you been, blud?' One of the fence panels was pushed aside and Derrick peered out through the hole. 'Come in, man!'

Nick laughed and disappeared through the gap, gesturing for me to follow him. With one last look along the deserted street, I took a deep breath and stepped into Derrick's back garden.

It was small and overgrown, consisting of a small square patch of grass and weeds and a rough concrete patio. Derrick was sitting on a folding beach chair inside a domed tent, wrapped in an enormous puffer jacket. He wore a beanie pulled over his head to his eyebrows and had about three scarves wrapped around his neck. In between his pinkish-red fingers, he held a lit joint, and in his other hand a can of Stella. He looked like he was freezing cold.

For a split second, surprise flickered across his face when he saw me. Then it vanished. Grinning, Derrick got up from his chair and grabbed Nick's outstretched hand.

'Yo, Nick, man! Where you bin hidin' bro? Long time no see!' he asked as the pair slapped each other on the back a little too hard.

'I just been busy, man,' replied Nick in an accent I'd never heard him use before. 'You know Sarah, right?'

Derrick's eyes shifted to me over Nick's shoulder and didn't blink. 'Yeah, we've met,' he murmured, a hint of a smile touching his lips. 'How's it going, Sarah?' he asked, his pupils black pin pricks, encircled by soulless bluish grey.

I smiled as sweetly as I could muster. 'Yeah, not bad thanks,' I said lightly, my voice barely more than an amiable whisper. My body stayed loose, but inside, everything tightened.

Just then, the pitbull slammed against the patio doors with a violent thud, its teeth bared, jaws snapping at the glass. I gasped and instinctively stepped back towards the fence. Nick reached out a comforting hand and rubbed my shoulder, and Derrick turned to the dog and grimaced.

'Rocco!' Derrick barked. 'Shut the hell up!'

But the dog didn't stop. It kept snarling, its spit smearing against the window pane.

'Mum!' Derrick shouted even more loudly.

The blonde woman stormed in and struck it hard across the head with a trainer. Despite the dog's hostility, I felt sickened. She glanced at me and gave a bright, brittle wave, as though nothing had happened. Then, she pulled the dog harshly away by its collar, and the pair were out of sight.

'Bloody dog,' Derrick muttered, but he was no longer looking at the dog. He was looking at me.

'Is Dyer here?' asked Nick curiously. 'His bike's out front.'

Derrick looked back at Nick. 'You just missed him. He's out on a *delivery*,' he winked, and I wondered what kind of delivery Derrick could mean.

'Oh, nice,' nodded Nick. 'Yeah, looks less dodgy to deliver it, rather than having people come around all the time. You only need one neighbour to call the Old Bill, and that's it,' he reasoned.

The pieces clicked into place. Derrick and Dyer were making drug deliveries together.

'Fancy a smoke?' suggested Derrick, holding out the spliff to Nick and gesturing for us to follow him into his tent.

'Nah, I quit, mate,' laughed Nick cordially, following him into the tent, nonetheless. Derrick nodded and glanced at me, his mouth flat. I hesitated, not wanting to be trapped in a smoky tent with Derrick, but not wanting to make my feelings too obvious either.

With a gulp, I stepped inside. Nick sat cross-legged on the floor and gestured for me to sit beside him. Derrick collapsed his deck chair and tossed it outside, where it clattered noisily on the concrete.

Even with the flap open, the tent filled with a light haze that stung my eyes. Positioning himself opposite Nick and me, Derrick looked back and forth between the two of us.

'So, what, are you two a couple now, then?' he asked dubiously.

Nick sighed. 'Nah, not a couple,' He nudged me playfully with his shoulder. 'Sarah's got a boyfriend.' Unable to stop myself, I smiled, and then Nick was smiling too. 'Sarah doesn't cheat. And I respect that,' he said, glancing up at me with a gentle expression that made my heart race and added to my guilt about James.

Derrick exhaled a large cloud of smoke and offered me the joint. Nick and I simultaneously shook our heads.

'No thanks, I don't smoke,' I said firmly, and beside me, Nick's smile broadened.

Derrick put the joint back in his mouth and looked at me flatly. 'Still behaving yourself, Sarah?' he said lightly. Then he glanced at Nick. 'Classy bird, this one. Didn't think there were any of them left. All the girls 'round here are slags.' His eyes took on a steely quality, and I shifted uncomfortably on the hard ground. Nick placed his hand on my back.

'You alright?' he asked casually, his concern for my welfare heartwarming.

'Yeah, just a stone,' I smiled, as Derrick continued to glare.

Turning back to Derrick, Nick moved the conversation on. 'Actually, mate, we were hoping to have a word with you about something, if that's alright?'

Derrick frowned. 'Course, mate. What's up?' he asked.

'You probably know this by now, but a few months ago Dyer told Sarah and Emma that I was going out with your sister,' started Nick, looking serious. 'But, I mean, obviously I wasn't.'

Derrick nodded, as though he'd expected this conversation to come up all along. 'Right, right,' he murmured, taking another drag on the joint, which had burned down almost to the roach. 'Yeah, I heard about that, mate.'

'But then, you thought I was seeing her, too?' Nick asked, framing the question in a non-accusatory way. I bit my lip nervously as I studied Derrick's face.

He shifted his weight and scratched his forearm gingerly. 'Yeah mate,' he confirmed, shaking his head apologetically. 'I thought you was. Dyer told me you two was an item, ya know? And I just believed him. I mean, you were always here. And she's a very pretty girl, my sister. So, why wouldn't I believe it?'

Against my better judgment, I considered it. But I had to know more about what Dyer had said before I knew what to believe. Drawing on all my courage, I shifted a little on the floor and looked directly at Derrick.

'But... what did Dyer say exactly?' I asked, my voice wavering a little. 'About Nick and Tiffany.'

Derrick turned his icy gaze towards me and thought for a moment.

'He made a few jokes. Had a few theories,' Derrick looked back at Nick before continuing. 'He said he saw you and Tiffany looking at each other funny. Said he saw you coming out of her room one time when you said you was going to the loo. Loads of little stuff like that. He was convinced that something was going on between you. You know what Dyer's like; he's got a theory about everything.'

Nick nodded confirmation and looked at me blankly for a moment. Even I had to admit that it did sound like Dyer.

'Mate, I've never been in Tiffany's room,' corrected Nick adamantly. 'I've never even thought of her like that. She's a kid. That's sick.'

'Yeah, well, she might be a kid,' scoffed Derrick defensively, 'but it's better if she has a boyfriend round here than if she got one round some other geezer's gaff, innit?'

I felt sick.

Nick exhaled loudly, his brows knitted into a frown. 'It's still a bit young to have an adult boyfriend, mate,' he insisted. 'Why wouldn't you have said something to me if you thought I was perving on your kid sister?'

I turned to Nick and felt pleased he'd taken a stand, even in the face of his friend, who also happened to be a violent drug dealer.

'Come on, mate. She's had *loads* of boyfriends,' shrugged Derrick. 'That stuff's up to my mum, anyway. It's girls' talk. None of my business. Jesus, the stuff they talk about. I don't wanna hear it.' Derrick put the expired roach in a tin can with some water, and it hissed as the burning ember went out.

As his words sank in, I wondered what had taken Social Services so long to pay this family a visit.

'Anyway. That's all sorted, now,' Derrick added. 'No more boyfriends thanks to Social Services, after somebody grassed us up.' Derrick's eyes found mine as he spat the words *grassed us up*, and heat flooded my face. I knew that if Derrick looked at me again, he'd know.

'Yeah, what happened with that?' asked Nick, his voice laden with confusion and concern. With a sudden jolt of panic, I realised Nick still didn't know that it was Emma's mum, with mine and Emma's help, who had reported the family to Social Services. Unless Tom had filled him in, because I certainly hadn't.

Derrick scowled down at his knees for a moment, running his finger slowly around the rim of his beer can.

'It was weird. Social Services turned up out of the blue one day, asking about Tiffany and her boyfriend,' he explained. 'Mum reckoned it was Jamie-from-The-Green. Said he'd been asking questions about you and Tiffany not long before. She told 'im nothing was going on between you two, but it looked like Jamie didn't believe it.'

'That *is* weird,' pondered Nick, thoughtfully. 'Doesn't seem like something Jamie would do.'

'Yeah,' Derrick's eyes lifted. They landed on me and stayed there a fraction too long. 'It doesn't.'

I kept my face blank and prayed that I wouldn't flush red again.

'So, why'd you beat him up then, Derrick? Jamie didn't deserve that,' pressed Nick, and Derrick thinned his eyes slightly like he was getting agitated. I glanced toward the opening of the tent, calculating how fast I could move.

But rather than kick off, Derrick cracked. He sighed and hung his head, rubbing his scalp under his beanie.

'I dunno. I just lost it. I couldn't stop myself. Mum was crying, saying Tiffany might get taken away,' Derrick looked up at Nick, a look of shame draping over his features. 'She says I gotta stop dealing weed from here, too, in case Social Services finds out. Then they might really take her away. So, I gotta move out.'

'You got him pretty bad, mate, he's got bruises all over his face!' Nick exclaimed, and silence fell in the tent. Derrick's face hardened a little, like his patience was wearing thin, but Nick didn't seem to notice. 'What are you gonna do now, then?' he continued.

'Not sure,' said Derrick frostily. 'Might move in with Dyer and deal together from our own place. Probably about time, anyway. Don't wanna get my mum in any more trouble.'

'What, even after all the bullcrap he told you about Tiffany and me?' exclaimed Nick, sounding taken aback.

Without thinking, I let out an indignant little snort, and both boys looked at me as though registering my contempt.

Then, Derrick shrugged. 'What can I tell ya? The geezer's an idiot. But we already knew that.'

Nick laughed. 'True,' he conceded, and the pair relaxed and regarded each other for a moment. 'Alright, mate. Well, thanks for clearing all this up,' he said, and apparently all was well between them.

'No worries,' nodded Derrick, already building another spliff in his lap. 'Pfffff. I guess I better patch things up with Jamie,' he sighed.

Nick nodded. 'Probably not a bad idea, mate.'

Much to my relief, we got up, made our apologies, and left. Nick held the fence panels back for me, and as I ducked through the gap—ecstatic at the thought of fresh air—I glanced back to wave.

That was when I saw it. In an upstairs window.

A pink rainbow catcher hung in the centre of the glass, its delicate spiralling crystals swaying gently.

Except... there was no wind.

The greying net curtains behind it were perfectly still, the room behind them completely obscured.

That must be Tiffany's room, I thought, my skin prickling.

From up there, the whole garden would be visible. The tent. The fence. *Us.*

I noticed that the window was ajar despite it being freezing outside. Remembering how my dad's words had travelled through my own open window the night he'd left my mum on the driveway, and how clearly I'd heard every word, I knew that if someone had been standing behind those curtains, they would have heard everything.

I kept my face neutral and kept moving.

27
The Confession

HOPPING BACK THROUGH THE HOLE IN THE FENCE, the air felt freer on the other side. As Nick hopped out behind me, I made a beeline straight for his car. Nick looked thrilled to have a satisfying explanation as to why his friends had sabotaged our budding relationship and the rest of his friendships—it had all been a big misunderstanding.

He jumped back in his car, and we sat for a while outside Derrick's house, Nick leaning his head back against the headrest, grinning from ear to ear. Then he turned to me and softened.

'So, it was an honest mistake,' he smiled, rubbing his eyes and looking tired suddenly.

I kept glancing back at the upstairs window. I couldn't shake the feeling that someone was at that window, and all I wanted was to get out of there.

'Do you mind if we go somewhere else?' I asked.

Nick smiled and put an arm around me. 'You know you didn't have to be scared of him while I was there,' he comforted lightly, like there was nothing more to be afraid of.

'I know,' I said. But I wasn't thinking about Derrick anymore. I checked the upstairs window again, then forced myself to focus on

Nick. 'Look, I'm really proud of you for confronting him the way you did. Especially how you stood up for Jamie like that. It was really something.'

At my words, Nick's face lit up, and he beamed as though he were proud of himself, too.

'Thanks, Sarah. That means a lot,' he paused, and took a deep breath as though steeling himself to be vulnerable. 'Um. There's something I still have to say to you,' he paused again, all of his bravery escaping him. And then he looked up into my eyes and found his courage. 'The worst part of all this, Sarah, is that I thought I'd lost *you*.'

As he spoke, I forced myself to stay present. His thumb gently stroked my cheek, but I struggled not to look at the upstairs window again.

'Nick,' I said quietly. '*Please.* Can we just drive?'

'Sorry,' he said gently, and turned the key in the ignition. 'Let's go somewhere.'

I took a deep breath, my fingers twisting together in my lap as he finally pulled away from Derrick's house. In the wing mirror, the upstairs window shrank and vanished into shadow. As the estate disappeared behind us, my shoulders finally loosened. And then I found myself looking at Nick.

He noticed me looking and smiled. I smiled right back, my thoughts drifting back to him—to us. Before long, we pulled up at a park in my hometown just as dusk was falling.

'Hey… before you go on, there's something you should know,' I said quietly as he shut off the engine. 'I only just decided this today, and I should probably be telling James this first... But I trust you, and I feel like I have to be honest with you.'

He watched me carefully, his face unreadable.

'I'm going to break up with James,' I admitted, the words spilling out now that they'd started. 'I've been trying to make it work, and it just… it isn't. And I'm tired of feeling like I'm asking for basic things and still being disappointed.' I gave a small, humourless laugh.

Something shifted in Nick's expression, like a door quietly opening. 'I'm so sorry,' he said gently, taking my hands in his fervently. 'I wish I could feel sad, but I… I just feel happy for myself. Is that selfish?'

I smiled, ashamed of myself for feeling pleased, and shook my head.

'That day I saw you in High Barnet when you ignored me, it really hurt me. It… changed something for me,' Nick confessed. 'I realised I couldn't stop thinking about you. About us.' He hesitated, then smiled, shy and hopeful, glancing at my lips before meeting my eyes again. 'It made me realise I… I want to be with you.'

Despite myself, an exhilarating thrill bolted through me. It was a moment I'd imagined so many times I could barely believe it was real.

'When I got home that day, I put my weed away. When Dyer called to get high, I said no. I haven't taken anything since. That's why Derrick said he hasn't seen me for ages. I haven't been around. I quit.'

I felt elated that Nick had turned his life around, and he had done it just for me.

'I don't want to do it anymore, Sarah. Not if it means losing you,' he said.

At this, he closed the gap between us and tried to kiss me, and I wanted to let him more than anything, but I couldn't. Instead, I pulled away and put my hand against his chest to stop him.

'Wait,' I said, overwhelmed, feeling the heat from his body on my fingertips. 'Just give me a minute, I need to think.' I had so many thoughts racing through my mind that it was difficult to know what to focus on.

Taking a breath, I thought about how, on that day when he had realised he wanted to be with me, I had just finished handing out pizza leaflets with his phone number on them. While he had been feeling softness and sweetness towards me, all I had been feeling was searing anger and resentment.

'There's something else you should know,' I began, without making eye contact.

'Yes, I know, you're not a cheater,' Nick started optimistically, pulling my hands eagerly towards him. 'But, Sarah... we've known each other for so long, and there's something really special between us. When are you going to tell him?'

I thought about going with the flow and taking the easy route out like my dad. But then I thought about who I wanted to be, and it didn't involve deceiving the people who trusted me.

I closed my eyes and took a deep breath. 'It's not that,' I whispered. 'Before I tell you, I want you to know that I genuinely believed you were a creep, a pervert and a misogynist. Dyer told me you said some terrible things about women, and I believed him.'

'Okay,' said Nick, looking confused. I closed my eyes, braced myself, and leapt.

'I thought you needed to be taught a lesson. So, I...' I gulped, unable to get the words out. 'So, I...'

'What? It's okay, you can tell me.'

'I... made a leaflet.'

'Okay.' Nick frowned. 'What does that have to do with me?'

'It had your phone number on it,' I confessed, pausing, not wanting to say the next part. 'And... I handed it out outside Barnet College.'

Saying it aloud, I felt absurd. Almost comical. I wondered if Nick would see the funny side, but silence filled the car as I watched his unmoving face.

'That's... not what I was expecting you to say at all...' he looked at me blankly. 'What kind of leaflet?'

'It was a pizza leaflet,' I answered meekly.

Nick's mouth dropped.

'I can't believe it,' he said, and for a moment, it looked as though he might laugh.

But then Nick's face hardened.

'That was *you*?'

His eyes moved away from me as though he were remembering fully, and then his gaze turned frosty as he looked back at me in a new light. 'I had to change my phone number because of that! I wondered what the hell was going on…'

'I'm sorry,' I said lamely, my hopes of us laughing about it shattering.

'Do you find it funny?' Nick looked at me hotly, his eyes filled with accusation. 'Wait, is that what you were doing in Barnet High Street that day you ignored me?'

Words escaped me, and I floundered, trying to find a fitting response.

'That day, when I realised I wanted to be with you… and I quit smoking and all the rest to try and win you back… That's the day the calls started...'

Wide-eyed and at a loss, I stared blinkingly at Nick without saying anything.

'Is that what you were doing? Sarah, answer me,' he demanded.

I nodded my head lamely, and Nick suddenly hit the steering wheel hard with his open palm, making me jump.

'I can't believe it! You of all people, Sarah,' Nick exclaimed, his face racked with disappointed. He threw his head back against his headrest and closed his eyes. 'Tell me you didn't call.' He looked at me angrily, offering me a single, final olive branch.

But I couldn't take it. I just sat quietly, staring at him, ashamed of my actions, knowing that he would have felt completely alone, friendless and paranoid about all of the strange calls.

'I'm so sorry, Nick,' I apologised from the depths of my panicking heart. I felt sure that I was losing him forever.

Furious, Nick started the engine and drove me back to my parents' house without saying another word. Feeling rotten, I climbed out of the car and turned morosely to say goodbye. Nick looked at me and beckoned me back to the window.

Smiling, hoping perhaps we could leave things on a better note, I approached.

In one swift motion, Nick tugged at my coral ring and broke the chain around his neck, leaned forward and put it in the palm of my hand. Then he turned back to the road and drove away.

Shocked, I glanced around and saw that I was standing in the exact spot where my mum had been abandoned for being too old, so I hurried inside and shut the door.

Upstairs in my bedroom, Dad came to check whether I was okay.

'No, I'm really not,' I said, being honest about my feelings for once, my voice cracking as the tears came.

I thought for a moment about everything going on in my life. About poor James, who, despite not being a very good boyfriend, didn't deserve to be messed around. About Nick, who had wanted to be with me and now hated me because of my own actions. About Andy, who was so mysterious and confounding, I needed to be 'Miss Marple' or the lady from 'Murder-She-Wrote' to have a chance at figuring him out. It all just seemed so exhausting. Yet suddenly, everything became clear.

'I need to break up with James,' I said with a sniff.

Dad looked at me with sympathy; the amusement from earlier evaporated. His expression told me he'd known this moment would come one day—that he'd been preparing himself for 'boy talk' for the past eighteen years. Then he went downstairs to make us a cup of tea so that we could talk all about it.

No Going Back

27
Gap Year

July 2000

IT WAS MID-JULY. I'd finished my A-level exams and said my farewells to Kate from school, who was going backpacking across South America for a year.

That summer, having drifted apart to study, the gang came back together with a vengeance. Nick hadn't spoken to me for five long months since I admitted to making the pizza leaflet. And even though Andy was as enigmatic as ever, he had at least started joining the crew's social gatherings from time to time. Meanwhile, Emma had yet again forgiven Dyer for his travesty of lies and taken him back, much to mine and Johnnie's mutual disgust. Even more astonishingly, Nick, Dyer and Jamie-from-The-Green were bosom buddies again, which was utterly mind-blowing to me.

As for me, with A-levels over and done with, I was happy that I could take part in another of Liam's plays, which was due for a week-long run in London fringe theatres in a few weeks' time.

One hot day, Emma and I were rehearsing my lines in her bedroom.

'That was really good, hon,' she said, closing the script and fanning herself with it after my final scene. 'Just remember to project your voice. I lost you on that last part,' she cautioned.

'Thanks. Yeah, I always forget,' I conceded, writing a note in my margin to 'BE LOUD' and then looking up at Emma happily. But to my surprise, she looked like she was going to cry.

'What's the matter?' I asked, throwing my script down on her bed and rushing over to her.

'I'm going to miss you, that's all,' Emma said, her lips turning down as tears started falling.

'Hey, hey!' I cooed soothingly. 'What are you talking about?'

'When you go to university in September. Everything's changing. Everyone's leaving,' she sobbed, tears falling harder.

'That's not true,' I said, trying to be comforting. 'Dyer and Andy will still be here—and Nick will still be around retaking his A-levels.' I realised as I was saying it that it sounded pretty lame.

'But you're going. And Johnnie and Tom are going,' she sniffed, her tears showing no signs of slowing up. 'And I'm just going to be here with Dyer…' she sobbed.

To be fair, I'd probably cry if I was left here with Dyer.

'…and you're going to forget about me. And everything's going to be about mortgages and stress and bills!'

I held her in a tight embrace as she wept on my shoulder. 'Well, I think you have to buy a house before all that,' I joked, and as she laughed, there was a break in her tears.

'Anyway…' I took a deep breath. 'I was thinking that I might take a gap year,' I announced, slightly uncertainly.

'Oh my God! Really!?' Emma exclaimed, pulling back excitedly, her face a vision of hope.

'Loads of people are doing it,' I declared, thinking of Kate and warming to the subject. 'Although I think most people spend their gap years backpacking around Australia or Thailand! But I don't really feel ready to leave you just yet. If I go now, I feel like I'll regret it for the rest of my life,' I shared truthfully.

I had been desperately craving more time to spend with the incredible friends who had saved me from social obscurity before the group completely disintegrated. Partly because Emma had decided to stay and find a job, and partly to be near Andy and Nick for another year—both of whom I still carried a torch for.

'Anyway, that way, I can keep going with Liam's new play and take it to the Edinburgh Festival next summer,' I pointed out, but I knew it was just an excuse. After that, I would finally study International Journalism at Leeds University, nearly two hundred miles to the North.

'That would be amazing,' she sniffed, hugging me and wiping her eyes. 'Wait, are you serious? Are you actually doing it?'

'Yes.' I decided right then and there that it was something I needed to do, and I felt wonderful about it. 'I absolutely am.'

I hugged her back, and we danced a little jig together in a circle. But at the back of my mind, an uncomfortable thought pricked at me.

God knows what Mum will think about all this.

***

As predicted, Mum was furious when I told her about my intentions, but she didn't stop me, and I didn't find out why she was so upset about it until much later. Then, at the end of August, just after Liam's play had come to the end of its run and we'd been named as *Time Out Critic's Choice*—I got home to find Mum and Dad waiting for me in the kitchen.

'Sarah, can you come in here a moment, please?' came Mum's serious voice, and my stomach did its usual flip. 'You too, Lucas,' Mum called out to Lucas, who was home for the summer and watching a fishing program in the living room.

In the kitchen, two serious faces were waiting—Mum at the table and Dad standing behind her.

'Hi! Have you been outside? It's so hot!' I said as Lucas breezed in, looking tanned, wearing a t-shirt with cut-off sleeves and Bermuda shorts. Finally, I caught the temperature of the room.

'What's up?' asked Lucas, running his hand through his blonde, Beckham-style curtains.

'Have you been waiting for me?' I asked.

Mum asked us to sit down in her patient and kind voice, which was her most terrifying tone. That was how you knew something horrendous was coming.

'Your father and I are getting a divorce,' she said softly, waiting a moment to let the information set in.

My mind reeled.

'Oh…' said Lucas softly. 'Why? I thought things were going well between you again?'

'It's perfectly amicable; we're still friends,' she continued. 'But Sarah and Bethany are going to come with me in September to a new house, and your father and Lucas are going to stay here.'

'How did this happen?' I managed, looking from one to the other.

'It was a mutual decision,' Mum said, but when I looked up at Dad, I could see that he had tears in his eyes, and I guessed that it was more mutual on Mum's side than his. 'It's for the best. We've agreed to share custody of Bethany. No courts or anything horrible like that.'

I glanced up at Dad again, who was looking down at his shoes, his bottom lip quivering as I'd never seen before. I didn't know what to feel. On the one hand, I felt so sorry for my dad. On the other hand, I felt so proud of my mum for finally standing up for herself and not letting him treat her the way that he had—although I wasn't sure why she had come to that decision now, after all this time since Dad's affair.

'Okay. But why now?' I voiced my thoughts aloud. I tried to keep the emotion out of my voice, but it was difficult, and it came out louder than I intended.

Mum sighed. 'It's complicated. We tried. Sometimes things just don't work out,' she said, and Dad nodded solemnly without looking up.

'Okay.' I nodded, not knowing what else there was to say. 'I'm really sorry,' I offered sadly, and Mum reached out and took my hand across the table.

'We haven't told Bethany yet, so we'd appreciate it if you didn't say anything,' requested Dad meekly.

'When are you leaving?' Lucas asked Mum solemnly.

'The last week of September—just before the unis reopen,' said Mum, glancing sideways at me. And as she said it, I realised that she hadn't wanted me to move in with her at all. I was supposed to be going to university.

Mum had timed her move because she wanted to make a fresh start without me.

28

Unfinished Business

THAT WEEK, TOM THREW AN EARLY GOODBYE BARBECUE for him and Johnnie in his back garden. Johnnie was going away on holiday for two weeks before Freshers' week at the University of Leeds—the same university where I'd deferred my place until next year.

'So, are you gonna miss me, then?' winked Johnnie at Emma as he handed her a burnt sausage.

'Soooo much, Johnnie! I'm going to count the days 'til you're back!' fawned Emma theatrically, reaching out and grabbing his sleeve imploringly. 'Don't go. Don't go!' she ended her little spoof by fake breaking down into tears while Johnnie regarded her flatly.

'Yeah, alright.' He turned back to the barbecue and rescued another black sausage. 'That's the last of my sausages that you're going to see, then,' he grumbled, and with that, Dyer came over and pulled her away (still laughing) with a whiff of possessiveness and sat her between him and Nick on the other side of the garden.

Standing with Johnnie and Tom, I regarded the trio curiously. Nick was looking tall, blonde and tanned, and I couldn't help but notice that he'd been working out, his chest and arms cutting an appealing muscular shape under his t-shirt.

'How is it,' I whispered to Tom, frustratedly, as Nick chatted happily with Dyer, 'that Nick still won't speak to me, but he's bosom buddies with Dyer again?'

Tom let out a low grunt. 'Ugh. You got me,' he moaned, as though the subject had been the topic of much chagrin. 'Nick is convinced that Dyer didn't mean any harm. That he really did believe what he said, and the whole thing was a big misunderstanding.'

I scoffed, trying my best to avoid looking bitter as I studied them from a distance—but I failed miserably. I didn't know what upset me more, that Nick had started getting high again at Derrick's or his seemingly indestructible bromance with Dyer.

Johnnie leaned in conspiratorially. 'Nick told me Social Services have been around at Derrick and Tiffany's mum's place quite a bit lately,' he said, to which Tom nodded in agreement, saying he'd heard it too. 'Derrick had to stop dealing and smoking drugs there,' Johnnie continued. 'They were going to put Tiffany into care if he didn't. So, his mum chucked him out.'

'About bloody time,' I moaned, happy to hear Tiffany would finally be protected from her family but sounding more sour by the second.

Tom piped up suddenly. 'So that's why Dyer and Derrick got a flat together?' he asked, as though a few things suddenly made sense.

'Yep. Derrick was piiiissed,' continued Johnnie, putting a few raw hamburgers onto the barbecue and then eating a very non-kosher pork sausage. 'He said whoever it was that called Social Services on his mum needs to watch their back.'

Tom and I exchanged worried glances. Derrick knew it was our group that was responsible, somehow. We just had to hope he would never find out it was Emma's mum, Emma, and me who had actually reported them.

A little later, as the sun started to dip and the light became warm and golden, Andy came home from work. After running upstairs to get changed, he swaggered out across the lawn to join us. He was sporting a backwards baseball cap, black aviator sunglasses, a black

Top Gun t-shirt and a long, baggy pair of khaki shorts that came to just below his knees.

'Hello, hello,' he greeted us with an understated smile and a wave, carrying a Corona with a lime wedge in the bottleneck. Everyone at the party turned and greeted him with reverence, and my pulse quickened as I watched his approach.

'What's this I smell?' he exclaimed, comfortably holding the floor and eyeing up the hamburgers on the grill. I felt my breath catch as he stopped next to me, and embarrassingly, Tom noticed it, too, giving me a knowing glance that left me feeling completely exposed.

'Miss Page.' Andy turned to me and nodded before looking at the grill ravenously. 'Don't mind if I do!' he smiled at Johnnie and helped himself to a burger, slathering it in ketchup before turning back to me. Johnnie and Tom turned to talk amongst themselves.

'How's it going, Miss Page?' he asked directly as he took a bite from his burger.

'Hi Andy,' I smiled, the familiar giddiness fluttering back into place.

'Are you ready to set off for university next week?' he asked, raising an eyebrow, and I felt incredulous that Tom hadn't mentioned I was taking a gap year already.

'Oh, no. I deferred my place for a year,' I said, and Andy thoughtfully chewed his burger.

'Interesting, Miss Page,' he said at last, a hint of a smile touching his lips. 'Very interesting. And what are you planning to do with your gap year, dare I ask?' he asked, lowering his voice slightly.

'Um. Most of it will be spent around here, I suppose,' I coughed, a lump of hot dog bread getting stuck in my throat.

Not wanting our conversation to end, I heard words start flowing from my lips as if from nowhere, as though I had no filter. 'We're taking my play—you know, the one I just did in London, that was *Time Out Critic's Choice?*'

Wait, did I tell him we were Time Out Critic's Choice already?

God, I sound like an arse.

'We're taking it to the Edinburgh Festival next year. Plus, Emma's here,'*...and you're here...*

Andy was studying my face intently as I spoke, looking from my eyes to my lips and my hair with his subtle, knowing smile. All I wanted to do was kiss him. Then, bite his bottom lip.

But I didn't.

'Yeah. So. Thought I'd stick around for a bit. You're not getting rid of me *that* easily!' I came to the end of my monologue and nodded animatedly, feeling hot.

Andy blinked. 'Well, Miss Page. I look forward to it,' he imparted, and at that, he pulled away from me and joined the rest of the party.

Fluffing my hair casually, I turned back to Tom and Johnnie, who were watching me with an amused look, and I saw that Nick had turned around and was watching me, too, from across the garden.

'Smooth. Real smooth, *Miss Page,*' mocked Tom, but I dared not react like I knew what he was talking about. The chemistry between his brother and me was never acknowledged, and Tom seemed to get a bit crabby when we flirted.

I looked back over at Nick, who was still watching me, and wondered if I had really been so conspicuous that I merited such a stare. Moments later, he turned away and ignored me.

My phone beeped in my bag. A message.

From Andy!

'What are you doing tomorrow?' it read.

My mouth dropped.

Is Andy asking me out?

I glanced over at him on the other side of the garden, where he was chatting with Jamie-from-The-Green.

'Are you listening?' asked Johnnie, who had been showing me how to keep the chicken legs from burning so he could take a break from barbecuing.

'Sorry, yes,' I said, trying to focus on how he was keeping them away from any flames, but getting completely distracted.

Crap! I thought. *I said I'd go to the pub with everyone tomorrow.* I didn't want to be one of those girls who cancel on their friends for a man. I chewed the phone aerial thoughtfully, considering what to write.

'We're going to The Bridge in New Barnet,' I wrote back. 'You should come.'

Johnnie shoved his barbecue tongs at me, and I reluctantly put my phone back in my pocket.

'Sorry,' I apologised and turned over a sizzling burger, the fat dripping down onto the coals with a satisfying hiss.

Moments later, another message arrived, and I put the tongs down apologetically and pulled out my phone to read it.

'Text me when you're done, Miss Page. I'll walk you to the bus stop.' My heart started beating a million times a minute as I imagined a secret rendezvous with Andy.

'Who is it?' asked Tom, picking up the tongs and regarding me suspiciously.

'Is it Derrick?' asked Johnnie, giggling. 'Or Nick, is it Nick?' he teased, and Tom laughed.

'Just a friend,' I smiled with a knowing air of mystery. 'Show me how to turn the kebabs again?' I feigned innocence, knowing exactly how to handle the kebabs (a moron could have done it, for goodness' sake).

'Fine,' Johnnie tutted, returning his focus to the barbecue, and I shot Tom a mischievous smile.

***

At the pub the following night, I felt a thrill of excitement as I slipped away early, telling everyone I needed to get home. Andy was waiting in the shadows across the street.

'Hello, Mr East,' I said coquettishly as I approached him, my legs feeling shaky with anticipation.

'Well, hello, Miss Page,' he smiled down at me, and we eagerly pressed our bodies against one another in a tight embrace. Andy barely hugged anyone, and in all the time I'd known him, I'd only been given a few, so each one was like a little gift to savour. But this time, he lingered, and the rest of the world stood still.

Andy pulled away and confidently led me in the direction of my bus stop, and I followed, eager but nervous.

Wait. Is he just taking me to the bus stop?

My heart sank as I imagined myself sitting on the next bus home, tragically mistaken about why he had messaged me.

But as we approached a triangular patch of grass surrounded by houses, with a ring of trees in the middle, Andy reached out a hand to stop me.

'You seem tense, Miss Page. Why don't you sit on the grass, and I'll give you a massage?

My stomach flipped.

'Okay,' I smiled, feeling so nervous that words escaped me.

Sitting down, the evening grass felt cool beneath me, and the trees sheltered us from the view of the houses.

As he positioned himself behind me, I felt a deep thrill that he was finally going to touch me. I'd thought about this moment for so long. As I felt his hands gliding down my back, I could sense how much he wanted me.

His fingers traced the curve of my neck, and as I sank into the feeling, I could feel his warm breath on my ear. Then his lips grazed my cheek, and as a growing ache inside insisted that I kiss him, he gently guided my chin around.

Slowly, lightly, his lips moved over mine, teased me, and finally kissed me.

Soft. Tender. It left all other kisses in the dust. Even Nick's.

I put my hands on his solid shoulders and felt the mass of him beneath his shirt, desire taking hold of me as I kissed him more passionately. Feeling his warmth and smelling his skin, I stopped for a moment, opened my eyes and saw that he was looking back at me.

We stared deeply into each other's eyes, kissed again, and then after some time, he simply got up, held out his hand to me and pulled me to my feet.

We walked in silence to the bus stop, then he kissed me again as I got on my bus and disappeared back over the hill.

***

A few nights later, Tom was packing for university and Emma and I went over to watch a film. With hopes of seeing Andy adding an extra spring to my step, I was disappointed when I saw he wasn't there; he was at work.

I moped around the living room with his Disney mug, wondering whether I should text him.

Finally, Andy came home at around midnight and greeted everyone from the living room doorway. He nodded at me, added a secret smile that sent my heart fluttering, then disappeared into the kitchen. Eager for his return, I waited for what seemed like an eternity, but when he emerged, instead of coming to join us, he went straight up to his bedroom.

I felt desperately disappointed. The night we'd kissed, he had messaged me to check I got home okay, but since then… radio silence.

Then, just as Emma and I were leaving, he slunk down the stairs and blocked my exit, his lean, muscular form looming over me as Emma and Tom filtered outside.

'And where do you think you're going, Miss Page?' he asked, his voice stern and his gaze intense and steamy. My face dropped; my body surged to attention. He laughed, pleased at his intimidating demeanour, and I hit him with relief as I realised he was playing with me.

'Shhhh!' he said, holding his hands up to block my blow and hiding behind the front door so that Emma and Tom—who were still lingering over goodbyes in the street—wouldn't see. 'Would you like to watch some TV with me?' he whispered, still laughing, and I nodded. 'Okay, hide in the front room and wait for my brother to go to bed, then meet me in the living room,' he instructed, and I nodded again, feeling a strange thrill from all the secrecy.

'Okay, I'll just text Emma so she doesn't wait for me,' I conspired.

'Good idea, I'll handle Tom,' plotted Andy, and I snuck inside the front room and closed the door as he headed back to the living room.

Watching Emma and Tom chatting in the street through the net curtains felt exhilarating. Normally, the room was used exclusively by Tom and Andy's mother, and we weren't allowed in there. When Emma finally checked her phone, she looked up at the window blindly with a conspiratorial smile and said her goodbyes to Tom.

When Tom returned to the lounge, he sounded surprised to find me gone already, and I felt sure that the game was up. My heart was pounding as I stood mere inches away from him on the other side of the wall.

'She went out the back,' explained Andy casually.

Goodness, Andy's quite a good liar, I noted.

'Really?' asked Tom incredulously. 'Why?'

'She thinks it's quicker. Plus, she didn't want to get bogged down in long goodbyes with Emma. You know how much she can blab.'

I bit my lip to stop myself from sniggering, but to my horror, Tom agreed.

'Oh yeah. She does go on a bit. She kept me out there for ten minutes!'

I held my breath and waited to see if he had bought it.

He had.

When he'd finally gone upstairs to bed, I abandoned my hiding place and crept towards the living room, the secrecy making my skin tingle and heightening all of my senses.

Andy was sitting motionless on the sofa, watching me carefully, his presence filling the room entirely as I entered.

I was about to sit down next to him, but for some reason, I became nervous and sat on the floor next to his legs. Staring straight ahead without looking at him, Andy didn't say anything, although I could feel that he was puzzled by why I was down there.

Neither of us reached for the television remote.

We sat in silence for a few moments before Andy asked me if I was alright.

'You didn't call me,' I uttered without looking at him.

'Oh, yeah. I meant to,' he started to explain, but trailed off. 'I thought about you,' he offered, and I felt a warmth within me ignite a smile that couldn't be squashed. 'Why are you down there instead of up here?' he asked gently.

'Just a bit tense, I suppose,' I said softly, pointing to a pain in my neck.

On cue, Andy slowly manoeuvred himself behind me, and his skilled hands got to work. It felt so good, I let out a small moan, spurring him on to explore further down my back. Then he slid his large frame off the sofa onto the floor, so that I was sitting between his legs, engulfed.

Something wild within me snapped, like I was finally unleashed.

God, I wanted him. I wanted him so badly.

I turned and kissed him passionately. Taking his hands in mine, I pushed him back against the sofa, kissing him harder and gently biting his lip. Smiling, Andy let me pin him down and responded to my passion in kind, edging forward so that he was fully on his back, with me on top.

I pulled back for a moment, we looked at each other, and then I hid my face in his shoulder, biting the fabric of his t-shirt in frustration, and then gently kissed his neck.

As much as I wanted him, I deeply feared the potential heartbreak of sleeping with someone only to be cast aside. Over the past two years, I'd gotten to know quite a lot about Andy, about how he was scared of commitment, scared that a woman he cared about would get to know him too well, better even than he knew himself.

If I slept with him and he wasn't interested in me afterwards, it would devastate me. But not only that, it would be the end of me hanging out at that house. It would probably be the end of Emma hanging out there, too, and it could potentially break apart the entire group.

If anything serious was going to happen between us, I needed the commitment of a relationship first. Even though it was the '90s and casual sex was everywhere, I believed that each person should do what was right for them, and I didn't feel comfortable with anything less.

'I only want to kiss… I'm sorry,' I said, hiding my face, scared that I might have teased him too much and fearing that he'd think me terribly old-fashioned.

'It's okay,' he said. 'I like kissing. I like kissing *you*.'

He pulled me back towards him so that I was lying completely on top of him and then flipped me over onto my back.

'My turn,' he grinned, and we spent the rest of the night kissing and wrestling, exploring a world of passion and play without taking any of our clothes off.

29
Strong Enough

September 2000

FEELING A BIT LIKE A STUBBORN WART that couldn't be removed, when September rolled around, Mum and Bethany moved into their new home and I tagged along with them. My bedroom was the box room that was meant to have been Mum's home office, and I could sense her disappointment that she had to give it up for me. That same day, Lucas went back to university, and Dad was left alone to rattle around in the empty family home. I couldn't help but wonder if he was going to be okay.

The day after the move, after breakfast, I went upstairs and found Mum crying on the floor next to her bed. Unsure about whether she would want me to comfort her or not, I froze. I wasn't exactly her favourite person, so I just stood in the doorway looking awkward.

Finally, I found my tongue.

'Are you okay, Mum?' I mumbled quietly.

Then, without saying a word, she got up and quietly closed the door. Sadness and rejection cut me like a blade dipped in vinegar. Then, like a ray of hope, Bethany came bounding out of her room full of excitement.

'Sarah! Sarah! Stephen Cherry wrote me a letter,' she beamed, grabbing hold of my sleeve and pulling me into her room. 'He's the most popular boy in school! Look!'

As Bethany showed me her letter—always the same bright, sunny attitude—I thought about all the changes in our family that she'd lived through: our brother leaving for university when she was eight, Dad leaving when she was nine. Now our parents were splitting up, and next year, I'd be gone too. I worried about how she was going to cope with it all as our mum recovered from her own immense loss.

But to my surprise, while our dad seemed to wither away, Mum positively blossomed. Within a few days, the first female friend I'd seen in years appeared. I'd just gotten home from working at the Chinese restaurant when Mum and Kimberley—Kim—a fellow teacher at her school, walked in carrying bagfuls of curtains, cushions, candles, and a chilled bottle of white wine.

'Hi, Sarah,' beamed Mum cheerfully. 'This is Kim; she's come over for dinner and to help me liven the place up a bit,' she explained. I jumped up from the sofa enthusiastically to greet them, excited to meet Mum's new friend. 'How was your day at work?' Mum asked.

'It was good, thanks,' I said, following the two women into the kitchen. 'I got a really big tip today, and they let me keep it. Usually, it goes straight into the till.'

Mum proceeded to open the bottle of wine and poured us three glasses just as Bethany came running in. 'Mum! Can I have some?' she pleaded, making a beeline straight for the forbidden wine.

'You can have a sip and then a juice,' conceded Mum. Then we three adults clinked glasses, pronounced 'Cheers!' and Bethany took a big sip of wine from Mum's glass, screwing up her nose with immediate regret.

That night, after dinner, Kim, Mum, Bethany and I had a surprisingly wonderful evening. Mum and Kim arranged the new cushions on the sofa, and Bethany and I played around with where the new candles should go. Then, Mum lit them ceremoniously and put on her new *Best of '90s* CD, forwarding it straight to Cher's hit *Strong Enough*, and we started singing and dancing with gusto.

I watched proudly as Mum added extra 'oomph' to some of the more poignant lines, as though singing them straight from the heart. I felt so sorry for my dad, but the fact that she had refused to stay and be humiliated by his lack of respect for her was inspirational for me, and it meant I didn't have to suffer the same fate if I didn't want to. She was not only back on her feet again, but she was living her new life with relish.

As Mum and I leaned in and danced together, I felt closer to her than I had in years, and a wave of optimism washed over me as I realised everything was going to be alright. That night, as Mum and Kim were putting up curtain poles with Mum's new drill and Bethany and I were making up a salsa dance to a new Ricki Martin song, my phone beeped. It was a text message from Andy.

'Everything okay, Miss Page?' I smiled at my phone screen. Things were looking up all around.

30

Don't Count Your Chickens

FROM THAT NIGHT ON, ANDY AND I USED TO SNEAK OFF to meet in secret without any of our friends knowing, which made everything feel naughty and forbidden. One evening, he walked me to the bus stop and took a detour so we could make out all night on top of a row of garages beside the train tracks, the ground trembling faintly beneath us as trains thundered past.

Another afternoon, we met behind a railway bridge and ended up climbing the fire escape of some flats, desperate for somewhere more private. At the top, we hopped a fence and ran across an abandoned penthouse floor until he caught me and pulled me down on top of him in our own secret hideout.

Once, we met by the church on his road, where he led me down into the basement through an unlocked door. Inside, I tied him to a chair in the boiler room and interrogated him like a captive Russian spy, teasing him until he laughed and begged for mercy. When we were apart, we'd meet online late at night on MSN Messenger, typing out the things we didn't dare say to each other in person.

Still, we never had sex, and the tension between us was palpable. But I wanted a relationship and knew Andy didn't, so I obsessed over the conversation we'd had about girlfriends when playing Truth or Dare. I took his admission to mean that if I slept with him, he'd either run—or, just as bad—keep me as his dirty little secret forever, rather than proudly be in a relationship with me.

I couldn't bring myself to do it. I didn't want to be Andy's secret. I wanted us to be together openly, proudly. The embodiment of young love in all its glory.

To keep myself in check, I resorted to the oldest trick in the book: I never shaved my legs when I saw him, and I kept my jeans on, as if they were superglued to my skin. And yet, despite my Victorian-era resolve, I thought about Andy every day; when I fell asleep, when I woke up; imagining him holding me, stroking my hair, choosing me.

I waited for Andy to tell me he wanted a relationship, and for a moment, it seemed as though he might. One afternoon, we were sitting cross-legged on the floor of his bedroom, he in nothing but his boxer shorts, me perched on top of him, my legs around his waist with my jeans stubbornly still on.

He looked at me with such happiness as I wrapped my arms around his neck and kissed his lips tenderly, then he asked softly what we were doing—whether we were 'going out'—which was London speak for being in a relationship.

I could have said yes.

It would have been so easy.

But I was terrified if I made things too easy, he'd go off me. So, I said we were *preparing to go out* because it sounded like what he wanted to hear, and because I wanted more than anything in the world to make him happy.

It seemed to work, because he smiled at me then and kissed me with what looked like love in his eyes, and my heart soared as high as it could go.

***

Later that afternoon, I left Andy's house on a wave of bliss, certain that we were headed for the relationship that I craved, just as Emma and Dyer pulled up on his motorbike outside. Dyer stared at me walking up the driveway as he dismounted.

'Oh. Hello, *Trouble*. What are *you* doing here?' he asked, intrigued by what I had been doing there without Tom being home.

Like a fool, riding on a cloud of happiness, I came clean about my budding romance with Andy. It turned out Emma had been keeping my secret loyally, and Dyer had no idea.

'Ahh, Page, you're so sweet,' he cooed, the look of laughing at an unspoken joke radiating from him like a beacon of darkness as he took off his helmet. He gave me a playful prod to the stomach. 'Do you want to get married and have his babies?' he joked.

'Of course, she doesn't,' tutted Emma, but still I rose to the bait.

'Oh yeah, Dyer,' I rolled my eyes, unable to stop myself getting wound up. 'About a million of them!'

'I'm really happy for you, Page.' He looked thoughtful and then smiled innocently. 'You know, we haven't seen you much lately. We're going to buy some weed in a bit, but later, we're going to a house party at Nick's—his parents are away. You should come. You can tell us all about you and Andy.'

I thought about it and wasn't sure. I didn't smoke cigarettes, let alone weed, and it had been ages since I'd seen Nick. As far as I knew, he was still angry at me for the pizza leaflet prank.

I shook my head sceptically. 'I really don't think he'd want me there,' I concluded.

'What!? Don't be silly, Page; he was just saying the other day that it would be nice to see you again,' smiled Dyer.

'Really?' I felt dubious but hoped that it was true, as it would mean that I'd been forgiven and we could be friends again. It would certainly make group dynamics a whole lot easier.

'You should come!' Emma piped up and elbowed me in the ribs. 'It's about time you two made up. Come on, I literally haven't seen you properly for about two weeks. Come out!'

'Well, if you're sure it won't be an issue,' I smiled, never able to resist a party with my bestie. 'But I've got to go home first—Dad's coming over—I'll call you later, Emma.'

'Excellent,' Dyer smiled, and the couple got back on his motorbike and sped off up the road to buy weed.

Later, I hopped off the bus in Friern Barnet to meet Dyer, who'd come to get me and take me to Nick's house party. I wasn't particularly in a party spirit, having seen Dad and noticing how much weight he'd piled on—his doctor prescribing a cocktail of blood pressure tablets.

The last person I wanted to see was Dyer. But there he was, leaning against his motorbike on the corner by a red phone box: the only man in Britain who could make a leather biker jacket look completely unappealing.

Dyer had already dropped Emma at the party, and she was waiting for us with drinks. We were just about to leave when he remembered something he'd forgotten.

'Oh, that's right. I meant to invite Andy,' he exclaimed with a glint in his eye, and suddenly I felt nervous. 'You don't mind if I invite him, do you? It would be great to see you together as a couple.'

'No, not at all, I'd love it if Andy came,' I agreed, hoping more than anything that he would.

Dyer pulled out his mobile and paused. 'Hmmmm… I don't have any credit. Just a minute, I'll call him from the payphone.'

He walked into the phone box and closed the door behind him. As he punched Andy's number into the keypad, he turned and smiled at me through the glass.

Anxiety gripped the pit of my stomach.

I couldn't hear any of their conversation, but when Dyer emerged from the phone box, he could barely contain his grin.

'He says he can't come but to have fun, *Miss Page,*' he gleamed.

'Okay. Well, I suppose I'll see him later, then.' I said, disappointed.

I pulled on Emma's helmet and climbed onto the back of Dyer's bike.

'Hold on tight. We don't want you falling off, do we?' Dyer giggled, and then we were away, whizzing through the traffic in the summer night air.

When we arrived at the party, Emma was sitting in the hazy living room in a circle of people from The Green, and Nick was passing a large bong around.

So much for a drug-free lifestyle, I thought as Nick looked up, surprised and seemingly annoyed to see me.

He got up discreetly from the circle and walked over to us. 'What's she doing here?' he asked Dyer in a hushed tone, pointing at me.

'I told her she should come,' said Dyer candidly, as Emma came over to join us. 'Don't you think it's time that you two kissed and made up?' he giggled. Then, turning to Nick, he added reasonably: 'If you're mates with *me* again, you should at least be mates with *her* again.'

At this, Nick turned to me, sceptically, as Emma pitched in.

'It's water under the bridge now, guys, if you ask me,' she said with a shrug. 'You both did some stupid things, now it's time to move on.'

I felt terribly awkward, suddenly aware that I might not be welcome after all, but to my relief, Nick sighed and gestured for us to join the circle.

'Put your drinks in the fridge and come join us,' he said, already sitting back down and picking up the bong. Then, he looked at me directly as he inhaled deeply on the pipe, the water bubbling as smoke filled the chamber.

I poured myself a vodka and cranberry, worrying briefly about how I'd refuse the bong when it came my way, then sat beside Emma and Dyer. To my relief, not everyone was smoking and it was a relatively even split. Soon, I was chatting to a girl called Louise, who felt the same way about smoking as I did.

'It just never really appealed, ya know?' she said animatedly, taking a big swig from a glass of vodka and Red Bull.

Overhearing our conversation, Dyer leaned in, wearing his slow, strange smile. 'But how can you comment if you don't even know what you're talking about,' he quipped. Neither of you has even tried it. Not once.'

I watched, amazed, as Emma picked up the bong and lit it with easy confidence. Clearly, she'd been practising.

'I don't need to try it,' Louise said, and I nodded my agreement, not able to peel my eyes away from Emma. 'Anyway, it's got tobacco in it…' she added.

'There is no tobacco in this,' assured Dyer, 'it's just the plant.' He looked across at Louise and sensed a moment's hesitation. 'Clean,' he continued. 'It's also not hot, because of the water, which purifies it.'

Just then, Emma finished with the bong and offered it up to Louise, who regarded it for a moment. And then took it.

'Good on ya, girl!' Dyer celebrated, and Emma, realising it was Louise's first time, showed her how to do it.

Inhaling deeply, Louise coughed—explosively—and a few people turned to smile and watch, while Dyer patted her on the back encouragingly.

'Keep it down, try and keep it down,' he instructed. 'Sorry, I should have warned you.'

Spluttering, Louise offered the bong to me, but I shook my head, unconvinced.

'No, I don't want it; it looks really strong,' I decided. 'Are you okay?' I rubbed Louise's back as she coughed again, and she nodded, seemingly pleased with herself.

Dyer looked at me. 'Well, you know, if you just want to try a little puff, I'm sure Nick would give you a blowback,' he smirked.

Intrigued and already off balance, I took the bait. 'What's a blowback?' I asked, and suddenly, I had all of Dyer's attention.

'It's when someone blows smoke into your mouth. It's much gentler. It's not like smoking at all,' he gestured over at Nick, who was rolling a joint in his lap. 'Hey, Nick, will you give Sarah a blowback?'

Pleasantly surprised, Nick looked up at me and smiled. 'Yeah, sure, give me a minute, I'm almost done.'

Startled, I began to object, but Dyer was quick to mollify me. 'Honestly, it's more like passive smoking than anything,' he said, looking at Louise, who was starting to giggle.

'You look so worried,' she said, pointing at me before bursting into hysterics, much to Emma and Jamie-from-The-Green's amusement.

Emma nodded. 'You'll be fine, hon. And Nick will just give you a little puff,' she reassured me.

Feeling strong-armed but not wanting to disappoint Nick or jeopardise his tentative forgiveness, I stopped protesting and plastered a big smile on my face.

Then, Nick came over cheerfully and sat cross-legged in front of me, his knees pressing against mine. He lit the spliff and inhaled deeply a few times. I watched him nervously and wondered if it was too late to back out.

'You ready, Sarah?' he asked, leaning closer. 'Okay, come here. I'm going to exhale, and you're going to inhale all the smoke,' he said, taking a long drag.

I parted my lips and inhaled as Nick blew a stream of thick, fragrant smoke into my mouth.

'Suck, Sarah! Suck!' cheered on Dyer loudly as I inhaled. 'Suck it all up!' he continued before Emma prodded him, and he fell back onto his elbow in silent laughter.

'Now, hold it,' instructed Nick, looking into my eyes, 'try not to cough, and let it out slowly.'

Struggling not to cough, I exhaled gently and, after a few moments, felt myself start to giggle, like Louise. It wasn't so bad, after all.

That was when Dyer pulled his phone out of his pocket, and, with a look of exaggerated surprise, turned it round to show us.

'Oh crap! I've pocket-dialled Andy by mistake!' he giggled as I saw that the call had been ongoing for over ten minutes. Nervously, I wondered how Andy might interpret what he'd just heard.

'Andy!' called Nick happily, reaching out to take the phone, but Dyer grinned at me and put it to his own ear instead.

'Heya, mate!' he said and then feigned a terrible shock. 'Well, that's rude!' he mocked, making deliberate eye contact with me, 'you speak to your mother like that?' Dyer's eyes sparkled, and then he stuck his bottom lip out in mock sadness. 'Oh. He hung up.'

'That's weird,' said Nick, oblivious to Dyer's little game.

'I thought you'd run out of credit?' I frowned, not feeling very in the mood for merriment anymore.

'Whoopsie! Looks like I did have some, after all,' giggled Dyer gleefully, getting up to refresh his drink from the fridge.

Just then, his phone beeped, and checking it, he giggled some more.

'It's from Andy, he relayed gleefully. He says: "F* you, man." Why the hell is he angry with me?' he asked, looking like the cat who got the cream.

Hazily, Dyer's intentions came into focus, and I realised he'd tried to sabotage mine and Andy's budding relationship. Panicking, I tried to call Andy, but there was no answer.

No longer in the mood to party, I called a cab to go home.

'Are you sure Dyer can't drop you back?' asked Emma, with strained patience, as I waited outside for my taxi to arrive.

'No, Em, he's been drinking. Plus…' I steeled myself. 'I'm really pissed off about the Andy stuff, actually. You realise he planned all of that, don't you?'

There. I said it.

'Oh come on. Don't be so sensitive. Why would he plan something like that? I'm sure he didn't mean to cause trouble, Sarah,' Emma soothed.

And as she made her usual excuses, I felt my jaw clench, and my hands ball up into tight little fists by my sides. I was getting pretty tired of her complete inability to see the truth.

Emma rubbed my arm and then turned to go back inside. 'Call me when you get in, okay?' she smiled.

I gritted my teeth—my mind reeling with a thousand things I'd like to say—and just nodded.

***

When I got home, fists still bunched in tight little balls, I walked into the living room, where Mum and Kim were sitting chatting. Bethany was staying over at Dad's.

'Hi, Sarah. What's wrong?' asked Mum, immediately sensing that I was upset. Despite my problems, a spark of happiness ignited within me. The fact that she sensed how I was feeling felt really special.

'It's this guy I know, called Andy,' I started to open up to Mum for the first time since I was little. 'I think I might have messed things up between us. He's not answering my calls…'

'Oh. Well, he sounds like a bit of a wally,' piped up Mum, capturing the situation perfectly with her Mum-speak.

'That's the thing. He's *not*. He's really amazing, and he's always looked out for me,' I sniffed, feeling hopeless and wondering where it had all gone wrong. 'I think maybe he got jealous and scared or something.'

Mum beckoned me over to the couch and gave me a deep, warm hug. She smelled just like I remembered—comforting like a woolly blanket, but with *Coco Chanel* perfume and lipstick mixed in.

'Not everything works out the way we deserve it to,' she said, pulling back from our hug after a long moment and holding my hands in hers. Then she smiled and brushed a strand of hair away from my face with her thumb. 'Take your father and me. I cooked him every meal; I raised his three kids; I even helped him run his business. Then, after forgiving him for leaving me for a twenty-one-year-old, I found out he'd been having affairs for years.' Mum paused and looked at me blankly. Her emotions all used up. 'I didn't deserve that. Nobody would.'

I was shocked. *Affairs for years?* I stared at Mum open-mouthed and then at Kim, who nodded kindly.

'How did you find out?' I asked, struggling to digest what I'd just heard. If Dad had been having affairs for years, then I didn't know what to think.

'She rang up. The girl. And left an answer machine message for me listing all the women he'd had affairs with,' Mum explained matter-of-factly, as though she had grown tired of the whole experience of knowing my father.

Mum stopped and patted my hand. 'Look,' she said. 'Sometimes, you can do everything right, and people still treat you badly.'

I paused, letting the horrible lesson sink in.

Then Mum got up from the sofa. 'Come on,' she said and held out her hand for me to join her in the kitchen. Despite everything going on with Andy, I felt immensely proud of my mum. No man was going to treat me and Bethany like Dad had treated her and get away with it.

But as Mum fixed us drinks, and we went back to the living room to Kim, candles and a comforting music collection, I simply couldn't forget about Andy.

Surely, Andy wouldn't treat me badly. Andy's one of the good guys.

Later that night, after I'd crawled into bed, I pulled out my phone. But I *didn't* call Emma. She could get stuffed. Instead, I tried Andy again.

But he didn't answer.

Then, after a restless night with little sleep, I sent a message to find out what was happening.

'Hi, Andy, is everything ok? R u home? Can't w8t 2kiss u!'

31

Down on the Floor!

October 2000

ANDY NEVER REPLIED. A week later, with Tom, Johnnie and Lucas away at university, and a new rift between my dad and me, I felt miserable. I had tried and failed to work out whether Andy was one of the *good guys*. And despite her denial that Dyer was one of the *bad guys*, Emma became my only source of comfort.

One evening I was hanging out at her house, as she got ready to go out to Dyer and Derrick's new flat.

'They've got really cool housemates,' she cooed as I lay on her bed, flicking through the latest copy of *Glamour* magazine. 'And it's right opposite Victoria Wines, so it's great for Matthew's work.'

I snorted openly. 'Still doesn't mean it was a good decision to shack up with a violent drug dealer, though.' I scoffed, wondering how relationships could work out for someone as nasty as Dyer, but not for Andy and me.

Emma stopped and stared at me angrily. 'Sarah, you know how it is with blokes. One minute, they're fighting; the next, all's forgotten,' she frowned. 'If Jamie-from-The-Green's moved on, why can't you!?'

'Sorry.' I replied on autopilot—mostly just sorry for myself.

Emma softened and sat next to me on the bed, gently playing with a strand of my hair. 'You should come tonight. Nick is going to be there,' she said, her voice laden with suggestiveness. 'He asked Dyer if you were coming. It's true. I overheard him this time.'

I glanced up from the magazine and pictured talking to Nick for a moment, that familiar feeling of excitement returning to my stomach. Then my mind drifted back to Andy.

I couldn't do it.

I frowned up at her. 'You *do* realise that Dyer and Derrick are dealing out of their flat?' I retorted.

Emma tutted. 'Yeah, yeah! I'm not saying he's perfect. But loads of people smoke these days, Sarah. It's great that you don't—each to their own and all that—but you don't have to act like it's beneath you.' She paused and took my hand, imploringly. 'Come tonight. There's no point moping around feeling miserable.'

I sighed. 'Not until I know what's going on with Andy and me,' I moped, and finally Emma dropped it.

'Fine, be boring, then,' she spat. 'But *I'm* still going.'

As Emma rushed around fixing her hair, I flicked aimlessly through the magazine. I paused at an advert of Kate Moss posing in a pair of expensive sunglasses and then turned to the 'Agony Aunt' pages. Perhaps I'd find some wisdom in there.

Just then, my phone rang, and my heart leapt when I saw that it was Andy.

'Andy!' I answered, trying not to sound too much like a puppet on a string.

Emma stopped drying her hair and came and sat next to me on the bed.

'Miss Page,' came the somewhat tepid reply, and instantly my guts wrenched.

Is he calling to break things off with me?

'How's it going? It's been a while…' Andy noted casually.

'It has,' I agreed and then paused. 'Where have you been? I've been calling you all week.'

'Yeah. Sorry. About that,' he began, and as he started to speak, I could feel my throat tightening and the tears welling up in my eyes. 'I think it might be an idea if we kept things casual,' he suggested. 'Figure out what we want.'

'But I thought we were going to go out?' I objected lamely.

'Yeah, so did I,' Andy agreed nonchalantly. 'But maybe we should just cool it…' he paused. 'We can still meet up,' he assured me as Emma placed a steadying hand on my forearm. 'I just think you should have some fun. You're young. You've only had one boyfriend. You haven't even had sex yet,' he said gently.

'Oh, great, well, thank you very much,' I replied sarcastically. 'I'm so thrilled that we can still "meet up". That's very nice of you.'

Emma tutted in disgust.

'You know what I mean,' he sighed, sounding tired suddenly. 'Maybe you should just sleep with Nick, or something.'

I couldn't believe what I was hearing.

'I don't want to sleep with Nick,' I said decisively, exchanging a look with Emma, her eyebrows raised in shock. 'And I don't want to keep things casual. I thought we were heading somewhere…' I felt myself almost give in to the mix of frustration and sadness that threatened to overcome me. All I wanted was Andy, and yet again, he didn't want me back.

'Look, I'll call you another time. Soon. We can meet up. Just—do me a favour,' Andy paused, and his voice took on a serious quality. 'Stay away from Dyer. I'm serious. And keep Emma away from him, too. One of these days, he's going to land himself in some serious trouble.'

'What do you think I've been trying to do, Andy?' I asked, imploringly, glancing at Emma and hoping she hadn't heard what Andy had said. 'And what gives you the right to tell me who I should or should not be hanging out with, when you clearly couldn't care less!?' My voice cracked with emotion as I became overwhelmed by the unfairness of the whole situation.

'Just promise me that you'll do as I ask,' he implored. And I paused, thinking how uncharacteristically unlike Andy he sounded.

'Take care, Sarah.'

Before I could reply, he was gone.

As the phone went dead, I stood motionless and dumbfounded.

Emma spoke first. 'That's bull crap,' she asserted. 'I can't believe what an arsehole he's being. He's just jealous because he thinks you like Nick. Sarah, are you okay?'

I nodded, numb.

I knew she was right, but I couldn't get my head around it.

Wasn't Andy one of the good guys?

Then anger slowly took over from the shock. 'He doesn't care,' I said, my thoughts clearer than they'd ever been with regard to Andy. 'He simply doesn't care. Nobody tells you to sleep with someone else if they care about you, whether they're jealous or not,' I reasoned angrily, wondering why it had taken me so long to figure it out. 'All he wants is to meet up in secret, and he thinks that one day I might sleep with him.'

It's like I'm his dirty little secret or something.

'Well,' I said abruptly, closing the door and pulling up the drawbridge. 'Screw him. If he thinks I'm going to meet up with him 'for fun', he's got another thing coming.' I wiped my eyes and looked at Emma decisively. 'Let's go to this sodding party.'

'That's the spirit!' Emma whooped.

Soon, we were in her car on the way to Dyer and Derrick's flat, dressed up to the nines with bottles of booze in my lap.

Emma glanced at me with concern as I took a gulp from a bottle of vodka in the passenger seat next to her. 'Just slow down on that bottle, okay?' she warned.

'Oh, shut up, spoil sport!' I laughed and took another gulp just to spite her. 'Why is it that everyone else can go crazy but not me?' I demanded, an edge to my voice that made Emma fall silent.

Before long, we pulled up outside an old Victorian house directly opposite Victoria Wines. In the window on the top floor, I could see Nick there already, sharing a joke with someone inside, but the sight of him didn't make me feel any better. I just felt hollow. Just as we were about to go in, Emma gave me a hug and pulled back to look at me.

'You know, we don't have to go in,' she said tentatively. 'We can go back home, if you like?'

'Ha! You've changed your tune!' I teased. 'Last one in's a rotten… king of the castle…' I slurred and banged my car door closed.

'Pffff!' Emma followed me into the building. 'That doesn't even make sense…'

'It does in my brain.'

'That's because you're mad…' laughed Emma.

One flight of stairs up, the front door to Dyer and Derrick's flat was wide open, and music was pounding loudly from a stereo. The place was packed, and yet my mind was elsewhere, lingering on the aftermath of my conversation with Andy. I glanced around, spotting familiar faces amidst the crowd.

Emma nudged me gently, her brow arched. 'You okay?' she asked, concern woven into her words.

I grinned. 'I'm more than okay, I'm grrrreatt!' I said, imitating Tony the Tiger. 'Let's get pissed!'

We navigated through the throng of guests until we found Dyer, who was dancing with a small group in the living room.

'Hey, baby, you took your time!' Dyer slithered his hands all over my best friend as he kissed her. 'Alright, Trouble?' he nodded at me dully, and I lifted my vodka bottle, smiling broadly.

'Fine, and dandy, thanks to you, *buddy*,' I replied sarcastically, and turned to the rest of the room. 'Who fancies a shot?'

Emma and Dyer exchanged glances.

'Er, yeah, go on then,' Dyer said, amused.

Dancing nearby, Derrick coughed suddenly, and Dyer jerked to attention as though remembering something important. He turned to me with a glint in his eye. 'Page, you remember Derrick, don't you?' he asked as Derrick came over to join us.

I must have missed it before, but that night, something about Derrick struck me as quite handsome.

What the hell. I thought. *I hate being me.*

'Of course!' I smiled. 'Fancy a shot?' I glanced at Emma, who shot back a look of horrified amusement.

Derrick studied me for a moment. 'Be rude not to,' he said, his scar deepening as he smiled. 'This way to the kitchen…'

In the kitchen, I lined up four shots.

'Bottoms up!' I shouted, and the four of us clinked our glasses and downed the harsh liquid in one.

Dyer smiled. 'I quite like this version of you, Page,' he said, and I smiled back.

'That's because you're such a *good* judge of character, Dyer,' I smirked, and looked sideways at Derrick, who didn't seem to grasp the fact that I'd just insulted him, and thankfully took it as a compliment.

Not long after, I was dancing with a bunch of people in the living room while Emma hovered nervously nearby. When Dyer grabbed my hands and spun me around, I let him. When Derrick joined in, pulling me in closer towards him, his hands all over my waist, I didn't stop him either.

At some point, I was standing on a chair, drink in hand, with Derrick holding my other hand, shouting the words to a song I barely knew, when Nick approached.

'Jesus! Someone's letting their hair down tonight,' he said, grinning up at me.

'Nick!' I exclaimed, dropping Derrick's hand and almost falling off the chair as I grabbed Nick around the shoulders.

'Whoa! Easy Tiger!' he joked, my drink already splashed down his shirt. 'Why don't you come down here and dance?' he suggested, exchanging an amused look with Emma.

'Fiiiiine—so boring!' I stepped down from my chair and into Nick's space, looking up at his chin from below. 'Ooh, I can see your nose hair from down here…'

Nick laughed and covered his nose. 'You're crazy, tonight!'

Put out, Derrick turned to size up Nick, gave him a reluctant nod, and resignedly stepped back, leaving us to chat for a bit. Or at least… Nick wanted to chat.

I… wanted to dance.

Wrapping my arms around Nick's neck, he reluctantly let me wind up on him for a moment before blushing and looking away.

'Okay, okay, calm down. You're like the Energiser Bunny tonight,' he said. 'How much have you had to drink?'

'Nowhere near enough!' I cracked up. 'Who wants a shot?' I asked, and Derrick and Dyer raised their glasses celebratorily.

'Don't you think you've had enough already?' he scolded, lightly.

I scowled. 'God! You smoke weed every day, and I'm the bad one?' I wobbled on my feet, and Derrick reached out gently to catch me. 'Everyone else always has fun, so why shouldn't I, for once?' I slurred, turning to smile at Derrick.

The two men exchanged a look, then Derrick shrugged and made a move towards the kitchen.

'Looks like the lady's made her choice, mate,' he gleamed, and I followed close behind him, flashing an insolent grin at a deadpan Nick as I went.

'Keep an eye on her, will you?' I overheard Nick say to Emma as we slipped away.

But before I made it to the kitchen, the room tilted.

The laughter grew too loud, the lights too bright, and my stomach rolled unpleasantly. I pushed through the crowd, giggling as I went, and staggered down the narrow hallway towards the bathroom.

I barely made it in time.

I dropped to my knees and retched violently into the toilet, my whole body folding in on itself. My hair fell forward into the bowl, and as I tried to fish it out, I was dimly aware of the door closing behind me.

'Jesus,' Derrick's voice drawled behind me. 'You alright there?'

I froze.

'Mmmmmm…' I tried to answer, but another wave of nausea hit, and I gagged again, clutching the rim of the toilet. The room felt like it was spinning, and I could hear him closer now, blocking the exit as the door clicked shut.

'Bit of a state,' he chuckled. 'Guess you finally let go, eh? Not such a good girl, after all, huh?'

I wiped my mouth with the back of my hand and tried to stand, but my legs wobbled uselessly beneath me.

Derrick took a step closer, not taking his eyes off me.

'Don't,' I managed weakly, not even sure what I was asking him not to do.

He leaned in, lowering his voice. 'Relax. Thought you might want some company.'

There was a metallic sound as Derrick undid his belt buckle and came up close behind me. Then his fingertips were in my hair, as though he were helping me hold my hair back.

'Wait…' I said, desperately.

But Derrick's hands were already sliding down my back. To my waist. And then they were on my hips.

Before I could say anything—before my brain could catch up with my body—there was a sudden thunderous bang somewhere in the flat.

Then shouting. Loud and sharp and unmistakable.

'Police! Stay where you are!'

The music cut dead. Screams rippled through the apartment. Heavy footsteps thundered down the hallway, and Derrick dove towards the door.

Then he was gone, leaving the toilet door wide open.

I stayed where I was, shaking now, my forehead pressed against the cool porcelain, trying not to be sick again—or cry—or both.

'Everybody down on the floor! Down on the floor! Don't move!' barked a female officer somewhere outside.

Moments later, the door creaked.

'Sarah?'

It was Nick.

I looked up at him, mascara streaked down my face, eyes bloodshot, clutching the toilet like it was the only solid thing left in the world.

'Hey,' he said quietly. 'Come on. Let's get you out of here.'

He held out his hand, and I took it without hesitation.

Emerging into the living room, Nick and I were the only two partygoers still standing, and I stared blankly at a number of police officers who barked at us to get down on the floor, which we did.

'We've got a search warrant for the address,' bellowed one officer, holding up a sheet of paper. 'Would the occupiers of this residence identify themselves!'

Dyer and Derrick got up and stepped forward along with their two other housemates. Then, confusion turned to shock as Dyer and Derrick were cuffed and led away, their faces twisted with disbelief and fury.

Outside, the street was flooded with blue lights and confusion. People were being herded out of the building two by two, pockets searched, bags tipped out onto the pavement. Dyer and Derrick stood off to one side with Emma, who looked like she was desperately trying to reason with a police officer.

After we'd been searched, Nick wrapped his jacket around my shoulders and guided me to his car. I didn't argue. I didn't say a word. I just sank into the passenger seat and closed my eyes as he pulled away.

The drive was quiet.

When we reached my place, he cut the engine but didn't move straight away.

'You okay, Trouble?' he asked gently.

I nodded, staring at my hands. 'Yeah. I think so.'

At least the world wasn't spinning anymore.

He hesitated, then smiled tentatively. 'I know you probably won't remember this in the morning. And I know it's probably been ages since you even thought about me, but do you fancy grabbing a drink sometime? Just us?'

For a moment, Andy's face flickered through my mind.

Then I looked at Nick. And I saw two of him. Not because I was drunk, but because I saw him as he was then, and I saw him as he was the first time I'd seen him. Outside the cinema—the moment I'd been struck by lightning.

'Yeah, I'd like that,' I smiled.

'Great,' he beamed. 'Text me tomorrow to let me know you remember!'

'Yeah. Good call,' I smirked, aware of how drunk I still was, and reached for the door handle.

As I watched him drive off, a mix of excitement and uncertainty bubbled up within me.

Nick.

32
Rock and a Hard Place

THE FOLLOWING WEEKEND, NICK AND I found ourselves in the cosy embrace of a local pub. The atmosphere was warm and inviting, with soft lighting casting a golden hue over everything. We sat in a corner booth, laughter and casual chatter creating a comforting backdrop.

'I'm so glad we did this, Sarah. I feel like we've finally turned a page and can move on from everything that's happened between us.' Nick reached out and held my hand across the table, and I felt a warmth ignite in my chest and bring a smile to my lips.

'Me too,' I conceded. 'I still can't believe we actually got here,' I chuckled. 'An actual, real-life second date!'

'I know! You've been a bit of a handful,' he teased, expecting a reaction and getting one.

I gasped and swatted him on the arm. 'Me!?' I exclaimed, and Nick sat back in his chair, pleased with himself.

'To say the least,' he prodded, smiling. 'Running away because I kissed Jennifer, leaving me without a kiss because you had *garlic breath* of all things—yes—Johnnie told me what happened that night quite recently,' he chuckled.

Oh God, he knows about the garlic breath!

As Nick tortured me with glee, I shook my head exasperatedly.

'What about you?' I rallied back. 'You've been way more difficult than me. Off with umpteen different girls, all of them *tooootally* in love with you…' Nick nodded proudly at this, so I persisted more urgently. 'Disappearing with weirdo Dyer and smoking anything you could get your hands on!'

Nick was having none of it.

'Ah yes, but I'm not the one who put your phone number on a pizza leaflet, am I?' he gleamed and took a sip of his beer as I deflated with guilt.

'Yeah.' I looked at him bashfully, remembering how awful I'd been. 'Sorry.' I put my hand on his arm affectionately and pouted. 'And yet you forgave me,' I said, hoping to hear that all was forgiven.

Nick paused and took my hand in his. 'How could I not?' he smiled. 'You've always wanted the best for me… *Except* for the pizza leaflet.' Nick stroked my hand with his thumb. 'I'm going to clean up my act. I promise. That raid at Dyer's place really made me think. I'm gonna retake my A-levels next summer and go to medical school in Leeds so we can go together.' Nick stared unblinkingly into my eyes. 'You're my girl, Sarah,' he said simply.

To hear him say all these things felt amazing—the 'me' of two years ago would have been doing cartwheels if she were watching us now—but there was something uncomfortable niggling me in the pit of my stomach.

What if he slipped again?

Unsure of how I felt, I realised Nick was leaning in to kiss me, so I quickly changed the subject.

'Speaking of girls, whatever happened to Jennifer, by the way? Do you ever hear from her?' I took a sip of my wine and acted naturally as though I hadn't noticed the imminent kiss.

Nick looked visibly disappointed. 'Um, yeah. I haven't heard from her in a while. I know she and Emma still aren't talking. But you know that. I think she has a boyfriend she met through her church group now.'

Despite everything Jennifer had said and done to sabotage my friendship with Emma and my connection with Nick, I felt pleased for her that she was doing well. I also felt pleased that Nick didn't hear from her much anymore, although I never would have admitted it.

Nick eyed the piano in the corner of the pub. 'So, do you think we'll ever spontaneously break out into a sing-song like in the old days?' he joked, a playful glint in his eyes.

I laughed and shrugged. 'Maybe if you start, I'll join in. But only if there's no one around to hear it.'

He grinned, leaning back in his seat, his easy charm coaxing me to relax. 'Deal. Next time, empty pub, we'll give it a shot. Same again?' he asked, eying my empty glass and getting up to go to the bar. I nodded appreciatively and smiled to myself.

This is shaping up to be a really nice evening.

But as Nick walked away, my phone started vibrating on the table. It was Andy calling. I hesitated. Then, reluctantly picked up.

'Hello?'

'Hey, Miss Page. What are you up to? Are you free to meet up?' Andy's voice sounded relaxed and casual, irking me more than I knew how to express.

'Hi, Andy. Actually, I can't. I'm on a date.'

Silence.

'Well…' Andy struggled to find the words for a moment. 'Can you make an excuse and leave?' He asked, his voice betraying a tone of surprise and disappointment.

The cheek!

'And why would I do that?' I retorted.

Silence.

'Because… I didn't mean for us to stop seeing each other,' he hesitated, 'I just thought that you should have a little fun.' There was growing urgency in his voice, but I was having none of it.

My pounding heartbeat filled the silence between us.

'You told me to sleep with someone else,' I stated calmly, trying not to show how upset I was. 'So, here I am, at the pub with Nick. And if you and I are just casual, then that's not something I need to explain to you.'

'Nick?' Andy snorted, and then the tone of his voice went up an octave. 'Sarah, you misunderstood. Look, can't you just come and talk?'

'I think I understood you perfectly,' I informed him, my voice harder than he'd heard it before. Whatever Andy had meant, his absence had spoken louder than words, and it didn't fit with what I wanted. As far as I was concerned, his effort was far too little, far too late. 'I have to go. Take care, Andy.' I said, then hung up the phone, feeling unhappy but extremely proud of myself.

Looking relaxed and content, Nick returned from the bar, drinks in hand. I decided to tell him about Andy. But for the next thirty minutes, try as I might to bite the bullet, the moment never seemed right.

Then, in a strange twist of fate, the pub door swung open, and my heart jolted unexpectedly as Andy walked in. And he wasn't alone. There was a pretty girl on his arm, with poker-straight black hair, a mini skirt and enormous gold hoop earrings, her laughter reaching out over the background chatter. My stomach twisted at the sight, and I immediately wished the ground would open up and swallow me.

Andy spotted Nick and me in our booth almost instantly. Casually yet confidently, he walked over to us, the girl trailing behind.

'Hey, Andy!' Nick turned and greeted our friend with relish. 'Fancy seeing you here,' he joked, knowing the pub was a regular haunt amongst all of us.

'Tom mentioned you two might be here,' Andy turned and gave me a little wave, and I sheepishly waved back. 'Thought I'd bring Natalie and come say hi,' he said, his voice calm and inviting. For a moment, his eyes sought out mine, a flicker of something mischievous crossing his face.

Nick, who still had no idea about Andy and me, gestured for the pair to join us at the table. 'The more the merrier,' he said with a grin. 'What are you drinking?'

As Nick got the drinks in, Andy slid in next to me in the booth, and Natalie slid in beside him.

'Miss Page.' He nodded with a slight smile as he introduced his date. 'Natalie, this is Sarah,' he gestured at me politely, and I smiled brightly and greeted her. 'Sarah is a friend of my brother's,' he explained, glancing at me as if to size up my reaction as he said it.

Outwardly, I smiled and stood to give Natalie a welcoming kiss on the cheek, but I struggled to mask the pain I felt at being referred to as a friend of 'his brother's' and nothing more.

This is exactly why I didn't want to sleep with him, I thought, feeling like I'd been punched in the stomach. *No one even knew we were seeing each other.*

Watching Natalie laugh and chat so easily with Andy stirred up a deep jealousy I hadn't expected and was completely unable to control. She was doing exactly what I had wanted to do with him—go out together as a couple—but what she had been awarded so readily, I had had to fight for and been denied.

I felt a knot tighten in my stomach.

As I went through the rigmarole of small talk and niceties, I felt like I had a coat hanger wedged in my mouth, and the muscles tightened around the edges of my smile.

Then Nick came back from the bar carrying an armful of drinks, and boxed me in from the other side.

This could be really awkward, I thought, making a small joke to myself and nearly laughing out loud. The swirl of questions, thoughts and emotions triggered by the two of them on either side of me was like being caught in a deafening storm.

Could Nick be trusted? What the hell was Andy doing there? Which one, if either of them, was actually one of the good guys?

I *needed* to get out of the pub and clear my head.

It was then that a surreal little twist of fate played out like an answer to my prayers when the pub door opened, and Dyer walked in. He and Derrick had been released by the police on bail a few days ago, and there was an urgency in his step as he approached our table.

'Hey, I've been looking for you,' he said, addressing me directly, his breath laboured and his demeanour earnest. 'I need to ask you a huge favour, Page—*please.* Can you take this package to Emma's place for me?' he asked, holding out a carrier bag with a shoe-box inside. 'She's been avoiding me, and it's really important.'

I blinked, startled by the unexpected request. 'What, *now*?' I asked, not sure why he was asking. 'How did you know I was here?'

It was like the universe had been listening to my private thoughts and sent me a way out of the pub just at the right moment.

Andy glanced over, eyes narrowing slightly. 'What's going on, Dyer?' he asked, suspicion lacing his voice, while Nick watched on easily.

'You know Emma,' Dyer shrugged, avoiding the question, a hint of plea in his voice. 'She won't talk to me. I need her to get this *tonight*. As in, right now. Please, Page. I wouldn't ask if it wasn't urgent.'

'Why can't you take it?' I pushed, weighing the situation. My gaze flicked to Andy, seeking his take on the matter.

'She doesn't want to see me,' whined Dyer. 'And her parents won't let me in any way; you know what they're like. *Please.* Call Emma if you want. She won't see me, but she's agreed to meet you if you'll take it for me. She's expecting you already.'

Nick leaned in encouragingly. 'Go ahead, Sarah, help him out. It's no trouble, right?' he said with a supportive smile.

Caught off guard by Nick's easy acceptance, coupled with my eagerness to escape the nightmarish situation, I nodded.

Dyer handed me the package with a grateful smile.

'Thanks, Page, you're a lifesaver,' he murmured before slipping away to the bar.

I lingered briefly to say goodbye to Nick, whose tender expression and easy manner made my head churn. He promised he'd call me when I got home and kissed me tenderly on the cheek. Then I turned to Andy and Natalie. Andy stood and gave me one of his rare hugs, his thick musky scent and knowing smile adding to my confusion.

Grabbing my coat, I decided I'd deal with all of this later. Tonight just needed to end. Feeling like there was a pressure cooker in my head, I escaped through the pub doors.

That's better, I thought, breathing the night air deeply.

Then, I took a few steps, running to put some distance between myself and the pub and pulled out my phone to call Emma. She answered straight away, sounding like she'd been crying.

'Emma, what's wrong?' I asked, feeling suddenly worried.

33

Signed, Sealed, Delivered

WHEN I RANG EMMA'S DOORBELL, it became immediately clear that since Dyer's arrest and release, her parents were keeping a close watch on her. Mrs McCarthy appeared in the hallway behind her, peering over Emma's shoulder to see who it was before relaxing and disappearing back into the living room.

Standing on the doorstep, I handed her Dyer's package and looked at her expectantly. She stared down at it for a moment, and beckoned for me to come inside, closing the door quietly behind us.

'I need to get this to Derrick,' she whispered at last. 'He's meeting me on the bench by the wooded bit.'

My stomach lurched. 'Derrick?' I repeated, struggling to process what she was saying. 'Why couldn't Dyer just meet him himself?'

Emma shook her head, pacing the hallway nervously. 'It's their stash,' she admitted, a note of fear in her voice. 'Dyer thinks the police are watching him, so he needed someone else to bring it.'

A wave of anger and disbelief surged through me. 'So... you've willingly turned me into his drug mule!?' I hissed.

'No! I mean, yes! I suppose so!' she cried, her voice wobbling, 'I didn't know what else to do. It's cocaine, Sarah. Turns out they've started dealing more than just a little bit of weed...'

'Jesus Christ! How much is in here!?' I weighed the bag in my hand, and it felt like a kilogram at least.

Emma ignored the question and carried on. '…It wasn't in the flat at the time of the raid, so the police couldn't charge them for it. But if they found Dyer with it now, he could get twenty years!'

'And what if they find *us* with it?' I shot back. I couldn't believe Emma would put either of us in that situation.

'They won't!' she insisted desperately. 'We just have to give it to Derrick, and that's it. He'll be here any minute; I just have to text him. Please, Sarah… don't make me meet him alone.' Her voice dropped to a whisper. 'He scares me… I think he knows it was us who called Social Services on his mum.'

Fear prickled along my arms, and I was suddenly very frightened. 'How could he possibly know that?' I asked urgently.

'I don't know. He always looks at me funny. Ever since the raid, he keeps asking Dyer about it.'

'He looks at everyone funny,' I muttered. 'He's a creep.' Emma let out a small, humourless laugh. 'God! Emma! How could you be so selfish!?'

'Shhh! My parents will hear you!' Emma scolded me in hushed tones. 'I'm sorry… Please, come with me. I'm scared,' she begged.

Despite everything, I couldn't bring myself to walk away and leave her alone with Derrick.

I gritted my teeth and let out a strangled groan. 'Okay! Fine!' I shout-whispered.

Emma beamed with relief and tried to hug me. 'Thank you, thank you, thank you!'

I shrugged her off. 'Let's just get it over with!' I said, frowning.

Together, we headed down the road towards the wooded patch until the trees loomed dark and close. The bench sat half-hidden behind the first line of trees, the shadows stretching long across the ground. Then, we sat down and waited, the package between us like a live grenade. Every snap of a twig made my heart race.

Why didn't I just stay in the pub? I thought, picturing the warm, welcoming booth, and the terrible trouble of having two handsome men to choose from. After what felt like an eternity, a shape moved in the darkness, and Derrick emerged from the shadows.

'Alright Ems? Sarah?' he sneered, his gaze dropping unabashedly to our chests. 'You got something for me?'

Emma nodded mutely and pulled the package from her bag, handing it to him with trembling fingers.

'Wicked. Thank you, girls,' he grinned, the scar on his cheek deepening. 'Now then. Why don't we all go into the woods for a smoke? My treat.'

'No thanks,' I said quickly. 'You know I don't smoke. We should just get going.'

'Yeah, sorry, Derrick.' Emma added hastily. 'My mum's waiting for us. She knows we're here.'

Derrick cocked his head to one side.

'Your mum knows you're meeting *me* here? Now?'

'Yes,' Emma said, too fast. 'She said I shouldn't be long.'

He chuckled darkly. 'Nah. Doubt that, Ems.' He stepped closer, the air around him suddenly oppressive. 'Come on. I won't bite.'

Then, slowly, deliberately, he pulled out a knife. The blade caught the faint light filtering through the trees, gleaming cold and sharp.

'Come on,' Derrick repeated lightly, as though we were being unreasonable. 'Just for a smoke. Come with me.' His mouth twitched into something that might once have been a smile. 'I'm not gonna hurt ya,' he added. 'Not unless you make me.'

My chest tightened as we followed him off the path and further into the trees. The branches closed in above us, blotting out what little light there was, the ground soft and uneven beneath our feet. I stumbled once and caught myself, my heart hammering so loudly I was sure Derrick could hear it.

We reached a small clearing, and Derrick stopped abruptly, turning to face us.

'Now, girls,' he said, his voice shifting, the friendliness draining away. 'You're gonna do exactly what I tell you to do.' He reached into his pocket and pulled out a roll of duct tape.

Panic surged through me.

'On your knees,' he ordered. 'Both of you. Now.'

For a split second, neither of us moved. Then fear took over, and Emma and I sank down onto the damp leaves, the cold seeping straight through my jeans. Derrick tore a strip of tape free with a sharp, ripping sound.

'Hands out in front of you,' he barked, stepping towards me.

I flinched and instinctively pulled back.

Derrick stopped. 'Arms. Out. Now.'

He loomed over me, knife still in his hand, and I felt myself shrinking under his gaze.

'I'm going to enjoy this,' he said quietly. 'It's been ages since I had myself a virgin.'

'What?' I asked, stunned.

'Dyer told me,' he sneered repugnantly. 'Said you were still untouched.'

'So?' I shot back, my voice shaking despite my efforts, as he grabbed my wrists and bound them together roughly with the tape.

'Virgins are my favourite,' he muttered. 'You know, Dyer was gonna set us up, you and me, but then, you liked *Nick*.' Derrick paused for dramatic effect. 'So, we said he was shagging my sister,' he laughed while watching my face.

My stomach dropped.

'You mean you knew Nick wasn't seeing Tiffany?' I demanded.

'Yep.' Derrick chuckled. 'Now, don't you feel silly?' he mocked, turning away from me and towards Emma.

Emma suddenly sprang to her feet and lunged at him with a feral cry, but Derrick was too quick. He reacted instantly, grabbing her arms and kicking her legs out from under her so that she hit the ground hard.

'Get up! Arms out front!' he snarled, but Emma didn't move.

A terrible stillness spread through me as she lay there, curled slightly on her side.

Derrick glanced back at me. '*Then* you went and got yourself a boyfriend,' continued Derrick, turning to me for a moment, 'so I thought the game was up.'

'You're disgusting,' I spat.

His eyes travelled over me slowly, deliberately, before turning back to Emma.

'Get up, Emma,' he snapped, nudging her with his foot.

She didn't respond.

He turned his attention back to me, and something dark flickered across his face.

'You started asking questions,' he went on, as if thinking aloud. 'About my sister. About Nick. And then Social Services turn up… eventually. We thought it was Jamie-from-The-Green. But it wasn't, was it?'

'What are you talking about?' I feigned innocence, hoping that my acting classes were paying off.

'First time you come to my new place, the police show up. Too many coincidences, Sarah. I don't believe in coincidences.'

He kicked Emma again, harder this time, and she let out a little yelp.

'Get up!'

Fear and fury tangled in my chest.

'I'm gonna get my own back on you,' he said calmly. 'And your little mate, too. But *you* first. *Frigid. Little. Snitch.*' Derrick spat out the last three words hatefully. 'I'm going to turn you into a *real* woman, and you're gonna *love every second of it.*'

He stepped closer.

'Take your jeans off,' he ordered, coming straight for me.

'Please, Derrick, don't do this,' I pleaded. 'Let us go. I swear I didn't call the police...'

'Sarah hasn't done anything to you…' wheezed Emma from the ground.

'Shut up!' Derrick snapped. 'I said take your jeans off, bitch!'

Derrick leant down and violently yanked at the waistband of my jeans. Shocked, I instinctively shielded my face as a blur burst out of the darkness from behind Derrick.

'And you, E…' Derrick continued.

But he never finished his sentence.

The blur slammed into him with bone-jarring force. Derrick went down hard, the knife dropping into the undergrowth as the two bodies crashed together.

For a heartbeat, everything froze. Then Emma was on her feet, tearing at the tape around my wrists with shaking hands.

'Let's go!' she pleaded.

As my hands came free, I looked up and saw Andy straddling Derrick in the dark, fists flying as he fought to pin him down, his face set with a ferocity I had never seen before.

For a moment, I couldn't move. I stood rooted to the spot, watching in disbelief as Andy grappled with Derrick on the forest floor, the two of them locked together in a tangle of limbs and grunts.

Then instinct kicked in.

'We can't go, we have to help Andy!' I shouted at Emma, my voice breaking through the chaos. 'We have to find something to hit Derrick with!'

We scrambled through the undergrowth, our hands clawing blindly at the forest floor, searching for some piece of wood or a rock that we could use as a weapon. Somewhere behind us, Derrick had found the knife again and was thrashing wildly at Andy, who ducked and swore, trying to keep his grip.

Suddenly, Derrick twisted free.

Andy stumbled backwards, losing his footing, and Derrick took the opportunity to scramble to his feet and bolt, crashing through the trees and vanishing into the darkness.

'This isn't over, Sarah!' he bellowed, his voice echoing through the woods.

I shuddered, the darkness oppressive, terrified that he might come back. Emma emerged from the shadows, clutching a fallen branch, holding it out in front of her as though her life depended on it. Then, Andy turned towards us, breathing hard, his lip split and swelling, but his eyes scanning us anxiously.

'Are you okay?' he asked urgently.

The relief that flooded me was dizzying, almost euphoric.

'Oh my God, Andy!' I cried, rushing forward. 'Are we glad to see *you*!' My voice cracked as the reality of what had almost happened caught up with me. 'What are you doing here?!'

'I'll explain later,' he said quickly, glancing over his shoulder. 'But we need to get out of here. Now. In case he comes back.'

He took my hand and started pulling us towards the path, Emma sticking close beside me, dragging the branch along the ground. As we ran, a strange calm settled over me—a sudden, crystal-clear understanding of how much it mattered to have people in my life I could truly rely on.

The feeling didn't last very long.

In the darkness, silhouetted between two trees, the unmistakable outline of Matthew Dyer stepped out in front of us.

'Matthew?' Emma called incredulously, dropping her branch. 'What are you doing here?'

Dyer didn't answer at first, his breath forming clouds in the night as the woods seemed to listen all around us.

Then, after a few moments, he spoke.

'It was her, Emma,' he said flatly, pointing straight at me. 'She's the snitch.'

'Don't be ridiculous,' Emma snapped. 'Of course, it wasn't her.'

'It wasn't me,' I insisted, my heart pounding. 'The police had a search warrant. It was a planned raid. Why would I call them when Emma and Nick were there, too?'

Dyer shook his head slowly, his eyes never leaving mine. 'I don't believe you. And you'd better watch your back, Page. Your little bodyguard won't always be around.'

Andy didn't move, but his voice cut into the darkness. 'It wasn't her who called the police, Dyer,' he said evenly. 'It was me.'

'You!?' Dyer roared, his face twisting with rage as he pulled out a knife.

'Matthew!' Emma screamed.

'Shut up, woman!' Dyer snarled. 'Men are talking.'

'And I didn't report you for dealing,' continued Andy, calmly watching the knife.

Dyer stared at him in disbelief. 'Then what the hell did you call them for?'

'For Tiffany,' Andy said. 'What you've been doing with her.'

Emma and I both turned to Dyer.

'What does he mean?' Emma shrieked. 'Matthew?'

'Nothing!' Dyer shouted, suddenly frantic. 'I ain't done nothing!'

'You have,' Andy said. 'She's a kid. You're the mystery boyfriend. And Derrick knows about it.'

'Mate, you've lost it. I don't know what you're talking about.' Dyer scoffed, but the bravado was slipping.

'I wasn't sure at first,' Andy went on, his voice tight with anger. 'But something about you and Derrick never sat right with me. The things you talked about at work. The way you laughed. Then one day, this young girl came in when Derrick was there, and when she'd gone, he asked me if I liked that sort of thing. I knew what he was asking. Scumbag made me feel sick. Turned out the girl was his own sister.'

Emma's hand flew to her mouth.

'I couldn't get it off my mind. My gut told me there was something going on,' Andy continued. 'So I reported it. More than once. Nothing happened. Then I told them you'd moved in together. And that night, I called again. They told me they had a warrant.'

Dyer stood motionless before us, his grip tightening on the knife.

'They found enough to put you away,' Andy finished. 'On both counts. You know what they do to kiddie fiddlers in prison, don't you?' he scoffed

As Andy spoke, we could hear someone crashing through the undergrowth towards us.

Dyer giggled. 'Derrick, mate! Over here!' he called.

As the crashing got closer, the three of us spun around, and in that split second of distraction, Dyer lunged, the knife disappearing underneath Andy's coat as he yelled and recoiled back. At the same moment, the dark outline of a man burst into the clearing.

'What the hell is going on?!' exclaimed Nick.

Dyer slashed at Andy again, but this time Andy dove out of the way, then fell forward, clutching at his side.

'Andy!' I cried, gripping his arm to steady him as he swayed, his hands covered in blood.

Seeing her chance, Emma hoisted up the branch and swung it straight at Dyer's crotch with everything she had, letting out a fierce scream as the branch connected squarely between his legs. A guttural cry echoed through the woods as Dyer folded in on himself, the knife slipping from his hand and disappearing into the leaves. Then Nick and Andy piled in on top of him, pinning him face-down in the mud as he thrashed and swore beneath them.

Emma, still clutching the branch, looked as though she were ready to strike again. I rushed to her and grabbed it.

'Drop it,' I said firmly. 'They've got him. Let's just call for help.'

She hesitated. 'You're not worth it, Matthew!' she cried, letting the branch fall from her hands where it landed inches from Dyer's face.

My fingers shook as I dug through my bag for my phone.

'I need an ambulance… and the police…' I said breathlessly when the line connected. 'We've been attacked.'

As I spoke, Andy kept his knee pressed into Dyer's back, forcing his face into the mud, while Nick wrenched his arms painfully behind him to keep him still.

'I knew something wasn't right,' Nick blurted suddenly, his words tumbling out.

Dyer wriggled on the ground, and we heard a vile giggle as he started to speak. 'Why don't you tell her why she's here, lover boy?' he laughed, his head twisting around in the mud and leaves.

Nick froze.

'What's he talking about, Nick?' I asked, a sinking feeling in the pit of my stomach.

His face crumpled. 'I'm so sorry, Sarah,' he said quietly, as Dyer thrashed beneath him. 'It was only meant to be a quick drop-off. Emma was supposed to hand the stash over to Derrick, and that was it. I swear—I never thought anything like this would happen.'

The words hit me like a slap.

'You!' I cried. 'You set me up? That whole date was part of Dyer's plan?'

'No!' Nick protested. 'The date was real. I asked you because I wanted to see you. But Dyer asked me for a favour. He said if the police found him with coke, he'd be inside for decades. Then, Andy ran off and Dyer followed him, looking dodgy as hell. It all seemed so weird… And you never know with Dyer… so I followed him,' Nick paused to catch his breath. 'Then I see him come in here, and there's all these noises in the bushes.'

Rage pulsed through me.

'So why couldn't you just take it yourself!?' I shouted. 'Why get me involved?'

'I couldn't,' he admitted. 'The police know my face. I've been stopped before. One of the coppers who raided Dyer's place recognised me. Dyer said he needed someone they'd never suspect.'

The betrayal landed fully then. Cold and unmistakable.

'Well, thanks a lot, Nick,' I said flatly.

'I'm sorry,' he pleaded. 'There wasn't meant to be any trouble.'

Dyer let out a sickening laugh from where he lay pinned to the floor.

Sirens began to wail in the distance, growing louder by the second. Moments later, police officers crashed through the undergrowth, and we shouted to alert them to our position. They took control quickly, hauling Dyer to his feet, handcuffing him and marching him out of the woods.

'Are you okay?' I asked Andy as Dyer was taken away. 'Can you walk?'

'I'm fine,' he replied stoically, clutching at his side again. Then, after a few steps, he changed his mind and let me help support him as he walked, bent double and clearly in pain.

We reached the road to a wash of flashing blue lights that felt violently out of place against the quiet suburban houses. The ambulance doors were already open. A paramedic jogged towards us as soon as he saw the blood.

'Who's injured?' he called.

'It's not that bad,' Andy muttered beside me, but his voice sounded thinner than usual.

'He's been stabbed,' I said, the word catching in my throat.

They eased him onto the back step of the ambulance and lifted his shirt carefully. I turned away for a second—then forced myself to look. The cut wasn't huge, but it was deep enough to make my stomach drop. Blood had soaked through his T-shirt and was still seeping sluggishly through the gauze they pressed against it.

'You're lucky,' one of the paramedics said calmly, inspecting the wound. 'The blade's missed anything major. But we're still taking you in, just to be on the safe side.'

Andy winced as they irrigated it. His jaw tightened, but he didn't make a sound.

I climbed into the ambulance without being asked.

Nick hovered just outside the open doors, his face pale under the flashing lights. Emma stood beside him, arms wrapped around herself, mascara smudged, eyes wide and glassy.

'Sarah,' Nick said quietly, stepping forward. 'I'll come with you. I'll sit in the back. Make sure you're both okay.'

The offer hung there—soft, almost hopeful.

And, for a split second, I felt the old pull. The familiarity. The thrill. The version of us that might have been. But then I looked at Andy. At the blood on his skin and at the way he was trying not to show pain, and something in me gravitated towards him.

'No,' I said gently, but firmly. 'I need to go with him.'

Nick nodded quickly. 'Yeah, of course. I just meant…'

'I need to talk to Andy. Alone.'

That did the trick. My words weren't cruel. But they were clear.

Something flickered across his face—understanding, maybe. Or acceptance, and finally, he stepped back from the doors.

Emma moved forward instead. 'I can come,' she said, her voice wobbling. 'I should. This is my fault. I…'

I couldn't look at her properly. Every time I did, all I could see was how easily she'd trusted the wrong people. How close we'd come to something far worse.

'I can't,' I said quietly. 'Not tonight.'

Her face crumpled.

'I'll call you tomorrow,' I added, softer now. 'Okay?'

Emma nodded, wiping her eyes.

The paramedic gave the doors two firm knocks. 'Right… we're off.'

The doors slammed shut with a hollow clang, cutting off the flashing lights and the others standing in the road, and the ambulance pulled away.

34
I'M YOURS

IN THE BACK OF THE AMBULANCE, Andy eased himself carefully onto the narrow stretcher while a paramedic secured the dressing at his side. I sat on the small fold-down seat opposite him, the harsh white lights humming above us. The enclosed space felt surreal after the chaos of the woods. The steady motion of the vehicle as it pulled away grounded me in a strange way, even as everything inside me trembled.

The adrenaline finally began to ebb, leaving me shaky and cold. One of the paramedics draped a thin grey blanket around my shoulders while checking Andy's vitals, then disappeared into the front next to the driver. I clasped my hands together to stop them shaking and watched as Andy lay back against the raised pillow, his jaw tight with controlled pain.

'Does it hurt?' I asked.

'It's manageable. They've given me something,' he grimaced, then looked up at me and paused. 'Try and relax a bit, Sarah,' he murmured, his voice low despite everything.

'You're the one who's been stabbed,' I whispered, horrified all over again.

'And you're the one in shock,' he replied quietly.

I nodded blankly, staring at the metal cabinets lining the wall. My thoughts strayed to Derrick, who was still out there somewhere.

'What if the police don't catch him?' I asked, suddenly terrified he might somehow appear again. That it wasn't over, just as he'd said.

'I really don't think he'll come anywhere near you now,' Andy said calmly. 'And even if he tried, he'd be stopped long before he got close.'

The certainty in his voice was soothing.

'But what if he does?' I insisted, remembering Derrick's harrowing face as he snarled at me in the woods.

'There's no way he's getting anywhere near you tonight,' Andy reassured me, reaching across carefully and brushing his fingers against my arm.

'Yeah. I guess you're right,' I said faintly, managing a small smile.

After a moment's silence, broken only by the hum of the engine and the occasional bump in the road, I asked him how he'd known where to find us.

Andy ran a hand through his hair and winced slightly before speaking, his expression serious.

'After you left the pub, Nick mentioned that the package Dyer gave you had coke in it. He said Emma was meant to hand it to Derrick because Dyer thought he was being watched. I confronted Dyer about it.' Andy's jaw tightened. 'He just smirked and said it would—excuse my language—"teach the frigid little snitch a lesson". That's when I knew he had something else planned.'

The words hung heavily in the air.

'I can't believe Dyer would go that far,' I murmured.

Andy shook his head with conviction. 'I can. I've known him a long time. If there's one thing he likes to do, it's mess with people. And if anyone messes with him, Dyer will make them regret it.'

I shuddered at the thought of his callousness.

'Derrick and Dyer had knives tonight. Derrick was taking us into the bushes and…' I stopped, unable to finish, tears welling up in my eyes. 'I can't believe Emma and Nick would do this to me,' I sobbed. 'I can't believe they went along with it. I thought they were my friends!'

Ignoring the discomfort at his side, Andy shifted and reached for me.

'They're still your friends,' he said gently. 'Just give it time.'

For a moment, I let myself lean forward, our hands clasped tightly between us, his presence solid and reassuring despite the clinical brightness around us. Then I straightened, needing to say what came next clearly.

'Thank you, Andy, so much for coming after us. I don't know what Derrick would have done if you hadn't shown up.'

'I wasn't going to let anything happen to you,' he replied simply.

He looked at me then. Really looked at me. And for a moment, it felt as though he might kiss me. The closeness stirred something deep and familiar. The warmth of his hand in mine, the intensity in his eyes, reignited the pull I'd never quite shaken. The thought of leaning across and melting into him felt wonderful.

But then I remembered how he had treated me. His words. The secrecy. The painful distance.

Sometimes, you can do everything right, and people still treat you badly, I thought, drawing strength from my mum's life lesson.

'Andy,' I whispered urgently, leaning closer so the paramedics in the front couldn't hear. 'What happened tonight doesn't change what you said before. It doesn't change the fact that you don't want a girlfriend. Or that you were too embarrassed to be with me in front of anyone. You kept us hidden. And I'm not going back to that. I deserve better than being someone's secret.'

He met my gaze, a mix of vulnerability and determination sparking in his eyes. 'I know,' he said. 'And you're right.' He took a breath. 'I wasn't avoiding you. I was avoiding how much I cared. It was easier to call it "casual" than admit how scared I was of getting it wrong. Of losing you.'

I stayed silent, letting him continue.

'I pushed you towards Nick because it felt safer than owning my feelings. That was my mistake. And I'm sorry,' he confessed, his thumb stroking the back of my hand. The honesty in his voice caught me off guard.

'I was never embarrassed by you,' he went on. 'Never. I'd be proud to have you as my girlfriend, Sarah. I've missed you. More than I knew how to admit.'

I smiled despite myself. 'What about Natalie?' I challenged quietly, remembering how he'd held her hand at the pub, and feeling a wave of jealousy and insecurity rise up in me again.

He grimaced. 'Natalie is just a girl I met. I brought her tonight because I was jealous and didn't know how else to handle it. That wasn't fair to her—or to you.' He paused, then looked away suddenly, as if remembering something. 'I should probably check that she's okay; actually, I just left her at the pub and followed you earlier.'

Shocked, I agreed he should, wondering where Andy was going with this and feeling a whisper of hope that it might be somewhere I wanted.

'Seeing you with Nick made me realise that fear isn't a good enough reason to walk away from you. Even if you and Nick had history, I needed to stop standing on the sidelines.'

I swallowed, my heart pounding.

'Andy, Nick sent me into a wooded area with drugs tonight,' I said. 'To help out his mate. And it nearly got me killed. You made a different choice.'

Andy tightened his grip on my hands. 'Just wait,' he said gently. 'I need to say this properly.' He hesitated, then looked at me with quiet resolve. 'I know that you are going away to university next year, and you'll probably forget all about me...'

'I would never forget about you; how could I?' I interjected.

'…and if you don't want to be with me, that's okay,' he continued. 'I'll understand. But you need to know that…'

He took a breath.

'I'm completely head-over-heels in love with you, Miss Page.'

The words seemed to fill the ambulance, bright and certain despite the sterile lights and bumpy ride.

'And if you do want to be with me, I don't want to keep us a secret anymore. I want all of our friends and family to see us and know. I want the whole world to know we're together.'

I smiled, the weight in my chest finally lifting.

'Yes,' I whispered. 'Yes, I want that too.'

Andy leaned forward carefully, mindful of the bandage at his side, and this time I didn't stop him. His lips met mine gently, full of promise. In his kiss, the chaos of the night, of the past few months, of my family, of Derrick and Dyer, all of it melted away. We were left only with the possibility of a new beginning.

Andy drew me carefully closer, and we stayed like that as the ambulance carried us through the night. No longer hidden. No longer uncertain. A shared understanding between us that whatever came next, we would face it side by side.

***

When we finally got back to Andy's house, it was gone two o'clock in the morning. Grimacing, Andy held the front door open for me and then led me into the living room. Then, he insisted on making us tea.

'You should be sitting down,' I protested.

'I am sitting down,' he said, lowering himself carefully onto the sofa before handing me his Disney mug with the broken handle.

I wrapped my hands around it.

The living room felt exactly the same as it always had. The place where I'd spent so many nights with my friends and with Andy felt so comforting after all of the night's chaos.

But it was as though everything had shifted. Andy looked at me across the small space between us. Not hidden. Not uncertain. Just open. I smiled… and Andy smiled back. For the first time all night, I felt something other than fear.

I felt chosen.

And safe.

And happy.

EPILOGUE

New Year's Eve, December 2000

WE GATHERED AT TOM'S AND MY PLACE, the music cranked high, and the lights turned low. My mates were ecstatic that New Year's Eve had finally arrived—there was so much for us all to celebrate. I danced with Sarah in the living room as she tilted her face up to me, laughing at something I hadn't even meant to be funny, her body fitting against mine as though it belonged there.

The girl who had chosen me.

I noticed Tom watching us from the dining table—pleased—as he chatted to Jamie-from-The-Green. Emma and Johnnie were dancing raunchily nearby. Nick was standing with Natalie, smiling broadly as he bent to say something in her ear, her gold hoops swinging wildly as she laughed and nudged him with her hip. I caught his eye briefly and lifted my chin in greeting. He lifted his glass back.

I turned my attention to Sarah again, but Tom waved me over, and I joined him and Jamie at the table, Sarah still dancing with Emma and Johnnie behind me.

'Alright, Andy?' Tom asked. 'We were just talking about Derrick and Dyer. Have you heard the latest?'

I watched, grinning, as Sarah danced in the middle of the room, her hair loose over her shoulders, her cheeks flushed.

I shook my head. 'No. What's happening?' I'd been trying not to think about them at all.

As Sarah laughed at something Emma whispered in her ear, I felt a deep, protective instinct rise in my chest.

'They've both been charged,' Jamie said. 'Two serious offences. Kiddie fiddlin' and intent to supply class-As.'

I nodded slowly. I'd expected it, but hearing it spoken out loud made everything feel heavier somehow.

'One o' the lads from The Green went to see Derrick,' Jamie continued, taking a long drag on his cigarette. 'He's saying that if—or rather when—they get out, they're coming straight for you for ratting them out.'

I held his gaze evenly. 'Let him,' I said, though a flicker of cold passed through me.

Jamie crushed out his cigarette and immediately lit another. Smoke curled between us.

Tom leaned forward. 'Derrick knows it was Sarah and Emma who reported his family to Social Services, too,' he added, his voice tightening. 'So he's coming for them as well.'

That landed differently.

My jaw shifted before I could stop it. I glanced over at Sarah again, suddenly aware of how small she looked across the room, how unaware.

'Yeah, but they'll be put away for years, surely,' I said, keeping my tone steady. The system wouldn't let men like that walk straight back out. It couldn't.

Jamie laughed softly. 'Anything could 'appen,' he said, amusement flickering across his face as Tom and I frowned. 'Never count yah chickens,' he warned, winking with an air of lazy authority.

Anything could happen.

I watched Sarah spin as the music changed, her hands thrown in the air. For a second, unease threaded through my chest, thin but undeniable. Just then, I checked my watch and looked up.

'It's almost midnight!' I boomed above the music and chatter, grabbing the TV remote and turning up the volume. The Bells of Big Ben had started their iconic chiming, and as Tom turned the stereo down, the room grew quiet as the countdown to midnight began.

'Ten!'

'Nine!'

'Eight!'

I reached for Sarah's hand.

On the stroke of midnight, we cheered uproariously and raised our glasses. Johnnie kissed Emma; Natalie let off a party popper before Nick pounced on her; and I pulled Sarah into my arms and kissed her, not caring who was watching.

She kissed me back, deeply and without hesitation.

My chest felt full. Certain. I knew that this was my girl.

'Happy New Year!' I shouted into the air.

When I pulled away, we hugged Tom and Emma, shook hands with Johnnie. Nick clapped me on the shoulder and muttered something I didn't quite catch while Natalie looped her arm through his as though keen to pull him back to her.

Out of the corner of my eye, I saw Jamie stand. It was strange. He didn't hesitate or hover. He just crossed the room directly towards us.

'Sarah,' he said lightly, and she turned toward him, still smiling.

Then, he leaned in and whispered something into her ear. I couldn't hear it, although Nick had gone quiet. She laughed at first. Then she stopped. Jamie leaned closer, his hand briefly touching her arm. I saw her nod once, frowning slightly, before he stepped back and returned to the table.

He caught my eye as he sat down, smiled and raised his glass. ''Appy New Year, mate!' he hollered, then lit another cigarette.

Sarah stood where he'd left her, staring after him for a moment. I moved back to her and slipped my arm around her waist.

For the first time that night, she didn't look happy.

TO BE CONTINUED...

PART 2 COMING SOON

www.ingramcontent.com/pod-product-compliance
Lightning Source LLC
LaVergne TN
LVHW091024080826
845145LV00002B/346